NEXT OF KIN

Dairy farmer Robin Meredith has just buried his Californian wife Caro who, though a central figure at the farm for more than twenty years, had remained a mystery to the family. With Caro gone, her adopted daughter Judy feels cut adrift. To Robin's brother Joe, Caro has been the emblem of a freedom he'd once glimpsed in America—a hopeful symbol that he could somehow dodge destiny—and his despair at her loss is far deeper than the family suspects. Robin and Joe's parents, entrenched in the adjoining arable farm, feel suddenly vulnerable to time and change as well. Into their midst comes Judy's London friend Zoe, whose disturbing directness, Robin privately reckons, is usually only found in animals. All underestimate Zoe's power as a catalyst for change.

NEXT OF KIN

Joanna Trollope

CHIVERS PRESS
BATH

First published 1996
by
Bloomsbury
This Large Print edition published by
Chivers Press
by arrangement with
Bloomsbury Publishing PLC
1996

ISBN 0 7451 5332 1

British Library Cataloguing in Publication Data available

Photoset, printed and bound in Great Britain by
REDWOOD BOOKS, Trowbridge, Wiltshire

CHAPTER ONE

At his wife's funeral, Robin Meredith was asked by a woman in a paisley headscarf, whom he didn't immediately recognise, if he wasn't thankful to know that Caro was now safe with Jesus. He, summoning all the courtesy he could manage at such a moment, said no, he didn't think so. He then went out of the church into the rain and looked at the black hole into which Caro was to be lowered.

'No cremation,' she'd said. 'I want it done properly. Brass handles. Full-length. In the churchyard.'

It was about the only instruction she had given as well as the only acknowledgement she had made that she was dying. There were planks on top of the hole, and long tapes of black webbing had been laid across them with which to lower the coffin.

'You OK?' Robin's daughter said, standing close to him, but not touching.

'Better out of there,' he said, meaning the church.

'Me, too.'

There was a pause, and then Judy said, 'Mum liked it, though.' Her voice shook.

'Yes,' Robin said. He put a hand out to take Judy's but both hers were deep in her coat pockets, her long, black, Londony coat which proclaimed, as did all her clothes, how far she had deliberately come from the land on which she grew up.

'You never—' Judy hissed suddenly.

'Sh—'

The undertakers, lugubrious and ungainly to the point of caricature, trod ponderously towards them.

1

They all wore spectacles and orthopaedic-looking shoes. The congregation, walking respectfully behind, began to fan out in a quiet circle, Robin's parents, his brother and sister-in-law, the herdsman from the farm and his wife, Caro's friends, people from the social advice bureau where she had worked, the man who ran the village shop, the woman in the paisley scarf.

Judy began to cry again. She left Robin's side and ran unsteadily through the wet grass in her high-heels to where her Aunt Lyndsay stood. Lyndsay put an arm round her. Robin looked up briefly and saw his mother watching him in the calm, mildly curious way she had watched him all his life, as if she could never quite remember who he was. He looked down again, at the coffin, now lying almost at his feet, which contained Caro. It didn't look long enough, not by inches. Caro, after all, had been almost six feet tall.

The Vicar of Dean Cross, a small, exhausted man with four parishes to run who refused ever to take a holiday, moved to the graveside under a black umbrella held up by his wife.

'"Happy are the dead who die in the face of Christ!"' he said, without particular conviction. He opened his prayer book and his wife moved the umbrella so that a shower of drops fell upon the open page.

'"In the midst of life,"' he read irritably, '"we are in death. To whom can we turn for help, but to you, Lord, who are justly angered by our sins?"'

Robin glanced again at Judy. She and Lyndsay were both crying now and his brother Joe had hoisted over them a vast yellow umbrella with 'Mid-Mercia Farmers' Co-operative' printed on it in black. Joe's face was set and he was looking straight ahead, his

2

gaze above the grave, above the thought of Caro.

'"We have entrusted our sister Carolyn to God's merciful keeping,"' the Vicar said, '"and we now commit her body to the earth—"'

If, Robin thought suddenly, he says 'Earth to earth, dust to dust, ashes to ashes', I will leap the grave and punch him.

'"—in the sure and certain hope of the resurrection to eternal life through our Lord Jesus Christ, who died, was buried, and rose again for us."'

The coffin sank down unevenly into the earth in its black slings.

'"To Him be glory for ever and ever."'

The undertakers stepped back, coiling up the webbing. Robin shut his eyes.

'"God will show us the path of life."'

He opened them again. Judy came forward and stooped to drop on to the coffin a posy of primroses and then the woman in the paisley headscarf gave a little dart and threw after it an artificial orchid whose plastic stem clattered on the lid.

'"In His presence is the fullness of joy,"' the Vicar said, '"and at His right hand there is pleasure for ever more."'

Joy, Robin thought flatly. Pleasure. He put his hand up to his black tie and tugged at the knot. He hated ties. He hated them as he did churches. The Vicar was looking at him across the grave, almost expectantly. Robin nodded at him briefly. Did the man expect him to say thank you?

'"Unto Him that is able to keep us from falling,"' the Vicar said, his eyes still upon Robin. '"To the only wise God, our Saviour, be glory and majesty, dominion and power, both now and for ever. Amen."'

3

'Amen,' everyone murmured.

'Nicely done,' Robin's mother, Dilys, said.

Harry, his father, moved closer. He looked at his son and then, briefly, at the open grave of his daughter-in-law. Strange woman. American. Never quite seemed able to involve herself with the farm and yet—Harry swallowed. He felt it might be an obscure and diverting comfort to mention to Robin that his new power harrow would cost over £6,000, but thought he'd better not. Not right now, at any rate.

'Judy's taken it hard,' Dilys said, her gloved hands easily clasped before her. She glanced across at her younger son. 'And so has Joe.'

Robin said sharply, 'Caro was Judy's mother. And my wife. Not Joe's.'

Dilys regarded him.

'I expect,' she said, calm and persistent, 'that it's almost harder if you've been adopted. Like Judy, you can't help waiting for the next loss.' She paused, looking towards the grave, and then she said, in the tone of mildly contemptuous pity she reserved for all those not truly part of her own family, 'Poor Carolyn.'

Robin jammed his hands in his coat pockets and ducked his head.

'I'm going to get Judy. See you back at the farm for tea.'

'Yes,' Dilys said. 'Yes.'

Harry leaned forward, and lightly touched Robin's arm.

'Bear up, lad.'

*　　　*　　　*

Robin had bought Tideswell Farm two months

4

before Caro had agreed to marry him. Harry had not offered to help him financially, nor had Robin wished to ask. With the proceeds of the sale of a small cottage he had previously bought, with the intention of living in it, and a huge bank loan, he had acquired those 200 acres running gently down to the River Dean and the farmhouse, a seventeenth-century stone house with gawky Victorian additions. The yard behind the house had been almost entirely decayed, overshadowed by an immense and collapsing Dutch barn, and with no hard standing for cattle. In those early months, a quarter of a century ago, Robin had poured concrete himself, all day and every day, and almost always alone.

The land proved, as he had hoped, reasonable for growing fodder for the cattle; grass on the lower slopes, maize on the higher ones. In spring, when the willows that lined the river banks were in soft, new, frond-like leaf, the landscape had a brief prettiness, and if the acreage, and mute swans arrived in pairs to lend the prospect a stately, almost park-like air. But at other times—and Caro Meredith had felt this sorely—the fields were just land, spaces of earth and grass divided by untidy hedges and fences with ugly, serviceable galvanised-metal gates opening on to the quagmires of mud the cattle and the wheels of tractors made.

The house stood at a mid-point between the river and the minor road down which the milk tanker came daily to empty the bulk tank outside the milking parlour. It was approached by a sloping track, either sticky with mud or cloudy with dust, along which Robin had planted, in a fit of early enthusiasm, alternate green and copper beech trees. At the end of the track, a concreted stretch led away on one side into the yard, and on the other a wooden five-barred gate, propped permanently open with a mossy boulder, gave on to a circular sweep of worn gravel in front of the house. There was a sundial in the centre of the sweep, with an engraved metal plate bolted to its surface. 'Onlie count,' the engraving ran, 'the sunny houres.' Caro had put it there. It had been her first Christmas present to Robin.

The drive now was full of cars. From over the pungent hedge of leylandii that screened it from the farmyard came the steady clank and whirr of the milking parlour where a relief milker, an efficient, sour-faced man sent by the local agency, proceeded with the afternoon milking. Robin, standing in the doorway to greet people with his funeral tie at half-mast, fought down the urge to go and see that the job was being done properly and that Gareth, Tideswell's herdsman, had indeed mended the puncture in the power hose as instructed.

Behind him, in the gloomy dining room he and Caro had seldom used, a vast funeral tea was spread out on Meredith family cloths, lent by Dilys. Judy, her red hair tousled and still in her black overcoat, was pouring tea, and Lyndsay was handing it round to people, the sugar basin in her free hand. There was an air of discreet excitement in the room at the sight of the food, unfashionable, childlike, teatime food, resting on mats of decoratively pierced white paper which Dilys had brought down to Tideswell and made plain she expected to be used.

Judy, struggling to make the pecan squares and chocolate brownies that had been so much part of Caro's American repertoire, had said defiantly that her mother never used doilies.

'But this is a funeral,' Dilys said. 'A family funeral.

6

We must do it properly.'

She emphasised the word 'family'. She had made several cakes, huge perfect fruit cakes glistening with cherries, flawless pale sponges decorated with improbably symmetrical segments of crystallised fruit. They lay on the kitchen table in hygienic plastic boxes, formidably professional, resolutely in the tradition of farmers' wives to whom anything not home-made is anathema.

'A family funeral, dear,' Dilys said again.

She had looked at Judy, at her long frame which might have come from either of her parents had they been her true parents; at her untidy red head and broad pale features, which certainly mightn't. Robin was as dark as Harry had once been, with Dilys's own father's narrow, harsh features. And Caro had been all brown—brown hair and eyes and pale-brown skin, even in winter. Not an English skin, Dilys had always thought, and certainly not a Meredith one. Even Joe's wife Lyndsay, with all that pale hair and those light eyes no Meredith had ever had, had skin not unlike Dilys's own; fine skin, clear-coloured. But Judy looked like none of them. Was like none of them.

'Take your coat off, dear,' Dilys said now.

'I'm cold,' Judy said. 'I'm cold from crying.'

'Leave her, Ma,' Joe said. He put an arm across Judy's shoulders. 'Leave her. You talk to the Vicar.'

Judy said in a fierce whisper, 'I never want to be buried like that.'

'Nor me.' He took his arm away. 'Burnt and scattered for me. Particularly scattered.'

She picked up the vast brown two-handled teapot, borrowed from Dean Cross village hall.

'On the farm?'

7

'No fear,' Joe said, 'in the river. Not on the bloody farm.'

Robin said beside them, 'Who's the woman in the scarf?'

Joe reached past Judy and took a slice of cake off a plate.

'Cornelius. A Mrs Cornelius. Bought the Chambers' old place. Rich and dippy. Caro used to visit her.'

Robin looked at him.

'Did she? Why? How do you know?'

Joe shrugged, holding one hand below the other to catch the cake crumbs.

'Dunno. Just did. She visited a lot of people.'

'She liked people,' Judy said, almost angrily. 'She *liked* them. All kinds of people.' She shot a look at Robin. 'Remember?'

He looked away from her. He looked across this table that he had rescued from a derelict chicken farm on the other side of the county—mahogany, nineteenth century, with nicely turned legs, being used as a perch in a barn—and saw his mother talking to the Vicar, and Mrs Cornelius talking to Gareth's wife, Debbie, and his sister-in-law Lyndsay, characteristically pushing combs back into her cloudy masses of hair, talking to three women Caro used to work with, competent women in their forties, competent women in competent clothes. He thought briefly, with a stab of longing and possible relief, of the milking parlour. Then he thought of what Judy had just said. 'Remember?' she'd said, as if it were a charge; 'Remember?' as if he'd forgotten in only a week, the week since Caro had died in Stretton Hospital of a brain tumour, what she was like, what she had loved and hated, what she had been. The

8

trouble is, Robin thought, detaching his gaze from Lyndsay's hair and allowing it to drift out towards the damp spring sky through the imperfectly cleaned windows, that it's too soon. It's too soon to remember because she hasn't gone yet. At least, not what was left of her. What didn't go years back. He held his teacup out to Judy.

'Please,' he said.

*   *   *

'No one from Carolyn's family?' the Vicar said to Dilys. 'No one from America?'

Dilys offered him a sandwich.

'Her father's dead. And her mother's in a wheelchair. Two strokes. And she's not seventy.'

The Vicar, who would have preferred cake, which he was never given at home, took a sandwich.

'Brothers and sisters?'

'Not that I know of.'

'Sad, isn't it,' the Vicar said, looking despondently at his sandwich, 'to die in a country that isn't your own and with nobody from home by you.' He had said this to his wife the night before, who had replied that it must have happened to Victorian missionaries all the time. There had been an edge of longing to her voice. She had wanted him to be a missionary, and when he had firmly declined in favour of provincial parish priesthood, had flung herself into forging her own links with Christian communities in Africa. The sitting room of the Dean Cross Vicarage was full of African artefacts, masks and statues and beaded hangings in red and black. The Vicar would have preferred water-colours, of boats.

'Very sad,' Dilys said, not thinking of Caro, but

9

thinking how terrible it would be if she, Dilys, had to die away from Dean Place Farm, away from people who knew the Merediths.

'I've never been to America,' the Vicar said. He looked at the nearest cake.

'Nor me,' Dilys said.

'But I felt I knew something of it sometimes. From Carolyn.'

'Oh?' Dilys said. She was eyeing Lyndsay, willing her to stop talking so absorbedly and do a little handing round. It was important to eat after funerals, to remind yourself of living. And to drink. She hoped Robin had remembered the sherry.

'Yes,' the Vicar said. He thought of those times Caro had sat in his study and asked him to find ways of accommodation for her, ways of coming to terms without complete submission, without the sacrifice of her deepest instincts.

'They're good people,' he had said to her, of the Merediths.

'What's good? Not being fornicators and abusers of the weak?'

'It's having integrity,' he had said. 'And principles. They do their duty.'

She'd said sadly, 'But that isn't enough. Is it?' and when he had stayed silent, she had insisted, more vehemently, 'Is it? Is it?'

He looked at Dilys now, grey hair waved, dark suit brushed, concentration given over entirely to the proper management of the funeral tea.

He said, only half meaning to, 'No, it isn't.'

Dilys didn't hear him. She was gesturing across the table to Robin with those well-kept, deft, domestic hands, a tiny drinking gesture.

'Sherry?' she mouthed. 'Time for sherry.'

10

Later, in the car, returning to their modern brick house on the edge of Dean Place Farm, Lyndsay said, 'We should have brought Judy back with us.'

'Couldn't do that,' Joe said. 'Couldn't leave Robin alone.'

Lyndsay took the combs out of her hair and put them between her teeth. Then she bent her head so that her hair fell forward over her face. Joe was right. Of course he was. Yet there was something about Robin that seemed to contribute to his own loneliness, to conspire to leave him in it, whatever one did—or didn't do—to try and help. She always thought of him as alone, somehow, driving alone, farming alone, standing alone at Stretton Market watching his cattle go through the ring. He was the only one of the Merediths to go in for cattle, too. Harry and Joe were arable farmers, as Harry's father and grandfather had been before them, tenant farmers on the same 250 acres even if the landlord had changed over the years from being a private individual to a company, a local manufacturing company, which had bought up several farms in the early seventies, when the price of land was low. Robin wouldn't be a tenant. Robin wanted to buy.

'Let him,' Harry had said. 'I shan't stop him, but I shan't help him either.'

Yet when Joe had needed a house for himself and Lyndsay, Harry had paid for that. He'd done a deal with the landlord and Lyndsay had been shown the plans, spread out on the table at Dean Place Farm.

'Utility room,' Dilys had said, pointing. 'Southern aspect. It'll make a lovely home.'

11

Lyndsay took the combs out of her mouth and shoved them back into her scoops of hair. It occurred to her, thinking of Robin, that Joe was solitary, too, in his way. She never quite knew what he was thinking, whether he was happy or sad. She knew he liked it when he was more successful than other arable farmers in the district, but that wasn't happiness, that was merely competitive triumph. Yet there was nothing odd in that, not round here. It might be difficult to get Joe to talk except on a factual level, but most farmers were like that, most farmers she knew didn't *talk*. Not like women talked. Or at least, some women. Dilys didn't talk that way either. She talked, as Harry and Joe did, about what was going on, on the farm, in the village. Happiness and unhappiness were for Dilys, Lyndsay thought, like the weather; emotions that happened or didn't happen, which were unpredictable and which, above all, had to be borne. If Dilys, in the manner of most wives, had ever had a moment of wanting to strangle Harry, she would have bided her time to let it pass, like waiting for the rain to stop. If you went to Dilys and said that you couldn't quite explain it, but you had the distinct sensation of being at the end of your tether, she would suggest you made chutney, or washed some blankets. Life had to be got through, great lumps of it pushed behind you, undigested if necessary. Life wasn't for battling with; the farm was there for that.

'Don't dwell on it,' Dilys would say to Lyndsay. 'Don't brood.' Had she ever said that to Caro?

'Will he be OK?'

'Robin?' Joe said. 'In time, I should think so. In time—'

Lyndsay said shyly, 'You were fond of Caro,

12

weren't you?'

There was a small pause, then Joe said, 'She made a change. Being American.'

Joe had been to America for a year, after agricultural college. Harry hadn't seemed to require him to take a serious job during that year—Robin had noticed this in silence—so Joe had roamed the great distances at will, picking up casual work in bars and diners and on farms in order to buy his passage onward. At one point, seduced by a girl and the mountains of Colorado, he had thought he might stay, but after a few weeks, he seemed to recollect his own legacy of knowing the difference between land and landscape, and had called from Denver to say he would be home by Christmas.

It was then that Robin had announced he was going in for cattle. One evening, at supper in the kitchen of Dean Place Farm, he had said that he had come to a decision, and that he'd be leaving home to start a dairy herd, and maybe a few beef cattle, too. Harry had put his knife and fork down and, in the harsh glare of the overhead light which Dilys saw no reason to soften because it was practical to work by, looked at his wife. Then he looked, much less intently, at Robin, and then he picked up his knife and fork again.

'Done your sums?' he said.

'Yes.'

Dilys held out a bowl of buttered cabbage.

'Joe will be home soon,' she said.

'I know.'

Robin waited for one of his parents to say that there wasn't room for all three Meredith men on Dean Place Farm, but they didn't. He took a spoonful of cabbage and said, rather more harshly

13

than he meant to, 'I want to do it, and it'll leave space for Joe.'

Harry grunted. Where Joe would go had been the chief preoccupation of most conversations he and Dilys had had since Joe had left for America.

'I've found a place. Land's not too bad but the yard needs a lot of work. I'd have to build a milking parlour.'

Harry looked up again, chewing.

'We've never had stock. Never.'

Robin said, 'But I'd like to.' It occurred to him to say, 'And you watch my profits,' but he thought he would neither tempt providence nor provoke his father. Instead, he said, 'I've got a loan. And a buyer for the cottage.'

Dilys got up to put a great wedge of cheese and a jar of pickle on the table. She said serenely, 'We wish you luck, dear,' and smiled at him as if he had solved a problem for her and she had known all along that he would.

Joe came home bringing a brief exciting aura of America with him to find Robin and some hired earth-moving machinery digging a slurry pit at Tideswell Farm. He also found that Robin had a girlfriend, a tall, brown-haired girl in jeans and cowboy boots painting window frames in the farmhouse.

'She's American, of course,' Dilys said. 'They met at Young Farmers.'

Dilys was doing the farm books, the ledgers and papers spread across the kitchen table weighted by the jam jars in which she kept the small change of housekeeping—egg money, newspaper money, money for the church collection and for shoe repairs.

'Seems nice enough.'

14

Joe thought she was more than nice. She carried with her something of that freedom he had known in America, that air of always keeping moving, keeping searching, that had briefly infected him like a sea fever. In the early weeks after his return, he tried to paint window frames with her, to keep America in his blood by being with her, but she sent him out to help Robin or home to take up his place beside his father. Even later, when she and Robin were married, she had retained a special quality for Joe, a reminder that there were places where life was different from this, where possibility was in the air, like oxygen.

Lyndsay said now, looking straight ahead through the car windscreen into the damp dimness of early evening, 'I never got to know her very well. I mean, we got on but we weren't close, were we?'

'She was older,' Joe said. 'She and Robin were married for twenty-four years. Judy's twenty-two after all.'

The lights of their house shone out suddenly as the lane turned between the hedges. Mary Corriedale, who worked at a paper factory in Stretton and lived in a bungalow in Dean Cross, would be there, putting the children to bed. Rose would no doubt already be in her cot, hurling toys to the floor as she defied the day to be over, and Hughie would be in his pyjamas and frog slippers commanding Mary to admire him while he balanced strenuously on one leg, his latest accomplishment.

Poor Caro, Lyndsay thought suddenly, with a stab of real pity, poor Caro not able to have her own children. What would she have done herself if she had discovered she couldn't have them either? Or that Joe couldn't? Being so much younger than Joe, she'd always assumed she'd just have babies when she

15

wanted them. And she had.

'Did Robin know,' Lyndsay said. 'Did Robin know before he married her that she couldn't have children?'

'I don't know,' Joe said. He turned the car off the lane and up the concrete slope to the house. 'I don't know. I never asked. It's not the kind of thing you do ask, is it?'

*   *   *

The milking parlour lay quiet, wet and orderly after the last hosing down of the day. The rubber and metal clusters of the mechanical milker were looped up next to the big reinforced glass milk jars—some of those, Robin noticed with his relentless eye, were still spattered with slurry—and the channels and ribbings of the floor along the stalls gleamed wet and clean. In the pit between the stalls the hose lay in the loose coil Robin required of it, the bottles of iodine and glycerine spray were lined up on the steps going down to the pit, the kick bars were hanging in a row on the wall at the far end. In the winter, if the river rose enough, the pit flooded and he and Gareth, swearing steadily, milked, heavily impeded by chest waders.

He turned off the fluorescent lighting, checked the bulk tank, and went into the barn. It was dark in there, apart from the dim washes of light cast by the low wattage bulkheads screwed to some of the timbers. Most of the cows were lying down in their cubicles, heads to the wall, their great black-and-white bodies spreading solidly between the rails. Some were standing up, back feet out of the straw and in the slurry channel; others were small enough to have got themselves the wrong way round so that

16

they'd drop muck at the head end and stand in it. He must remind Gareth to put some lime down.

Out in the yard beyond, where some of the cows chose to spend their aimless days, two of the outside cats were crouched on the fodder trough, containing the remains of the day's ration of feed made from chopped wheat-straw, given to bulk out the maize. The cats fled at his approach, streaking through the darkness towards the feed store where their harvest of vermin lived. Robin looked up at the sky. There was a moon, but a soft-edged one, presaging rain, and a few stars. In the business of the day, he'd hardly heard the weather forecast, that accustomed obsession. He sniffed deeply. The wind was soft, but there was rain on it, and soon.

He went back through the barn and the parlour to the stretch of concrete that led to the yard door of the house. By the door, the house cat waited, a rusty tortoiseshell, permitted inside because she was house-trained, possessed no anti-social feral attributes, and was a consistent mouser. Robin stooped to take off his boots and scratch her head.

'Hi,' he said.

She murmured politely, arching under his hand, and then shot in ahead of him as he opened the door.

Judy was still at the kitchen table, where Robin had left her twenty minutes before. She had cleared away the supper things, but had returned to her chair and was now sitting in it, elbows on the table, staring down into the glass of red wine Robin had given her. She didn't look up when he came in.

He pushed his socked feet into slippers.

'All well,' he said.

'Good.'

'A hundred and ten now. I'm trying to build up the

17

Dutch ones. Three to calve next week.'

Judy said, still staring at her wine, 'What happens if they're bull calves?'

'You know that,' Robin said. He poured himself some wine and sat opposite her. 'You grew up here.'

'I've forgotten.'

'They go to market.'

'And then?'

'You know that, too. They go as store cattle or to the slaughter house. Unless of course some rat gets hold of them and sends them for forty hours to Italy.'

'Mum once said to me that one of the first things she learned about farming was that the male of any species was only of any use for his semen. And meat.'

Robin said nothing. He turned his glass in his fingers. Supper had been difficult, largely because he didn't know what Judy wanted of him. She had said, at one point, pushing the casserole Dilys had made for them round her plate, 'I don't think we're even mourning the same person.'

'Of course not,' he said. Such a situation seemed utterly clear to him, and not at all surprising, but he had offended her by failing to rise to her implied accusation. She had twitched her grief away from him, as if he might sully it by trying to touch it and inevitably misunderstand it.

Now she said, 'Dad—'

'Yes.'

'I want to ask you something.'

'Yes?'

Her mouth quivered.

'Did you love her? Did you love Mum?'

'Yes.'

She said, 'You said that too quickly.'

Robin got up, and leaned on his hands on the table,

18

his face towards Judy.

'I don't think I could say anything to your satisfaction just now.'

She looked up at him.

'If you loved her—'

He waited.

'If you really loved her—'

'Yes?'

'Then why are you so angry?'

CHAPTER TWO

Carolyn Bliss was born in a small, peeling wooden house, painted duck-egg blue, in Sausalito on the Marin County side of the Golden Gate Bridge in San Francisco. Her father was a painter, a peaceful, aimless, pot-smoking man whose instinct for moral relativity was so strong that he had never, Carolyn's mother decided, made up his mind about anything. She came from further up the coast, from a featureless little place on the Washington State border, a girl of strong, tall, Scandinavian-settler stock. Her roots were agricultural. She wanted to move back up to Oregon with the painter and their baby and start a vineyard, a little 12-hectare vineyard planted with Cabernet Sauvignon grapes. The blue wooden house, in Caro's childhood, was filled with manuals on viniculture, leaflets on pruning techniques, photographs of bunches of grapes hanging dusty with bloom in harvest sunlight.

Caro grew up with the strong impression that life—and therefore the world and the future—lay over the Golden Gate Bridge. The skyline of San

Francisco shimmered across the bay like the towers and spires of a mythical city of dreams, the place which, if only one could reach it, would turn out to contain one's own personal Holy Grail. Her mother's talk of Oregon reinforced this feeling that the blue wooden house was only a starting point, no more than a nursery nest, and that it had nothing at its back, either literally or figuratively, only the bay and the bridge and the city beckoning before it; that was the only reality. In the summer, the pretty coastline around the blue house filled up with people who owned second homes there, people with children whose fathers didn't spend the winters in a dopey haze on the waterfront getting in the way of the fishermen, and whose mothers sailed and swam and cooked barbecues, instead of hacking at the earth behind the blue house all year, as if determined to wrest productivity from it by brute force.

There was a week or two of mild euphoria when Caro's father left. He just vanished, taking with him his paints, a stash of the marijuana he had grown painstakingly himself in one of his wife's clearings, and the small hoard of dollars she was putting by for the vineyard in Oregon. The police added his name to their interminable list of the missing, but perhaps they sensed that neither his mistress nor his daughter felt very urgent about his discovery, and after some months it was assumed, without needing to say much about it, that even if he were alive he would not return. Caro had a water-colour of his, a small blue oblong of seawater, and sometimes she would look at this patch of water and wonder if he was in it, lying tranquilly on the floor of the bay with a joint in one hand and a paintbrush in the other. She did not miss him. He had not allowed enough of himself to be

20

known to be missed.

Carolyn's mother sold the remainder of the lease on the blue house to a Chinese family from San Francisco who wanted it for the summers and moved herself and her daughter northwards. Caro was eleven. Somewhere on this journey, Caro's mother acquired a friend, a small tough woman called Ruthie who seemed to share the dream of the vineyard. They bought a battered trailer, and fixed it up for sleeping in, and for four years Caro rode the roads of North-west America looking for the 12 hectares. At some point in these travels, it occurred to her that she had never crossed the Golden Gate Bridge to the future, so that, although she was definitely away from Marin County, she was still within the thrall of the blue house, waiting for life to begin in earnest.

She did not like Ruthie. In the course of some of her brief bouts of schooling, girls her own age said Ruthie and Caro's mother were sleeping together. Caro saw no sign of it, but then she took care not to look too closely, just as she took care not to observe the welfare-food stamps, nor her mother and Ruthie's itinerant labouring lives, vine-pruning in January, pea-picking in June, the backbreaking harvesting of late summer. She kept a corner of the trailer her own, with fierce possessiveness, and drew endless pictures of houses with yards and picket fences and apple trees and dog kennels, houses absolutely hedged about with all the paraphernalia of a settled domesticity.

When she was fifteen, she had had enough. On a grilling late August day, she braided her hair into a fat pigtail, dressed herself in clean clothes she had ironed by putting them under her mattress and then sleeping on it, and went to ask the wife of the farmer

21

her mother and Ruthie were then stripping corn for if she might live at the farmhouse that winter, and go to school in a regular fashion in nearby Harrisburg. She would earn her keep, she said, cleaning the house, looking after the poultry, doing the dishes and minding the children. The farmer's wife looked out wearily from her brood of five sons under nine years of age and said yes. A fearful row ensued. Ruthie tried to lock her in the trailer and her mother took away her shoes. But Caro moved into the farmhouse before the end of the month and viewed her austere bedroom, on whose every surface dust from the fields lay pale and thick, with profound satisfaction.

She stayed there for a year. When it was up, she moved in with the family of a schoolfriend, and then, for her final grade, with a teacher who taught history at her high school. Two or three times a year, her mother and Ruthie and the trailer turned up at these various addresses and were entertained with cookies and root beer or pizzas and low-calorie Cola before Caro judged they had trespassed on her life long enough and dispatched them. They were growing alike as they got older, gruff in manner and mannish in speech. Neither of them ever suggested that Caro should rejoin them and return to her corner of the trailer. She would have rejected the idea out of hand if they had.

When she was eighteen, she got a state grant to do a course in graphic design at an art college in Portland, having something of her father's artistic aptitude, overlaid by her own stoutly defended desire for order. She did not like being in Portland, however, and found that she did not like the course much, either, and the idea began to haunt her that she was in the wrong place to get anywhere in the simplest geographical sense, and that, if she did not return south and cross that damned Bridge, she was never going to have a real life, nor a future, and that all the efforts of her adolescence in forging a way forward would be thrown away.

She sold most of her possessions to buy a long-distance bus ticket back to California, and to have a few dollars by her. Back in Sausalito she paid a cursory visit to the blue house—now painted hot pink—and then, with her backpack, walked the whole length of the Golden Gate Bridge back into the city. It took her twenty-seven minutes. After that, and prompted by the memory of the welcome extended to her by the educational community in Harrisburg, she hitched a series of lifts out to the University of Berkeley and got herself a job in one of the futon stores that abounded there among the banks and bookstores and purveyors of hippie beads and ginseng and magic mushrooms.

Two things of immense significance happened to Caro as a result of working in the futon store. The first was that she made friends with an English couple, a professor of semantics and his physicist wife, in Berkeley for a year as part of an academic exchange programme. They came into the store to buy a couple of futons for their apartment in order to have somewhere for their visiting adolescent children to sleep, and a friendship was struck up in the big, light store among the pale, quiet rolls of bedding that led to Caro's going round to their apartment for meals, and then for weekends.

The second thing was Caro's first love affair. It was with a Japanese student at the university who worked in the store on Saturday mornings and, at odd times, on the order books with the manager, who spoke no

Japanese and did not understand all the invoices. The student was called Ken. He was tall, for a Japanese, but still much shorter than Caro, and they made love in the stock room behind the store on futons due to be returned to the factory because of faults, mostly in the stitching. She found his skin and hair especially attractive, and also his courtesy. He escorted her to the student clinic to obtain her first ever prescription for contraceptive pills. She began to believe that she had crossed the Bridge.

But then she fell ill. At first she felt tired and queasy, which she attributed to getting used to the contraceptive pills, and then she felt worse, and her periods ceased. She no longer felt like making love and Ken, though unfailingly polite, made it plain he did not simply wish to lie on the faulty futons in the stock room with her and smoke. He withdrew himself a little, and then announced that he must find himself another outlet for his natural impulses and took himself off to a different Saturday job, in a sushi bar, where he sat behind the till, wearing a green waistcoat and matching bow tie, taking the customers' dollars.

Three days after his departure, Caro fainted at work. Brought round, she said the pain was simply terrible and fainted again. She was taken to hospital, where tests revealed that both her fallopian tubes were blocked by a chronic inflammation caused by infection, and that the same infection had gravely affected both ovaries. She was operated upon at once, informed that she was now, regrettably, infertile and sent away to convalesce on one of the futons she had sold to the English couple.

They were good to her. She was, they said, the age of their eldest daughter, now studying law at an English university Caro had never heard of called

24

Exeter, and that alone aroused their sympathy. They nursed her back to health, found her work in the bookstore of the student centre and then, as a twentieth birthday present, gave her an economy-class return air ticket to London. They had friends and relations in England she could stay with, they said, and she would have a chance to see her life and her country from another perspective. It would help her, they said, to make up her mind. To Caro, it was the most extraordinary present she had ever been given, not just for its generosity but because it appeared to prove that, despite Ken, and despite the operation—whose consequences had as yet hardly dawned upon her—the promise of the Golden Gate Bridge still held good.

*　　　*　　　*

In April 1971, Caro Bliss arrived in England with a modest bag of clothes and a list of addresses. She spent ten days with her benefactors' relations in a suburban house near Richmond Park, and then went to stay in chaotic student lodgings—a rented farmhouse with lukewarm hot water and intermittent electricity—outside Exeter. The culture shock of both places was immense. Even the language seemed to divide more than it united. For three weeks Caro endured the incomprehensible loud rompings of English students at play—so different in every way, from the spaced-out laxity of their counterparts at Berkeley—and then, leaving a stilted thank-you note in her simply turned American hand, set off into the mysteries of the English railway system to her third address, a farm in the Midlands.

It was a big, commercial place, raising pork and

beef and growing fruit and vegetables for a series of farm shops. The family who ran it—father, mother, grown-up son and two daughters—had known the physicist at Berkeley since she was a girl. The farmer's wife's mother, now dead, had been her godmother. They took Caro in as if tall, homeless American girls without particular direction came their way every day of the week and included her, without fuss, in their life and work.

They didn't, as the students in Exeter did, talk all the time. They talked when necessary, about subjects that affected their working lives, the life of the farm. This suited Caro. Living, as she had since she was fifteen, on the edges of so many other people's lives, she had become used not to talking much herself, as if to talk was to thrust herself into the limelight, into the centre of attention in lives that she depended upon for sustenance and thus could not afford to alienate by the wrong sort of behaviour. Even before that, Caro's childhood had not been an eloquent matter. Her father's articulateness, such as it was, lay in his painting, her mother's in an urgent practicality, designed to wrench some kind of reality out of romantic dreams. On this large, efficient commercial enterprise in the English Midlands, Caro found much to recognise as trustworthy. Cautiously, feeling her way through the unaccustomed rhythms of the days and the peculiar food, Caro began, despite herself, to relax.

Some evenings and at weekends, the son of the house and his girlfriend—a vet specialising in pigs—took Caro with them on outings with the local Young Farmers' group. She attended lectures on farm management, competitions on stock judging and an enormous number of evenings in the pub where she learned to play darts and failed to learn to like warm, strong English beer. It was often the same crowd, friendly, cheerful and healthy, a youth group of a kind Caro had never encountered before, with scarcely even a nod to urban life. They were the farming children of farming parents; for most of them the decision to devote themselves to the land had scarcely been a decision at all but rather an acceptance of the preordained path of things. Looking around the smoky bars of pubs and clubs, Caro saw, with a kind of awe, that she, the nomad, had at last come to rest among settlers, among people who identified themselves more by place than by personality or trade. And, to her surprise, she liked it.

Robin Meredith watched her for five weeks before he spoke to her. Being tall himself, he was struck by her height, and then by the exoticism of her accent. She was a different build to English girls, and she used her body differently, and her hands. He was told she was a hired hand in the farm shop at Thripps End, so he supposed she was part of the itinerant community of international students postponing both the return to the familiar and facing the future. When he finally bought her half a pint of cider, he discovered that she was neither a student nor in work. She had come to England, she said, at someone else's suggestion, and because of their generosity.

'Why?' he said.

She shrugged. 'To look, I guess. To look at over there from over here.'

'Why?' he said again.

She had paused and looked down into her cider. Then she said, with her new-found self-knowledge, 'Maybe to see if I really am a nomad.'

He didn't know what she meant, but he asked her

27

out anyhow. He drove her through the countryside pointing out farms and crops and woodland planted especially for the rearing of pheasants. He took her to the cinema, where he sat with his long thigh pressed to hers but did not take her hand, and to the local annual horse fair where she saw the first gypsies of her life, and to the top of Stretton Beacon where he showed her the county laid below them like a map, orderly and tamed from this height, the agricultural spaces punctuated by the roofs and chimneys and spires of settlements. Up there, in the wind, he kissed her and told her he was leaving home to set up his own dairy herd.

'Down there,' he said, pointing at the grey loops of the River Dean winding below them. 'Down there.'

'I've never touched a cow,' Caro said.

'I'm starting with twenty,' he said. 'Twenty. I'll build a herringbone parlour.'

She looked down at the landscape below her. She'd seen lovelier landscapes, certainly, more dramatic, more powerful. But had she ever seen landscape that seemed to offer itself so benevolently for people to live in, and use? Had she ever seen any place so manageable, so involving, so harmonious? And it just lay there, at her feet, 20 or 30 square-miles of peaceful, tractable cultivation, not fighting mankind, not riven with exaggerated weather and earthquakes, not elusive because of impossible distances. It was a world down there, a complete world of man and land and beast under an unremarkable, unthreatening English sky. Caro put her hands into her jacket pockets and shut her eyes. How was she to fashion, with no means at her disposal except the simple fact of herself, the chance to stay?

28

A week later, Robin drove her to Tideswell Farm. They inspected the house and the derelict yard, and they walked through the neglected fields down to the river where ducks and coots and moorhens prattled among the reeds. It was late March, and the willow trees had their yellow-green spring haze about them, and on the opposite slope, a tractor was ploughing the red-brown earth into a satisfactory ribbing, like corduroy.

'What about the house?' Robin said.

Caro watched the tractor. A decorative flock of gulls was wheeling above the turned earth in the wake of the plough. Robin's house was almost too strange for her to have an opinion of, so old, so solid in its stone walls, so rambling, with its gaunt, chill Victorian additions, that passage with the mosaic-tiled floor in red-and-ochre, the bay-windowed room with the wooden-fire surround like a Gothic church.

'I don't know,' she said. 'I haven't anything to compare it with—'

'Does that matter?'

She looked at him.

'No,' she said slowly, 'I don't suppose it does. It's just when you keep travelling, you keep comparing. You can't help it. It's what all the differences do to you, it's how you think.'

He reached up into the willow above their heads, and broke off a long, smooth, flexible twig.

'What's the best place you ever lived?'

'Oh,' she said, 'I haven't found that yet. I'm still looking.'

Robin bent the twig into a circle, a willowy coronet, and skimmed it out across the water like

29

a quoit.

'You don't have to wander,' he said. 'You don't have to.'

She looked at him. She looked at his rough, near-black hair and uncompromising features, at his corduroy trousers and his boots and battered weatherproof jacket with the collar turned up around his ears. She thought: Do I know him? and then, almost simultaneously: Who have I ever known?

He turned to look back at her.

'I said, "You don't have to wander." Not any more.' He gestured back up the fields in the direction of the house. 'You could live here. I'd give you somewhere to live. You could—' He paused and then he said, 'You could marry me.'

CHAPTER THREE

Velma Simms stood at the sink in the kitchen at Tideswell Farm and washed up Robin's breakfast dishes. Caro had installed a dishwasher, but Velma never used it. She didn't use it because she disapproved of the fact that it in turn used electricity. By the same token, she preferred using the mechanical carpet sweeper to the vacuum cleaner and to performing almost all tasks in the half-light. In her council house, the electricity meter, resentfully fed with coins, was regarded as an ill-intentioned household god forced upon her by the authorities. Anything Velma could do without submitting to the tyranny of electricity seemed to her a blow struck for personal victory over a force of darkness.

Behind her, at the kitchen table, Gareth sat eating

a bacon sandwich. Debbie made him a stack of them late each night for the following morning, and Gareth had taken to eating them in the farm kitchen after the first milking, to save going home. Home, a three-bedroom brick tied cottage that Robin had built for the previous herdsman, was only a few hundred yards away, but the farm kitchen made a change from his own, and fifteen minutes in it daily meant that he kept up with everything that was happening. When Caro was alive, he hadn't liked to do this, being dimly aware at some level that he was intruding on territory that was both mysteriously female and forbidden. Sometimes, he had stood in the doorway in his boiler suit and stockinged feet, and left messages for Caro to give Robin about a cow with mastitis or the failure of the artificial insemination technician to show up, but he'd never intruded further. He was always struck by the refrigerator. While he was talking to Caro, he kept his eye on it in wonder, this huge, double-doored American thing, big as a wardrobe.

'You should see it,' he said to Debbie. 'You could get a couple of blokes in there, easy.'

He sat with his back to it now, chewing. Without Caro there and its cavernous spaces only housing Robin's utilitarian supplies, the refrigerator had lost its magic. Its chief purpose now was for taunting Velma, to try and get her to open the door or, even better, both doors. She hated opening the doors because it made the lights come on.

'Waste of electric!' she'd shriek, slamming them shut almost before she'd got the milk out.

'He won't eat cooked,' Velma said now, parking a cereal bowl in the plate rack. 'He was doing himself a cooked breakfast right up till she died but he won't

31

do it now. Mugs of cold tea he's forgotten sitting about all over the house and these everlasting cereal bowls.'

'Better than the bottle,' Gareth said. He eyed Velma from behind. She wore purple leggings and a black jersey—not long enough—and turquoise trainers. 'Me daps,' she called them. Her bottom, Gareth decided, reminded him of his mum's.

'He thought the world of her,' Velma said firmly. 'The world.'

'Did he?' Gareth said. The Robin he knew was not, he considered, the kind of man to think the world of anything or anybody. He'd never go that far. He just wanted things to work, jobs to be done properly. When Debbie complained, as she frequently did, that all he, Gareth, ever thought about was the cows, he said well, he had to, didn't he? With Robin on his back day and night, he hadn't exactly got a choice, had he? Debbie wanted him to stop being a herdsman, and go back to college to learn some modern skills with computers and business studies. She wanted to see him in the management side of farming, not in a mucky boiler suit with hands and arms that had spent half the day up something she'd rather not think about. But Gareth liked cows. He didn't mind the hours and he didn't mind Robin. In any case, the thought of computers made him panic.

'Where's he gone then?' Velma said.

'Milk quota meeting.'

'Load of nonsense, all this quota stuff—'

'Yeah,' Gareth said. He stood up, screwing the foil in which Debbie had wrapped his sandwiches into a ball. He said, 'Funny here now. Isn't it?'

Velma took her hands out of the sink and dried them on a tea towel. She looked round the room, at its sunny, fruity, American colours, at the extravagant fridge, at the poster of an enormous swooping bridge photographed black against a sunset under the slogan, 'California Dreamin''.

'She never settled,' Velma said. 'Not really. Me mam's sister was like that. Went to New Zealand to marry a sheep farmer and she never really took to it. Homesick till the day she died, always pining. At least,' Velma said, wiping a handful of spoons, 'my auntie knew what she was pining for. I don't think our madam here ever did.'

'Who's that?' Gareth said. It was time he was back out in the yard, getting the three cows whose feet needed attention into the metal-framed crush so he could inspect them, but there was something about this conversation that was oddly alluring. And now, beyond Velma's outline at the window by the sink, he could see a Land Rover in the yard.

'Joe,' Velma said. She tugged down her jersey. Good-looking fellow, Joe.

'What's he doing here?'

Velma went over to the kitchen door and out through the porch where the boots were kept, to the yard.

'He's out!' she yelled at Joe.

'That's OK—'

He came past her into the kitchen, boiler-suited like Gareth in dark-blue drill and wearing army-fatigue boots.

'Morning, Gareth—'

Gareth nodded. He picked up his flask and his copy of the daily paper he preferred, partly for its obsessive football coverage and partly for the daily tits shot. Debbie had had tits once, but they seemed to have vanished, subsiding in a gradual and puzzling

33

way as each of her three children was born. Pity, really.

'I'm getting back to the yard—'

'Yes,' Joe said.

Velma came back into the kitchen saying, 'Coffee?'

'No thanks,' Joe said. 'I just want to look for something.' He paused and then he said, 'Upstairs.'

'I'll show you—'

'No,' Joe said. He put a hand out, as if to stop her. 'I know what it is. I know my way. See you, Gareth.'

They watched him go out of the kitchen.

'Take your boots off!' Velma shouted.

His tread, still booted, went up the stairs.

'What the heck—'

'I dunno,' Velma said. 'I dunno. I shouldn't have let him. But I couldn't stop him, could I? Robin's brother and all—'

'Sh—' Gareth said. He looked upwards. Velma looked, too. Above their heads, across the floorboards of the room above, Joe's boots moved slowly, and then stopped.

'Blooming cheek!' Velma said. 'He's in her room! What the hell's he doing there?'

The footsteps moved again, very slowly and carefully.

'He's in her room!' Velma said again. 'In Caro's room! I haven't been in since she went, only to dust and that. I'd better go up—'

'No,' Gareth said. He put a hand on her arm. 'Leave him.'

'But he—'

'You don't know,' Gareth said. 'You don't know what he wants. He wouldn't take nothing. Maybe—'

'What?'

'You just leave him,' Gareth said. He gave her arm

34

a squeeze and let it go. 'He wouldn't have come in, bold as brass, would he, if he was up to anything? You just leave him.'

He moved towards the door, rolling up his paper into a baton, his flask under his arm.

'See you, Velma.'

She picked up her tea towel again, shaking her head as if to rid it of unnerving vibrations.

'Weird,' she said.

*   *   *

In Caro's bedroom, Joe leaned on the footboard of her bed and looked at where she had lain. He had seen her there, several times, during the fast and frightening progress of her illness, wearing candy-striped nightshirts with her hair plaited slightly to one side so that she could lie comfortably. That is, while she still had hair. Before the treatment.

He held the polished wooden rail of the bed and stared at the curve of the pillow under the red-and-white patchwork quilt. He wasn't wholly certain why he was here, but only that he had obeyed a sudden impulse to say goodbye to Caro, to explain to her—by being in her bedroom rather than by saying anything—that his mental absence from her funeral, from anything to do with the fact of her death, had nothing to do with *her*. It had to do with something much darker and more alarming, a fear that had settled upon Joe the moment Robin had rung from Stretton Hospital to say that Caro had died twenty minutes before—and hadn't left him since. He had felt, standing at the graveside and holding the yellow umbrella over Lyndsay and Judy, something close to panic. He had felt it again, on and off, ever since, had

35

found himself driving the long way round through Dean Cross in order to avoid the churchyard and almost barking at Lyndsay every time Caro's name came up in conversation. Ten minutes ago, driving down the lane between Dean Place and Tideswell, but heading home, the panic had fallen so violently upon Joe that he had, for a fraction of a second, almost blacked out.

'I'll nail it,' he'd said aloud to himself, gripping the steering wheel. 'I'll go and stand in her bedroom and I'll bloody well *nail* it.'

But her bedroom offered him nothing. It was tidy, almost austere, furnished with a random collection of things she had picked up at auction sales over the years; neat things, almost prim. There was no sign of Robin in the room, no evidence of his having shared the bed with the patchwork quilt. But then there was no sign of anything much, least of all the element Joe had so urgently wished to find—a sign of life.

'Caro,' he said to the empty air.

Nothing stirred. He went over to the window and looked down into the yard from it—a view she had presumably chosen—and saw nothing there, either, not even cows. There was something literally unbearable about her removal, something deeply cruel, as well as fatal. He put his forehead against the glass of the windowpane. It was the fatality that was so terrible. Without Caro there, without her living self being there as proof of this other world, this other life of hope and movement that she had carried about with her like an aura, the fates could just close in. He swallowed hard. Something about Caro, about who she was, where she'd come from, had made him feel—why the hell had she made him feel it?—that he could dodge destiny, that he—if he kept running—

36

was the fleeter of foot.

She'd even made him feel that the money didn't matter, that his seeming ability to manage the farm's finances was not running away with him. He had never spoken to her openly about his fears, about the secret loans, about his tendency to feel that, if he spent more money, he would somehow see a return on it automatically, but he had hinted at it. And she had smiled at him. She had smiled that calm but perceiving smile and told him not to be afraid of the short-term; the short-term was always full of shocks, it was the long-term you had to focus on. And now she had gone, and the consolation of the long-term had gone with her, and he was left here alone with the shocks.

He took his forehead away from the glass, and rubbed it. Below him in the yard, Gareth went by at some distance, holding a cow either side of him on halters. Robin was good at training cows to halters, had rigged up some device like a whirling clothesline where the young heifers were broken in to being led. He said it made them better to show and in the saleroom, that a well-behaved cow was more likely to attract a buyer's eye. Robin ... What would Robin think if he were to come home now and find Joe in his dead wife's bedroom with no explanation to offer for it? And there wasn't an explanation, was there, not a solid one, not one you could hold out to a sceptical brother who, after all, was entitled to any manifestation of grief he cared to indulge in? Whereas he, Joe, brother-in-law to the deceased woman only, husband and father of living beings, had no such entitlement. No right at all, no claim except this sensation that appalled him so, that she had somehow held a key to the future for him, and

37

that when she had died, she had taken it with her.

He went out on to the landing. The house was very still. Velma would be still in the kitchen, too, affecting to wash up but in reality waiting for Joe to come down and explain himself. Velma hadn't come to the funeral. Said she never did, couldn't take the things. 'Morbid,' she said. 'When you're gone, you're gone. Funerals is sick.' What had she said to Robin, Joe wondered, if anything? 'Sorry to hear of your loss' or, 'I'll miss her, that's for sure' or simply, 'You want me to get you another jar of coffee? This one's nearly gone'?

Across the landing, the door to Robin's room was open. His bed was made, after a fashion, but the two wooden chairs Joe could see were heaped with clothes and there were shoes and newspapers on the floor and scattered copies of dairy-farming magazines. Odd, really. Robin had always been so orderly. There was a photograph of Caro on the chest of drawers against the far wall, a black-and-white picture taken of her leaning on the gate from the garden to the fifteen-acre field where the young heifers were first put out, close to the house where an eye could be kept on them. Joe couldn't see the picture very clearly from this distance, but Caro's hair appeared to be loose and she was wearing something checked.

'You OK?' Velma called.

She was standing at the foot of the stairs, holding a duster and a can of spray polish.

'Find what you want?'

'No,' Joe said, 'I didn't. Doesn't matter.'

She said, 'Better come down then.'

He descended the stairs, slowly, while she watched him.

'Robin'll be home dinnertime—'

'Yes.'

'I'm leaving him a slice of veal-and-ham pie,' she said and then, firmly, 'I look after him.'

At home, Joe thought, Lyndsay would be cooking lunch for him and the children, the proper, conscientious lunch she cooked for them every day, with plenty of vegetables. They would sit round the kitchen table, he and Lyndsay and Hughie with Rose in her high chair, and they would eat cottage pie or casserole or cheese-and-potato flan, and Lyndsay would try and talk to him and make him encourage Hughie to talk. She attempted to dissuade him from having the radio on, for the farming news and the weather. She said he could hear that all day, in the Land Rover, on the tractor, that mealtimes were for communication, for paying attention to one another, for talking. Rose couldn't talk yet but she made up for that by urgent shouting and banging of spoons on her high-chair tray. On Joe's darker days, there was a lot to be said for Rose.

'I'll be off,' Joe said to Velma.

She looked up at him. He'd always had a bit of an air of the young John Wayne about him for her, that rugged look. She said, 'You could try smiling, Joe. Life's got to go on.'

He paused a moment, gave her a fleeting smile which never got near his eyes, and then went past her through the kitchen and out to the yard.

*   *   *

Robin's slice of pie lay under a sheet of tightly stretched plastic film beside the salt and pepper mills and a loaf of bread under a muslin dome. Dilys had given Caro several of these domes, to protect food in the larder from flies, but Caro had never used them, any more than she had used the larder, since she kept everything perishable in the great Westinghouse refrigerator that Robin had given her, via an importer in London, when they had been married for twelve years.

The house cat had plainly attempted forced entry to the pie, and failed. She now sat on the stack of newspapers by the back door destined for Robin's next journey past the recycling bins, and waited for developments. Robin pointed at the plate.

'Mine,' he said.

The cat pretended she hadn't heard. She stared at him levelly. Robin peered at the pie. It had the off-putting pallor of all processed food kept at room temperature because Velma preferred to risk its going off rather than supposedly consume electricity by storing it in the fridge. Robin peeled off the film and sniffed. A marked smell, not exactly rancid, but pungent, rose from the pie. He picked up the plate and carried it across to the pile of newspapers, setting it on the floor beside them.

'All yours,' he said.

He moved across to the fridge and took out a block of cheese. He seemed to be living off the stuff, cheese and cereals, anything bulky and easy. When he was a boy, Dilys had kept a house cow who'd provided all the butter and cheese they'd eaten, and the skim milk went into the bread. Now Dilys bought cheese and bread like everyone else. The economics of keeping a house cow were hopeless.

Velma had left a list of messages on the table.

'Man rang from farming development scheme. Said you knew what about. Gareth says new slurry

40

pipe's come and he's got four cows bulling. Salesman came about the fertiliser. I said come back Wednesday. Joe came but I don't know what he wanted. Got the doctor tomorrow morning but I'll be down later. Sitting-room chimney needs the sweep.'

Robin turned the radio on, heard the prediction of strong westerly winds he'd heard on the way home and turned it off again. He lifted the muslin dome off the loaf and looked at it. What had Joe wanted? What had he wanted he couldn't say on the telephone? He picked up the bread knife and began to slice thick, practised, even slices from the loaf. The meeting had been depressing, as such meetings tended to be these days, with all the big dairies reporting turnover down for the half-year and government health guidelines urging the public to consume less dairy fat. He hadn't needed to go to the meeting to be told that, nor to have salt rubbed in the wound of his own vulnerability. Those early years of farming, he thought he'd had it made, with profits on the herd doubling year after year so that the sleep-disturbing loans, for a brief and heady period, had seemed they would melt like sugar. Some hope, he thought now, putting cheese between the bread slices, some hope, with costs going up all the time, Gareth on £13,000 plus his house, cows needing several hundred pounds' worth of bought-in feed a year each, interest rates ... and now this cold wet spring would mean the maize would go in late. He took a single bite and then put the sandwich down. It tasted of nothing and the texture was as dry as dust.

*   *   *

Out in the yard, all was quiet. In an hour Gareth
41

would be back to herd the cows into the collecting yard, and then go round the barn and all the hard-standing scraping away the slurry with a great rubber fender attached to a tractor. It was an ancient tractor, Robin's very first, third-hand even when he'd had it. You couldn't buy a tractor tyre these days for what he'd paid for that tractor. He liked old things, like the experienced cows, often stubborn as hell, who went to the same stall in the parlour every milking, regular as clockwork, and the same cubicle in the barn. They had an authority about them that he respected, that calmed the young ones. He liked to put a few old girls among the young ones for that very reason even though old was hardly the word for them these days. He'd have liked to think of them going on for thirteen or fourteen years as was their natural span, but nowadays they didn't make much more than five.

The cows watched him with the peaceableness of familiarity as he climbed into his Land Rover and set off past them down the farm track to the river. Because of the spring rain, the pollution-control people were in a ferment about slurry getting washed down into the river, and if it wasn't the pollution-control people, it would be something about health-and-safety regulations, inevitably involving the spending of money he didn't have.

'I haven't got any money,' Caro had said to him, all those years ago on the river bank. 'Not a cent.'

'Nor have I.'

'But—' She had gestured up the sloping fields behind them, to where the house stood beside its ruined yard.

'I'm borrowing it,' he said, understanding her. 'All but £6,000. Borrowing every other penny.'

He swung the Land Rover off the track and

stopped it in a field gateway. The field, this close to the river, had been flooded until early March and lay bleak and starved-looking, desperate for warmth for the new growth of grass. Borrowing! That had only been the beginning. Borrowing had become a way of life, hadn't it, borrowing for animals, for machinery, for buildings, for tractors and fertilisers and parlour equipment all on hire purchase, all gone or obsolete before he'd ever got to the end of the payments.

'Do your own milking,' Harry had said, over and over. 'Save on a herdsman. What d'you want with a herdsman on a herd that size?'

Because of Caro, had been the reply, but Robin had never uttered it. He'd never uttered it because it was nothing to do with Caro in a way, she'd never asked him to give more time to her and to Judy, never declared, as he knew Lyndsay did, that she felt excluded from this arduous, dedicated, relentless farming life of his. It was he who had wanted it, he who had employed herdsmen he could ill afford, to try and be part of Caro's life, to make himself available to her, to be something other than a farmer for her if only for a few hours.

'Why do you want to farm?' she'd said to him at the beginning, and he had replied, almost shyly, 'Because I like producing things,' and she had looked at him for a long time with a kind of quiet sorrow that he hadn't understood at all.

He got out of the Land Rover, and made his way across the field towards the further hedgerow—which needed attention, he noticed—down which a small brook, not much bigger than a ditch, ran from the slope below the slurry pit to the river. The pit needed enlarging, he knew that, had needed it for a year or so, as well as the installation of a new dirty-

43

water pump. Next thing, the rivers authority would be down on him and fines would be added to that pile of bills he now kept in a plastic storage box in the kitchen, and which he only paid any attention to when the red demands came.

Caro had never kept his farm books. He had wrested them from Dilys with great difficulty, hoping that Caro would take them up, would learn the prices of feed and water rates and straws of bull semen so that the farm would become a reality to her, a commitment of his that might naturally turn into a commitment of theirs. But she declined, gently but firmly. She said she was no good at figures.

'But you'd learn—'

'No,' she said, smiling, 'I wouldn't.'

She had set aside a room for him, for a farm office, a narrow room like a slice of passage, on the ground floor, with a window looking out on to the drive. She had fixed shelves for him there herself, and made curtains and cushions, and set out filing trays as if encouraging a child to believe that homework is fun. Obediently, for twenty years, until Caro's death, he had confined the farm's paperwork to the narrow room, had withdrawn there to read agricultural ministry pamphlets and market reports and articles on new feeding systems and, when it became unavoidable, to write cheques. These came from a cheque book stamped 'Tideswell Farm Account'. Caro thought it was some kind of piggy bank. Robin knew it was only a record of debt.

He reached the hedgerow, and pushed his way through to look at the brook. The water, running freely in its narrow channel, looked clear enough, but that meant nothing much. There could be seepage down through the sodden earth and he would rather

44

find that out for himself before the authorities officiously found out for him. What he would do when he discovered he was indeed polluting the river, he didn't know. But then, he didn't know right now what he was going to do about anything.

He straightened and looked up the long slope of the hedgerow towards the point on the horizon where the roofs of the farmyard were outlined against the persistently grey sky. In the weeks since Caro had died, it had been grey, day after day, deadening to the spirit and failing to nourish the chilled earth. It had rained, too, as it did at her funeral, cold, sharp rain that had held up the spreading of fertilisers and had made him feel, at some obscure level, that he was out of step with things, that he was being punished.

Judy had almost accused him of not loving her mother. He had denied it, badly, not because he didn't believe in his own denial but because the story went back so far, was so complicated. Perhaps he should, fatigue of heart and mind after the funeral notwithstanding, have tried to explain to Judy, have at least attempted to describe how much he had once loved Caro and how much he himself was at a loss to know when that love took a wrong turn and then persisted in its wrongness. Yet he hardly knew himself. He just felt, looking back on those years of an endeavour he believed he'd put his whole heart into, the endeavour of Caro, that there was a moment he realised he'd grown to like being on his own and to be quite calm—even indifferent—about the unending puzzle of understanding her. Judy would probably call it a betrayal; that was the sort of language she went in for, defiant, unhappy language. But there was no deception, Robin believed, in what he had done, no treachery or base abandonment;

45

only a struggle to live with something one had chosen and which had then turned out to be both entirely different from one's expectations, and utterly intractable.

He began to walk slowly up the rough bank of the little brook, head bent, eyes fixed upon the mud and the water. Judy had declared that he was angry. Well, he was, in a way, in a complicated way borne of years of battle and effort. Anger at specific things, such as Caro's failure to tell him until they were married that she couldn't have children, or the sudden demand he should meet her mother's hospital bills in America, had long since faded. Hadn't they? But he was angry about her illness, that anyone should have to die this ravaged, distorting way, a slow cruelty that seemed to put most other hideous cruelties in the natural world to shame. Yet was he angry with her, for leaving him, by dying, and for subjecting him, before she left, to this long life of the form of companionship without the content? Was it that? He put out a hand at random and grasped a supple young rogue sapling sprouting from the hedge, bending it over decisively and weaving it through the nearest stout upright stems. No, he wasn't angry about that, or at least only as by-product of the thing that had really cut him to the quick, really caused him the most bitter pain and mortification. And that was that she had never, despite all his efforts and even at the beginning, ever loved him. What is more, he wondered now, had she ever even tried to?

He looked back down the long slope to the river, which ran dark and shining between the muddy banks, only raggedly defined now after the ravages of the floodwater. Slightly to the right of the point where his hedgerow reached the bank, the straggling

46

line of willows began, stooping and craning over the water in their oddly oriental way. It was beside one of those willows that he had proposed to Caro, had said that she could live in his house because by saying that he had believed she would know that he wanted to look after her. He did. Even after she had withdrawn from him to the little bedroom over the kitchen, he had still wanted to look after her. Was that love? Judy would call it possessiveness and male patronage, but would she be right? Wasn't the desire to cherish and protect, even in the face of the death of many intimacies, in fact a kind of love?

He turned resolutely back towards the hill and resumed his progress upwards. Pollution was his problem, *must* be his problem, he must not be deflected by these futile searchings back into the past, opening doors into rooms Caro had just abandoned, following paths that she had left before he reached her. Grief, the Vicar had said in his one, brief, embarrassed visit to Robin after the funeral, took many forms and he must try to remember that even the most disconcerting reaction was perfectly normal.

'Perfectly,' he said, rising to his feet to show that the interview, to his intense relief, was over. 'No need to blame yourself.'

Robin watched him in silence, as he had at the funeral.

'The answer,' the Vicar said, pulling on a dark-blue anorak with a drawstring waist, 'is probably, in your case, work. Work is a great healer. Work is often the answer to troubles of the spirit.'

He held his hand out to Robin. Robin stood, slowly, and took the offered hand for a mere second.

'I know that,' he said. His voice was full of a

contempt he took no trouble at all to hide. 'I've known that all my life.'

CHAPTER FOUR

Through the window beyond her office desk, Judy Meredith could see a wall of dirty white brick, the corner of a balcony too small to stand on where someone had left a nondescript plant in a plastic pot to fend for itself, a further wall of brown brick and a T-shaped slice of sky. The sky was the only thing in the view that ever changed, and during the winter months, it hardly seemed to trouble itself even to do that. Indeed, during this last winter, while her mother was dying, the slice of sky seemed determined to reflect the relentless strain of Judy's life by being steadily dark, even at midday, and either weeping with rain, or threatening to.

Judy's desk was made of pale-grey plastic with a matching computer screen and keyboard fitted into the surface. On the computer she sub-edited features for the interior design magazine for which she worked. Sometimes she was permitted to write feature pieces herself, on decoupage, or Shaker tinware, or the revival of interest in eighteenth-century stripes and checks. Her last piece, written really for Caro, on American quilt-making, had received a postbag of twenty-seven letters from readers congratulating her and wanting to know more, and a warm note from the editor on one of the buttercup-yellow cards which were her speciality. Judy had saved the card to show Caro when she went up to Tideswell for the weekend, but the weekend never happened, only the Thursday-night call from Robin for Judy to come to Stretton Hospital without delay. When she got back to the office, after the funeral, Judy tore the yellow card up and put it in her grey plastic wastebin. It was too reminiscent of sharing.

Besides the computer, Judy's desk held a tier of filing trays, a pile of the magazine's back numbers, a mug that a porcelain company hoping for promotion had given her, patterned with classical columns and which she used for storing pens, a photograph of Caro, and another one of Tideswell Farm photographed from below. It was summer, and the pasture in the foreground was full of young heifers. A small figure in the distance by the Dutch barn was probably Robin, but might have been Gareth. Caro had sent the photograph soon after Judy had first gone to London, and had written 'Home Sweet Home!' on the back. Judy wondered now about the possible irony of the exclamation mark.

The desk was orderly. Either side of her, at slight angles, two other sub-editors worked at desks of monumental chaos. Papers, coffee mugs, vases of dead flowers, galley proofs, empty crisp packets, fabric swatches and a confetti of little yellow memo notes were layered haphazardly across the surfaces, and out of the muddle, the computer screens rose calmly like periscopes. While Caro was dying, the inhabitants of these desks, Tessa and Bronwen, had showered Judy with attention and treats, as if she herself were some kind of invalid, bringing her flowers and fruit and single cream cakes, in paper bags. Now that Caro was dead, they were paralysed by not knowing what to do instead, and in consequence did nothing, averting their gazes from

49

the photograph of Caro and whispering into their telephones as if by withdrawing in awkwardness they were somehow conveying both respect and sympathy.

'How chronic,' Zoe said.

Zoe was Judy's new flatmate. She had arrived the week after the funeral, on the recommendation of a sister of Judy's last flatmate. 'She's great,' they'd said. 'You'll like her.'

She had dark-brown hair dyed claret-colour and cut very short. Her possessions were all carried up the four flights of stairs to the flat in carrier bags and cardboard boxes except for a fuchsia-pink Chinese silk quilt which unrolled to reveal two wooden herons at least half life-size.

'I don't cook,' she said to Judy. 'Can't. So no stink of vindaloo.'

Judy had told her about Caro the first evening.

'I can't help it. I can't think about anything else. I feel I'm going about with "My mother's just died" written all over me. I expect I shouldn't mention it. People seem terrified I'm going to, and they'll get put on the spot. The girls at work are just pretending I'm not there till I get over it and everything's normal again.'

'How chronic,' Zoe said. She glanced at Judy. 'You look worn out.'

'I can't sleep. I'm tired all the time and I can't sleep.'

'It's sorrow,' Zoe said. She put her herons either side of the blocked-up fireplace in their little sitting room. 'Just sorrow. Worse than stress. Do you mind them there?'

'Have you had anyone close to you die?'

Zoe looked away from the herons and at Judy

50

instead.

'My father.'

Judy seemed to sag with physical sympathy.

'Oh—'

'Three years ago. In Australia. He left my mother when I was eight, so I never knew him. We had two days together when I was seventeen and my mother just *freaked*. But I went all the same, and he was great. He was *fun*. He never said a bad thing about my mother all those two days. And then he went and *died*, the sod. I could kill him for that.'

Judy had wanted, then, to say, 'I'm adopted,' but had held back with immense self-control. If she'd said it, she'd remember Caro saying to her, when she was five and first at school, 'Now look, Judy. I chose you. I *chose* you.' And that would bring on the tears again. However sympathetic Zoe promised to be as a flatmate, one mustn't start such a relationship by crying all over it.

Now, sitting at her desk and ostensibly working on a piece about a fashion designer's country retreat in Brittany—it had big white sofas which for Judy had become the carelessly impractical benchmark of the very rich—Judy gazed at the list Zoe had made her. It was written on a long strip of green paper in Zoe's showy, rather childish hand, and it was headed 'Sorrow', in capital letters. Underneath, Zoe had written, each word precisely below the one above, 'Grief, Distress, Woe, Affliction, Pain, Ache, Misery, Unhappiness, Agony, Broken Heart, Ordeal, Shock, Depression, Gloom, Mental Suffering.'

'That's why you feel bad,' Zoe had said, putting the list into Judy's hands. 'That's sorrow for you. And that's only *some* of the symptoms.'

Judy held the list away from her.

51

'Why do I need this?'

'Because you've got to look it in the eye to get better. *All* of it.'

Caro would not have said that. Caro would have said, 'You have to go on. That's all there is to do, sweetheart, just go on. Hold tight to yourself and on you go.' She'd talked that way after both the broken love affairs that Judy had had since she came to London, neither of them spectacular things, being more the product of Judy's hopes than of much reality, but both had been ended by the men.

'Sorry, Judy, sorry, really sorry. You're sweet, but I—'

'Judy, I'm not ready for this kind of relationship. It's not you, it's just that I can't cope with commitment, not yet—'

She had gone straight home to Caro on both occasions, and railed at herself for her height and her red hair and her untrendiness and her being adopted and anything else she could lay her racing mind on as the reason for first Tim and then Ed just walking away—slowly, certainly, and full of excuse and apology, but *away*. Caro had listened, Judy remembered, she had always listened, but then she had simply said, in her quiet, slow voice that had lost none of its Californian character, that Judy must simply light her candle again and walk forward into the dark. Caro loved that image, of the candle. She was always quoting it. Even as a little child, Judy was told she had a candle inside her nobody could snuff out, *nobody*. It was her candle. If only Caro had known, Judy thought, how she, Judy, had striven to believe her, had struggled to feel, even for a moment, that she had an inner flame that was both unquenchable and hers alone. All she had felt was that she had failed Caro in some way, and the fact that two profoundly unremarkable young men like Tim and Ed could ditch her was a kind of proof, however illogical, of that failure.

After Tim and Ed, she'd tried a bit of a vamp phase, wearing red lipstick and sleeping with men she didn't know very well. She never told Caro any of this; indeed had a feeling that, if she kept quiet, she would somehow break free of Caro and the burdening sensation of being her chosen daughter, but not essentially her daughter all the same. 'We don't have rows,' Caro had once said of herself and Judy, to Lyndsay, 'we just don't row.' Even then Judy had wondered if not having rows was a mark—an almost fatal mark—of the courtesy in their relationship, the courtesy between the chooser and the chosen. She remembered Lyndsay had looked at her very carefully. Lyndsay had been pregnant then, with Hughie, and was wearing a smock Caro had made for her, cream cotton printed with stiff little blue cornflowers. Caro had been very generous when Lyndsay was pregnant.

But this list ... Judy held the green slip up and looked at it. She couldn't quite tell why, but it impressed her. It wasn't exactly unsympathetic but it was blessedly free of the anxious, soggy, *caring* quality of the expressions on colleagues' faces when she caught their eyes inadvertently in the lift or beside the water fountain. Zoe's list was practical, almost brisk. It seemed to imply that these feelings were the ones inevitably attendant upon the condition and therefore there would be something the matter with you if you *didn't* feel them. Only a freak, Zoe's list seemed to say, would not feel all these terrible things after the death of their mother. Failure—a sensation

53

Judy was painfully accustomed to—lay, in fact, in insisting on keeping your candle alight when a time in the pitch-black was actually the right and proper thing to do.

Judy laid the list aside with a small feeling of respect, and turned back to her screen. The fashion designer said her heart absolutely *sank* every time she had to leave her Brittany paradise and return to her shop in Bond Street. 'Devastated,' she said. 'There's no other word for it. It's heart-breaking.' Judy was strongly tempted to add a sardonic sentence in brackets about the effect of this confession upon the fashion designer's loyal clientele who had presumably previously supposed that her commitment to their clothes was the centre of her life, and whose wardrobes had also paid for the white sofaed house in Brittany. She glanced aside at Zoe's list. 'Agony,' it said. 'Broken Heart. Ordeal.' She glared at the screen.

'You stupid cow,' she said aloud to the fashion designer. 'You stupid, ignorant *cow*!'

*   *   *

That night, Zoe came home from her job as a photographer's assistant with a spinach tart in a cardboard box.

'I just passed it. They'd taken £1.30 off the price because the shop was closing. D'you hate spinach?'

'No,' Judy said. 'Only swede.'

She had drunk two glasses of white wine since she'd got home, and eaten half a box of matzos which were strangely unappetising and appetising all at once. She had done this in front of the news on television followed by a game show and a programme

54

proving that plants have feelings. Even swedes?

'Good day?' Zoe said. She was dressed, as Judy was, all in black but boyishly, with heavy boots and a biker jacket.

Judy pulled a face.

'Not good, but less bloody, maybe. I've got a commission to write a piece on marble.'

'Halls?'

'And walls. And bathrooms and kitchens and no doubt snug little marble bedrooms, too.'

Zoe held out the box.

'Shall I heat this?'

'Yes.'

'Can't turn the oven on.'

Judy heaved herself out of her chair in a shower of matzo crumbs.

'You're hopeless.'

'So my boss says. I think I'm going to evening classes to learn Spanish.'

'Why?'

'Then I could go and take my own pictures of donkeys and hot villages instead of holding all the kit while someone else takes art shots of dustbins and tube trains.'

Judy went out to the kitchen. It was very small and she had painted it California yellow in homage to Caro, but rather badly so that shadows of its former royal blue showed through. Zoe had added nothing to the kitchen since she came, not a mug, not a spoon, not a poster. She bought food every day, for immediate eating, and ate it wherever she was, often standing up. Otherwise, she drank water out of the tap in one of Judy's mugs.

'Don't you like coffee?'

'Yes. Course I do.'

'But—'

'I'll go out and buy you as many gallons as you want,' Zoe said. 'I just don't want to make it.'

Judy turned the oven on and slid the tart inside on a baking tray.

She shouted, 'Want some wine?'

Zoe appeared in the doorway, holding Judy's box of matzos.

'I don't drink.'

'Heavens. *Don't* you?'

'Don't like the taste. Judy—'

'Yes?'

'Have you got a boyfriend?'

Pause.

'No,' Judy said and then, 'I bet you have.'

Zoe took one of the matzos.

'Yes. But it isn't working. It isn't going anywhere. It isn't even very interesting. He's called Ollie.'

'Like an owl,' Judy said, pouring more wine.

'No. More like a run-over stork. He was nice to me when my dad died.' She shot Judy a direct glance. 'What about your dad?'

Judy said quickly, 'He's a farmer.'

'A *farmer*? Wow.'

Judy began opening cupboards in search of plates.

'Why wow?'

'Well, a *farmer*. I mean, most fathers do insurance and banks and computers and stuff. Not tractors. I don't need a plate.'

'He's a dairy farmer. He has cows.'

'Where?'

'In the Midlands. Going towards Wales a bit.'

'Did you grow up there?'

'Yes.'

'Can you milk?'

56

Judy said shortly, 'Machines do it.' She stooped down and opened the oven door and laid a finger on the tart.

'So your father's alone on this farm with these cows now your mother's dead?'

'There's Gareth. And there's Joe and Lyndsay. And Granny and Grandpa.'

'Sounds like Postman Pat,' Zoe said. 'Why are you sulking? Why are you talking as if you hate all these people?'

Judy shut the oven door and pushed past Zoe into the sitting room, holding her wineglass.

'I don't belong there. I never did but it was OK while Mum was there because she didn't belong either. It isn't home, it's just where I had my childhood. Most of it, anyhow.'

She stopped. Zoe turned in the kitchen doorway, so that she was facing Judy, and leaned against the frame.

'You adopted then?'

Judy nodded violently.

'It's a lot, isn't it?' Zoe said. 'To be adopted and then to lose your mother? It's a lot for one person to carry. What about your real mother?'

'She lives in South Africa. She sends me birthday cards with proteas on and tells me about the weather.'

Zoe put the cracker box down on the floor and came to stand in front of Judy.

'You want to get a hold on all this mess,' she said. 'You want to sort of get your arms round it. It's no good pretending it isn't there.'

Judy held her wineglass tightly with both hands.

'I'm not part of the family. You don't understand about farming families. They're different. They're all

57

tight together, you have to be born in them to belong.'

'Can I have a look?' Zoe said.

Judy stared at her.

'A look at what?'

'At this farm. At your dad, and these cows and everything.'

Judy said, 'Are you saying you want to come to Tideswell?'

'Yes.'

'For the weekend?'

Zoe shrugged.

'I suppose so.'

'That tart's burning,' Judy said suddenly, pushing past her.

From the kitchen she called, 'It's pretty boring, the farm. There's nothing there, just fields and cows.'

'Nothing's *really* boring,' Zoe said and then added reflectively, 'except possibly Ollie. Can I come?'

Judy appeared in the kitchen doorway, holding half the tart on a plate, and half in the cardboard tray in which it had arrived. She held the latter out to Zoe.

'OK.'

Zoe sat down in Judy's armchair and balanced the cardboard tray on her knees.

'What's your dad like?'

'Tall. Dark. Grumpy.'

'Grumpy—'

'Most farmers are grumpy.'

Zoe said, holding up the half-tart in one piece and biting out of the centre, 'Can I come next weekend?'

'OK.'

'Will you ring? Will you ring your father?'

Judy put her plate down on a pile of magazines. She hadn't rung Robin for ten days, although on

58

each one of those ten she had been sharply conscious that she should. She thought of the kitchen at Tideswell Farm, and Robin eating supper there— tinned soup maybe, or something Dilys had cooked—and the telephone going and him getting up to answer it with a little murmur of annoyance, leaving his reading spectacles to mark the place he had got to in a farming-magazine article about getting tricky heifers in calf. 'Yes?' he'd say sharply into the telephone. 'Yes? Tideswell Farm.' What would he make of her request? Even more, what would he make of Zoe with her wine-red hair and her knucklefuls of silver rings, having a look at him with her big, penetrating eyes?

'I'm no trouble,' Zoe said. 'I can sleep anywhere.'

'It isn't that—'

'Look,' Zoe said, chewing, 'I'll get a return ticket on the coach and if I'm a disaster, I'll push off after one night. OK?'

Judy nodded. She said, as if to make up for deficiencies of hospitality, 'There's a river. And a big hill quite close. Sometimes it's quite pretty—'

'Just ring him. Just ring your father and say I'm bringing a friend down. Why don't you? Why don't you do it now?'

*   *   *

Robin had fallen asleep in front of the nine o'clock television news. Along with the box of farm papers, he had brought the television into the kitchen since Caro died and an extra electric heater. He set the television up so that he could see it from his accustomed place at the big central table, and at night, while attempting to eat the pies and stews Dilys

59

sent up to Tideswell via Velma or Joe, would often slide into sleep where he sat, and wake some twenty minutes later with his head on a bent arm and the food cold on his plate. Yet when he finally abandoned the evening, offering his supper to the house cat and making his last customary round of the cows chewing and dozing in the barn, he couldn't sleep. When finally he reached his bed, he would fall into it, dog-tired, every limb complaining, and on still nights, hear the steady far-off chimes of Dean Cross church clock marking off hour after unyielding hour. The pattern was then for him to plummet into fathomless slumber half an hour before the alarm clock shrilled at five-forty-five and almost threw him out of bed with its impact. In the faint light of dawn in his bedroom, the thought of Caro waited for him, as it did in the bathroom and down the stairs to the kitchen and then out with him to the yard and the tractor parked under cover in the feed store against the great rough brown wall of maize. Not her face, not her voice, just some essence of her, fragmentary, unmistakable and painful. And finished, he told himself over and over. *Finished.*

When the telephone rang, Robin was down in a pit of sleep full of the deep reverberations of the television news. He came up to the surface as if through thick oil, and sat for a moment gazing stupidly at the screen and wondering why, during an interview with the Foreign Secretary, nobody bothered to answer an insistent and interrupting telephone. Slowly, it dawned upon him that the telephone was his own, the mobile phone he had bought when Caro became so ill, and that he had carried about with him all that time, and which was now ringing manfully away on the table under

60

scattered newspapers and a discarded sweater.

'Yes?'

'Dad—'

'Judy,' he said.

'Don't sound so surprised—'

'Sorry,' he said. 'I was asleep. I'd gone to sleep in Granny's fish pie.'

There was a pause. In London, Judy watched by Zoe, and at Tideswell, Robin watched by the television, waited for the other to say, 'How are you?'

'I was wondering—' Judy said.

'Hang on,' Robin said. 'Can't hear. Just going to turn the telly down.' When he came back, he said, 'What can I do for you?'

'Can I come down? Can I come down this weekend?'

'Course!' he said. His voice sounded too hearty to him. 'Lovely.'

'And bring a friend—'

'A friend?'

'My new flatmate. Zoe. She's a photographer.'

'Why not,' Robin said. 'Why not.'

'Good.'

'A photographer?'

'Yes. We'll come on Friday. We'll get the coach to Stretton.'

'I'll meet you,' Robin said. 'Tell me which coach and I'll meet you.'

'Thanks. I'll let you know. Don't—don't do anything, go to any trouble—'

'Velma can make beds,' Robin said. 'And no doubt Granny can do her bit for three instead of one.'

'See you Friday then,' Judy said.

'Yes. Yes,' Robin said, aware with sudden keenness of the inadequacy of the conversation. 'See you Friday.'

He put the telephone down again. He thought, with an abrupt rush of feeling, poor Judy, poor bloody Judy with a father like me, a father she despises for having all the wrong attitudes, the wrong feelings. She'd fought him off, all her life, as if she knew, even as a tiny child, that he was doomed to be a stranger to her always, a misunderstanding, alien stranger who filled her often with apprehension and sometimes with distaste. From the moment of her arrival, a watchful red-haired baby of eight months, Joe had been better with her, easier, than he, Robin, had. Joe had seemed quite relaxed with her, able to talk to Caro about her in a way that Robin couldn't do naturally. He remembered finding Joe lying on the kitchen floor one day, in his boiler suit, holding Judy in his arms high in the air, and she was shrieking with laughter and her legs were going like pistons. Robin had never done that, had known it would be false in him to behave that way. But he had tried to read to Judy, to show her things on the farm and in the hedgerows, to lay her small spreadeagled hand on the broad wet nose of a cow. Every time, she endured him tensely for a few minutes and then became convulsed with the determination to go back to Caro, straining at his encircling arms, her face and eyes closed against him.

But then Caro intimated—and Caro's intimations were as plain as most people's declarations—that Robin's mind was closed against Judy, long before she came. Caro had announced, in her quiet way, that she would like to adopt a baby and only after Robin, in amazement and confusion, had asked why, had said that she would very much like a child and that, as she couldn't have one herself, she would have to do it

62

this way.

She had said this standing by the first cooling system that Robin had installed in the milking parlour. It was like her not to wait until mealtimes to say anything of significance, but instead to come in search of Robin wherever he was, in her queer unhurried way, and simply make her announcement.

He had stared at her, his hands dropping from the gauges as if they had become disconnected from his brain.

'You can't have children?'

'No,' she said. She stood before him in her denim shirt and her jeans and her cowboy boots, with the end of her plait tied with a red bandanna. 'I had an operation when I was nineteen as a result of an infection. I'm infertile.' She spread her hands. 'Nothing works.'

He tried to control himself, to react to this bombshell with some semblance of civilization, but instead found himself shouting, 'Why didn't you say? Before we were married, why didn't you *say*?'

'I thought you were marrying me and not my child-bearing potential.'

'I was, Caro, I *was*, but—' He stopped, silenced by unhinging bewilderment.

She said, voicing his unspoken thoughts, 'But all normal men want children. All normal women have children. That right? That what you mean?'

'I didn't mean you aren't normal, I didn't mean that—'

'But I'm not normal. I was once, but I'm not now. I'm just normal enough, still, to want a child. That's all.'

He said again, almost in a whisper, 'Why didn't you say?'

'I didn't think to. I wanted to stay here and stop wandering and I didn't think to.'

'Don't you think you should have? Don't you think you should have thought of me?'

She considered for a moment, and then she said, not unkindly, 'Maybe.'

He had shouted again, then. He had shouted about being deceived, about the impossibility of being married to someone who behaved so unilaterally, about there being no heir for Tideswell, his farm, that he had made, with his own hands, his own money. Then he had yelled, 'I don't want to adopt!'

'It's the only way to have a child,' she said. 'Do you really want us not to have a child?'

He had turned away from her and put his hands flat against the milking-parlour wall where the pale-blue wash he had painted it with was already beginning to flake away.

'I don't know,' he said, and then, miserably, 'I just assumed we'd have one. When you had settled. I suppose I was just waiting for you to be ready.'

'But I am ready,' she said reasonably to his back. 'That's why I'm talking to you about adoption. I'm ready for a child now.'

He closed his eyes. He thought of making love to her—she never initiated sex but she almost always acquiesced—and how he had been thinking one thing all those times, and she had known something quite different. There was no point in shouting at her any more, no point in raging; she had the inexorableness of some natural force which knows no laws but its own. He took his hands away from the wall.

'OK,' he said.

'You want it?'

'No,' he said between clenched teeth, 'I don't mean

that. I mean, given that you will do it anyway, go ahead and do it. But don't expect me to join in just yet. I can't go from believing one thing to having to accept another in a flash, I can't—'

He stopped.

'What can't you?'

He turned slowly and looked at her.

'What else haven't you told me?'

She said, 'You know everything. I just forgot that. Robin, I'd like a daughter. I would most terribly like a daughter.'

He opened his mouth to say that he didn't know much about girls, and closed it again. What was the point of restating something that the previous twenty minutes had made so manifestly plain? He knew nothing about girls, *nothing*. He didn't know what they wanted, because he couldn't even fathom how they thought. And yet he wanted to. Standing there in the milking parlour that summer afternoon and looking at Caro's smooth brown face, he would have given anything to understand her, to know why she did some things, so tellingly, and omitted others, with equal significance. And then a desolation came over him, a great black wave of it, that he would never have a child by her, that they would never, essentially, be able to do even this together, and he turned away from her and went through the parlour and out into the collecting yard, where the cows waited for milking.

Poor Judy. What kind of start was that for any child, even a child disadvantaged by first being conceived so carelessly and then given up with such palpable relief? Robin stood up at the kitchen table and tried to marshal the clutter on it into some kind of order so that Velma would have less to get her teeth into in the morning about his state of mind. As it was, she read his recent habits of life like tea-leaves in a cup. Velma. He must leave her a note to make up beds for these girls, look out bath towels. Yawning, his reading glasses pushed up into his hair, Robin began to hunt through the confusion for a serviceable piece of paper.

CHAPTER FIVE

Rose was resisting clean dungarees. Her face suffused with scarlet determination under the halo of fair curls which gave her such a misleading air of amenability, she thrashed and screamed in Lyndsay's arms.

'Tiresome,' Hughie said. He stood watching his sister, wearing a pirate's hat they had made at his playgroup out of stiff black paper.

'Very,' Lyndsay said.

'Nah, nah, nah!' Rose yelled.

'Can't she just be in her nappy?'

'No,' Lyndsay said, thrusting a stout kicking leg into the dungarees, 'because Judy is coming with a friend and Judy gave Rose these dungarees for Christmas.'

'I suppose,' Hughie said, eyeing the rose-printed dungarees, 'that they are meant for girls?' He leaned forward as if to make a point. 'I would *not* like flowers.'

'Nobody shall make you. Rosie, you are a *devil*.'

She bent the baby, still roaring, over her right arm and pulled the dungarees up over her bottom.

'I imagine I was quite a good baby,' Hughie said.

'Yes, you were.'

66

He stooped and picked up the grey plush seal that Joe hated him carrying everywhere.

'He's only three,' Lyndsay said. 'And with Rose—'

'Three's a little boy,' Joe said. 'Not a baby.'

Hughie tucked the seal comfortably under one arm, and put his thumb in.

'Hughie—'

'I must,' he said, round his thumb.

'Daddy won't be pleased.'

He looked at her, still sucking, then he turned and went steadily out of the room. She heard him go along the short landing to his own bedroom, and then the sound of the flimsy door shutting decisively behind him. He would then, she knew, sit on his bean bag under his paper hat, pressing Seal to his side, and suck and suck.

Rose, bored with protest, struggled now to get down. She was a big baby, a big square baby with Meredith colouring, Meredith build. Dilys had a photograph of Joe, taken on his first birthday, dressed in a romper suit with a sailor collar, which looked astonishingly like Rose. She looked especially like him when she smiled, which was often. Bright sunshine, or thunderstorms, that was Rose. If only, Lyndsay thought, getting up to clear away Rose's dirty nappy and discarded clothes, there was a bit more sunshine about Joe these days, just a little lightness of heart, a gleam of humour. But he seemed unable to shake something off, something that dogged him and dragged him down, made him inert and silent at home, lumpy.

It was as if he had a great preoccupation, something bitter and unresolvable, that ceaselessly stalked his mind. She had tried, occasionally, asking him—diffidently because she knew nothing about

67

farming—if there were business problems, money worries, debts.

'No,' he'd said, flatly and firmly. 'No. Nothing like that.' He'd sounded almost angry. 'Nothing like that at all.'

Lyndsay left Rose crawling busily along the landing towards the gate which prevented her from falling downstairs, and which she liked to shake and shout at, and went into the bathroom to find some make-up. She looked at herself in the mirror above the basin, and caught her anxious eyes before they remembered to change their expression to something more optimistic. Well, she *was* anxious. Being married to Joe had given her far more cause for anxiety than she had ever imagined; indeed, she'd supposed that marrying a man fifteen years her senior would be a good insurance policy against anxiety. He'd seemed so certain, so calm, so big and reassuring and adult. 'Strong and silent,' Lyndsay's mother had said, meaning it as a compliment.

It was the silence now that was the trouble. Lyndsay let her hair down and brushed its pale masses, and then piled up the top half again with combs. They'd only had one conversation that was even remotely to the point in the last few weeks, and that had been so unsatisfactory, almost surreal, that it had merely added to Lyndsay's concern. She'd said, confronting him in the utility room while he put his boots on after lunch two days ago, 'Joe. Joe, *please*. What is the matter?'

He'd grunted, tugging at the laces.

'What's eating you? What's getting at you?'

'Nothing.'

'Yes, it is. It *is*. You'll hardly speak to us and you sit staring at the telly in the evening like a zombie. Is it

68

the farm?'

He shrugged and stood up. Lyndsay darted past him and stood with her back against the outside door. She said again, 'Is it the farm?'

Joe pushed the poppers together up the front of his boiler suit.

'Maybe.'

'Oh Joe, tell me. It doesn't matter what it is, but *tell* me!'

He put his hands out and took hold of her shoulders. Then, very gently but firmly, he moved her away from the door.

'I've always had it too easy,' Joe said, not looking at her. 'Always. And now the farm is hard.'

She cried out, 'Because of Caro? Because of Caro dying?'

He looked at her penetratingly for a moment, and then he put his hand on the door handle and turned it.

'I don't know,' he said impatiently. 'Why should I know a thing like that?'

And then he had opened the door and gone out, almost running.

Lyndsay opened the bathroom cupboard and took out a pot of grey eyeshadow and a brush. She'd been trained as a beautician, with dreams of opening her own salon, when she met Joe. She'd never been so attracted to anybody in her life—she wouldn't have cared what he did for a living. Farming, about which she knew nothing, seemed a wonderful idea; he was so good at it, the first farmer in their district to get three and a half tons to the acre, he'd be around all day, she'd see him, be with him. But the reality was different. He was never around. She felt, almost from the beginning, that she had no claim on him. Their first Christmas Day, their very first Christmas

69

together, he'd gone top-dressing all the daylight hours, because the weather and the soil conditions were right. When she had protested, he'd said, 'I can't waste it, Lyn. I can't waste the time and the money.'

She took another brush out of the cupboard, for lipgloss. It was comforting, doing this, performing this practised ritual of painting and shading and blending. Along the landing Rose was bellowing and banging the stairgate, but she was loving it, loving the noise. Lyndsay's mother said Rose was out of control. She was right, Lyndsay reflected, drawing the brush round the curve of her lower lip, Rose was out of control, quite a long way out, but then so was Joe, her wonderful Joe, who was, quite simply, her world—and she didn't know in the least what to do about either of them.

*   *   *

From her kitchen window, Dilys watched Judy drive into the yard at Dean Place Farm, in Robin's car, and stop it, rather awkwardly, by the shed where Dilys used to keep the poultry feed. The yard at Dean Place had been full of poultry once, forty or fifty rare breeds like Welsummers and Leghorns and Old Dutch Bantams. Dilys had won prizes at poultry shows, notably with her Black Orpingtons. But those busy times were long gone. The yard lay swept and bare these days, ornamented only, in summer, with two tubs of geraniums in municipal scarlet, ferocious both in colour and regimented tidiness.

Judy's friend looked to Dilys very odd. She got out of the car and stood looking interestedly about her, her cropped head turning this way and that. She wore those legging things that Dilys so lamented seeing the

70

village people in, and a peculiar top, partly a jacket and partly a sort of tunic, that put Dilys in mind of a drawing of the Pied Piper of Hamelin she'd had in an illustrated poetry book when she was a child. Judy had on black jeans and a long green sweater with a gauzy-looking scarf wound high at the neck. Dilys liked to see Judy in green. In her opinion, green was an appropriate colour for redheads. It was nice to see Judy with a friend, too, and even she, Dilys, had learned that in the modern world you couldn't judge by appearances as you could in the old days, you just had to wait for people to reveal themselves. That is, if they chose to.

She went to the back door and opened it, joined by Harry's old springer spaniel, now promoted to house dog since his shooting days were over.

'Granny,' Judy said. She bent forward to kiss Dilys and caught the scent of laundry and flour that had been Dilys's for as long as Judy could remember. 'This is Zoe.'

'Hello, dear,' Dilys said. She held out a hand.

'Hello,' Zoe said. She was smiling. She had smiled most of the weekend. 'It's great here,' she kept saying to Judy. 'Isn't it? Why don't you think it's great?'

'Come on in,' Dilys said. 'I've got the kettle on.'

'We've just had tea,' Judy said. 'With Lyndsay.'

Dilys shot her a look.

'Did you see Joe?'

'No. He was working. Why?'

Dilys said, 'He's a bit down in the dumps. That's all.' 'I'm worried sick,' she'd said to Harry the night before, making their bedtime tea. 'I really am. He's miles away. It isn't natural.'

She put the lid on the teapot.

'It isn't as if there's anything to worry about. Not

71

on the farm. I do the books, after all. I should know.' She lifted the pot. 'The books balance nicely. Like they always have.'

She led the way into the kitchen. A blue-checked cloth had been laid at one end of the long table, and on it was a plate of shortbread, arranged in a fan.

'Granny, I don't think—'

'I'm sure you can manage another cup of tea,' Dilys said. She looked at Zoe and then gave a little nod in the direction of the shortbread. 'I made that this morning.'

'Brilliant,' Zoe said, 'I'm eating all day here. I had two breakfasts so I don't see why I shouldn't have two teas.' She sat down at the table and put her elbows comfortably on the blue-checked cloth. 'I never had tea to eat in my life before anyway.'

'How did you find your father?' Dilys said to Judy, pouring boiling water into the brown-glazed teapot banded with flowers on a cream background that was so familiar to Judy it almost hurt to look at it.

'I don't really know,' Judy said, 'it's so difficult to tell. He's pretty thin.'

'I send a hot meal down there every day,' Dilys said reprovingly. 'And he gives it to the cat. Velma finds the plate on the kitchen floor in the morning.'

Zoe helped herself to a piece of shortbread, biting into it and scattering crumbs.

'Why should he eat,' Zoe said, 'if he's grieving?'

Dilys's lips tightened. This was speaking out of turn.

'He's a working man,' she said to Zoe, putting the teapot down on the table on a mat of linked wooden beads.

Zoe said, quite undismayed, 'Doesn't mean he isn't a feeling one, too.'

72

'If you're a farmer,' Dilys said firmly, 'you can't give in. You can't give way to things. Time and tide wait for no man.'

Judy, taking a chair opposite to Zoe's, tried to catch her eye and motion her to shut up.

'He isn't giving in,' Zoe said, ignoring Judy, 'he is going on. But he's suffering. You can see it.'

'Zoe—' Judy said.

'You should know,' Zoe said, turning her big gaze on Judy. 'You should sympathise with him.'

Judy looked down. Dilys began to pour tea out of the brown pot into cups patterned with Indian pheasants that had been part of her wedding service. She disapproved of mugs. Harry was only permitted a mug mid-morning, when he came in from getting in Joe's way about the place, and arguing about modern methods of doing things. 'You mustn't upset Joe,' Dilys said to him, over and over again. 'Joe knows what he's doing. Joe thinks long-term which is more than you've ever done.' She didn't want Harry's elderly obstinacy being a clog upon Joe, or a trouble to him. Dilys had always been able to bear trouble for Harry or for Robin, but trouble for Joe made her flinch, as if the skin of her feelings had been flayed.

'We don't talk of suffering here, dear,' she said. 'We don't indulge our feelings. We're practical people.'

Zoe looked round the kitchen, shabby but spotless, crammed with objects all in order, each cup and jug upon its appointed hook.

'Yes. I can see.' Her voice was quite neutral.

'It may be the farm,' Judy said quickly. 'He had a bad day at market on Thursday. He had to bring three calves back because they were scouring. Or so the auctioneer said.'

73

Dilys clicked her tongue. She pushed the shortbread towards Zoe.

'Do you work with Judy, dear?'

'No,' Zoe said, 'I'm a photographer. At least, I'm learning to be.'

She'd got up at five-thirty that morning to take pictures of Gareth in the milking parlour, the double line of great black-and-white bodies with the snaking hoses of the milking machine and the big glass jars filling visibly with milk, warm and off-white. Gareth had liked having her there, had been perfectly happy to pose when she asked him to, fitting on the clusters, spraying the teats afterwards, driving the column of cows back out into the yard and the pale new morning light. She'd worn a boiler suit like his; she'd just found it outside her door when she went to the lavatory at five-thirty-five, folded up on the floor with a pair of thick marbled wool socks, the kind her father had worn with the heavy shoes he preferred. She supposed Robin had left them there. If so, it showed a real but minimal approach to human relations that Zoe appreciated.

She said now, to Dilys, to soothe Judy, 'I took pictures in the milking parlour this morning. And some of Lyndsay's little kids just now. That's a lovely little boy.'

'He is,' Dilys said. 'Takes after his mother to look at. Now Rose is a real Meredith. A Meredith through and through.'

Judy picked up her teacup and bent her face into it. She wanted to go, wanted this strange and awkward little occasion to be over, to get Zoe away to a place where she couldn't break the rules she didn't even know existed. You could see Dilys was disconcerted by Zoe, and therefore did not care either for her

74

appearance or her outspokenness. Lyndsay had warned her it would happen.

'Don't alarm Granny,' she'd said.

'I can't help it. We've got to go.'

She said now, her face still bent into the warm steam of her teacup, 'Where's Grandpa?'

'Hedging,' Dilys said. 'The ten-acre. He wanted to pull the hedge up to make ploughing easier right across but Joe wouldn't let him. Says he's got to put the headlands back, too.'

Judy put her teacup down and stood up.

'Maybe we'll go and find him.'

'He'd like that,' Dilys said. 'You can take him a new flask of tea. He'll have drunk his.' She looked across at Zoe. 'Nice to meet you, dear.'

Zoe looked back.

'You, too,' she said.

*   *   *

'Jesus,' Judy said, turning the car out of the yard. 'Sorry about that.'

'What d'you mean?'

'Granny, of course. She's got such fixed ideas—'

'I liked her,' Zoe said. 'She mightn't think like me but that doesn't stop me liking her. You don't think like me either.'

'No,' Judy said enviously. 'I don't.'

'Talking of like,' Zoe said, putting her feet up on to the edge of the passenger seat and holding her bent knees in her arms, 'why don't you like it here?'

'Zoe, you don't know it—'

'Of course I don't. But I see it. I see it as a hard place. But not a place to hate.'

'I don't hate it,' Judy said.

75

Zoe looked at her for a moment, and then back out of the windscreen.

'Don't you? Well if you don't, all I can say is you give a pretty good imitation.'

*   *   *

Harry had done seven yards of hedge along the far side of the 10-acre field, the side where the north-east wind got you if it saw the smallest chance. He worked in the leather gloves his father had given him forty years ago for hedging, stiff as boards until you got them warmed up, and a mass of splits. He could have bought new ones any day but he liked the old ones, he liked their associations.

He wasn't much of a hedger, never had been. His father had taught him the old Midland way of laying a hedge, cutting the main stems almost through with a billhook, and then bending them horizontally for strength and density. But there were always too many splintered raw ends in Harry's hedges and he didn't weave tight enough to provide proper protection. But he did all right. It had always been enough for him to do all right, he didn't have Dilys's desire to do better, or even best, the desire she'd passed on to Joe. But not to Robin. Robin, as far as Harry could see, just had the desire to do things differently. You couldn't make Robin toe the line, you just had to shrug your shoulders and let him go his own way, even if that way was full of difficulty and debt. In Harry's view, Robin ought to sell the milk quota, and the herd, and the house and land, and then lease it back as a tenant arable farmer. Give someone else the headaches. But he'd never say it, any more than he'd say to Joe these days, 'What's up, lad?' You couldn't

76

do that in life, you just couldn't. It wasn't so much a matter of respecting another man's privacy, even that of your sons, but more of recognising that each man was for himself, solitary and responsible, destined to resolve or just bear whatever came his way.

A car came slowly down the lane beside the field, and stopped in the gateway twenty yards away. Harry straightened up. It was Robin's car. What did Robin want with him on a Saturday afternoon? Two car doors slammed, and then Harry saw Judy's red head above the hedge as she climbed the gate, and another head, darker.

She jumped down on the field side and waved a flask at him.

'We've brought you some more tea!'

'Champion!' Harry shouted. 'Champion!'

He began to walk stiffly and quickly along the hedgerow towards her, pulling off his gloves and stuffing them into his overall pockets. He'd forgotten Judy was coming, forgotten everything on account of the plaguey row he and Joe had had that morning when Joe had refused, point blank, to let him grub up that hedge.

'It'd only take me a couple of days. With a digger.'

'No, Dad. No. *No*. I'm putting things back, not taking them out. Can't you ever think beyond tomorrow? Can't you ever see further than your bloody nose?'

'Grandpa,' Judy said, with pleasure. She put her arms round him and felt his hard old frame, like a tree or a piece of rustic furniture.

'Good girl,' Harry said, patting her. 'Good girl.'

'And this is Zoe.'

Harry grinned.

'Hello, Zoe.'

Funny little object. Girl's face and boy's hair. She was looking at the hedge, at the yards he'd split and woven.

'That difficult?'

'Not so difficult as I make it,' Harry said. 'Seen Granny?'

'Yes.'

'And Joe?'

'What's all this about Joe?' Judy said. 'Granny asked us, too. No we haven't. We just saw Lyndsay and the kids.'

Harry grunted. He looked across at Zoe. 'Your first time on a farm?'

'Yes,' she said.

'It's a terrible life,' Harry said. 'Terrible. We must be mad to do it.'

'I think so,' Judy said.

'Why do you do it then?' Zoe said.

Harry grinned at her.

'Can't do nothing else. It's bred in you, father to son. Even in the war, when I got caught up in Italy, all I could think about was the dratted farm. And I wasn't nineteen then.'

'Mum—' Judy said, and then stopped.

Zoe looked at her.

'Go on.'

'Mum said, even on holiday, Dad was only looking at the scenery to see how it was farmed. She said the only time he didn't was when they went to Tunisia, when I was seven and I came to stay with you, and there was no farming to look at there, only sand and camels.'

'Obsession,' Zoe said. 'Obsessions are interesting.'

Judy said, 'And scary.' She held the flask out to Harry. 'Your tea, Grandpa.'

78

He looked at her for a moment as he took it, and his eyes suddenly looked very old to her, faded in the centre with a ring of dull colour outside. It struck her, with a shaft of pain, that he was the age to die, the proper age when things begin to wear and dim and weaken, not Caro's age, not the age where you've still got things to do, people who need you.

Harry said gently, 'I'd better get on, girls.'

'Yes.'

'Or I'll have your Uncle Joe on my back.'

Judy leaned forward and kissed him again.

'We might see you tomorrow.'

'All right,' Harry said. He lifted his hand to Zoe. 'Bye for now, dear.'

She smiled at him.

'Bye,' she said.

As the two girls walked away from him along the hedge, and back to the car, Harry saw Zoe put a hand out to indicate his day's labours.

'I bet,' he heard her say, 'I could do that. I bet I could.'

*   *   *

'Do you think,' Robin said, 'that between us we could do something about that?'

On the kitchen table, a supermarket chicken lay trussed up in plastic and rubber bands.

'I might eat it,' Zoe said, 'but I couldn't cook it.'

'That's rather how I feel. Judy?'

'OK,' Judy said, 'if you wash up. Are there any potatoes?'

Robin indicated a plastic keg of cider that stood on the dresser.

'In the larder, I think. Drink, girls?'

79

'Zoe doesn't,' Judy said.

'Doesn't she?'

'No,' Zoe said. 'Don't like it.'

Robin looked at her. 'Uncommon,' he said.

'Thank you for the boiler suit. And my socks.'

'No trouble.'

'I liked it—the milking,' Zoe said. She perched on the edge of the kitchen table. 'I think I'll do it again tomorrow.'

'After you've peeled some potatoes,' Judy said.

Robin turned the spigot of the plastic keg and ran cider into a glass. He held it out to Judy. She almost met his eye when she took it.

'Thanks.'

'You look better,' he said to her.

She turned away from him and began to peel the plastic off the chicken. She said, 'You wouldn't really know.'

Zoe leaned forward across the table.

'Hey, hey, no need to bite his head off—'

Judy said nothing. Robin looked better to her, too, this evening, less haggard, his eyes less shadowed. He needed a haircut—at least, he did by his usual standards—and the longer hair became him, softened his face. But she didn't want him buttering her up in front of Zoe. That was cheating.

'I'll get the spuds,' Robin said. 'How hungry are we?'

'Not very. We've been eating tea ever since lunch. At Lyndsay's and then at Granny's. And before you ask us, we didn't see Joe.'

Robin, his hand on the larder door, opened his mouth to say that nobody saw Joe much these days, and shut it again. He had in fact called in to try and see him after the girls had left his house that

80

afternoon and had found Lyndsay helping Hughie to write his name at the kitchen table, while Rose crashed about the room in a wheeled walking frame.

'Look,' Hughie said. 'The big J. That big H is me.' Robin stooped.

'Not bad, old son.'

Lyndsay looked tired, with the transparency of fatigue that affects true blondes.

'I'm afraid Joe isn't here. I can't remember what he said he was doing this afternoon but I don't expect he'll be back before dark.'

'It can wait,' Robin said.

Rose careered across the room, bellowing, raising her arms for Robin's attention.

'Hello, Rosie.'

'She's been awful,' Lyndsay said. 'All afternoon.' She had always felt a little shy of Robin, of his height and his darkness and his solitariness, and in consequence, apologetic for things she felt he might disapprove of, like Rose's unruliness. But he stooped now and lifted Rose out of the walking frame. Rose was delighted.

'Yah,' she said to him. 'Yah, yah, yah.'

'You are a solid woman,' Robin told her.

She beamed. Robin said, 'What did you think of Judy's friend?'

'Nice,' Lyndsay said. 'Unusual. Hughie loved her.'

'I did not,' Hughie said with emphasis.

'Good for Judy. Lightens things. She was up at five-thirty for the milking.'

Rose put her hand on Robin's cheek.

'You're sticky,' he said.

'She's always sticky,' Lyndsay said and then, in a burst of confidence inspired by the unique sight of Robin with a baby in his arms, 'Robin, I'm a bit—'

81

She remembered Hughie and stopped. 'Joe,' she mouthed over Hughie's head. 'I'm worried about Joe.'

He nodded.

'I know.'

'And your mother—'

'Yes.'

'Can—can you talk to him? Can you? See what's the matter?'

Rose began to roar to be down again. Robin bent and lowered her back into her frame.

'I can try.'

Lyndsay stood up. She looked at Robin standing there in her kitchen in his working clothes and had a sudden impulse to step forward, children or no children, and lean on him, her face pressed into the navy-blue drill of his boiler suit, and say, 'Help me, help me, I don't know what to do, I'm at the end of my tether.'

'I must be getting back,' Robin said. He put a hand on Hughie's head. 'Keep writing. And tell your dad I'd like a word with him, will you?'

'What about?' Hughie said, drawing rapid Hs in scarlet crayon.

'Fertiliser,' Robin said. He touched Lyndsay's arm. She'd looked so close to tears only a moment ago. 'I'll see what I can do.'

It wouldn't be much, he thought now, opening the larder door. How could it be, since he didn't know what to ask and Joe probably didn't know what to reply? By the outward look of things, Joe was doing fine. The fields at Dean Place were clean, the boundaries mended, the bills got paid. At least, Robin supposed they did. In Dilys's hands, they could hardly avoid it. Robin and Joe, by some

82

unspoken agreement, never discussed money, indeed, almost shied away from it, but it was unthinkable that, with the farm in the outward shape it was, and Dilys doing the books, money could be Joe's trouble. If Caro was still here, she'd probably know what ailed him by instinct, but then if she was here, whatever was the matter mightn't be the matter in the first place. We are cursed by our reticence, Robin thought suddenly, surprising himself, cursed by it. It's like being in leg-irons. He stooped to scoop potatoes out of their dusty paper sack. He could hear Judy laughing a little in the kitchen, presumably at something Zoe had said. He rather liked Zoe. She had a boldness about her, a directness you usually only found in animals. Or children. Like Rose that afternoon, wanting to be picked up, wanting to be put down, no shilly-shallying, no complicated accommodation of other people.

He went back into the kitchen and dumped the potatoes in the sink.

'All yours,' he said to Zoe.

'OK,' she said. 'What do I do them with?'

'A peeler.'

'Wet or dry?'

Robin looked at her.

'Where did you grow up?'

'In a flat in Tottenham. I'm the original take-away kid. That's why I'm so wizened, like a First World War squaddie. I'm seriously malnourished.'

'Take no notice,' Judy said. 'She eats all day, like a horse.'

Robin grinned. He opened the kitchen drawer and hunted about in it for a potato peeler.

'There,' he said, holding it out.

She made no attempt to touch the peeler.

'Nasty,' she said. 'Looks like the kind of thing they used for the forcible examination of nineteenth-century prostitutes.'

'Zoe!'

'Get over to that sink,' Robin said. 'And run it full of cold water.'

'*Cold* water?' Zoe said. 'I *knew*, I knew why cooking was a bad idea.'

'Hurry up.'

She went over to the sink and put the plug in.

'Potatoes don't look like this in London. They have cheese in and live in take-away ovens.' She looked at Robin. 'Well, show me.'

Judy paused in putting half a lemon and a lump of butter—'sweet butter', Caro had always said—inside the chicken, and looked across the table. Robin was bending over the sink at an angle, a potato and the peeler in his hands, and Zoe, her elbows propped on the draining board, was watching him with the absorption of a child in front of television. Was she sending him up? Or was she flirting? And why, with her in the room, should the shadows seem fainter, gauzier, as if a little life had been allowed back in as well as the memories? She turned the chicken over and laid it on its breast in a roasting tray, just as Caro had always done, as Caro had taught her.

'Right,' Robin said. Judy heard the splash of the peeler being thrown into the water. 'Right. Over to you.'

CHAPTER SIX

Stretton Cattle Market lay off the ring road, between an ice-cream factory and the offices of the Regional Electricity Board. It occupied a vast site, an untidy complex of auction houses and car-parks, and had a reputation for being good for live weight stock sold on the hoof. At one end, a large new building housed the main auction rings for cattle and calves; at the other an immense roof spread over the pens in which sheep and pigs were packed like dates in a box. Between the two ran a pedestrian precinct lined with banks and agricultural suppliers, horticultural shops and pet-supply stores and at either end, marked by a menu board propped up outside in the shape of a great white bull, an eating place, called the Charolais Diner, served all-day breakfasts for £2.95.

Robin drove the trailer into the park nearest to the main auction building and drew up next to the sales-times notice-board: 'Butchers' sheep: 10.15. Beef cows and sucklers: 10.45. Beef calves: 11.15. Store cattle and barren cows: 12 noon.' In the trailer, five fortnight-old bull calves stood with their heads to the far wall, as far from the tailgate and the alarming business of being loaded and unloaded as possible. Robin and Gareth had loaded them in an hour before, running them up into the trailer holding their makeshift collar halters of baling twine in one hand and their tails in the other.

'I never like this,' Gareth said. 'I never like seeing them go.'

Robin grunted. He didn't like it either, not these days with the eighteen months of fattening life ahead

85

of the calves so uncertain; but he liked it even less with the barren cows. There was something about sending a cow off to market for a failure that was entirely not her fault that affected him more as he got older, not less. But he wasn't about to have a discussion on stock-farming ethics with Gareth, who would then stop what he was doing in order to lean against the nearest upright and expound. There was something in Gareth that made him incapable of talking and working simultaneously, and Robin, though considerate of Debbie and the children in many ways, was ever mindful of the fact that Gareth was paid to work.

'I don't want to come back,' he said, 'with less than seven hundred for the lot of them.'

He climbed down now from the Land Rover and went round to the back of the trailer to unhook the bolts. Two market herdsmen in flat caps and buff overall coats came up to line hurdles between the trailer and the pens in which the calves would wait until it was their turn to be herded, by a boy relatively not much older than themselves, through the clatter and shouting of the auction ring. One of the men held a bucket of glue and a wooden paddle to slap an auction label on to each small rump as it emerged from the trailer.

'Robin—'

Robin, his hands still up against the tailgate, turned to look over his shoulder. Joe was standing there, in working clothes, his hands in his pockets.

'What are you doing here?'

Joe said, 'Nothing much. Maybe looking at some beef cattle—'

'What do you want to do that for?' Robin said. 'Here, give us a hand with this—'

'I thought I'd like it,' Joe said, moving to take the weight of the far side of the tailgate. 'I thought maybe I'd like some animals, maybe the farm would be better with some life on it. Just a few store cattle.'

'Does Dad know?'

'No.'

'Why not?'

'Dad doesn't want anything to change.'

'If it's change for its own sake—'

'I don't know,' Joe said. 'I don't know about that. I just know I want a change.'

The tailgate swung slowly down to form a ramp and the five calves pressed themselves against the farthest wall.

'Poor little sods.'

'Don't you start. Gareth's bad enough. You'd think I was taking his children to the auction.'

Joe watched Robin climb into the trailer and manhandle the calves one by one towards the ramp, their winglike ears pierced with plastic identity tags. He remembered bringing Lyndsay to the market during their engagement to show her the reality of farming, the inescapable fact of cows driven dazed through the clanging gates of the auction ring and sold off to buyers for slaughterhouses and meat-packing stations at so many pence per kilo. She had cried all the way back to Dean Place, mortified both by what she had seen and by the death of her own romantic preconceptions of farming.

'It was the calves,' she had sobbed to Caro, fetched by Joe in an effort to console her, to reconcile her to the reality of food production.

'I know,' Caro had said, 'I know. They're just far too pretty to be sensible about.'

'Perhaps I shouldn't have taken her,' Joe had said

87

later. 'Perhaps I should just have let her think farming is fields of oats. After all, that's about all she'll see.'

'I don't know,' Caro had said slowly. He remembered her veiled brown gaze. 'I don't know. I don't think I'll ever really know how much truth is good for us.'

The hurdles swung into place behind the last of the calves.

Robin said, 'I just always hope they'll go to a beef unit in this country.' He looked at Joe. He was standing gazing after the calves with an expression of studied remoteness, the expression Robin had caught on his face at Caro's funeral, as if he were driving his mind through and beyond what he was looking at in order not to have to react to it. Robin went down the straw-littered ramp and put his hand on Joe's arm.

'Want to say anything?'

Joe shook his head.

'Want to look at the ring? I'll come with you—'

Joe sighed.

'I should be getting back. I don't quite know what I'm doing here—'

'Looking at beef cattle. You said.'

'Yes.'

'Because you want to make things different.'

Joe said nothing.

'So do I,' Robin said. 'I want things to change. I want this—time to be over.'

Joe looked at him, a long, dark, unhappy look.

'If buying cattle'll help,' Robin said, 'you buy cattle.'

'I can't be sure—'

'No,' Robin said, 'none of us can. It's the first time we've done it. It's the first time I've lost a wife.' He

88

looked away from Joe. It was on the tip of his tongue to say that he craved Caro back, not so much for herself, but so that he could ask her things, demand answers to his questions about abandonment, about betrayal of trust. But it wouldn't be fair. Whatever Joe was struggling with was plainly all he could manage just now. Revelation of all that was seething unresolved in Robin's mind was the last thing Joe needed.

Joe said suddenly, 'I didn't love her. I mean, not like that, not *love*—'

Robin waited. The straw on the ramp lifted in little eddies of wind and blew about their legs.

'I just—' Joe spread his hands and then clenched them into fists. 'It seems, now she's gone, that she held things together, somehow, that she made things kind of hopeful.'

Robin hesitated. A small anger at Joe's impudence began to smoulder at the edges of his sympathy. He took the Land Rover keys out of his pocket and jingled them in his hand.

'Watch it,' he said.

'I never meant—'

'No,' Robin said, 'no. I don't expect you did. But just don't make too much of it, OK? You've got it all on a plate, you always have had, so don't go and make too much of *anything*.'

*   *   *

He left the Land Rover and the trailer in a car-park next to a very similar vehicle in which a yellow-eyed sheepdog sat alert and upright in the passenger seat, and made for the auction ring. It was housed in a big, plain, glass-and-concrete building, like a bus station, with internal staircases that led up either side to the top of the amphitheatre of great tiered steps from which to watch the auction ring below. There were perhaps thirty or forty people scattered about these steps and leaning on the metal guard rails, farmers of every age and type, with a few women, dressed much like the men, among them, and a handful of hard country girls in rubber riding boots, pushing long hair off their faces with one hand and holding cigarettes with the other.

Below them, on fixed stools around the ring itself, were the bidders, some farmers buying for themselves, others buyers on commission from abattoirs. They sat there, market day after market day, dressed winter and summer alike in shapeless, weatherproof country clothing the colour of mouldy thatch, elbows propped on the edge of the ring, making those infinitesimal gestures of the practised bidder, taciturn, businesslike and tough. To their left, cattle were herded one by one through an automatic weighing crate which flashed each cow's weight in kilos up on to a screen above the auctioneer's head, and then the animals were goaded through the ring for only a matter of seconds, blundering and turning in the clanking confusion of metal gates, before being driven out again, weight sold, fate sealed, to the herding pens behind the rings.

'Morning, Robin,' someone said. 'You got business down there?'

Robin shook his head.

'Only calves today.'

The man, bulky in a padded waistcoat over shaggy layers of knitting, said, 'Not much quality this week. Even the best won't make much more than ninety pence.' He looked keenly at Robin for a moment.

There'd been rumours for years that Caro Meredith had been an odd one, but rumours or no rumours, a wife was a wife and her loss was a loss all the same.

'You keeping all right?'

Robin nodded.

'That's the spirit.' He looked back down towards the ring. 'Now there's a grand cow, that straight Angus. That's Jim Voyce's herd.'

Robin touched his arm.

'I'll be off, Fred. Only came in for a second.'

Fred James touched his cap.

'All the best, Robin. Give my regards to your father. Keeping well, is he?'

Outside in the air once more, he found it was beginning to rain, small, constant, cold rain. He turned his collar up and cursed himself for leaving his cap in the Land Rover. Why had he been in the ring, he wondered? Why had he obeyed that impulse to help Joe, when he did not believe that to diversify into stock was going to help Joe in any way? Why, for God's sake, should he help Joe when Joe had had everything, right from the start, without even needing to stretch out his hand to ask for it? The rain was, steadily and unmistakably, getting harder. People were beginning to hurry towards cover, people who spent their lives working in the rain but who reacted to it differently in a built-up environment. Robin hunched his shoulders and sank his chin deep in his collar. He must buy some wheat straw before he left, if he could get it for under £25 a ton, delivered.

*   *   *

Judy lay on the sitting-room floor of her flat, her head

and shoulders propped uncomfortably against an armchair, watching a play on television. Zoe had said she must watch it because a friend of hers was the assistant cameraman, and had then gone off to a two-day photography course in Birmingham, leaving Judy to watch it alone. Of course, Judy told herself, she didn't have to watch it. She could wash her hair or read a book or do a bit of cleaning instead, but somehow, in the last few weeks with Zoe as a flatmate, she had grown used to doing things with Zoe. Zoe had a way, Judy had discovered, of making her, Judy, use her time.

It wasn't, anyway, as if it was a very good play. It was about two teenagers on the run from the police in an unspecified northern city, but the reason for their being on the run was never explained and there was more breathless panting than dialogue. It was also shot either in the dark or the half-dark, so that it was difficult, on Judy's small television screen, to appreciate the skills of Zoe's friend, the assistant cameraman. She lay there, her chin on her chest, and willed herself to summon the energy to get up and turn the play off.

The two teenagers, androgynous-looking girls, were now stumbling along a railway line in the dark. One of them had a haircut rather like Zoe's. Zoe had hers cut every three weeks and rinsed with a vegetable dye to bring it back to the deep burgundy colour that Judy was now quite used to. Basically, Zoe had said, her hair was brown. Not rich glowing brown with tawny highlights and the sheen of a new conker, she said, but plain brown like dead leaves, boring brown. She had dyed it black once, long ago, having seen a video of Liza Minnelli in *Cabaret*, but she said black was too much and made her look phoney. Judy reached up and pulled a lock of her own hair down so that she could see it. Red hair looked pretty phoney to her even in its natural state.

Someone rang the doorbell. Judy sat up slowly. It would be the elaborately spaced-out man from the flat below wanting a loaf or a light bulb or another look at Zoe. He appeared three nights out of five these days, grinning and languid, a rolled-up £5 note between his fingers, which he had, Judy noticed, no intention of ever letting go of. She stood up and, without any hurry, turned the television down, but not off, and went to the front door, opening it the four inches the security chain would allow.

There was a young man standing there, a thin young man in jeans and a leather jacket. He wore spectacles and was carrying a cone of the shadowy printed cheap giftwrap beloved of flower sellers.

'Hi,' he said.

Judy regarded him.

'Who are you?'

'I'm Oliver,' the young man said. He held out the paper cone of flowers. 'I'm looking for Zoe.'

'She's in Birmingham,' Judy said.

'Oh.'

'She won't be back until Friday.'

'Oh.'

Judy said heartlessly, looking at the flowers through the four-inch crack, 'They'll probably be dead by then.'

'Yes,' he said, and then, 'Would you like them?'

Judy slid the bolt at the end of the chain to release it.

'Well,' she said, 'I don't want them to die.'

'Thanks,' Oliver said. He stepped in through the door and stood in the tiny hall, looking uncertain. 'I haven't see her for three weeks. Not since she moved in here.'

'No,' Judy said, 'I don't expect you have.' She smiled at him. He had a sweet face behind his round, modish spectacles and the kind of clean, smooth, childish hair you saw on choirboys. Ollie the run-over stork. She said, 'Like a coffee?'

'Yes,' he said. 'Please.' He pushed the flowers at her. 'Do take those. They make me feel a geek.'

Judy led the way into the sitting room and turned off the television.

'Don't do that,' Oliver said. 'Not if you were watching.'

'I only half was.'

'I expect,' he said resignedly, 'you know why I've come.'

'Well—'

'Girls always know about each other.'

Judy ran water into a jug and unrolled the flower paper to reveal several fragile stalks of yellow freesia.

'These'll smell nice.'

'Is she avoiding me?' Oliver said.

'Maybe—'

'You mean yes. Why doesn't she just say?'

'I don't know,' Judy said. 'You'll have to ask her. It's none of my business.'

He leaned against the kitchen doorway, as Zoe always did.

'What's your name?'

'Judy.'

'Hi, Judy,' Oliver said, 'Shall I put the kettle on?'

He moved past her as she inserted each long green stem into the jug, and plugged the kettle in.

'Now what. Where's the coffee?'

Judy jerked her head.

94

'There.'

'Have you noticed,' Oliver said, 'how Zoe can't even boil a kettle? Or won't?'

'My dad made her. He got her peeling potatoes and frying bacon. He made her fry him some bacon after milking.'

'Milking?'

'He's a farmer,' Judy said.

'And your mother?'

There was a tiny beat.

'She's dead,' Judy said.

'Oh,' Oliver said. 'Oh, oh I am *sorry*.' He turned round in the small space of the kitchen and put his arm around Judy's shoulders. 'Poor you,' he said, holding her. 'Poor Judy. Poor girl.'

She looked fixedly down at the freesias.

'Six weeks ago. Brain tumour.'

'Awful,' Oliver said. 'You must have had such a bloody awful time.' He squeezed her shoulder. 'Poor girl,' he said again.

She glanced at him. His eyes, clear and guileless behind his glasses, were looking straight at her.

'Zoe's been kind—'

'Well, she knows how it is. She lost her father—'

'She said you were kind to her about that.'

'Did she?'

Judy moved gently out of his embrace to rescue the steaming kettle.

'Yes.'

'It isn't hard,' Oliver said. 'No one in my family's died, but I can imagine how I'd feel. At least I think I can.'

'Most people,' Judy said, 'are frightened to. So it's like some contagious disease they think they'll catch if they come too close. Do you want milk?'

95

'And sugar. Two, please.'

Judy held out a mug.

'It's nice when someone isn't afraid. Like you.'

'I'm afraid of heights,' Oliver said, 'and depths. And I could do with a world without spiders.'

Judy went past him into the sitting room and set the flowers down on the empty hearth between Zoe's herons.

'I gave her those herons,' Oliver said. 'They come from the Philippines.'

'I like them,' Judy said. 'So does she.'

'Good,' Oliver said. He took a noisy swallow of coffee. 'Good. I'm glad she does. But I don't think, somehow, that I'll be giving her anything else.'

* * *

From her sitting-room window, Gareth's wife Debbie watched Robin's Land Rover emerge from the yard and turn up the drive towards the road. It was the fourth time he'd been out that morning; she'd counted them. This time, as far as she could see, there was nothing in the back of the Land Rover, no hay bales, no calf with its bony little rump turned towards the tailgate. You weren't supposed to carry livestock in an open trailer like a Land Rover, but Robin Meredith was not the kind of man who seemed much interested in what you weren't supposed to do. He'd got a reputation locally for being bloody-minded but Gareth said that wasn't fair. He said he just didn't say much.

Debbie sprayed a blue mist of window polish—'contains real vinegar' the label on the bottle said—on to the wide expanse of picture window against which the dust from the track past the cottage blew so relentlessly. She had a list of seven household chores to do before she went to Dean Cross Primary School for her daily job of helping serve and wash up fifty-seven school dinners. Velma had got Debbie the job when she and Gareth first came to Tideswell, before Eddie, now four, was born. Her elder children, Rebecca and Kevin, were both at Dean Cross School already and didn't like their mum appearing at dinnertime in the school kitchen in an apricot-checked overall with her hair done up in a muslin bag with an apricot peak to it. They wouldn't look at her when she ladled out their mashed potato and pasta bake but shuffled on down the queue, heads bent, as quick as they could. Gareth told them they were nothing but a pair of little snobs.

Gareth was good, Debbie reflected, at standing up for her against the children, against Kevin wanting a television in his bedroom and Rebecca wanting her ears pierced for her tenth birthday. He was good in other ways, too, not smoking, not getting drunk except very occasionally, buying her flowers on their wedding anniversary, handing his wage packet over each week except for a few quid he kept for himself, just as Debbie's father had done. Gareth said she was a good manager. Well, she was, she'd always been good with money, even if she'd felt that this was a sensible rather than a sexy quality. She used to pride herself on being sensible, and was critical of Gareth for his lack of desire to be responsible about money, but just recently, she felt she'd changed. Just recently, since Caro Meredith died, as she'd watched Robin's lonely light from the farmhouse kitchen window at night, she'd been conscious of things she'd never thought of before, of the fragility of life, of what it would be like if Gareth died and left her alone with

Rebecca and Kevin and Eddie. For years, she had told Gareth that sex once a week was quite enough, on a Saturday night because he didn't have to milk on Sunday mornings; Robin did Sunday mornings. But now, something about Robin, something about the spectacle of his solitude, almost as if he had been excluded from ordinary life by Caro's dying, made her want to make love to Gareth, even on Tuesdays or Thursdays, as if by loving him physically she could somehow put extra strength into him, extra life, like an insurance against fate.

She stood back from the window and surveyed the glass for smears. She never said any of this to Gareth, though she knew he was surprised at the change in her. 'What's this all about?' he'd said two nights ago, when she'd turned to him, on a Wednesday. 'What's up, Debbie?' But he'd sounded pleased, he'd been pleased. It made her colour a bit now to think of, but she couldn't help herself. Nor could she say anything. Saying things was so difficult; it was much better to let cards and flowers say what you couldn't say yourself. She had spent £25 on a wreath for Caro's funeral, a wreath of pink carnations and white chrysanthemums, and sent a special funeral card to the farmhouse which said, 'To Robin, thinking of you in your sad loss. Gareth, Debbie and family.' She didn't know if Robin had seen it, but even if he hadn't, she knew she'd done her best, said what was in her heart to say, with the wreath and the message. Robin's Land Rover appeared again at the top of the drive and came back down towards the yard. He'd only been ten minutes. Poor Robin, Debbie thought, poor Robin. Gareth said he and Caro hadn't shared a bedroom in years.

In the kitchen at Tideswell Farm, Velma had left a packet of powdered mushroom soup and two sausage rolls in a cellophane packet that had plainly been squashed under something much heavier in her plastic shopper. Beside the food lay the morning's mail which he had opened by tearing the envelopes with his thumb, and which Velma had arranged, as she always did, in a graded line, the biggest envelope at the back. In the front of the pile—the smallest letter—lay the one item he did not wish to see, a single sheet from the River Authority to say that their inspectors would be down on the River Dean below his property on the morning of the 17th to verify the findings of their previous, unannounced, inspection.

Robin put the mushroom soup down on the River Authority letter and dropped the sausage rolls in the bin. Then he opened the fridge. There were no surprises there and he shut the door again. He wandered over to the window and stood looking out into the yard, rattling the keys in his pocket. He was restless rather than hungry, had been all week, fidgety and unsettled. Ever since that strange little encounter with Joe at Stretton Market something had tugged at him, disquieted him, some elusive little trouble that had nothing to do with grief, with Caro. It was more that he felt there was something the matter that Joe wouldn't tell him, something specific that he ought to know, that affected him, and because he didn't know it and couldn't get it out of Joe, it buzzed in his mind like a wasp in a jar. He'd been in and out like a yo-yo, up and down to the village, to Dean Place Farm, to the river bank.

'Trying to wear your tyres out?' Harry had said.

It was only half a joke. Harry wasn't in much of a joking mood this week since someone had reported to him seeing Joe at Stretton Market, hanging round the store-cattle pens, and, when confronted, Joe had flown into a rage and said that where he went and what he looked at was his own bloody business. It had bothered Harry, both Joe's attitude and what he might be planning. Two years ago, Dilys and Joe had persuaded him that they only needed two signatures out of the three on the Dean Place Farm cheque book since Joe did most of the buying these days. Suppose Joe did have some tomfool scheme about cattle in his head? Lord knows what did go on in his head right now, and Dilys had always been foolish with him, soft, she'd never refuse him her co-signature on a cheque if he pleaded with her. It made Harry edgy. So did Robin, driving in and out of the yard at Dean Place like something from Wells Fargo, and never for an errand Harry could see any sense to.

Robin knew Harry was troubled. That last visit to Dean Place, he'd tried to say something comforting, that they'd all settle down again, that Joe was just toying with a few ideas like all farmers did. But Harry had simply grunted, tinkering on with his spanner at the old drilling machine Joe had wanted to replace for two years.

'We all do it,' Robin said. 'We all think about change, about shaking things up a bit.'

Except Harry, Robin thought now, looking at the yard and the clumps of docks in the corners he kept meaning to spray. Harry had farmed the same way all his life and would never wish to do otherwise. Harry liked things to be the same, manageable and familiar. What would happen, Robin wondered, if something Harry really couldn't manage happened, something

100

alien that really touched him, affected his life? Would he simply go on imperturbably, ignoring the problem as far as he could, like an oyster wrapping a grain of sand in layers of pearl? Or would he, instead, fall to pieces?

A car had turned off the road at the end of the drive and was coming down towards the house. It was a taxi; Robin could see the red dome of the taxi's illuminated telephone number on the roof. Who would be coming here in a taxi, and at lunchtime? Velma sometimes used a taxi, but she used the local man from Dean Cross who drove an orange Vauxhall Astra with 'Dean Cross Taxis' painted on a piece of thick cardboard propped up behind the windscreen. This taxi looked like one from Stretton. It passed the yard gate and vanished behind the leylandii hedge to the front drive and the front door.

Robin went out of the kitchen and down the long-tiled passage to the Victorian part of the house and the front hall. It was dark, as it always was, illuminated only by a panel of coloured glass above the front door, a stylised pattern of tulips in pink and red with stiff green leaves. Robin switched on the light to find the front-door key, unused since Caro's funeral tea, and kept in a drawer of the hall chest among outdated maps and single gloves. The light shone down on the results of Velma's unillumined housework, upon random swirlings of a mop in the dust, like scribblings with a stick in sand.

Robin put the key in the lock and turned it. It needed, as it ever had, a wrench to open the door. Outside, on the drive, and moving away as if she meant to go round to the yard and the back door, was Zoe holding a metal camera case and a black haversack.

101

'Hey!' Robin said. 'What are you doing here?'

'Sorry,' she said. She put the camera case down. 'I didn't mean to make you open that door. It was the taxi. He wouldn't go into the yard in case it made the cab mucky. I was in Birmingham.'

'Yes?'

'And I saw a coach to Stretton at the bus station. And I thought—'

'Yes?'

'Well,' Zoe said. She didn't sound in the least uncertain of her welcome. 'Well, I thought I'd come and see you. So I have.'

CHAPTER SEVEN

'I don't want to interfere,' Dilys said, 'but you ought to take Joe off on a bit of a holiday. Fishing, maybe.'

She sat at Lyndsay's kitchen table with a cup of tea in front of her. She had refused a slice of the banana bread Lyndsay had made. All her life, Dilys had eaten regular amounts of excellent old-fashioned food without really thinking about it, but just recently she had noticed that her clothes were tighter, that, when she stooped to pick things up from the floor, or unplug the Hoover, her lungs felt as if they were being compressed from within, by bolsters. This was a pity. The banana bread looked just as she liked it, nicely risen with sultanas scattered through it. That was exactly how it ought to look, mind you. After all, it was she who had taught Lyndsay to make it.

'Harry and I went to Ireland once, fishing. On the West Coast. It was beautiful. I expect these days you

102

could fly straight there, from Manchester.'

Lyndsay said, 'He wouldn't come.'

'What do you mean?'

'He won't think about holidays. You know that.'

'I know nothing of the sort,' Dilys said sharply.

Lyndsay finished cutting banana bread into strips for Hughie and small squares for Rose, and laid them in front of each child. Dilys had rung that morning saying she'd be in Stretton that afternoon and was there anything Lyndsay wanted? No, Lyndsay had said, mindful of Dilys's tendency to buy you the things she thought you ought to have rather than the things you had actually asked for. In that case, Dilys had said, she'd just call in to see the children on her way home anyway, and Lyndsay, who had intended to spend the morning investigating a new part-time hairdressing course at Stretton College, had made a banana loaf instead.

'Where did the banana go?' Hughie asked, looking at his bread.

'I mashed it up, and then it got cooked in the bread.'

He pushed his plate away.

'I must *see* it.'

'Now, now,' Dilys said.

Hughie got down off his chair and retrieved Seal from the top of the vegetable basket. He put his thumb in. Lyndsay held her breath.

'Now,' Dilys said to her grandson, her hands calmly folded on the table, 'are you a man or a mouse?'

Hughie regarded her. He took his thumb out long enough to say, 'A mouse,' and then he put it back in again.

Dilys looked at Lyndsay. Lyndsay looked at Rose

103

who was packing her cheeks with banana bread, like a frantic hamster.

'I didn't hear you ask to get down,' Dilys said to Hughie.

Hughie sidled sideways behind Lyndsay's chair until he was hidden from Dilys's view. Rose took a deep breath and blew a sodden lump of banana bread out of her mouth across her high-chair tray and on to the table, where it landed wetly not far from Dilys's teacup.

'Rose!'

'It's Joe,' Lyndsay said desperately, carelessly.

Dilys took the spoon off her saucer and began to scrape Rose's banana bread off the table.

'What's Joe?' Her face and voice were tight with outrage.

'Everyone's upset,' Lyndsay said, not caring. 'Can't you see? We're all feeling it. And nobody will say, nobody will say what's the matter. Especially not him.'

Dilys got up. She walked round the table to Lyndsay's chair and picked up Hughie, still sucking, still clutching Seal. For a moment, he hung in her hands like an amazed, petrified rag doll and then he found himself back in his chair, in front of his untouched plate. He couldn't move. He was paralysed by terrified surprise.

'There's nothing to say,' Dilys said, 'because there's nothing the matter. Except he's overworked. He works all hours, and he's got Harry to contend with. Harry never was a forward thinker. And you've got tense. I can see it. We can all see it. It hasn't been easy since Caro went and you've got yourself into a state. You need a holiday. You both need a holiday. I'll look after the children. Mary can help me with

104

their bedtime.'

Hughie put Seal up to his face so that his hot, alarmed tears could leak silently into Seal's plush.

'It's not me!' Lyndsay cried. 'It's not me! If I'm tense, it's because of him!'

She sprang up and seized Rose out of her high chair. Rose, enraged by being picked up when she hadn't demanded it, began to yell.

'Look at you,' Dilys said. 'Just look at you. And these children. Is this any way to bring these children up?' She had wanted to say 'Joe's children' with a harsh, proud, possessive emphasis.

'Please go,' Lyndsay said, almost gasping. She began to dab madly at Rose's face with a cloth and Rose roared in response. 'Please go. I can't bear any more of this, I can't cope, I can't take you all pretending everything's fine, I can't stand this conspiracy, this family conspiracy—'

Dilys stood up.

'You've had nothing but support, dear. Ever since you came into this family, you've had everything anyone could ask for. This house, help with the babies, no responsibility on the farm—'

'The farm!' Lyndsay screamed. 'Oh, the farm, the farm!'

'Ow,' Hughie wailed inaudibly into Seal. 'Ow, ow, ow, ow, *ow.*'

'It's no good shouting,' Dilys said. 'When did shouting ever get anyone anywhere? And it's no good blaming the farm. The farm's the Merediths. Where would we be without it?'

She moved to the door, where she had laid her handbag and wicker shopping basket on a nearby chair.

'Now listen,' she said. 'Just listen. You're a good

girl, Lyndsay, but you've let yourself get all worked up. And it's affecting Joe and it's affecting the children. Joe needs a holiday and you could do with one, too. And a tonic, maybe. You might be anaemic, it's very common in young women. I'll talk to Joe and then we'll see.' She put her handbag into her basket beside the paper bag of fresh yeast and the packets of tea and darning needles. Then she stooped and kissed the top of Hughie's head.

'You be a good boy, now. No more upsetting your mother.'

'He doesn't upset me,' Lyndsay said, her face against Rose. 'He doesn't. He's good. It's—' She stopped.

'I'll ring you,' Dilys said. 'You make yourself a fresh pot of tea. Bye-bye, Rosie! Bye, dear.'

When she had gone, Lyndsay set Rose on the floor.

'Nah!' Rose bellowed.

'Please—'

Rose considered for a moment and then twisted herself on to her knees and began to crawl vigorously towards the vegetable basket. In two minutes the floor would be a rolling sea of carrots and onions, as it always was since Lyndsay had run out of places to put things out of Rose's reach. Lyndsay went back to her chair and put her elbows on the table and her face in her hands. Hughie watched her over the damp, warm body of Seal.

'She loves us,' Lyndsay said faintly. 'She does. She wants to help us. But she doesn't know how. None of them do.'

Hughie laid Seal beside his plate and slid off his chair, to come and lean on Lyndsay. She took an arm off the table to hold him.

'I love you,' Lyndsay said.

He waited. After a moment or two he said, struggling with himself, 'And Rose?'

An onion hit his ankle.

'Yes. And Rose.'

Hughie nudged the onion away. It was pale brown and satiny, but it had horrible little wavering roots sticking out of it at one end, and Hughie didn't want them to touch him.

'And Daddy?'

'Oh yes,' Lyndsay said. She gave a long, sighing breath. 'I love Daddy, all right. Daddy's just about everything there is to me.'

* * *

Mary Corriedale's husband, Mac, had just finished his fortnightly mowing of Dean Cross churchyard. It was only the second cut of the year, and he had mowed as he always did, in great broad swirls, leaving the headstones of the graves in ruffs of long grass. Later, in May, they would stand in a froth of cow parsley, and then in tall buttercups. The Vicar would have liked more precision in the churchyard, more clipped edges, more the air of a garden than a half-tamed field. He said this, tentatively, every summer at Parochial Church Council meetings and was told that if he could find anyone other than Mac Corriedale prepared to cut the grass all summer for nothing he was welcome to try. The Vicar, who found asking anyone for anything, especially God, appallingly difficult, continued to endure the clumps of nettles and the stands of willowherb and Mac's haymaking mowing methods.

Zoe thought it was lovely. She liked the haphazard look of it and the cool, earthy smell of it, and the way

107

that the mown places were casually punctuated with molehills. The old graves were especially appealing, crusted with lichen, their lettering weathered into almost nothingness, faint grooves you could only make out as words when the sun was low and the light struck at just the right angle. The modern gravestones were often made of marble, polished slabs of black, or pink like potted fish paste, and some were shaped like open books and had flowerpots cemented in front of them with grilles in the top to hold the flowers upright. These graves, Zoe noticed, didn't mention death. 'Passed away', they said nervously in bright gold letters, 'Went to sleep', or just dates, so that you could make your own assumptions. Some graves were marked with crosses and one with an angel, whose head had been vandalised, thereby giving it a strangely pagan look, like the Winged Victory of Samothrace. Caro's grave, which Zoe had gone looking for, wasn't marked at all.

'You can't,' Robin had said. 'You can't put a headstone up for six months at least.'

'Why not?'

'Because the grave sinks.'

'Why?'

'Because the coffin lid falls in as the body decays.'

'God,' Zoe said. And then, 'Can I go and see her grave, all the same?'

He had looked at her.

'Of course.'

It was a shallow mound. The grass hadn't yet had time to grow and it and the earth looked patchy and ragged, irregularly dotted with clumps of flat weeds. At one end, a jam jar of dead late daffodils leaned against a small white plastic pot, fashioned in crude imitation of a Grecian urn, planted with big blue pansies.

Zoe bent down and touched the pansies. Robin would never have put those there, he didn't know anything about flowers, didn't notice them. Perhaps it was his mother, Dilys, or that pretty sister-in-law with the little kids who Zoe had seen driving through the village the day before, looking haunted. She had mentioned seeing Lyndsay to Robin, but he'd only grunted. He was reading some letter from the River Authority at the time—she could see the letterhead through the paper from the back—and had hardly heard her. She hadn't repeated herself. Two nights under Robin's roof had already taught her the futility of that.

He had made no fuss about her staying. She had moved her camera case and her rucksack into the room she'd been given when Judy had brought her to Tideswell and then she had gone out into the yard to find Gareth. He was preparing a shed outside the barn for two cows about to calve, and she picked up a pitchfork and helped him. His little boy, Eddie, had appeared and shown Zoe his set of plastic warriors who could be transformed into robots by twisting their helmets.

'Don't you touch,' Eddie said. 'You just watch. I got them off of the telly.'

Zoe had taken pictures of him. She took her camera everywhere. She had brought it up to the churchyard now and had taken some shots of good angles of the church buttresses and the lych-gate and the gravestones. It wasn't a pretty church, but it was squat and old and looked indomitable. Caro's grave didn't look in the least indomitable. It looked forlorn. It looked, Zoe thought, as if the person

109

underneath had just been tossed aside because there was, quite literally, no more the living could do except futile things like give them pots of blue pansies. Robin said his wife had been American, a Californian, and here she was in this English churchyard, with a field of cows on one side and the village-school playground on the other and a grey sky above like a soft, dense lid. It was like her father, born in England, buried in Australia. Except he wasn't buried. He'd left instructions for his ashes to be scattered somewhere in the outback miles and miles north of Sydney. His girlfriend had done it. She wrote Zoe a long, long letter about it saying it was a place where they'd had a wonderful camping trip once, and slept under the stars, and how Zoe's father wanted to be scattered under those same stars. Bloody cheek, Zoe had thought, reading, bloody nerve. She had torn the letter up.

She moved to the head of the grave and picked the jar of rustling, dead daffodils up. Then she nudged the pot of pansies with her foot, so that it was central. Nice flowers, pansies. They had faces, like sunflowers did. She'd wanted to go to Italy last summer, or Spain, and photograph all those sunflowers, fields and fields of them, all facing the east and the dawn, like good little kids all listening to their teacher. But she hadn't done it. Like she hadn't done a lot of things. She looked down at the dismal jar. But she must. She must start doing things before she, too, became stuck somewhere, getting by, like Caro seemed to have done, like her father had done, working as a mechanic in a Sydney garage when he was really a qualified engineer, living with a girl half his age so's not to be lonely.

110

'Bye,' Zoe said to Caro's grave. 'Judy sends her love.'

*   *   *

Joe didn't get home until after nine. Lyndsay had given up waiting for him for supper and had taken her mug of soup—leek and ham, made with leeks from Dilys's garden—to the sofa in front of the television, which she had turned on, for company, but not really watched. Instead, she read a novel that had come bound with a plastic cummerbund to a woman's magazine, a pretty-looking novel, with a white shiny cover showing a bright water-colour of an idealised country kitchen with the door open to a garden beyond and spires of delphiniums and a beehive. The story concerned an unhappy woman moving from the city to the country and finding self-fulfilment there. And a lover. Of *course*, Lyndsay thought irritably, a lover. The country world of the book bore no resemblance to anything Lyndsay had ever encountered in country life, it was a wish-think world of birdsong and caricature villagers, a honey-for-tea idyll. It wasn't what Lyndsay knew. It wasn't those relentless greedy acres at Dean Place Farm and always the wrong weather and loneliness and worry and family and Joe. And it wasn't either, a world where you couldn't *say* anything. In this novel people talked all the time, about their feelings and frustrations and desires and longings, they explained themselves to one another over and over again, while drinking chilled white wine and filtered coffee. What the hell, Lyndsay thought savagely, hurling the book from her, is the matter with bloody instant coffee, for Christ's sake?

'Hi,' Joe said, from the sitting-room doorway.

111

She sat up.

'Where've you been?'

'Spraying. I said. I told you.'

'But it's gone nine. It's been dark nearly two hours. I told Hughie—'

'I went to Mum's,' Joe said.

Lyndsay swung her feet slowly to the floor so that her back was to him.

'Oh.'

She got up and switched the television off.

'D'you want some supper?' she said, her back still turned.

'No, thanks. I ate at Mum's.'

Lyndsay turned round.

'Why didn't you ring?'

'Mum said you knew she wanted to talk to me.'

'But not tonight!' Lyndsay cried. 'Not without telling me!'

'Lyn—'

'I'm your *wife*. I'm not some child you and your mother have to decide things for. I'm the mother of your children and your *wife*. I'm the one you should talk to—'

Joe came further into the room. He was still in his boiler suit, the front open and showing his checked work shirt, those shirts she ironed even though there was no point to it considering the state they got into. But she ironed them because they were his shirts and she was his wife.

'I didn't mean to talk to her. I meant to come home. But she cornered me. I was having another go at Dad about those hedgerows and she got me there. About this holiday.'

Lyndsay put her hands up to her hair and took the combs out.

112

'She came here at teatime.'

'I expect it was on her mind, then.'

'It isn't,' Lyndsay said, shaking her head so that her hair fell cloudily over her face, 'any of her *business*.'

'She says she'll have the kids.'

'I know. Hughie cried.'

'She's trying to help.'

Lyndsay pulled her hair back hard and jammed the combs in, first one side, then the other.

'What did she say?'

'What do you mean?'

'Did she say I'd got in a state and you'd better take me away for a bit? That I wasn't coping with the children?'

He said nothing.

'I'm not coping,' Lyndsay said. 'She's right there. But it's *you* I'm not coping with. I can't. You won't let me.'

'I've agreed to this holiday.'

'Fishing in Ireland?'

'If you want.'

'I don't know if I want it. I just know I want you to talk to me. If we go to Ireland, will you talk to me?'

He looked at her. His face was heavy with fatigue, dragged down by it so that she could suddenly see how he would look when he was an old man, Harry's age.

'I'll try,' Joe said. 'But I don't know what you want.'

He put his arms out suddenly and pulled her against him, against the cloth she laundered so endlessly and which now smelled, as it did at the end of every day, of sweat and oil and all the chemical processed things he worked with on that hateful land.

113

He held her there for some minutes, hard, uncomfortably hard, straining her against him, her head jammed under his chin which he had lifted a little as if he was staring upwards. She had the feeling that his eyes were closed.

'Joe—'

He let her go as abruptly as he had seized her.

'You go to bed,' he said.

'But—'

'I want to catch the headlines at the end of the news.'

'And the weather?'

'OK,' he said. 'The weather.'

'Hughie asked me if I loved you today,' Lyndsay said, 'and I said yes, I did.'

Joe looked away.

'Thanks,' he said.

*   *   *

Dilys lay beside Harry in the bed in which both Robin and Joe had been born. It was an old-fashioned bed, with a footboard as well as a headboard, and a new interior-sprung mattress resting on the old steel-mesh base stretched across the frame. The mesh crunched faintly when she turned over, as if it was grinding its teeth. There were sheets and blankets on the bed, and an eiderdown that had belonged to Harry's mother and which Dilys had re-covered herself in a satin-finished furnishing cotton patterned with roses. The same cotton hung at the windows and made a stout petticoat curtain for the dressing table. Dilys had bought a roll of it fifteen years ago, in Stretton Market, beating the stallholder down to £2 a yard.

114

Fifteen years ago, Joe hadn't been married. He hadn't met Lyndsay and, if Dilys was honest, she'd been thankful when that meeting finally happened. You couldn't have said that Joe had been straightforwardly sweet on Caro, but he was kind of fascinated, almost spellbound by her. It was, Dilys thought at the time, this American thing. He hadn't got America out of his system when he came home and then there was Caro, at Tideswell, an emblem of all the freedom he thought he'd left behind.

He'd told her something of America. Sitting at the kitchen table for mid-morning coffee—'Men's tea' it had always been known as on Dilys's father's farm between the wars—he'd talked a bit about the size of it, the great spaces, and the way so much of it couldn't be tamed and managed, all those rivers and mountains and deserts which made men realise they weren't masters of the universe after all. Dilys wouldn't have stood this kind of talk from Robin or Harry, but she listened to Joe. Joe had an ambition in him, a driving force she recognised in herself, a desire that things should be as good as they could be—and then better. Yet there was more still, in Joe. There was something restless and hungry in him, a quality of dark need that made him vulnerable. This vulnerability made Dilys wince. She saw it in the way he went at the farm, more as if it were an enemy than a challenge. She'd hoped—oh, how she'd hoped—that marriage and fatherhood would calm him, would channel some of this dangerous emotional energy into a harbour at last, a safe place, out of the storm.

She turned over carefully and the steel mesh ground complainingly under her. She wouldn't wake Harry by turning over. Nothing ever woke Harry. All

115

their married life Harry's behaviour had been as steady and regular as a metronome.

'He ain't going to give you no surprises,' Dilys's father had said when she announced their engagement. 'If that's what you want.'

She had wanted it. It seemed to her, in those dark, depressed, uncertain years after the end of the war, that Harry promised a security that was all too rare a commodity then, a security for her to be what her mother had so singularly failed to be, a good farmer's wife and then the mother of farmers. She'd done all that. Harry had given her every chance to be that, and she'd taken it. When the boys were young, and the poultry yard was full and the house cow—a Jersey—was in calf and the windows of Dean Farm glittered across the fields in the searching spring sunlight, Dilys knew with every instinct that she'd done the thing that was right for her.

But it was harder now. Harry was older and his regularity had stiffened into fixed habit and obstinacy. The boys weren't comprehensible, manageable children any more, but grown men with complicated lives and hidden personalities. Even the farm, that land whose changelessness had been one of the sources of Dilys's greatest contentment, was different, hedged about as it now was with impossible bureaucracy, with rules and regulations and subsidies and fines. The land seemed now as defenceless as an element in Joe had always been, no longer a source of security and livelihood but a capricious, helpless thing governed by arbitrary forces far away, and no longer by the men who farmed it.

Dilys raised her head and pushed her pillow about to plump it up. She shouldn't have blamed Lyndsay that afternoon, she shouldn't have told her it was she that was upsetting Joe. When she'd seen Joe later, shouting at Harry in the open store where the fertiliser was kept, she'd known she'd been wrong. It wasn't Lyndsay's fault. Yet it wasn't Joe's fault either. Nor Harry's. They were only trying to get by, all of them, only trying to live life with the hand they'd all been dealt. Just as she was. And Robin. Her eyes flew open suddenly. What about Robin then? And that girl? Velma had come in just before supper to return a pie dish that had been sent down to Tideswell and said that that friend of Judy's had turned up, just out of the blue, and was staying there, cool as a cucumber. What was Robin doing with that girl in the house?

*   *   *

In his bed at Tideswell Farm, Robin lay and watched the moon through undrawn curtains. It was roughly half full, and the clouds were speeding past it in rags and tatters on the wind that was rattling the climbing rose against the house below his window, a yellow rose Caro had put in because it was called 'Mermaid' and she liked anything, in this landlocked place, that reminded her of the sea. With any luck, the wind would keep the rain away, or blow whatever rain there was quickly past. Robin didn't need more rain. The maize and grass wanted warmth now, steady, quiet warmth. All that had been steady that day had been the drizzle.

'Stone Age weather,' Zoe had said at supper.

'What?'

'Can't you see them, all huddled up in caves and stuff, in this weather? Toes like monkeys, hair all

117

matted, just staring out into the murk. Waiting for a mammoth. How many people would a mammoth have fed?'

'Lots.'

'A hundred?'

'Maybe.'

He took a forkful of Dilys's steak and kidney. Zoe seemed to be eating only potatoes. And watercress.

He said, 'Where did the cress come from?'

'The river.'

'Don't eat it.'

'Why not?'

'Fluke. It carries fluke. Gives sheep liver-rot. It's a worm.'

Zoe looked at her plate.

'Spuds OK?'

'Perfectly. Did you cook them?'

'Yes. I remembered how.' She picked up the thick sprigs of watercress and dropped them on the side of her plate.

'You laid the table back to front. Forks go on the left.'

'Does it matter?'

Robin looked at her. He grinned.

'Nope.'

'Gareth says that cow is barren. She didn't take last time either.'

'I know.'

'Seems unfair, doesn't it. I mean, she can't help it. It isn't her fault. Can I come to market with you when you take her?'

Robin took a long swallow of water.

'And can I ask how long you're staying?'

Zoe looked at him.

'D'you want me to go? Am I in the way?'

118

'No. But there'll be talk. Velma knows you're here, so does Gareth.'

'You mean your mother will disapprove—'

'She'll think it's odd. I hardly know you.'

'Well,' Zoe said reasonably, 'you know me better than you did the day before yesterday. I'm just a friend of Judy's who likes it here. It's kind of interesting. I'll go whenever you say.'

Robin put his fork down.

'Does Judy know you're here?'

'No. She thinks I'm in Birmingham. I'll ring her. I'll go and see your mother. There isn't a mystery. Put me to work if,' Zoe prodded a potato, 'you think I ought to earn my keep.'

'I don't think that.'

'Well then,' Zoe said.

'I just wonder why you came.'

Zoe had looked across at him. Her eyes were large and their expression was at once straightforward and penetrating.

'Look,' she said, 'it's perfectly simple. I wanted to see you again. When I came with Judy, I liked it here and I liked you. So I came back. See?'

Simple, she'd said. I liked the farm and I liked you, so I came back for more. Simple as that. That's the truth. For a moment, outside his window now, the moon hung clearly in an unclouded space, a simple silver disc except for its blurred unfinished edge, polished and pure. Robin pulled a hand out of his bedclothes and scratched his head, hard. Two rooms away, down the narrow landing, Zoe slept, her strange red head dark on a white pillow, sleeping because—being Zoe—that was what the night was for. You did what you needed to do and didn't mind who saw you. There was nothing to hide. Life was for

119

living and there were many, many ways of living it. Zoe lived hers her way and let other people do the same. Simple. See?

CHAPTER EIGHT

The girls in Judy's office were loud with relief that she'd got a boyfriend. He rang every day, sometimes twice, and now Bronwen, or Tessa, answering Judy's phone if she had gone for coffee or to the lavatory, said, 'Oh hi, Ollie! How are you?' in voices bright with enthusiasm. They left messages for Judy on yellow and pink adhesive notes: 'Ollie called! Ringing back 12.30!' with little smiley faces drawn underneath, and sometimes kisses. They commented on the flowers he gave her—always freesias—and asked what she was going to wear for the next date at the cinema, at a wine bar, at the weekend. They told her she was thinner. Bronwen gave her the address of a really good aerobics studio and Tessa said black suited her, honestly. Ollie, whom they had never met, who was no more than a slightly diffident voice on the telephone, had erased for them the awkward fact that Caro had died and left Judy motherless.

Judy herself wasn't sure if Oliver was, indeed, her boyfriend. She liked him—you couldn't, she thought, not like him unless you were simply being perverse— and she liked his attentiveness, but something in her held back from him. He had been not only so recently Zoe's, but even more recently discarded by Zoe. He had tried to explain that he had been fascinated by Zoe, attracted by her otherness, but that he was sure it hadn't been love. After he'd said that, he stopped

120

and gazed at Judy as if willing her to understand how different it was with her, how at home he felt, how companionable. She had looked back at him for a moment and thought that, for all his sweetness and openness, she couldn't trust him yet. If only Caro had been there, to run past, like a pony in a sale ring. And to show her that she, Judy, wasn't solely dependent on Caro for praise and appreciation, even for love.

Oliver encouraged her to talk about Caro. After films they'd seen, or pictures they'd stood in front of in galleries, he'd say, 'Would your mother have liked that? Did she have modern taste? Mine doesn't. Mine got stuck about 1965. It's quite endearing, really.'

Judy liked the game. It was better, easier, to think of Caro with this small degree of objectivity that Oliver brought to her, Judy's, memories. It made Caro more of a person, somehow, less of a mother, and that was a relief.

'Is it,' she said to Oliver, 'easy to please your mother? To live up to her expectations?'

'Oh yes,' he said, 'easy as anything. She thinks my sister and I are wonderful. She can't believe that we've actually managed to walk and talk at the same time on our own. She's amazed by us.'

'But then, perhaps, she isn't a disappointed person.'

He glanced at her.

'No,' he said carefully, 'I don't think she is.'

'Rare—'

'Very.'

'So you can't really fail her.'

'I think,' Oliver said, taking her hand, 'that you should stop thinking about failure.'

'Like Zoe.'

'Zoe doesn't think about success or failure. Zoe

121

just lives.'

Zoe had been in Birmingham for over a week. The course she'd gone to—perspective in photography, she'd said—had lasted two days, but she'd been gone for ten, nine of which had now been occupied for Judy by Oliver. She'd sent Judy a black-and-white postcard, of a line of pylons across an empty stretch of moorland, and on it she'd written, 'Going missing for a bit. Will ring. Course grim but good people.' And then a row of kisses half an inch high and a big Z. The inference was that she had gone off with some of the people on the course for a few days. Judy propped the card on the sitting-room mantelpiece above the wooden herons, one of whom Oliver had adorned with a baseball cap. He had offered to help redecorate the sitting room.

'I'd like to. Really. Promise. I'm no good at wallpaper, seem to get paste on both sides, but I am a *wizard* with a paintbrush. You'll see.'

'Should I wait till Zoe gets back?'

'No. Why?'

'She lives here, too.'

'Not like you do. You don't even know where she is, do you?'

Judy said, looking at the herons, 'No. But I don't need to, it isn't any of my business. Anyway, I expect she'll ring.'

Zoe rang Judy, on the eleventh day after her departure, in the office. Judy was working on a directory of craftsmen, a list of gilders and restorers and French polishers which was going into the July edition of the magazine under the heading 'Five Star Remedies'. When the telephone on her desk rang, Judy expected it to be a two-woman team of easel-painting conservators who had been doubtful that

122

they could take on any more work just now, and it was Zoe.

'Hi!' Judy said, at once, in a tumult of surprise and of remembering that Oliver was now hers, and not Zoe's. 'Where are you?'

'At Tideswell,' Zoe said.

'What?'

'At Tideswell. I've been here since Friday.'

'What the hell are you doing at Tideswell?'

'Staying,' Zoe said.

'But you never said, you never told me—'

'I didn't need to. You live in the flat. I'll tell you when I'm coming back to the flat.'

'Listen,' Judy said, incredulous and angry, 'what are you playing at? You can't stay there with my *father*—'

'He doesn't mind. I hardly see him anyway.'

'Why did you go there?'

'I wanted to. I told you I liked it here. I just saw a bus that said Stretton, so I got on it.'

'Zoe—'

'What?'

'You can't do this, you can't just go to my house—'

'I've been to see your gran. She was fine. She just said I wasn't to get in Robin's way, but I'm not. You couldn't if you tried. He wouldn't let you. I was just ringing to say I'll probably be back after the weekend.'

'You owe me rent,' Judy said in revenge. 'Two lots of seventy-three quid.'

'OK.'

'Is Dad there?'

'No. He's been out since six. Shall I get him to call you?'

'No,' Judy said. '*No*. He's my father and I'll call

123

him when I want to.'

'Judy,' Zoe said, 'cool it. Just cool it, will you? I'm not taking anything that's yours. I'm just here, having a look, being here.'

'But it's weird—'

'No, it's not,' Zoe said, 'it's your attitude that's weird. I'll see you Monday. Or Tuesday, maybe.'

Judy heard the receiver go down the other end, on the Tideswell telephone in the Tideswell kitchen, below the poster of the Golden Gate Bridge that Judy had given Caro seven years ago, when she was only sixteen. Caro had had it framed, in dark-green stained wood, and now Zoe was standing beside it, looking at it, touching the telephone, touching the table and chairs and wooden spoons and mugs and plates, being familiar with everything in that kitchen, the kitchen Judy had known all her life. She picked a black felt-tipped pen out of her pen mug and drew a grotesque shape on the nearest piece of rough paper. Then she gave the shape eyes and huge ears and big crude teeth and stubbled hair, like an old-fashioned convict. Then she threw the pen down and reached for the telephone to ring Oliver at work in the gallery a friend of his owned, specialising in modern lithographs and woodcuts, and where she had never, as yet, telephoned him.

'Oliver?' a laconic voice said at the other end of the line. 'Oliver Mason? Sorry, he's gone out to lunch.'

*   *   *

'I don't know,' Velma said, rinsing dusters, 'what you think you're doing here.'

'Everybody says that,' Zoe said. 'Everybody asks.'

Velma drew the dusters out of the bowl in a

124

dripping mass and twisted them into a clumsy rope, squeezing out the water.

'It's not as if you were any *use*—'

'No,' Zoe said, 'but I'm not any trouble either. And I'm company.'

'He never was one for company,' Velma said. 'Always been a loner, all his life.'

'You can tell that,' Zoe said, taking no notice of Velma's tone. 'You can tell by the way he speaks. Like you were a dog or something. Kind but a bit distant.'

'Well,' Velma said, shaking out the damp dusters and draping them over the nearest radiator, 'mind you *keep* your distance. That's all.' She looked at the clock. 'He'll be in for his dinner in ten minutes.'

'I'm going back to London in a few days,' Zoe said.

Velma grunted.

'I put a pasty in the larder. No point buying two with you being funny about meat.'

'I only eat peacock,' Zoe said, 'and swan. Stuff like that. Do you want me to take your picture?'

Velma stared. She pulled down her yellow acrylic jersey, as if to protect herself from the prying eye of the camera.

'Not bloody likely! What would I want my picture taken for?'

After she'd gone, Zoe opened the great refrigerator and took out a paper bag of tomatoes and the huge yellow cube of cheese that seemed to be a staple for Robin. She had bought them at the village shop, with guidance from Gareth's Debbie, who had found her there, standing lost in thought in front of the cardboard boxes of cabbages and carrots.

'He said tomatoes,' Zoe said. 'But I wonder how many? Two? Twenty? If I want a tomato, I just buy
125

one and then I eat it.'

The thought of buying tomatoes for Robin made Debbie too feel she was on unfamiliar territory. As did this odd-looking girl with her ears and fingers loaded with silver rings and her red hair, not red like nature intended, but red like a beetroot. Gareth said there wasn't any funny business going on between her and Robin but the very fact that she'd come and not been sent packing seemed to Debbie quite funny enough without any extras. And she wasn't sexy, this girl. Debbie eyed her covertly. She was thin and flat, like a boy; there was nothing pretty about her, nothing feminine.

'I should get six,' Debbie said, looking at the tomatoes. 'And two pounds of cheese. Gareth says cheese is about all he eats.'

Now, Zoe put the cheese on the table in the waxed paper she'd been handed it in, and the tomatoes, in their brown-paper bag. She paused, looking at them both. Then she picked up the paper bag and dropped the tomatoes into the sink and ran water over them violently, splashing her clothes. Then she turned the tap off and picked the tomatoes out of the sink and made a little pile of them on the tabletop, like a miniature cairn. They looked good there, on the table, with drops of water hanging roundly on their tight, shining skins. Two of them still had their little curling green tops on. She thought she might take their picture.

The back door to the yard opened and Robin came in, boiler-suited and in his socks. He was carrying a newspaper, a 200-millilitre blue plastic bottle of anti-parasite fluid, and a dosing gun. He dropped the bottle and the gun on the table beside the cheese and the tomatoes.

126

'I'd got eleven to go,' Robin said, 'and I ran out of bloody needles.'

Zoe looked at the dosing gun.

'What's it for?'

'Worms,' Robin said, 'lice. Mange mites. Should stop them scouring. I should have done it before the winter but—'

He stopped. He wondered for a moment if Zoe would say, 'Caro was too ill?' but she didn't. She said, 'Velma's left you a pasty.'

Robin ripped open the poppers down the front of his boiler suit and began to extricate himself from it.

'Thanks. I'll just have bread and cheese.'

'I rang Judy.'

He grunted.

'And I borrowed Gareth's bike and went to Dean Place. Your mum gave me a hot cross bun.'

Robin glanced at her. He threw his boiler suit into a corner, and the house cat, who had heard the word 'pasty', settled herself on it, to wait.

Zoe put a sliced loaf on the table, upright in its tailored plastic bag, and a plate and knife for Robin. He went past her and began to wash his hands at the sink, splashing water on to his face and hair. If Dilys had given Zoe a bun, that meant she had asked her in, not left her on the doorstep as she did with vagrants now and the poor half-witted boys who came around selling flimsy dusters and badly made clothespegs. In the old days, Dilys had had her pet tramps, who'd visited annually and regularly, like the gypsies, and she'd kept old clothes and shoes of Harry's for them, and given them a hot meal in the poultry-feed store. But not now. 'It's got nasty now,' Dilys said. 'I'm not risking more than the doorstep now.'

Robin went back to the table and sat down.

127

'Did you see Dad?'

'Yes,' Zoe said. 'He said he'd heard you'd got two cows calving and he said that was a bit late, wasn't it? He said you should have done it by January.'

Robin said, pulling bread out of the packet, 'Dad likes to have a go.' He paused, and then he said, 'Everything got a bit late this year.'

Zoe offered him a lump of cheese on a knife.

'Because of Caro.'

'I thought you were going to say that five minutes back.'

'I thought of it.' She leaned forward. 'Have you been up to her grave?'

'No.'

'Why don't you? Why don't you come up with me?'

He looked at her briefly. She wasn't looking eager, more matter-of-fact.

'You men,' Zoe said, without rancour. 'You men. As long as things look all right, you never bother to find out if they really are. Did you ever try and imagine what Caro felt like, what it was like to be her?'

He put the bread and cheese he had halfway to his mouth down on his plate.

'I couldn't. I tried, and I couldn't. If it's any business of yours.'

'I can't help thinking about her,' Zoe said, entirely unoffended. 'I keep trying to imagine what it was like for her here, what she was like.'

Robin said, without meaning to, 'Nobody knew.'

There was a little pause. Zoe picked up a tomato and bit into it.

'I wondered,' she said. 'I wondered that.'

Robin got up and went back to the sink, picking two tumblers out of the draining rack and running

128

water into them. He put one down beside Zoe.

'You've still got to say goodbye,' she said. 'When you lose things, that's what you have to do. Otherwise you don't go on. It's like all those graves up at the church, just pretending all those people are sleeping. Well, they're not. They're dead and they're not coming back.'

Robin said, still standing, holding his glass of water, 'Sometimes, pretending it isn't final is the only way you can stand being left behind.'

'Do you feel that?'

'I don't know.'

'You do,' Zoe said. 'You do know. Even if you just feel confused, you know you feel confused. Why don't you want to talk about it?'

He said, almost shyly, 'I never have. It isn't my way.'

'But don't you want to ask her things?'

He swallowed his water in two gulps and put the tumbler down.

'Maybe.'

'I want to ask my dad stuff, all the time. I want to ask him why he left us, why he went to Australia, why he stayed there, whether he regretted it. I get so angry he went and died before I could ask him. He's got away with it, you see—'

'Maybe he hadn't,' Robin said slowly. 'Maybe he never had the chance.'

Zoe stood up.

'You can make chances, can't you? If you really want them. You know what?'

'What?'

'It really bugs me I wanted to ask him this, but I did. I wanted to ask him if he loved me.' She looked at Robin. 'Do you want to ask Caro that?'

Robin moved past her to where the plastic bottle and the dosing gun lay as he had dumped them. He picked both up, and then he crossed the kitchen and pulled his boiler suit out from under the cat. The words 'I always wished she did' rose up in his mind, and hung there across the darkness inside his skull like a string of lights, bright and urgent but unspoken.

'I'll see you later,' he said. 'Seven-ish, maybe. Got to go into Stretton and get more needles.'

'Bye,' Zoe said.

He didn't look at her.

'Bye.'

*　　　*　　　*

On one of Judy's sitting-room walls, Oliver had painted a big square of pale grey. Opposite it, above the fireplace and the herons, he'd done the same in dark blue.

'Keep looking at them,' he said. 'See which you like. Or if you don't like either.'

He'd met her after work, and come home with her and drunk three cans of diet Coca-Cola and painted the squares and then gone off to have supper with his father.

'I kind of ought to. He never comes to London, as a rule.'

When he had gone Judy made herself some toast and sat down to eat it in front of the blue square on the wall. It was a good blue, a summer-night sky blue. She'd never had a blue room. There was no blue at Tideswell, except the milking parlour where blue was supposed to ward off the flies. Caro had painted things yellow and green and red and melon pink, like

130

ripe fruit and vegetables, sun colours. In her opinion, blue wasn't a sun colour, even if sea and sky were blue. She used to say that blueness was just for contrast really, like that awful blue swimming pools always were, artificial and harsh as if emphasising that the water in them wasn't naturally there, but had been trapped there, by people, in rectangles and squares, for playing in, not using. It was like so much on Judy's magazine, pages and pages of objects and fabrics and furniture that were eagerly amassed by people for quite other—and often bizarre—reasons than those best and basic ones that they were either useful or beautiful. Yet dark-blue walls were not really useful. Staring at Oliver's bold, rough square, Judy wondered if she really thought they were beautiful either.

'What if they're a mistake?' she'd said.

'Then I'll paint them again. It wouldn't *be* a mistake. Stop thinking things are mistakes. It's an experiment. Most of life's an experiment, otherwise how do you know if anything's going to work or not?'

Judy got up and took her toast plate out to the kitchen. She had thought, for a moment, that Oliver was going to ask her to meet his father. But then he hadn't. She didn't know if she was glad or sorry, whether she'd have felt cornered if he'd asked her rather than—unfairly—mildly disappointed now that he hadn't. She went to the window and looked down into the small dark courtyard of the building where three dustbins lived and an old sink containing a broken plastic bucket and a fern, a brilliant green fern which thrived down there on the damp and the dimness. Oliver is so nice to me, Judy thought, so *nice*. Why is he so nice?

Behind her, from the tiny hall across the sitting

room, a key turned in the front-door lock.

'Hi!' Zoe called. The door slammed.

Judy went to the kitchen doorway.

'Hi.'

Zoe looked exactly as she had when she had left, boots, and a black-leather jacket over a black T-shirt and jeans with the knees ripped across, showing Zoe's skin. She dropped her rucksack and camera case on the floor.

'It took all day. All bloody day. There were roadworks everywhere.' She looked at Judy. 'I got a coach from Stretton. Gareth ran me in.'

'Oh.'

Zoe glanced about the room. She gestured towards the blue square on the wall above the fireplace.

'That's nice.'

Judy said deliberately, 'Oliver did it.'

'Ollie?'

'Yes.'

Zoe said, without effort, 'Good.' She put a hand into her jacket pocket and pulled out a handful of notes. She held them out to Judy. 'A hundred and forty-six quid. That I owe you.'

'Doesn't matter—'

'Judy,' Zoe said. 'It's my rent and I owe it to you. Take it. And—'

'And what?'

'I said good, about Ollie. I meant it. *Good.*'

Judy took the money slowly and put it, without looking at it, into her pocket. She said, by way of manners, 'He came to bring you some flowers. The day after you went. And then—well, it just sort of happened.'

'I know,' Zoe said. 'Things do. I'm glad. He likes looking after people.'

'Do you think I need looking after?'

Zoe stooped and loosened the neck of her rucksack.

'Yes. You do. So does your whole family. You all need looking after.'

'My family,' Judy said with emphatic precision, 'is tough.'

Zoe found a thin white plastic bag containing something light and bulky. She held it out to Judy.

'If you say so. These are for you. From your Gran.'

'What is it?'

'Buns,' Zoe said.

'You mean my Gran gave you buns to give me?'

'I offered.'

Judy took the buns and dropped the bag on the nearest chair.

'It really annoys me you went to Tideswell.'

Zoe looked up at her, from her squatting position beside her rucksack.

'You don't want to go.'

'I might——'

'Don't be such a bloody child.' She gestured. 'They're nice people. Can't you see that? They're nice people, getting on with living. It's not their fault they didn't understand your mother. And they miss her. They tried to make her one of them and they didn't succeed but they miss her.'

'Where d'you get all this from?'

'I just thought it. I noticed. Perhaps I can see better, being an outsider.'

Judy sat down on the arm of the chair where she had dropped the bag of buns from Dilys. 'Outsider' had been one of Caro's words. She had made it seem mysterious and glamorous, as she had the word 'nomad', another of her favourites. She had also

133

made Judy feel that this quality of not belonging to a tribe, of not being shackled to an inherited orthodoxy, was a desirable one. 'Poets are outsiders,' Caro had said. 'They have to be.' She had inferred that to be adopted was to be part of this elusive, enviable, moving band, roaming through life with their eyes full of visions. But Zoe had described herself as an outsider, too. At this moment, Judy did not want to feel that Zoe was any part of anything that Caro had been part of and had, with her particular inscrutable charm, included Judy in.

She said, unable to keep the bitterness out of her voice, 'Why don't you mind about Oliver?'

'Mind?'

Judy waited.

'Why should I mind?' Zoe said. 'I'm not in love with him. I like him, he's a nice guy. I like you. Why should I care if you two get together?'

Judy said, 'What did you get up to at Tideswell? What did you *do*?'

'Nothing,' Zoe said. She looked straight at Judy with her wide uncomplicated gaze. 'I ate and I slept and I took pictures and I helped Gareth a bit and I talked to people.'

'And my father?'

'You've got a dirty mind,' Zoe said. She stood up and lifted her rucksack on to one shoulder by a single strap. 'Your mother's left your father in as bad a state as she left you in. It's just that he's quieter about it.'

Judy yelled, 'He didn't love her! He never loved her! He never knew what she was like!'

Zoe stepped sideways a little and retrieved her camera case.

'Oh yes he did,' she said. 'He loved her all right. You've got that in common.'

134

'We've got nothing in common!'

'His trouble is,' Zoe said, as if she hadn't heard Judy's cry, 'his pain is that she didn't love him back.'

'She couldn't!' Judy shouted. 'How could she?'

Zoe paused a moment, looking at the floor under her boots, at the worn golden-yellow carpet left by the last tenant. Then, without saying another word, she turned away and went into her bedroom, closing the door behind her and leaving Judy quite alone.

*   *   *

In the morning, Robin decided, he would turn the cows out. The weather would be fair, and the grass, though not wonderful, had come on better than he had hoped in the last week or two. It would also give him and Gareth a chance, with the cows out to grass, to do some work on the cubicles in the barn, enlarging some, mending head rails and brisket boards which the cows had damaged, lunging forward to get up. 600 kilos of Holstein could do a fair amount of damage, quite inadvertently, in seconds.

Gareth said five of them had laminitis. Robin remembered an old general in his boyhood, a retired soldier of the old school who had tried to run Dean Cross village like a military operation and met resistance at every turn. 'Army?' Robin had heard him bellow once. 'Army? Wonderful career, if it wasn't for the soldiers and their bloody feet!' Something of the same, Robin thought, could be said of farming and cows. Cows always had something the matter with their feet. Cows' feet cost the dairy industry over thirty million lost pounds a year, succumbing to diets that were too high in

135

concentrates or not high enough, to standing in slurry or knocking into corners or each other, to broken surfaces, to hazard. This last month, Robin's bill from the vet had been almost £600, and most of that for feet, for ulcers and inflammation and digital dermatitis, those crusty sores at the back of the foot that gave cows such misery. And now it was laminitis.

'Shouldn't have given them that barley,' Gareth said.

Robin, bent over a cow's rear foot as she breathed heavily above him, clamped in the metal crush, said nothing. He had continued to say nothing for ten minutes and then he had simply said that he wanted a footbath set up, between hurdles, at the exit to the milking parlour. And that he would turn the cows out, after.

The kitchen seemed oddly quiet without Zoe, even though she had hardly made much noise, hadn't been talkative. She'd left a note on the table that morning, thanking him for having her, 'for letting me just stay'. He hadn't minded her staying. He'd quite liked it in so far as he could like anything just now because she had asked nothing of him and yet she could see things, sometimes, without his having to explain them. It was as if she respected him not particularly as Robin Meredith the farmer, but just as a man, as a human being with his own right to pain and joy and privacy. It came to him—and surprised him—that Caro would have liked her, Caro would have warmed to the fact that she didn't pry, didn't seem to need something from you. If only he could have been like that, if only he hadn't needed to need . . .

He stood up at the kitchen table and pushed his half-eaten plate—Dilys's sausage casserole—into the welter of papers and booklets that littered its surface.

136

He would go out into the barn, he decided, and look at the cows, well and sick, watchful of them and comforting himself. The house cat, seated on the newspaper pile, courteously regarded him pulling on his boots and jacket, waiting, with no impolite show of impatience, for his departure. Robin stooped to scratch her head. He indicated the table.

'You won't,' he said, 'like the onion.'

The barn was as he liked it best, dim and quiet except for the gentle crunchings and gruntings of the cows who had not yet settled themselves. He ran a hand over one or two of them and inspected the rear feet that he had trimmed earlier that day, hollowing out the underside of the claws to keep them self-cleaning.

'Good girl,' he said. 'OK, old lady? That's my girl.'

The cows shifted and grumbled, banging into the bars of their cubicles. But nobody kicked him. Robin hadn't been kicked for years, not since the early days before he knew what cows were like, what they'd take and what they wouldn't. It had amazed him then, he remembered, discovering about them, how brutal they were to one another, picking on the sick or weak ones and knocking them over. But he loved them. He'd learned to love them. And, not being genetically harnessed like pigs and poultry whose stockmen had become not much more than technical engineers, they'd managed to stay lovable, being still within the natural, human range of things.

He went slowly up and down the aisles between the cubicles. The cows, as used to him as they were to one another, took virtually no notice. At one end, an old favourite, a red-and-white cow who dropped her sturdy calves as easily as laying an egg, turned and eyed him for a moment comfortably, as if he were no

137

surprise to her, but merely a familiar unremarkable part of her accepted world. Then she turned her head away and forgot him.

Outside in the yard Gareth, having had, in his own view, a small triumph over the barley in the feed, had cleared up with extra assiduousness. The grooved concrete was scraped clean, as were the feeding troughs and the passageway he had created from the milking parlour through the footbath that he and Robin had dug and concreted together three years before. There was a small wind and in it various things gently flapped and clanked, bars and gates and sheets of zinc and plastic, the result of years of mending and patching, of making do. But the night was fine and the wind would keep any showers that were about on the move. Robin walked to the edge of the yard, and put his hands on the wall and looked over. Below him, the fields, dense in the darkness, and apparently unmarked by hedge or fence, ran down to the river. Only the line of water gleamed visibly at the foot of the fields and beyond it the land vanished again, thick and black, until it met the sky. Robin held the wall and stared out into the dark, moving air.

It was only crossing the yard some ten minutes later that he became aware that the telephone was ringing, inside the house. For some reason, he had the sudden feeling that it had been ringing for some time, insistently, and he began to run, opening the back door and the kitchen door and running through, clumsily, still in his boots. The house cat, sitting neatly on the kitchen table beside Robin's almost empty plate, stopped a careful washing to watch.

He seized the telephone.

'Hello? Hello? Tideswell Farm—'
'Robin?'
'Yes,' he said, 'Lyndsay, yes—'
'I need you to come,' Lyndsay said. 'I need you to. *Now.*' Her voice rose almost to a scream. 'Come now, Robin, come now. Joe's done something terrible!'

CHAPTER NINE

It was Harry's old dog who had found him. Harry's custom, at around nine-thirty every evening, was to take a heavy-duty torch and go round the yard and the buildings, accompanied—very slowly now—by the old spaniel. He'd been an active dog once, perhaps the best rough-shooting dog Harry had ever had, but arthritis had seized his back legs and slowed him up, and there were cataracts forming in filmy discs in both his eyes. But his sense of smell was as good as ever. Slow and stiff, he creaked behind Harry on those nightly rounds, his nose on the ground, never missing a detail.

He had halted beside the store where the fertiliser was kept. It was a big open shed, roofed in corrugated iron where the great solid white 500-kilogram sacks of woven plastic were stacked in double columns, slightly higher than a man's height, leaving narrow aisles between for access. The dog had paused by the entrance to one of these aisles, head down, intent.

'Come up, lad,' Harry said, from 20 feet further on.

The dog took no notice. Despite his age and decrepitude, a kind of urgency seemed suddenly to seize him and he began to sniff with the concentration that had made him once so useful in the field. Then he

139

gave a curious little whine, a sound both of excitement and distress, and thrust himself with force and purpose down between the white sacks towards the back of the shed. Harry retraced his steps.

'Come on, lad, come on. Out of there. What've you got?'

The dog was scuffling frantically at something in the darkness. Harry raised his torch and shone the beam down the gleaming white corridor created by the fertiliser sacks. There at the back, slumped sideways in the narrow space, was something bulky, and horrible. Harry took an unsteady step forward, and forced himself to shine the torchbeam directly in front of him. It fell on Joe, still in his work clothes, slumped behind an old twelve-bore lying askew against his shoulder, and shot through the mouth.

* * *

'Dr Nichols is here,' Dilys said. 'And the police are coming.'

She was sitting at the kitchen table, bolt upright under the harsh overhead light. Opposite her, Harry sat in his usual chair with his eyes closed. Between them, her head down on her arms, Lyndsay half lay across the table, her hair spread over her face so that Robin couldn't see it.

He stooped by his mother and put his arm round her. She accepted his embrace but did not in any way relax into it.

'One shot, Dr Nichols said. Just the one. He took Dad's gun.'

Harry said in a whisper, not opening his eyes, 'I didn't lock it. I didn't lock it up. I was going to have a go at them crows. In the morning.'

140

Robin moved round the table and put his hand on his father's. Harry seized it.

'I didn't lock it—'

'It wasn't your fault,' Robin said. His voice sounded harsh and loud. 'If he wanted a gun, he'd have got one. Yours was just handy.'

Tears were streaming down Harry's face. He opened his eyes and looked intently at Robin, and then he opened his mouth, too, and jabbed a forefinger inside it and his wet eyes widened in horror and rage.

'Dad,' Robin said, 'it wasn't your fault. It wasn't anybody's fault. It wasn't even Joe's.'

'It was mine,' Lyndsay said. Her voice seemed to come from miles away, as if her cloud of hair was muffling her mouth, like a duvet.

'No,' Robin said.

She sat up partially, staring at the scrubbed tabletop between her spread arms.

'I didn't see,' Lyndsay said. 'I didn't see how bad it was for him. All I could see was how bad it was for me.'

Robin left his father and crouched by Lyndsay's chair.

'It *was* bad for you,' he said. 'It was bad for all of us, but especially for you.'

She turned sideways then, and put her arms around his neck and fell against him, heavy and helpless. He stood up with difficulty, holding her, feeling her despair in the yielding weight of her body.

'I loved him,' Lyndsay said. 'I loved him more than anything in the world.'

Dilys made a tiny sound in her throat, but her position never changed.

'I know. He knew, too.'

'No,' Lyndsay said. 'No. I couldn't reach him. He couldn't hear me. And I didn't keep trying, I didn't keep helping, and he got so lonely, didn't he, he got so lonely he couldn't bear the pain, and he knew I couldn't help him, I wasn't strong enough, he knew he'd chosen someone who was wrong for him, someone who'd let him down in the end, who'd leave him to be alone—oh God,' Lyndsay said, gasping and crying, sagging against Robin. 'Oh God, oh God, what have I done?'

Robin glanced across the table at his mother. Dilys nodded and got up.

'Brandy. And I'll put the kettle on.'

'Old Kep found him,' Harry said, rolling his head back and forth across his chairback, his eyes closed again. 'Old Kep did. I thought it was rats he was after, just rats—'

'I didn't think,' Lyndsay wept. 'I just didn't think! He didn't come in for supper but he often didn't. I was watching television. I was just watching television when Dilys rang. Oh I hate myself, I hate myself, I do, I do, I do—'

Dilys put a flat half-bottle of brandy on the table and a handful of tiny glasses, rimmed in gold and painted with mallards.

'Tea coming up.'

Robin adjusted his embrace of Lyndsay, and lowered her gently into her chair again. He reached past her, and poured brandy into two of the glasses, pushing one towards his father.

'Drink this.'

Lyndsay's hands were shaking as violently as if they had an existence of their own, uncontrolled by her. Robin bent and put an arm round her shoulders and lifted the brandy to her mouth.

'Just a sip. The shock of drinking it will steady the rest of you.'

Lyndsay swallowed and coughed.

'I don't want to live without him, I can't, I can't—'

Robin held the glass up again.

'Just drink.'

She obeyed and then pushed his hands away, putting her own up to her face so that it was quite covered by them.

Harry said, leaning forward and speaking urgently to Robin, 'I should have locked that gun up, lad. I should have. I *should*.'

Robin said gently, 'We never lock our guns up, Dad. Do we? We're supposed to, and we never do. Shouldn't think Joe's is locked up, even now.'

Dilys said from the far side of the kitchen, pouring boiling water from the kettle into the teapot, 'You're wrong there. Quite wrong. Joe did things properly. He always did things properly.'

Robin reached out to touch both Lyndsay and Harry's shoulders, either side of him, and then he went across the room to his mother. He put an arm around her again, pressing her towards him.

'I know,' he said.

She gave him a quick, glaring glance.

'You none of you knew,' Dilys said, bending away to put the lid on the teapot. 'You never understood.'

Robin waited, his arm still about her unyielding shoulders. He glanced behind him and saw that Harry had reached out across the table, to hold Lyndsay's nearest wrist, even though she wasn't looking at him, couldn't see anything but the blackness behind her hands.

There was a sound of cars approaching, and two

143

sets of headlights, their beams full on, swung into the yard outside the kitchen window. Dilys moved herself out of the circle of Robin's arm.

'There,' she said. 'The police.'

*　　*　　*

The night after Robin's call, Judy couldn't sleep. She lay alone, not daring to close her eyes, terrified of the images that printed themselves immediately, luridly, on the insides of her eyelids.

'How,' she had said to Robin, hating herself, paralysed by shock, 'how did he—'

'He put the barrel of Grandpa's shotgun in his mouth. The shot took off the back of his head and went into the sack behind, the fertiliser sack he was leaning against. The police—the police said the shot hadn't gone far because he'd, well, he'd such a thick skull—'

Robin had offered to come to London.

'I'll come and get you. You shouldn't be alone.'

'I'm not, Zoe's here—'

'Good,' Robin said.

'Dad—'

'Yes?'

'Why?' Judy wailed, her voice rising to a sobbing scream. 'Why? Why?'

'I don't know,' Robin said. 'I can only guess.'

'And Lyndsay? And the kids?'

'Not good. She's got some sedative. Mary Corriedale's there for the children.'

'What's going on?' Judy yelled. 'What's going on with first Mum, now Joe?'

'It's—it's just how things go,' Robin said. His voice was faint with fatigue. 'Sometimes. It's just

144

chance. And people. Different people. Some of us can cope with things, some can't—' He broke off. 'Sure you don't want me to come?'

'Yes.'

'I'll ring you tomorrow.'

'OK.'

'Judy—'

'Mmm?'

'Judy, I'm sorry it's me that makes these calls. I'm sorry it's always me.'

Oliver had offered to stay. He had made her tea and tried to make her eat and said that he would sleep there, just for comfort. But she had felt that she could bear nobody there, not even Oliver, that she couldn't bear kindness and sweetness and sympathy, that such comforts were in another, and temporarily irrelevant, realm from the thing that Joe had done, to himself, to all of them. It was something beyond horror, beyond outrage, because it spoke of a pain Judy couldn't even conceive of, and of despair. In all her own wretchedness, in all her own insecure, self-loathing miseries, Judy knew that she had never seen the face of the despair that Joe had known. She had seen the greyness of disappointment and anxiety and doubt; he had seen the blackness of no hope, no hope whatever now and not the remotest possibility of hope in the future, a prospect that quite simply broke his heart and mind and spirit.

So he had decided to end it. It was so easy, Judy thought, for farmers to act, once they had decided that any more life was out of the question. Those hours of solitude, whole stretches of day alone on the land, and, in Joe's case, alone without living things, without cows and sheep and pigs and all their needs and noises and dependencies. And then those stores

145

of drugs and poisons, bottles and sacks and sachets and phials of remedies for pests and diseases, a whole liquid and powdered armoury for self-destruction. And guns. In Judy's childhood, Harry's gun had lived on two hooks screwed into the wall by the kitchen door, angled to hold it when it was broken. Guns for vermin, for rats and crows and rabbit, guns for the pot, for pigeon and pheasants, guns for that ancient instinct for self-defence, of land and family and livelihood; guns, as a final gesture of defiant independence, against all the accepted laws of human behaviour, to turn upon oneself.

The handle of Judy's bedroom door turned slowly, and the door opened three inches.

'You awake?' Zoe whispered.

'Of course—'

Zoe crept in. She wore an oversized grey T-shirt and her feet were bare.

'This is bad,' Zoe said. Judy felt her slight weight as she sat down on the end of the bed. 'This is so bad.'

'I can't stop thinking, picturing—'

'Me, too.'

'It's so violent—'

'Death is violent,' Zoe said. 'There must be a moment of dying when it is for everyone, even for people who just die in their sleep. But this is the worst.'

'I can't imagine how he felt—'

Zoe drew her feet up and pulled her T-shirt down over her bent knees so that her outline became a rough cube to Judy, silhouetted against the light from the street lamp that shone up through the curtains.

'I hope we never can,' Zoe said, and then, after a pause, 'Do you believe in God?'

'No.'

146

'Me neither.'

'Nor does my father,' Judy said. 'He thinks that if there is anything up there it's definitely against him and not for him. If he's ever in a church you can see he can't wait to get out.'

Zoe put her head down on her knees.

'Will Joe have a funeral?'

'I don't know. I suppose so. Gran and Grandpa would expect it.'

'Poor them—'

'Gran thought the sun rose and set with Joe. You could see, when she just looked at him.'

'I won't come to the funeral,' Zoe said.

Judy waited.

'I didn't know Joe,' Zoe said. 'I'd look like those people who stop and gawp at car accidents.'

'I don't want to go alone—'

'Take Oliver.'

'He doesn't know any of them—'

'He knows you.'

Judy sat up slowly, propping herself on her arms.

'I hurt, Zoe. I hurt all over.'

Zoe looked at her, and even in the dimness of the room, Judy could see the shine of her eyes.

'It's grief again, Jude. I was thinking about it, lying there trying not to think about Joe. And I thought that one of the things about grief is change, it changes your life and the people in your life, it makes you move on when you don't want to. And that hurts. It's the change you don't want that hurts.'

*   *   *

Hughie sat on his bean bag behind his closed bedroom door, leaning over Seal with his eyes tightly closed and his thumb in. He wore his pyjamas still, and his anorak and the red-and-black baseball cap Lyndsay had been given at Dean Cross garage with her petrol coupons. She had wanted two mugs instead, which were also on offer with coupons and which she had thought Joe could take outside with him as it wouldn't matter if they got broken, but the garage had run out of mugs and she had to settle for the baseball cap instead. In any case, Hughie had made a fuss about it, pleading and whining like a baby, knowing Lyndsay wouldn't want a scene in public, in the garage shop.

He had refused to let Mary Corriedale dress him that morning, or to dress himself. She had laid out his jeans and checked shirt and a green sweatshirt and socks and his new trainers with the Velcro strips to fasten them, and he had, when her back was turned, stuffed the clothes down the back of his bedroom radiator. He could see bits of them sticking out, the top of his jeans, a green sweatshirt arm, and the dark lump of his socks. His trainers, being new, he had left on the floor but he had covered them up with his dressing gown so that he needn't see them.

Across the landing, Mummy was in bed. Her curtains were pulled. She had been in bed a lot ever since Daddy hadn't been there, except for getting up in her nightie and sitting at the kitchen table either staring or crying. If Hughie wanted a cuddle, she would cry. If he just watched her, she stared, not back at him but at nothing much, like a piece of wall or the milk bottle. She had told Hughie that Daddy was dead and wasn't coming back again.

'What's dead?' Hughie said.

'It's not living any more. It's not breathing and walking about. It's like a sleep you don't wake
148

up from.'

'Was he killed?' Hughie said, thinking of things he trod on in panic, in the garden, beetles and centipedes and woodlice which you killed to stop them creeping and scuttling.

'Yes.'

Hughie remembered scenes on television before Lyndsay had swooped down to turn it off.

'With a chopper?'

'No. With an accident.'

'What's an accident?'

'Something that shouldn't happen. A mistake. A mistake that does damage, like falling out of a window, or a car crash.'

Hughie put Seal on his head.

'Can I see him?'

'No, darling. I'm afraid not.' Her voice was very peculiar, Hughie thought.

'Why not?'

'Because he's gone. When you die, you go away, your body isn't here any more.'

'Where is it, then?'

'In heaven,' Lyndsay said uncertainly.

Hughie gave up. At the playgroup in Dean Cross where he went three mornings a week, there'd been talk of heaven at Christmas, when they'd made angels for their mothers with paper doily wings. Angels lived in heaven, and heaven was somewhere in the sky. With aeroplanes, Hughie supposed. And now Daddy, Mummy said. She couldn't seem to explain better than that, nor how he stayed up there, nor why he wasn't coming down again.

This not coming back was about the only thing Hughie began to have sight of. He didn't want to see it. He had an idea that, if he stayed somewhere very

149

still, holding Seal and sucking his thumb, he would find, when he stopped being still and started moving again, that the world would have gone back to normal again as well. And Daddy would be there. He pulled the baseball cap down hard until he and Seal were huddled together in the privacy under its peak. He didn't know how long he would have to stay there, but he didn't mind. It would just take as long as it had to.

*   *   *

Lyndsay had Rose in bed with her, while Mary Corriedale cleaned up the kitchen and did some cooking. Lyndsay didn't want any cooking done because she wasn't hungry, but Mary said Dr Nichols had said she had to have some soup, and a bit of fish if she could face it. She couldn't. She couldn't face anything now except the pills he'd given her which sent her to sleep as if she were being drawn into it down a black velvet tunnel.

Rose was difficult to face, too. Because she was only a baby, and naturally ebullient, she seemed heartless, rampaging across Lyndsay's bed on her hands and knees and crashing shouting into the pillows. Lyndsay couldn't leave her to go in search of Hughie because she would immediately do something wild and destructive, and it wasn't possible to bring Hughie into bed, too, because, at the moment and even more than usual, Rose was anathema to him. Lyndsay knew most things, Hughie knew some things and feared and dreaded others, but Rose knew nothing, which made her terrible.

Lyndsay knew that Hughie was shut away in his

bedroom trying to work some kind of magic, and her heart bled for him. Her heart bleed all the time just now, she could feel it, could feel the dark, hot liquid seeping out of it and leaving it shrivelled up inside her like a dried-up nut kernel, dusty and dead.

'Grieving is a journey,' Dr Nichols had said, his narrow young face turned seriously towards her. 'When you're through—and you will be one day, I promise—you won't be in the same place as you are now.'

Lyndsay had gazed at him. She wasn't in any place, that was part of the pain of it, she was just hanging somewhere suspended in nothingness and, now that Joe was dead, always would be. Dr Nichols was kind, and he didn't talk to you as if you were mentally subnormal, but for all his kindness and respectfulness, Lyndsay couldn't tell him that Joe had been everything to her, that, even if she couldn't talk to him, she never stopped adoring him, *needing* him. Nor could she tell Dr Nichols of a new suspicion that had come to haunt her, a hideous suspicion that she couldn't get out of her mind where it clung like some revolting fungus, and that was that, if he had lived, Joe's fatalism would in the end have damaged his children. And she, Lyndsay, would then have had to decide between them.

*   *   *

Harry stood in the space where Joe had died. The police had taken away the sack of fertiliser against which his head had rested and Harry had cleaned up the remainder himself. He had wanted to. There wasn't much to do, only a few smears of blood on nearby sacks and some scuffing on the dirt floor to

151

rake over, and although he wept silently while he worked, he wanted to be there in that narrow space where Joe had last been.

'Sorry, lad,' he kept saying to the empty air. 'Sorry, lad. Sorry.'

The police had taken his gun away, too. He hoped they never brought it back. He'd got another old twelve-bore that would do for rats and rabbits, the gun he'd taught the boys to shoot with. They'd both been quick learners. If Harry had to put his hand on his heart and choose between them, he'd have to say Robin was the better shot, cool and accurate. But Robin had never had Joe's style. It used to give Harry pleasure watching Joe handling a gun, he looked such a natural; he made a gun look an innocent thing somehow, graceful.

Harry put his two hands against the sacks where Joe had leant and then his forehead on them. He didn't seem to want to be anywhere but here, he couldn't think of anywhere but here, where Joe was.

'Don't worry, Dad,' Robin had said. 'Don't try to do anything just now. I'll see to the urgent jobs.'

Robin was out right now on the tractor, on the 12-acre field Joe had planted with peas. He'd put in a lot of peas this year, nearly 50 acres of them, and more barley than usual, and linseed whose flax-blue flowers Lyndsay had always liked. Harry had only seen Lyndsay twice since Joe died, calling in at the house out of some instinct he couldn't define, and being tongue-tied when he got there, even with the children. Lyndsay looked like a ghost, as if she didn't belong to this world any more and didn't want to. Poor girl, Harry thought, poor girl. A widow and she isn't even thirty. She'd always seemed such a child beside Joe, so much smaller and younger, so dependent. Joe shouldn't have done it, Harry thought, watching Lyndsay making a sandwich for Rose with infinite, weary slowness, he shouldn't have left them alone like this, three little corks cast away on the ocean. But then he, Harry, shouldn't have left his gun unlocked either.

He felt that that thought was in Dilys's mind, all the time. Ever since the accident, as she called it, he had felt she was blaming him. Their lives had outwardly gone on much the same except that neither of them had any appetite to speak of, but Harry felt in some way that Dilys had banished him from being her husband, from being Joe's father. Joe had always been the topic that brought them together. For forty years and more, delight and anxiety about Joe had been a bond between them, the subject they could always feel themselves quite united in. But now it seemed that Dilys didn't want Harry anywhere near either her grief or her memories of Joe. He knew, at night, that she was lying beside him as wakeful as he was, and as preoccupied with the same thing, but if he spoke to her, she just said, 'You get your sleep. Harry. It'll be six o'clock before you know it,' and left him there in his grief and loneliness, pulling away from him into her own. Harry had never known real grief before. Once or twice, in the last few days, he had wondered, without alarm, if it might kill him, and had known, simultaneously, that he would, at the moment, be glad if it hurried up and did.

He raised his head and looked at the shed roof. It was made of corrugated iron, and Joe had replaced some sheets in the autumn, but more needed it already. In some places, the iron was perforated with as many holes as a caterpillar leaves on a cabbage, and the rain had come in and left the fertiliser sacks

153

dotted with rusty orange speckles. He'd have to get Robin to see to it, and to the blocked drainage ditches that Joe had never got round to. 'I will, I will,' he'd say each week when Harry reminded him, and then something else had come up and they'd been forgotten. Like making a barn ready for these beef stores he'd set his heart on suddenly—days and days he'd spent on that. £400 apiece, he'd reckoned he'd have to pay for medium weight, maybe more. And he'd wanted twenty, Hereford or Limousin. Harry had set his face against the whole scheme, said he'd never had stock and he wasn't about to start. He hadn't shouted but he'd been obstinate, as obstinate as an old rock, an old root. It sickened him to think how obstinate he'd been, how resentful and unhelpful. And over twenty head of cattle, too. That was all. That was all Joe wanted. And he was prepared to do all the work himself, he wasn't asking Harry for anything except the initial investment. Harry leaned against the sacks again and closed his eyes. He couldn't bear it. He couldn't bear the way he'd been to Joe over those cattle. And he couldn't bear the fact that now, because of what Joe had done, he couldn't make it right.

* * *

Dilys put tea and cherry cake in front of the Vicar. It was his third visit since the accident and he still, Dilys observed, hadn't the first idea of what to say. He'd had some idea that Dilys might be worried about the sinfulness of suicide. She'd hardly known what he was talking about.

'What do you mean, talking of·sin?' she said. 'What's sin got to do with it? Joe had his accident

154

because he was driven to it. If you're driven to do something, you're the victim. Victims are innocent.'

The Vicar had wondered whether to outline the difference between innocence and helplessness, and decided against it. Instead, he had eaten a slice of cherry cake and complimented Dilys on it. She was being wonderful, everyone said so, going about her life as if nothing had happened, not hiding but being plainly, ordinarily visible, shopping in the village, baking cakes.

'I am praying for you,' the Vicar said. 'Daily. And for Harry and Joe and all your family.'

Dilys didn't snort exactly, but she looked as if she had never heard such an ineffectual suggestion in her life. She reminded the Vicar of an old woman from Dean Cross whom he had visited once as she lay dying of pneumonia in Stretton Hospital and to whom he had also said that he was praying for her. 'Praying?' she'd said. 'Praying? Prayer never buttered no parsnips.'

'If you would ever like to talk to me,' the Vicar said now to Dilys, 'any time, about anything, you only have to pick up the telephone.'

Dilys looked at him.

'Grief is natural,' he said, looking at his teacup. 'But it can frighten us by taking forms we were not looking for. And God—'

'No,' Dilys said. 'Not him.'

The Vicar sighed.

'You are very brave,' he said. 'But you cannot rely on your own strength alone.'

'Can't I?' Dilys said. 'Can't I?' She stood up, indicating that the visit was over. 'If you'll excuse me, Vicar, that's the one thing I've left to me. The one thing.' And then she took his teacup away and put it by the sink.

CHAPTER TEN

The day of Joe's funeral dawned as clear as crystal. Even Robin, who was disposed to look at the weather with a remorselessly practical eye, felt obscurely that there was almost a cruelty in the brilliance of the light, as if it was pointing out that there could and should be no hiding from the manner of Joe's death.

Robin regarded himself without much recognition in the bathroom mirror while he shaved. He shaved with an old-fashioned razor, scraping away the dark shadow of stubble that had always appeared again by evening and which Caro, in the early days when she was still looking at him with some interest, had wanted him to remove a second time. He'd been up since four, woken by the thought of the day ahead, by the memory of the days behind and the people in them—Lyndsay, his parents, poor little Hughie. And he himself. He hardly knew what he felt himself, except that reality had simply drained out of things, that, even though he could still observe places and objects, they had lost their true nature and become extraneous. Nobody had asked him how he was. He hadn't expected them to.

It had been assumed—indeed, he had assumed it himself—that the painful work of the last ten days would be his, that it would be he who would identify Joe's body, that it would be he would supplied information for the police report confirming that there were no suspicious circumstances, that Joe's mind, ever prone to darkness and disturbance, had tilted fatally from such equilibrium as it had ever had, and had fallen. He had detested that. He had abhorred the descriptions of his brother's personality which honesty had compelled him to confirm; it had seemed a terrible disloyalty, as if he had prevented Joe from taking an essential precious privacy to the grave. But it had to be done, just as a post-mortem had to be done, and a toxicology test to establish that Joe had been neither drunk nor drugged, and an inquest opened by Stretton Coroner to establish the cause of death, and the identification of the body, before a cremation order could be issued as Joe had wished, as Joe had actually articulated as his wish to Judy within Robin's hearing at Caro's funeral.

'Burnt and scattered,' he'd said. 'Particularly scattered. And in the river. Not on the bloody farm.'

Had he really thought of his own death? Had Joe stood at Caro's grave and known, at some unarticulated level, that her end meant his, too, that she had been his last thread of hope? During the fitful night that had preceded Joe's funeral, Robin had been deeply preoccupied with the idea that, as he, Robin, grew to pin fewer and fewer hopes on Caro, Joe by contrast was pinning more and more. Couldn't help it, couldn't even help himself. Any more than he could help looking at Dad's gun, and seeing it as a way out, the only way out. Yet he'd looked calm enough in the mortuary, relieved almost. Robin had emphasised that sense of relief to Lyndsay to try and soothe her, and then immediately regretted it. Who could, he realised too late, be comforted by knowing that their dead husband, whom they felt they had ultimately failed, looked relieved to be dead?

Such thoughts had plagued Robin in half-sleep
157

and half-wakefulness until his alarm clock showed four in the morning. He'd got up then, and made tea and done a bit of paperwork (final demands only) and still been in the milking parlour before Gareth. Gareth hadn't been pleased. He didn't like getting out of bed at five-fifteen if he didn't need to, and he didn't like having Robin around if there wasn't an emergency. Robin did things slightly differently, brought another atmosphere, and the cows knew it and took advantage of it, banging about in the collecting yard, jostling and shoving.

In any case, Gareth hadn't slept well either. Debbie had burst into tears just as they were getting into bed the night before and said, between gulps and sobs, that they had to leave Tideswell.

Gareth, half into bed, had paused with one knee up and said, 'What d'you mean, leave?'

'We've got to get away from here,' Debbie said. She had collapsed on to the edge of the bed and was holding herself and rocking backwards and forwards as if she had a pain. 'You've got to get another job!'

'You mad?' Gareth said. 'What are you on about? You daft, or what?'

'It's haunted, here. It must be. First Caro and now Joe. And suicide—Gareth, I can't get it out of my mind, I can't stop thinking about it. We mustn't stay, we mustn't. Not with the kids and all. It's like there's some sort of curse on the place, it's like we're being picked off one by one—'

Gareth got into bed and lay flat, pulling up the duvet.

'You've been watching the kids' videos—'

'I mean it!' Debbie shouted. 'I mean it, I mean it!'

He glanced at her. She didn't look like his Debbie at all, but like some wild thing, with her mouth open

158

like that. He reached out to flick back a corner of the duvet her side of the bed and patted the sheet.

'Get in, then,' he said. 'You get in and we'll have a cuddle. You don't want to go putting two and two together and making seven.'

She had cried for a long time, talking raggedly in between sobs about Lyndsay and Caro and loneliness, about being left to cope with life when you couldn't. At last she had gone to sleep, heavily, damply, against his shoulder and left him wakeful instead of her, staring into the darkness and listening to the silence of the quiet night, which suddenly seemed not peaceful but mildly threatening, as if some great force out there was holding its breath before unleashing its power. When the alarm had gone off, Gareth had been deep, deep down in the final exaggerated slumber and had felt almost sick to be awakened. Debbie had slept on, her face half buried in her pillow, her eyelids moving slightly.

And then he had found Robin in the parlour.

'Something up, then?'

'No,' Robin said. 'Only me.'

'Could've told me,' Gareth said. 'Could have said you'd do first milking. Couldn't you?'

Robin didn't look up at him.

'Didn't know myself.'

Gareth clumped down the concrete steps into the pit. The milking machines clanked and thumped, the steady sound interrupted every so often by the erratic splatter of slurry.

Robin said, fitting on a cluster, feeling the cow's teats with his hand, 'What's up here? She lost a quarter?'

'Yes,' Gareth said, sulking. 'A month back. She's fine. She milks fine on three.'

159

Robin gave the cow a slap.

'Funny old girl. Always gets herself in the same place. Always gets herself at number four.' He glanced at Gareth. 'I'll leave you then. I'll go and give myself a shave.'

Gareth said nothing. Robin went up the steps out of the pit and paused, holding on to the battered metal rail at the top.

'Gareth,' he said. 'Are you coming today? You and Debbie?'

'I expect so—'

'You don't have to,' Robin said. He paused and then said awkwardly, 'If—if—it's all a bit difficult, if you can't—'

Gareth turned away, and jabbed at the buttons on the control panel for the automatic feeder.

'We'll be there,' he said, and then rudely, 'What else did you think?'

Nothing much, Robin thought now, scraping at his chin, only maybe trying to spare you something, a second death in the family in only months, a different kind of death, one about which there was nothing to say, no murmurs of comfort, only endless, endless things to ask.

'Why,' Judy had said, all the evening before at supper. 'I know it's no good asking, but I can't stop. Why? Why then? Why that way? Why didn't he think of Lyndsay and the children?'

Judy had brought a friend with her, a boy this time, a tall, gentle-mannered young man in spectacles who called Robin 'Mr Meredith' and cleared plates from the table without being asked. Robin had been mildly surprised to see him, but soon saw why Judy had brought him. Or had, at least, brought somebody. He had wondered, briefly, why she had not brought Zoe,

160

but he had said nothing and nor had she. Zoe hadn't been mentioned. At bedtime, Judy had shown Oliver to the bedroom Zoe had slept in and a few minutes later Robin had encountered him on the landing, holding a towel and a toothbrush, without his spectacles on. His eyes had looked soft-shelled without them.

Robin dipped his razor into the basin of hot water and swirled it clean. In the bedroom next door, his only dark suit hung on the wardrobe door, brushed by Velma. She had also polished his black shoes and left a white shirt out. She hadn't done that for Caro's funeral, but then Caro hadn't been Joe, Caro had never become a part of Velma's fixed order of things. But Joe had been part, from boyhood, big and golden and good-looking and haunted, a figure of romance, even in his overalls. And Velma had known it, felt it. Robin wondered, letting out the scummy water thickened with soap trails and bristles, if Velma would break her rule about funerals and come to Joe's. Not because of death, not because of respect or sympathy or manners or anything else; but because, quite simply, of Joe.

*   *   *

Dilys stood bolt upright in the front pew of Dean Cross church between Lyndsay and Harry. Beyond Harry, at the end of the pew, was Robin, and behind them all were Judy and the young man Judy had brought. He seemed a nice enough young man but he should not, in Dilys's opinion, have been there at all. This was not an occasion for strangers.

It was, instead, an occasion for a display of family strength, solidarity and proper behaviour. It was an

161

occasion for making it impossible for the world to pity the Merediths. They had had Joe; now they had lost him, but they had been unique in having him in the first place. This unquestionable fact must be reflected in everything, from the brushing of hair, through the firmly affirmative prayers, to the immaculate sandwich lunch which awaited the mourners at Dean Place Farm, garnished with parsley, and radishes cut like roses, and safe from flies under pristine domes of white muslin.

She glanced along the pew. Robin looked almost as she would have wished—his hair, however, was too long—and he held himself well, he had her father's carriage. Harry, brushed and polished and starched until he gleamed, had shrunk down inside his clothes as if they were quite foreign to him as well as too big, and although he was obediently wearing them, they didn't fit him, either in body or mood. She had trimmed his hair in the kitchen and inspected his fingernails. He had submitted to this like a docile child, but he hadn't looked at her; his gaze had been far away, milky and detached. She looked back towards the altar and the big coffin of pale oak with Lyndsay's lilies on it. Dilys had wanted to put her own flowers on as well, flowers from the Dean Place garden that Joe had known all his life, but Lyndsay had flared up out of her torpor and refused.

'No,' she'd said. Her eyes were glittering. 'He was *my* husband and the father of *my* children. Just *my* flowers. Flowers from Hughie and Rose and me.'

Dilys didn't even glance at Lyndsay now even though her right shoulder was less than a foot away. She knew what she'd see, anyway, and she knew she wouldn't like it. She'd see Lyndsay's misty pale hair scooped up into its combs as it always was, half

162

hanging down her back, instead of tidily, appropriately, put up into a smooth French pleat, and she'd see a long dark-green coat—green, at a funeral!—which Lyndsay insisted on wearing because it was Joe's last present to her, the previous Christmas. It might have been, Dilys said to herself, but it was wrong, utterly wrong. It had a black velvet collar and cuffs and dull gold buttons. It wasn't a funeral coat, it wasn't even a spring coat. It was just upsettingly, defiantly, the wrong coat for this day.

'Let us pray,' the Vicar said.

The church was immediately full of creakings and rumblings as the congregation knelt. It was a big congregation, Dilys had noted, very big and much bigger than the congregation for Caro's funeral. The whole village seemed to have come, and Gareth and Debbie, and even Velma, and all manner of people from the local farming community as well as the National Farmers' Union County President and the chief auctioneer from Stretton Market. Dilys put her forehead against her clasped gloved hands and closed her eyes. She hoped there would be enough sandwiches. Perhaps, when they got back from Stretton crematorium—none of this sentimental business of full burial for Joe such as Caro had had—she ought to get some sausage rolls out of the deep freeze and thaw them in the oven. Robin could deal with the drinks—Harry had never had a grasp of it—and Judy's young man could help him. Thwarted of putting them on his coffin, Dilys had put flowers from the garden on the dining-room table, flowers from Joe's garden, from his home, where he had grown up and belonged.

'"For ever and ever,"' the Vicar said.

'Amen,' Dilys said loudly. 'Amen.'

*   *   *

There was a starched white cloth on the table, and flowers in a silver rose bowl, and Dilys's best cut glass, and a neat regiment of bottles, and plates and plates of precise sandwiches, crustless triangles of white bread and brown bread, with little flags stuck in them on cocktail sticks, little banners cut out of white writing paper, with 'Egg and Cress' printed on them in Dilys's careful hand, 'Salmon and Cucumber', 'Ham and Mustard,' 'Celery and Cream Cheese'. The chairs had been pushed back against the walls, and the windows polished and the Turkey carpet brushed by hand until the pile stood straight upright, and the colours glowed.

'Open the sherry,' Dilys said to Robin.

'Shall I wait until people come?'

'No,' Dilys said. 'Open it now. To be ready for them.'

She was very pale, Judy thought, but then, no doubt, they all were. Judy stood in the bay window of the room with Oliver, and was obscurely grateful for him. He hadn't taken her hand during the service, but he had, once or twice, just touched her lightly to reassure her, to keep living in view. He was being extraordinary, she thought, just accepting things, just quietly, kindly being there, in this funny over-furnished old-fashioned room, with her grandparents and her father all rendered mute by the intensity of the occasion. And it was awkward that Lyndsay wasn't there, that she had refused to come, saying that she must get back to the children. Of course she must be with them, especially Hughie, but her absence somehow felt pointed, as if she was

164

making some kind of statement, of separateness.

'Here's the Vicar,' Dilys said, looking out past Judy towards the drive. 'Always the first, the Vicar.'

They all turned and watched him climb out of his car, slowly and tiredly, and then his wife got out of the other side and looked towards the farmhouse with apprehension.

'Oh!' Dilys said, and her voice had an edge of surprised gratification to it. '*She's* come! Well, that's something.'

Robin went out into the hall, where the seldom-used front door had been propped open with a cast-iron doorstop he had been very fond of as a boy, shaped like a rampant lion. The Vicar and his wife came slowly forward.

'Good of you to come,' Robin said. His hand went instinctively to his throat, to loosen his tie. 'Are there more behind you?'

The Vicar's wife looked up. She had been a pretty woman once, but seemed to have decided at some moment that it was a pointless asset, being pretty, that it availed her nothing, so she had resolved to let it quietly fade, like a party frock kept in a cupboard and rotting to rags because there were no parties to go to.

'I didn't see anyone,' she said. She looked at her husband, as if he somehow had had a different perspective and had seen something she hadn't seen. 'Did you?'

'No—'

'Nobody coming?' Robin said. 'Nobody following you from the village?'

'Well, there was the gap, you see,' the Vicar said carefully. 'The gap, you know, while we went to the crematorium. I expect they went then, I expect a lot of them had to get back to work, you know, after

165

their dinner hours—'

Robin said slowly, 'I see.' He looked at the Vicar's wife. 'But they all knew; there was an announcement. They all knew they were expected back here, that Mum expected them—' He paused.

The Vicar looked up at him.

'How can I put it, how can I—' He stopped and then said softly, 'This is a different kind of funeral, you see. It creates—it creates an apprehension.'

Robin stood for a moment, thinking. Then he said, 'Will you come in, at any rate? Will you come in, while I tell my mother?'

They nodded, moved behind him into the house and along the polished floor towards the dining room.

'Ah,' Dilys said. She seized a glass of sherry and a plate bearing a white paper napkin, folded into a triangle, and held it out to the Vicar's wife. 'Now you must help yourselves. Just go ahead and help yourselves.'

The room seemed very quiet.

'Mum,' Robin said.

Dilys turned from the Vicar and his wife.

'Well?'

Robin moved a step or two and lifted his arm as if to put it round Dilys's shoulders. Then he let it fall again.

'Mum, I don't think there's too many people coming. We didn't think of the time we took at the crematorium. They had to go back to work. We didn't think of that.'

Dilys gave him a bright, hard glance. Then she picked up a second glass and plate and thrust them at the Vicar.

'Nonsense,' she said.

166

'Nobody came,' Robin said. 'At least, almost nobody. Five or six. Mum was expecting fifty.'

He sat on the edge of the sofa in Lyndsay's sitting room, still in his funeral clothes, with his tie pulled down and his elbows on his knees. She had given him a glass of whisky and he held it loosely between his hands, and stared at the carpet.

'Poor Dilys,' Lyndsay said.

'She wouldn't take it. She wouldn't accept it. We sat there till gone four, just waiting.' He raised his glass and took a swallow. 'It was Judy in the end, it was Judy who had the courage. She said, "Gran, I don't think anyone's coming now. It's time we cleared up and stopped waiting." And then she just got up and took things out to the kitchen. Mum didn't say anything but she didn't try to stop her. She just sat there while we went in and out with all the plates. Enough food to feed the village.'

'And Harry?'

Robin looked down at the carpet again.

'He was outside. Where he always is. In—in the store.'

'Where Joe was,' Lyndsay said. 'Where he found Joe.'

'Yes.'

'I keep wondering what I'd have done, if I'd found him. Sometimes—sometimes I think I envy Harry, for finding him.'

Robin glanced at her.

'Don't do that.'

'And why didn't he shoot himself here? Why didn't he do it at his home, our home, where he belonged?'

167

Robin gave a tiny shrug.

'Perhaps that's why.'

Lyndsay leaned forward in her chair and put the mug of tea she had been drinking from carefully on the carpet beside her feet.

'I feel—oh Robin, I feel so sorry, so bad, just utterly bad that I couldn't cope—'

He said slowly, 'Maybe it was him that couldn't cope. Maybe he couldn't cope with being a farmer but he knew there was nothing else. You might hate the land, but you can't leave it either.' He paused and then he said, even more slowly, 'I should think suicide isn't far from a lot of farmers' minds.'

She stared at him.

'Robin!'

'Not many farmers have anyone to turn to,' Robin said, looking down into his whisky and observing his fingers, splayed and amber-coloured, through the side of the glass. 'And then they grow to doubt relying on themselves. You begin to think whatever you do is likely to go wrong, you decide to spray or not to spray and then the weather turns and all your time and money is wasted. You feel fate's against you. You feel the land is fate.'

She said, 'Do you feel that?'

He sighed.

'I see it, but I don't feel it. At least, not often. I'm not the same kind of animal as Joe.'

'But do you feel that about farming, about the land?'

He sighed again.

'I suppose so.'

'Are you trying to tell me,' Lyndsay said, 'that Joe was just an accident waiting to happen?'

'Maybe.'

'Oh my *God*—'

'But more,' Robin said, 'more I'm trying to make you see it wasn't your fault.'

'But I'm his *wife*. I'd have done anything in the world for him—'

'There were things you couldn't do, Lyndsay. Nobody could. He'd got to the point where nobody could help him and he couldn't help himself.'

'Somebody can *always* help!'

Robin looked at her.

'I don't believe that. And what's more, apart from the pain he's caused you and his family, I don't think Joe necessarily did a wrong thing. In the end, your life is your own. It's all you've got that really is your own. It isn't something you owe other people.'

The sitting-room door opened a little way, and then stopped.

'Hughie?' Lyndsay said.

Seal came round the door, held by a pyjamaed arm, and was wagged at them.

'Hughie,' Lyndsay said. 'Do you want to come in?'

'Who is it?' Hughie said, still outside the door, his voice thickened by speaking round his thumb.

'It's Robin,' Robin said.

'Oh.'

'You know *me*,' Robin said.

'Where is Daddy?'

Lyndsay got up and crossed to the partly opened door, standing looking through it to where Hughie stood, in his pyjamas and the red-and-black baseball cap.

'You know where Daddy is. Daddy died. He went to heaven.'

'I don't want that,' Hughie said.

Lyndsay stooped down and picked him up.

169

'No, darling.' Her voice shook. 'None of us do.' She put her face into his neck, by the soft red knitted band that finished the neckline of his pyjamas. 'We have to bear it, Hughie. We have to get used to it.'

'Bring him,' Hughie said. '*Bring* him.'

Robin stood up. He put his whisky glass down on top of the television and moved towards Lyndsay and Hughie.

'Would you come to me, old son? Would you come and give your old uncle a hug?'

Hughie shook his head.

Robin said, 'I wish you would.'

Slowly, still sucking, Hughie swivelled his head and looked at Robin, the fingers of his free hand working, tiny, busy movements in Seal's plush side. Robin held out his arms. Hughie bowed his head, submitting to the transfer, and was carried to the sofa.

'It's a change,' Robin said, settling Hughie against him. 'That's what's frightening. Nobody likes things being different.'

Hughie lay against him, his face invisible to Robin under the peak of the baseball cap.

'But you'll get used to it. Like you got used to going to playgroup. Like you got used to Rose being here.'

Hughie took his thumb out to say distinctly, 'I didn't,' and put it back again.

'You just have to wait,' Robin said, holding him. 'That's all we can do, all of us. We have to wait until we're used to it, until it feels normal that your dad's not here. We have to wait until we feel better.'

Hughie took out his thumb and pressed his face and, uncomfortably, the peak of his cap into Robin's chest and held himself there, tensely and silently. Robin waited. He looked up and caught

170

Lyndsay's eye.

'Poor chap. Poor old chap.'

He put a hand up and cradled Hughie's head against him.

'You just wait,' he said.

*   *   *

Before she went to bed that night, Lyndsay removed the two pillows from Joe's side of the bed, stripped off their covers to wash and put the pillows in the airing cupboard. She had promised herself that she would do this, on the night of his funeral. Then she got into bed, and told herself that she would give herself half an hour before she swallowed one of the sleeping pills Dr Nichols had given her. After fifteen minutes, she got up again and retrieved the pillows and their covers and got back into bed with them and lay holding them against her while she wept.

Some time later, she put the pillows back where they had been all her married life; and went along the landing to the bathroom. Both the children's bedroom doors were open. Rose lay on her back, her stout arms flung above her head, lost in sleep. Hughie was on the floor of his room, curled up on his duvet, still wearing his baseball cap. Lyndsay adjusted the duvet, so that there was enough to tuck round him, and put his pillow against his back, for comfort. It had been Robin who had finally put him to bed, and he hadn't protested. In fact, he had been so submissive as Robin carried him from the sitting room that Lyndsay would have given a good deal to have heard a roar from Rose, a roar to remind herself that there were other emotions in the world than the grinding ones of pain and pity.

Lyndsay did not look at herself in the mirror above the washbasin. She had decided not to, for a week or two, to spare herself the signs of her grief that seemed to her to have quite distorted her face. In the cupboard, whose door the mirror formed, Joe's shaving things still stood, beside her creams and lotions, and the indigestion tablets in their royal-blue plastic bottle that he had chewed all day, every day, ever since she had known him.

'Shouldn't you tell the doctor?' Lyndsay had said. 'Shouldn't you tell someone that it never stops?'

'No,' Joe said, 'it's fine. I don't think about it. It's nothing.'

Lyndsay went out on to the landing again. Nothing had ever been nothing to Joe, and nothing had really ever been fine, either. She leaned against the wall, the wall papered by Joe with the paper of her choice—clumps of daisies on a cream satiny ground—and felt suddenly quite overwhelmed, not just by the present or the future, or even by Joe's suicide, but by the past and by all she hadn't understood about it and couldn't have changed, even if she had understood it. It had all been too much for her, all along, and only her incomprehension had enabled her to keep going. She sank down where she was, still leaning against the wall, the landing carpet—only a cheap one, to Dilys's disgust—harsh on her thighs through the thin cotton of her nightgown. She closed her eyes and let the sad silence hum in her ears. Was this growing up?

*   *   *

Judy and Oliver were waiting for Robin in the kitchen at Tideswell Farm. They had made coffee and were sprawled either side of the kitchen table, sometimes briefly touching hands across it. Oliver had taken off his sweater, and thrown it on one end of the table across the litter of papers that lived there now, and on this the house cat lay, curled up but watchfully, waiting to be told to go.

'I thought you'd be in bed,' Robin said. He had been wearing his black funeral tie loosely round his neck all evening, and now he pulled it off and dropped it on the table.

'We were waiting for you,' Judy said.

'I was with Lyndsay—'

'Yes.'

'Trying to tell her she wasn't to blame.'

'Are you hungry?' Judy said.

He shook his head.

'Coffee?' Oliver said.

'No, thanks. I had a whisky at Lyndsay's and I feel as sick as a dog.'

Judy said uncertainly, 'You've been good to Lyndsay. And Gran.'

Robin grunted.

'Poor old Gran—'

'Do you mind that?' Judy said. 'Do you mind what Gran thought of Joe?'

Robin said, 'It's no good minding. It's what is. Was.'

The telephone shrilled.

'Shall I go?' Oliver said.

He stood up, pushing his spectacles up his nose as if to see better was also to hear better.

'Hello?'

He waited a second or two and then he held the receiver out to Robin.

'It's for you. It's your mother.'

173

Robin put the telephone to his ear.

'Mum? Everything OK?'

He paused, listening. Oliver moved round behind Judy's chair and put his hands lightly on her shoulders.

'You'd better come,' Dilys said, her voice clear across the Tideswell kitchen. 'You'd better come at once. I can't find your father.'

CHAPTER ELEVEN

Eight feet in front of Zoe, the string quartet posed inside a huge gilded cage. They were all young women, and the cage was their trademark, since they called themselves Birds in a Cage. They were about to appear at the Royal Albert Hall, playing Venetian Baroque music, which was their speciality, and dressed in vaguely Renaissance clothes made of rich dark satins and brocades, which they had made their speciality, too. They were being photographed for posters and programmes, and, influenced by the vogue for portraying classical singers and musicians as sirens, they were getting as much sex appeal into the session as possible, as much hair and teeth and potential trouble as the photographer would let them get away with.

The photographer was loving it. Zoe had never worked with him before but had marked him down immediately as flash on account of his custom-built Hasselblad and lizard cowboy boots. He called her darling, as if they'd known each other for ever, had worked on a hundred shoots together before, but he never looked her in the eye, she noticed. She did what

174

she was told, setting up tripods and huge dull gold reflector discs and taking light-readings, but she wouldn't speak to him. One of the girls in the quartet, a thin viola player with dead straight black hair like a curtain, caught Zoe's eye and winked.

The studio, in a dingy street off High Holborn, was completely white, ceilings, walls, floor, with long white blinds that could be pulled down to obscure the angles. The four girls inside their fragile cage looked as if they were suspended in space, as if the cage might indeed be hanging somewhere outside the known world, in some removed fantasy. Zoe had been into the cage to arrange the folds of their dresses, so that the shadows fell as lushly as possible, and the satin caught the light, and had felt that there was a different atmosphere inside, an atmosphere that was more than just an illusion. Those girls had been very clever in choosing their cage; it gave them mystery and it gave them power. Zoe, crouching outside it holding a huge, light nylon reflector, looked back at the viola player and grinned.

'Turn your faces towards me,' the photographer said, 'and your eyes to the side, and when I say "Now!" flick your eyes towards me, right at me, right into the camera. Give the camera all you've got.'

At this moment, Zoe thought, while we're in here giving our all to four girls in fancy dress, there are people out there selling newspapers and lottery tickets and going through litter bins and gazing out of office windows and counting the half-hours till lunchtime, till end of office time—

'Now!' the photographer shouted.

—and there are kids in school and people getting into lifts and aeroplanes and picking up telephones and we're poncing around here with all this kit and a

Hasselblad—

'Brilliant,' the photographer said. 'Brilliant. You babes have it. What it takes you *have*. But I need it one more time. Faces to the camera, eyes to the left a little. Mouths a little open? Relax those lips, relax; let me see the teeth, just a glimpse of teeth.'

—and while we're doing this, Gareth is probably mucking out the cubicles in the barn and Robin's out somewhere on the farm and Velma's in the kitchen spraying air freshener everywhere; Mountain Pine, her favourite—

'Hold it up, darling, would you?' the photographer said to Zoe in quite a different voice. 'As you were? No, darling, no. As you *were*. Now, girls, now, my lovely girls, I want your instruments between your knees, legs spread. Let's see some leg, let's see it.'

I bet, Zoe thought, tilting the reflector so that a warm glow lit the girls' faces from underneath, I bet none of this lot have ever touched a cow. I bet they don't think about cows. I bet they just put milk in their coffee and never think about where it came from, about how cows live, who looks after them. I'd like a cow to walk in now. I'd like her to come straight in and just stand there and see what they'd do, see if the cow made them look stupid. The cow wouldn't look stupid, she'd just go on being a cow—

'Darling,' the photographer said, 'can you concentrate? Can you please just give us a fraction of your attention?'

Zoe looked at him. The girls in their cage, holding their instruments lightly between their spread legs, looked at Zoe.

'Perhaps,' the photographer said, sensing a chance for point-scoring, 'perhaps you'd like to share your thoughts with us? Would you, darling? Would you

176

like to tell us all what you were far away thinking about?'

Zoe didn't blink.

'Cows,' she said.

*   *   *

Later, in Judy's flat, eating a baguette stuffed with salad out of the long, thin paper bag in which she had bought it, Zoe decided she would get another three days' work from the agency that had given her the string quartet job, and then she would go down to Tideswell. Three days' work on top of what she had earned this week already would pay the rent and her bus ticket. Her mother hated the way Zoe regarded money, hated her short-term view of what she needed, wanted her to put money by, to make for herself some small security, even if only a few hundred pounds.

'What for?' Zoe said. 'What'm I putting it by for? I might be dead tomorrow.'

Zoe's mother put money by for things, for washing machines and a video recorder, for a nest of occasional tables, for a microwave oven.

'Then you've got them,' she'd say to Zoe. 'Then they're yours,' meaning that possessions were somehow a defence against insecurity, evidence of existence in a world where invisibility of some kind, non-existence, threatened at every turn.

'But I don't want them,' Zoe said. 'I don't like them. I like *not* having things. I like being able to move about. Maybe,' she'd said, in the last conversation of this kind with her mother, 'maybe I'm naturally a wanderer. A nomad.'

Nomad was a new word for Zoe, a new idea. Robin

177

had used it to her. He said that nomad had been one of Caro's words, that she had believed herself to be one, to be a person who would always be a traveller in essence, a person you couldn't settle even if outwardly you thought you had. Zoe liked that idea, had turned it over in her mind and looked at it as one might a shell or a pebble in one's hand, especially at Caro's grave. That fascinated her. Why should a nomad, of all people, seek the final refuge of someone who identified themselves ultimately by a particular place, a place in the end as specific as 6 feet of earth? It seemed to signify a contradiction in Caro, but then, Zoe reflected, she was learning fast about contradictions, about how inconsistencies dwelt in everyone and flung them about and made it impossible to expect anything from them except what they chose to hand you at any given moment. Look at Judy, loud in condemnation of her childhood at Tideswell, yet touchy and jealous of Zoe's interest in the farm and her father. Look at Zoe herself, urban through and through, steeped in the knowledge and landscape of the streets, and now fascinated by the complete opposite, by the rooted inevitable ways of the countryside where weather and season presided like gods. Like *bad* gods, Zoe thought now, retrieving a slice of cucumber from her lap, gods that don't want to help, but want to test you. Joe's death had made her think that and she'd thought a lot about it. And about Robin. Robin was the age, roughly, that Zoe's father would have been, if he'd lived; yet Robin wasn't like a father. Perhaps he wasn't for the simple reason that he wasn't Judy's physical father, but only her father by legal arrangement and so part of him had never been exercised by blood fatherhood, as part of Zoe's father had, or part of Joe. It had kept

178

Robin separate, hadn't it? Not exactly undeveloped, but full of potential still, like someone young, someone who still had lots of basic things to do with their lives, with themselves. And didn't that make Robin a bit exciting, a bit unconventional, a bit, well, a bit capable of something he hadn't done yet, but might? Fathers were one thing; men who were fatherhood age but not actually fathers were something else.

Zoe opened the last 3 inches of the baguette and peeled out the sliced vegetables, rolling them into a damp parcel inside a lettuce leaf and cramming them into her mouth. Had Robin envied Joe for having kids? Especially Hughie, with farmers still so stuck in their ways about what girls were good for? And if he had, Zoe thought, chewing, had he just got on with his envy like he got on with milking and mowing and making silage? She stood up, crumpling the paper bag in her hand. A shower of breadcrust crumbs fell on to the floor and the scuffed toes of her boots. Maybe nobody had ever asked him. Maybe, in that funny world where everything seemed so practical and necessary, nobody ever discussed anything that wasn't central to the sheer business of farming. Maybe, Zoe thought, treading crumbs into the carpet on her way to get a drink of water from the kitchen, nobody had ever told Robin that it was OK to have feelings, that everybody had them and nobody should be afraid of them. And if nobody had ever told Robin that, perhaps it was time someone did.

* * *

Harry lay on his side, his teeth in a glass of sterilising solution on the locker beside his bed, and stared out

179

of the window. He could see the long brick wall of Stretton Hospital punctuated by neat windows at regular intervals, and the tops of a row of pink cherry trees that marked the edge of the visitors' car-park. Beyond that he could see the grey tower of a financial services company building and the Victorian spire, encrusted with pseudo-Gothic crockets and finials, of the parish church of St Mary the Virgin and a few roofs and wall-angles and, in the far distance, the peering crane-like floodlights of Stretton Football Ground. It was an ugly view, despite the cherry trees. He didn't like it. He didn't like looking at bricks and mortar. He wanted to be at home. If he had to be in bed—and he couldn't see why he had to be in bed, he was only tired, for God's sake—he'd like to be in his own bed, thank you, with its view of sky and trees and the 10-acre field Joe had left for set-aside this year, where the partridges were nesting.

He wasn't ill, after all. Observation, they said, they were keeping him in for observation. There was nothing to observe, was there? Nothing he couldn't have told them, if they'd asked, but they didn't ask and he wasn't bloody going to volunteer anything. When he'd gone off the night of Joe's funeral, he hadn't meant anything, hadn't intended to do anything, he just needed to be out there, where he and Joe had done things together and where something of Joe still lingered, he was sure of it. He'd been asleep when Robin found him, tucked under the lee of a hedge and sleeping like a baby. He couldn't remember much after that except how angry they all were, especially Dilys, about the mud on his suit, the rip in his jacket. He'd been in his chair in the kitchen while they all shouted at him, and he'd gazed at them all as if he hardly knew them. It occurred to him that

180

it didn't actually matter if he didn't know them. In a minute, Joe would come in and explain. Joe would tell them why Harry had been under a hedge with his eyes shut wearing his best suit at ten o'clock at night.

Now, lying in his hospital bed and looking at the weather-vane on St Mary's steeple, he knew Joe wasn't coming. Dilys came, and Robin came, but Joe wasn't coming. Not now. He supposed he'd known that all along, at some level, but not believed it, like knowing you're going to die some day but not believing that either. The thing was, Joe shouldn't have died. Joe was Harry's son, and fathers died before their sons, didn't they, so that they never had to be without them. The loneliness of Joe not being there, of being without Joe, was something Harry couldn't look at yet except in tiny glances, appalled. It was easier to look at the cherry trees and the grey office block. You could at least hate them. You could hate them for being the wrong view, for not being what you wanted to look at. You could hate them for being town, not country. You could hate them, above all, for being there still, when Joe wasn't.

*   *   *

'You five?' Gareth's Eddie said. He sat at the kitchen table at Tideswell Farm wearing a 'Batman For Ever' T-shirt and a sun visor of green transparent plastic.

Hughie said nothing. He stared at his plate on which Eddie's mother Debbie had put a scattering of potato crisps and a cold sausage like a dead finger.

'Hughie?' Lyndsay said gently, promptingly.

'Three,' Hughie hissed. Seal was on his lap, under the table. Hughie gripped him.

Eddie rolled his eyes to the ceiling.

181

'Three? *Three*? I haven't been three in *years*.'

'One,' Debbie said.

'I'll be five come July. July the 13th.' He flipped his visor up. 'Don't you forget.'

Debbie said to Lyndsay, 'Take no notice. It's the age gap that does it, with Kevin and Rebecca being that much older.'

'I got a football,' Eddie said to Hughie. 'Gary Lineker signed it. What you got?'

'A cricket bat,' Hughie whispered.

Eddie collapsed sideways.

'Cricket? *Cricket*? Only nerds play *cricket*.'

'That's enough,' Debbie said. She had been anxious about this meeting, but her anxiety had been dispelled by the sight of Lyndsay looking so fragile, so drained, so vulnerable, Debbie said later to Gareth, like someone who needed looking after, who was ill. Yet when Robin had asked Debbie to come to the farm, because Lyndsay needed to get out of the house, needed a distraction, and this was all he could think of to divert her just now, Debbie had been very doubtful.

'What'll I say?' she'd said to Gareth. 'What'll I do? I mean, she's kind of like the boss's sister-in-law, isn't she, I mean what do I say to her? I can't—well, I can't talk about him. Can I?'

'Take Eddie,' Gareth said. 'Eddie's never stuck for something to say. He'll be company for—' He stopped. He'd been going to say 'For Joe's little lad'. He said, 'For their kid. For their boy.'

'What you got there?' Eddie demanded, pointing a sausage at Hughie. 'What you got on your lap?'

Hughie bowed his head.

'It's a seal,' Lyndsay said. 'It's company for him. Have you got something for company?'

182

'Nah,' Eddie said scornfully.

'Not Panda?' Debbie said to him. 'Not Pink Panther? Not Sonic the Hedgehog?'

Eddie glared at her. He put his sausage down and got off his chair, hitching his jeans up round his skinny waist.

'I'm going home.'

'OK.'

'I'm gonna see my dad.'

Debbie flinched. She couldn't look at Lyndsay.

'My dad,' Eddie said to Hughie with emphasis, 'drives *tractors*.'

'That's enough,' Debbie cried sharply. 'Enough. Go on home, go on, go on before I belt you one—'

The kitchen door slammed, and then the outer one, to the yard.

'Sorry,' Debbie whispered.

Lyndsay said, 'He couldn't know. How could he know?'

'He shouldn't have said it. He shouldn't have said it anyway—'

'It doesn't matter,' Lyndsay said. 'He was just being normal. It's good for us to see people being normal, it's what we need.' She stooped over Hughie. 'Are you going to eat your crisps?'

He took one, the size of a small shirt button.

Lyndsay said, 'We aren't very good guests. It's so kind of you to be here. I think Robin—' She stopped, and then she said in a rush, 'Nobody knows what to do with us,' and then in almost a whisper, 'We don't know what to do with ourselves.'

Debbie waited, clenching her hands in her lap. The sight of them made her want to cry again, she could feel the tears bunching up in her throat, hard and uncomfortable. She wanted to say she'd do anything

183

to help, anything, but she couldn't trust herself to open her mouth or the tears would burst out and then they'd all be at it. She shook her head helplessly instead, and crushed her fingers together until the bones shone white through the skin.

'Try another one,' Lyndsay said to Hughie. He chose a second crisp, even smaller than the first. Lyndsay said to Debbie, 'We left his sister with Mary today. Didn't we, Hughie? Sometimes we like just being the two of us.'

Debbie said unsteadily, 'Rebecca was wild with jealousy when Kevin was born. I couldn't leave them alone together, not for a minute. She had him once, with the fire tongs.'

'Rose is just a bit noisy,' Lyndsay said. 'Isn't she, Hughie? And sometimes we need a bit of peace and quiet. But she's only a baby—'

Debbie leaned forward, releasing her hands from one another.

'I'll help you with her. I'm only up at the school dinnertimes. I'll help. You only have to ask, I'd like to, I'd like to help.'

'Thank you,' Lyndsay said. 'You're really kind. Thank you.' She looked across at Debbie. 'I—I don't know what I'm going to do. Maybe a job. I don't know, I can't think. Not yet.'

'No—'

'Dr Nichols says it's shock. He says it was shock for—for Joe's father, too, that's what did it. He called it a blow to the nerves.'

'How is he?'

'Still in hospital,' Lyndsay said. 'They'll let him come home when he's eating again. He won't eat yet.' Her voice shook. 'I don't blame him. We none of us want to eat. There doesn't seem any point,

184

somehow.'

Debbie said, glancing at the clock and reminded of Gareth's tea, 'I'm ever so sorry, but I ought—'

'Of course,' Lyndsay said, 'of course. You go.' She stood up, slowly. 'We'll clear up. Won't we, Hughie? We'll clear up and then we'll wait for Uncle Robin.'

'I meant what I said,' Debbie said. 'About the baby, about helping with the baby—'

Lyndsay put a hand on Hughie's head. He shrank down from under it, pulling Seal up to hide his face.

'Thank you,' Lyndsay said, 'I won't forget.'

*　　　*　　　*

'Take Hughie home,' Robin said. He had on a jacket and tie, the knot loosened below the open collar of his shirt.

Lyndsay paused in her slow wiping of the plates the children had used. Hughie, sitting beside the house cat on the newspaper pile, sucked his thumb and watched.

'Why?'

'Is Mary there?'

'Yes, but—'

'I want you for half an hour. I want you to do something with me.'

'What?' Lyndsay said.

Robin glanced at Hughie.

'Come into the yard a moment,' He said to Lyndsay. 'I've something to show you.'

'Will you wait there?' Lyndsay said to Hughie. 'Will you stay there just for one minute with the cat?'

Hughie said nothing.

'I'll only be a second. Just one second and I'll be back. Don't move.'

185

She followed Robin out into the yard. His car, the battered estate car Caro had used as an alternative to the Land Rover, was parked close to the yard door. Its back seats were folded down flat, to give the maximum carrying space, and Lyndsay could see a coil of rope and some old newspapers and a roll of pig wire and an empty gas cylinder. There was also a small neat cardboard box.

Robin went round to the tailgate of the car and lifted it. He pulled the box towards him and opened the flaps. Inside, Lyndsay could see a container, like a big square instant-coffee jar, made of bronze plastic with a screw-top lid.

Robin said, 'I went to the undertakers' in Stretton this afternoon.' He made a sketchy gesture towards his tie. 'As you see.'

Lyndsay gazed at the container. Robin lifted it out of the box and held it in his hands, not quite holding it out to her.

'Joe's ashes,' Robin said.

She swallowed.

'Not all of them, of course,' Robin said. 'All of them would have been—' He stopped. He looked at Lyndsay. 'We have to scatter them,' he said. 'It's what he wanted. He wanted them scattered in the river. I think we should do this together unless—unless, of course, you'd rather do it alone.'

She shook her head. Her eyes were filling again. Robin put the container back in the box. He straightened up and put his hands on Lyndsay's shoulders.

'It's what he wanted. I heard him. We have to do it. I can't leave him—them—here in the car.' He paused, about to say that driving Joe's ashes back to Dean Cross had been unbelievably hard, one of the hardest

186

things he'd done in all these long, hard months, but he refrained. 'Take Hughie home,' he said. 'Take him home to Mary and meet me down by the river in half an hour.'

He dropped his hands from her shoulders. She raised her eyes to his for a second and he saw she was about to run away. He raised a finger to her and she flinched.

'Lyndsay,' he said angrily, not caring. 'Lyndsay, *do* it. Stop thinking of yourself and bloody *do* it.'

*   *   *

She was there before him, waiting. She had parked her car fifty yards up the track from the river and had walked down to the bank and now stood there beside a willow tree that Judy had played on as a child, which had grown out so horizontally from the bank that it made a natural saddle to bestride.

'Hughie OK?'

'I think so,' she said. 'I mean, as much as he can be. Sometimes I wish he wasn't so quiet, so good. Sometimes I wish he'd just yell so I knew what he was thinking.'

Robin grunted. He had the container of Joe's ashes in the crook of his arm. Lyndsay looked at it.

'Should we have asked your mother?'

'Not unless you wanted it—'

'I don't,' Lyndsay said. 'I expect I shouldn't say it, but I don't.'

'There's no should or shouldn't,' Robin said, 'there's only what is. For the moment anyway.'

He took the container in one hand, and gently unscrewed the lid. He held it out to Lyndsay. He was still, she noticed, wearing his tie, a dark-red tie with a

187

small tidy pattern on it, very conventional. It was probably one of not more than three or four he owned altogether. Joe had hardly owned any ties, either, only the ones she had given him for parties, frivolous ties in bright patterned silks, and a black one. There was something odd, and touching, to see Robin standing there on the river bank in his tie. She looked, with apprehension, at the open container.

'They're very soft,' he said. 'I felt them. They're softer than wood ash.' He held the container a little closer to her. 'Put your hand in. Put your hand in and take some.'

'I can't—'

'You can,' Robin said. 'You must.'

She dipped her hand into the neck of the container. What was inside was indeed soft, almost silky. Her fingers went down into it, into . . .

'It isn't Joe,' Robin said. 'Don't think that. It isn't him.'

'It *must* be—'

'Then let him go!' Robin shouted suddenly. 'Throw him on the river and let the poor bugger go!'

She snatched her hand out of the container and a plume of ashes, pale pinkish grey, streamed out after it and blew away like smoke across the water.

'More,' Robin said.

She dug her hand in again and flung it wide across the river, and then again and again, letting the arcs of ashes melt into the air above the water. She thought she was screaming. She saw Robin put his hand into the container and take out a lot, a big handful, and then he set the container down on the ground and moved to the water's edge and stooped down, so that his hand almost touched the water and the ashes slid

188

away from him into it, quite silently and swiftly, and were gone. She heard him murmur. She cried out.

'What did you say?'

He turned.

'Just goodbye.'

Lyndsay bent and picked up the container. It was still half full. She carried it down to the river and knelt beside Robin on the muddy grass. Then she leaned forward and let the remaining ashes pour smoothly from the jar, vanishing into the water as they touched it.

'That's it,' Robin said. 'That's the way.'

He stood up. Lyndsay stood up, too. For a moment, they stood side by side, watching the water, this unremarkable small brown river full of pebbles and soft mud and chub where Joe had asked to be scattered. And then Lyndsay turned to Robin and put her arms around his neck.

He held her back. She could feel the surprise in his arms, in that they were not quite relaxed. She pushed herself against him.

'*Hold* me.'

'I am.'

'Properly,' Lyndsay said.

He felt different from Joe, the same height but more wiry, less solid, less permanent. She turned her face so that it lay against his shoulder and moved her arms to hold him across the back.

'He knew I needed him,' Lyndsay said. 'And he left me. He knew I'd blame myself and he's let me do it. He knew I can't live alone, he *knew* it. He made me lean on him, he let me do it.' Her arms tightened around Robin. 'You mustn't let me down, Robin,' Lyndsay said. 'You mustn't.'

She felt his arms loosening.

189

'Don't,' she said.

'I'm the wrong person to talk to like this—'

'What d'you mean?' she demanded, looking up. 'What d'you mean, the wrong person?'

Robin said awkwardly, 'I'm his brother, and in any case—'

'What?'

'I don't know about—love.'

'Nonsense!' Lyndsay cried. 'Absolute nonsense! Everybody knows about it! It's the one thing everyone knows about!'

Without warning, she moved suddenly and kissed him on the mouth. It was a hard kiss, a startling one, and he felt her tongue fleetingly against his lips. He dropped his arms. He was shaking slightly.

'Time you went home—'

'No!' she shouted.

'You must get back to the children.'

'What do you know about it? What do you know about children, about what I should and shouldn't do? What do you bloody know?'

He took her arm, gripping it.

'Nothing,' he said. 'I told you. I never said I did.'

Lyndsay began to cry.

'Sorry,' she said, sagging against him. 'Sorry, sorry, I shouldn't—'

He put an arm round her.

'No shouldn't,' he said. 'I told you that, too. No should.'

'I want to kill someone,' Lyndsay said. 'I want to make someone pay for this.'

He began to propel her slowly up the track back to her car.

'Robin—'

'Yes?'

'I'm sorry about just now. I'm sorry I gave way like that—'

'It doesn't matter.'

'I don't know what I feel. Or think. Or anything.'

She stopped walking and turned to face him, her hair in the light evening wind blowing about her in a cloud.

'You'll stand by me, though, won't you?'

He looked at her.

'You will, won't you, Robin? You'll help me sort myself out, what I do, where I go? You won't leave me to deal with—with, well, with your parents alone, will you? You'll stand up for me?'

He sighed. A feeling of dread slid abruptly into his chest like a small cold knife.

'Of course,' he said.

CHPATER TWELVE

Dilys stood in the bedroom that had been Joe's, all his life, until he had left it to marry Lyndsay six years before. It was an odd room, L-shaped because of the big airing cupboard that jutted into it and contained the house's hot-water cylinder, but Joe had liked it because it had a double view. He had done his homework here, and collected his model aeroplanes and had had measles and chicken-pox. On the walls still hung team photographs from his school days, framed in black against the cream emulsion paint. He'd been a rugby player at school, the best scrum-half Stretton Old School had had in a decade, and his strip still lay in the bottom drawer of the big chest between the windows, laundered by Dilys and then

191

put away and left there. There were some things from the past you couldn't touch; there was still too much life left in them.

Dilys came into Joe's room every day, sometimes twice. She brought a duster with her and gathered up the spinning half-dead flies that collected daily on the windowsills, and polished the small looking-glass— she still felt a thrill of pride that it had had to hang so high on the wall, to accommodate his height—and smoothed the bed, as if someone had rumpled it since her last visit, by sleeping there. She allowed herself five minutes, ten at the most, and then she would stand just inside the door for a moment or two, quite still, eyes wide open, before she went out and closed the door behind her.

Now, standing facing the bed, she could hear the murmur from the kitchen below. That was the men from the agency, the men Robin had hired while Harry was still in hospital, while they sorted themselves out and decided what they'd do. They were nice enough fellows, even if one wasn't much more than a tractor driver, and since they came some distance each day to work—office hours, Dilys thought scornfully, eight to four-thirty—she allowed them to eat their lunch in the kitchen. That way, she could keep an eye on them, too, see that they really were doing what Robin had told them to, and not slacking. The thought of anyone slacking on land that Joe had put his heart into was anathema to Dilys.

So, to her great discomfiture, was the thought of having Harry back at Dean Place. Every day, when the men had gone home, Dilys tidied herself up and drove in to Stretton Hospital and sat by Harry's bed for an hour. She took him fruit and home-made biscuits and bottles of lemon-barley water. She also took the newspapers, both national and local, and the weekly farming journal he subscribed to, and the Stretton Market reports. She would mix his barley water for him and then she would read to him and tell him what had happened on the farm and peel him an apple, or a banana, and try to get him to eat some. Then, when the hour was up, she would fold up the papers, and put the fruit peels into a plastic bag, and stoop and kiss Harry on the forehead.

'Now you try and sleep,' she'd say. 'And eat your supper. You must try and eat your supper. I'll be in again tomorrow.'

Then she'd go and find her car in the visitors' car-park and drive home to Dean Place Farm with a feeling of relief, a feeling of having escaped from someone whom she had had to make conversation to, but who no longer spoke the same language.

Yet she didn't like seeing him in hospital. She didn't like the way hospital seemed to have aged Harry, and made him helpless, diminished him. Dr Nichols had said it was shock that had sent him off the night of Joe's funeral, that grief could cause shock, could be traumatising and could immobilise ordinary functions and patterns of thinking. Dilys could see that, but it didn't make her feel any more warmly towards Harry, but rather added to her obscure but powerful feeling that he had betrayed her, had let her down in the one part of her life where he knew—he *knew*—she had required unswerving loyalty. It had been almost a pact between them, an unspoken pact, that Joe was the centre of things, the centre of their world, the cradle of their hopes and wishes. Joe had bound them together in a way that Dilys had always assumed Harry understood as well as she did. And then he'd left his gun unlocked. He'd worked alongside Joe all those days and months and years and seen how things were for Joe and still he'd left his gun unlocked. His mulishness in the face of Joe's progressiveness Dilys could forgive, also his readiness to have rows with Joe, to deny him developments he'd set his heart on—but not the gun. Something about the unlocked gun stuck in Dilys's throat and made her thankful for that bed in Stretton Hospital, and for Harry's continuing refusal to eat more than would keep a hamster alive. When they sent Harry home, Dilys wasn't at all sure how she was going to live with him.

'Missus!' one of the men called from downstairs.

Dilys went out of Joe's room, closing the door, and out on to the landing. At the foot of the stairs, the younger of the two men stood, a gingery young fellow, who lived, he'd told her, with his wife and two young children in his parents-in-laws' council house the far side of Stretton.

'I'll be off, then,' he said.

She started down the staircase.

'Off where?'

'Promised the wife I'd take her mother to the hospital later. For her check-up.'

'You're supposed to be here until four-thirty,' Dilys said. 'You know that.'

He scratched his head.

'Sorry. Sorry about that—'

'Did you tell Mr Meredith? Did you tell my son?'

'Slipped me mind—' He shifted, in his stockinged feet. 'Can you give him a message? Can you tell him the harrow's playing up?'

'It's new,' Dilys said.

He grinned at her.

194

'That's OK, then,' he said. 'Isn't it? It'll still be under guarantee.'

She put a hand on the newel post at the foot of the stairs. She was suddenly tired and worse, slightly fearful. She said, 'You go, then.'

He nodded.

'Might be a bit late in the morning. Nine-ish, maybe—'

Dilys turned her head away.

'Cheers,' he said. 'See you tomorrow.'

She waited until he had padded back through the kitchen and out into the yard. He was calling to the other fellow, she could hear him, cheerful and careless. She felt her way slowly back into the kitchen and saw that, although they hadn't left any actual mess, there were two chairs askew by the table, and a screwed-up ball of plastic film and an apple core. She put a hand on the doorframe and leant there. Harry's old dog, from his basket by the back door, raised his head and scented her presence. He was seeking Harry. She closed her eyes. Blind and deaf, old Kep was still seeking something he wanted and needed which wasn't there. Just like me, Dilys thought. She felt the silence of the kitchen surge round her, cutting her off. Just like me.

*   *   *

'You OK?' Bronwen said, passing Judy's desk with a mango in one hand and a plastic cup of black coffee in the other. 'You look really tired.'

'I am a bit—'

'Want a mango?' Bronwen said.

'No, thanks. No.'

'You should book a holiday,' Bronwen said. 'You

195

need a break. I'm going to Formentera this year, renting a villa with some friends. It's supposed to be really unspoiled.'

Judy looked at her computer screen. 'The mood this autumn,' she had written, 'is childlike. The room in all our minds will be the nursery. Think gingham and painted furniture. Think farmyard friezes and rag rugs. Think rocking horses.'

Awful, she thought, awful, *awful*. She clicked the mouse to wipe out the sentences. 'Do you,' the computer asked politely, 'wish to save this document?'

'No!' Judy said, almost shouting.

Bronwen, back at her desk and slicing into the mango with a fragile plastic knife, looked up.

'Sorry,' Judy said. 'Sorry. I just wrote such complete crap, that's all.'

'Did you hear me?' Bronwen said. 'Did you hear what I said about a holiday?' She held the mango up so that its thick yellow juice ran down her wrists. 'Christ, I always forget you can only eat these things in the bath.'

'I've had so much time off,' Judy said. 'So much, just lately—'

'But that was *family*. That wasn't holiday. They can't penalise you for—well, for—'

'For relations dying,' Judy said.

Bronwen manoeuvred a desk drawer open with her elbow and extracted a dented box of tissues.

'Can't you go somewhere with Ollie?'

'I don't know. I haven't asked him. I mean, he's done so much just lately, so much propping up—'

Bronwen sank her teeth into a mango-half and tore out a chunk of slippery flesh.

'Probably likes it. What about Zoe, then?'

196

There was a tiny pause.

'Not Zoe.'

'I thought,' Bronwen said, biting again, 'I thought Zoe was great.'

Judy remembered the list of grief words on green paper, the midnight talks, Zoe's undemanding, unjudging, almost invisible presence in the flat.

'She—well, she was.'

Bronwen dropped the skin of half the mango into her wastepaper basket with a wet flop.

'So what went wrong?'

Judy hesitated. She looked at the photograph of Tideswell Farm, with the heifers in the sunny meadow and the figure who might have been Robin and whose identity, up until now, she hadn't really troubled herself about. Now, looking at the photograph, she wanted the figure by the barn to be Robin definitely, to be able to be certain of it. She peered a little closer. It was too tall a figure for Gareth, but the hair didn't look dark enough for Robin. Gareth's hair was brown, pale mousey brown like weak tea. Perhaps the man by the barn wasn't Robin or Gareth, but Joe. Judy put a hand out and edged the photograph sideways so that the light caught the glass and blotted out the picture. If the man was Joe, Judy could not quite look at him just yet.

'Well?' Bronwen said. She had finished the second half of her mango and was now licking her fingers, sliding the whole length of them into her mouth, one by one. It was somehow revolting to watch.

'She's—well, she'd got kind of hooked on my family—'

'What d'you mean?'

Judy bent her face towards her desk and shielded it

197

from Bronwen with her hands.

'She wanted to come and stay, to see the farm. So I took her. And then she went back, without telling me, on her own. And now she's gone again.'

'Wow,' Bronwen said.

'She did tell me this time,' Judy said and then, struggling to be fair, 'and she wouldn't come to my uncle's funeral because she said it wouldn't be right. But she went again yesterday. She got the bus.'

Bronwen held her hands away from her.

'Biz*arre*,' she said, laying emphasis on the second syllable.

'I keep thinking she has to be after something. She says she isn't. She says she just likes it.' Judy stopped. What Zoe had actually said, yesterday morning, before departing for the bus station was, 'It isn't me who has to answer these questions, Jude. It's you. It's you who said you never liked the place, it's you who said your family stifled you. Well, I like it and they don't stifle me. I'm not taking anything that's yours. I'm not even *taking* anything. I'm just going to be there. If your dad says I'm to go, I'll go.'

Judy said now, to Bronwen, 'There's a bit missing. It all seems so simple when she says it, but it doesn't hang together.'

Bronwen was losing interest. She stood up, holding her sticky hands away from her, fingers spread like Struwwelpeter.

'I'll have to wash. I've got the bloody stuff almost in my armpits. Shall I bring you a coffee?'

Judy looked at her blank screen. She was supposed to have 500 words as a first draft by twelve for the features editor.

'No, thanks.'

'OK,' Bronwen said. 'Just answer my phone for

me, would you? Shan't be a tick.'

Judy nodded. Then she reached out and laid the photograph of Tideswell Farm flat on its face, so that she couldn't see the house or the cows or the man by the barn at all. 'It isn't my home,' she'd said once to Zoe, almost irritably. 'It's just the place where I spent my childhood.' Well, Judy said to herself, picking up the computer mouse again, *well*. True or false?

* * *

Robin's shotgun lay on the kitchen table. It was broken, and a scatter of cartridges lay beside it that he had taken out of his pocket and dropped there. Zoe had never seen a gun before in real life, and certainly not a long-barrelled gun like this, with its wooden butt and chased-metal plates. It was a completely different thing from guns in the movies, much more old-fashioned and elegant and countryfied. Zoe touched it now and then. Robin said he was going to clean it later, after he'd sorted out some problem he thought he had with the total bacterial count on last month's milkings. It seemed to be very high, he'd said to Zoe, averaging nearly 20. He'd got to go and see somebody about it; check the feed. She didn't know what he was talking about. Sometimes, when he talked farm jargon, she asked him what he meant, but this time she didn't. She had instead looked at the gun lying on the table and wondered if it was the same kind of gun that Joe had used, to kill himself.

Robin had been using his gun last night, he said, to shoot badgers. They were protected, of course, he said, by misjudged town-bred legislation, whose perpetrators didn't have to live with the results.

199

Badgers were fine, Robin said, at a distance and in moderation.

'But they're dirty beasts and they're coming closer to the house every day, and fouling up the pasture. And they carry TB. Bovine TB. I don't want them round my cattle.'

He hadn't looked at Zoe while he said this. In fact, she noticed, he hadn't looked at her at all since she had arrived three hours before and he had found her in the parlour with Gareth at the end of the afternoon milking.

'You back?' he'd said, just as Gareth had.

'Yes.'

He hadn't smiled. He said merely, 'We could do with extra hands just now,' but he directed the remark more at Gareth than at Zoe.

Gareth was less talkative than usual, too, and his face looked older, somehow, sterner, as if his head was full of harsh, preoccupying thoughts. He said he didn't know what was going to happen, what the future held, what Robin was going to decide, what they'd do over at Dean Place Farm. The old man, Gareth said, looping a milking cluster out of the way to let a cow move on, was still in hospital. Suppose he couldn't farm again? He wasn't very old, Gareth said, but suppose this had knocked him sideways, knocked the stuffing out of him? Robin couldn't run two farms. And he didn't like the arable anyway.

'Hasn't got any heart to it,' Gareth said, slapping a cow to make her move into a stall. 'Not like stock. It's a different thing altogether from working with stock.'

It had been on the tip of Zoe's tongue to ask Gareth if he was thinking of leaving. But something in the atmosphere held her back. The whole place felt different this visit, less settled, less certain, as if the

200

future was not in fact the simple and sturdy matter it once had seemed. The mood made Zoe herself feel less certain, too, less able just to ask questions when she felt like it, or climb in and out of these seemingly stable lives at whim, observing them and photographing them as if her presence affected them no more than the touch of a butterfly alighting on a wall. When she left the milking parlour, she had come back into the kitchen and hung about in it, awkward and restless. Before, she would simply have been there, existing, and taken pleasure in the unaffected ease of that. Now, hovering uncertainly round the table on which Robin's gun lay, she felt she was in some alarming nursery fable, and that the forces that ruled the weather and the land had taken the roofs off the houses, too, and soon would blow the walls down, just on a whim, and watch all the little people inside scurrying out in a panic.

She looked into the sink, to find a mug to rinse out, for water. Robin's lunch plate lay there, and a knife, and a tumbler. They looked, to Zoe, incredibly lonely, evidence of an existence rather than a life. She picked up the tumbler, and rinsed it under the tap, and then filled it with water and drank it off in a single draught. It tasted faintly metallic. Zoe swilled the tumbler out, and then rinsed the plate and the knife under the tap, too, and put them in the draining rack, and then she picked up the disposable cloth Velma always left folded in an exact square and polished the sink, and then the taps. She had never done such a thing before in her life and was amazed at the brilliance of the chromium. She leaned forward and peered at her distorted reflection in the mixer tap. She had enormous eyes and a vast nose and a minute mouth and no chin or neck to speak of. She tilted her head and put her tongue out and it swelled across the whole reflection like a wet pink balloon, huge and hideous.

Behind her the telephone rang. Robin had an answering machine which he often forgot to put on. Zoe waited. Two rings, three, four, five. He hadn't put it on. She crossed the kitchen and picked up the receiver.

'Tideswell Farm—'

'Who is that?' Dilys said sharply.

'Zoe,' Zoe said.

There was a beat.

'Zoe? What are you doing there?'

'I just came,' Zoe said.

'I should have thought,' Dilys said, 'I should have thought you'd have had more tact at a time like this. I should have thought you'd have seen this is no moment to come. Where's Robin?'

'Checking the cell count, or something. In the milk. He's gone somewhere—'

'I wanted to leave him a message,' Dilys said. 'I wanted to leave him a message about his supper.'

'I'll take it.'

There was another pause.

'It doesn't matter,' Dilys said. 'It doesn't matter now. I'll speak to him later.'

Zoe shifted the receiver against her ear.

'I'll come up and get it. I'll bring his supper down. I'll borrow Gareth's bike.'

'I'm going out,' Dilys said. 'I'm going to the hospital.'

'Now?'

'In half an hour—'

'I'll be less than half an hour,' Zoe said. 'I'll be ten minutes.'

202

'All right,' Dilys said. Her voice was uncertain. 'All right. It's only a pie, a slice of pie—'

'Ten minutes,' Zoe said. 'I'm starting now.'

She put the receiver down and ran out through the doors to the yard. Gareth had finished the milking, and was standing above the pit directing the hissing blast from the power hose at the stalls where the cows had stood. Zoe went as close to him as she could and cupped her hands round her mouth to amplify her shout.

'Can I take your bike? To go up to Dean Place?'

'How long'll you be?'

'Half an hour!' Zoe yelled.

Gareth nodded. He didn't look at her. The water from the hose swirled and slapped against the concrete.

'It's in the feed barn. Behind the tractor. Don't you mess up my gears.'

She ran out to the barn, past the bulk tank where the milk was stored. There was no sign of Robin. Gareth's bike, a battered early mountain model, lay on its side against the maize feed. Zoe seized it and ran it out into the yard, so that there was a momentum going for her to mount it, swinging her right leg over the cross bar which Gareth had wound with fluorescent tape, for visibility at night.

It was good to be on a bike again. Zoe hadn't ridden a bike in years, not years and years, until she'd borrowed Gareth's the last time she'd been at Tideswell. There was a freedom to it, and a sense of participation, and the hedges, in which the flat, coarse, creamy plates of elderflower were now opening, had a different perspective at this height, this speed. She bent her head into the small wind she was creating and pedalled like fury, as if she were on a

203

mission, as if something vital depended upon her, the messenger.

Dilys was waiting at the kitchen window. She saw Zoe come flying into the yard, and wrench the bike to a skidding halt as if it were a runaway pony. She looked exactly as Dilys remembered her, and just as disconcerting, all in black with her hair as short as a boy's. You shouldn't, Dilys thought, be able to see a girl's neck like that, not the actual skin of the neck. It wasn't decent, somehow, it looked too naked. Zoe propped the bike against one of Dilys's geranium tubs and came running up to the door.

'There's not that hurry,' Dilys said, opening it. 'It's not life or death.'

Zoe was panting.

'I didn't want to make you late—'

'You won't,' Dilys said.

She led the way into the kitchen. On the table a plate lay neatly covered in aluminium foil, and beside it, a plastic box.

'I've put up enough for two,' Dilys said, indicating the plate and box. 'And a bit of salad.'

'Thank you,' Zoe said.

Dilys looked wretched. Zoe remembered a confident woman, a woman of health and purpose, a woman in control. She looked now like an echo of all that, her tidy clothes and tidy hair and tidy kitchen almost mocking the destruction that had taken place within.

Zoe said, 'Did you say you were going to the hospital?'

Dilys began to refold a dishcloth, opening it up, and then folding it again exactly as it had been.

'Yes.'

'How is he?'

204

'He's not well,' Dilys said. Her voice was odd, almost as if she were stating something she was pleased about, grateful for. 'They can't make him eat. He won't eat.' She laid the dishcloth back where it had been, in the exact centre of the rim of the old-fashioned white sink. 'They put him on a drip yesterday.'

'Oh—'

'He can't come home,' Dilys said, again with her air of queer triumph. 'He can't come home until he's off that drip.'

Zoe looked at her. She noticed that her hands were shaking as she put the dishcloth back.

'D'you want me to come in with you?'

Dilys stared.

'What?'

Zoe said, 'Shall I come in to the hospital with you? To see him? I can't drive but I'd be company.'

Dilys said, 'But I don't know you—'

'You do,' Zoe said. 'A bit anyway.'

Dilys moved to the table and began to realign the plate and the plastic box.

'It—it wouldn't be suitable.'

'Why wouldn't it? It'd be better if I came. Much better. It'd be easier to leave, easier to come home.'

'Oh,' Dilys said, too quickly. 'Coming home's easy, it's not the coming home—'

'I know,' Zoe said.

Dilys raised her eyes from her busy hands at the table and looked at Zoe.

'You never know,' Zoe said, 'what's going to scare you. Do you? It just sneaks up when you're not looking, and there you are, scared.'

Dilys said nothing.

'I can bike these down,' Zoe said, 'on the carrier on

205

Gareth's bike, and then you can follow me, in the car. And then we can go together.' She paused and then she said, 'I'd like to go. I'd like it.'

Dilys touched the foil on the plate lightly. She dropped her eyes from Zoe's face.

'You take that bike back. I'll bring these down in the car. Don't want the pie spoiling, being knocked about.'

Zoe grinned.

'OK,' she said. 'OK.'

She moved towards the door. Dilys was still standing by the table, her gaze directed at it but not seeing it.

'Ten minutes?' Zoe said.

*   *   *

Harry didn't mind the drip. In some odd way, being connected up to it reminded him of Robin's milking parlour, with all those tubes and hoses, except in that case milk was flowing out, and in his case, they'd said, glucose was flowing in, glucose and some vitamin or other. Harry wasn't much bothered, to tell the truth. He'd never concerned himself much with vitamins; new-fangled things they'd invented in the war because of the food shortages. There'd never been vitamins in Harry's childhood, there'd been the pig and there'd been bread and cheese and potatoes and cabbage. In Harry's childhood you would tell the days of the week and the hours of the day by what you were eating. When Harry or his sisters fell sick, his mother brewed up one of her concoctions, nettles and sorrel and mint and stuff. Harry lay and looked at the delicate engineering they'd harnessed him to, and thought of his mother's back kitchen. She'd have forty fits to see him now. She'd have been able to think of nothing but the cost of it, the expense.

'Harry,' Dilys said. She was standing at the end of his bed, as she always did when she arrived, so that he had to squint to see her. 'Hello, dear.'

'Hello,' he said.

'I've brought a visitor,' Dilys said. 'You remember Judy's friend, Zoe?'

Harry shut one eye, to narrow the squint. Dilys moved sideways out of his view and Zoe replaced her. She was smiling.

'I saw you down by the hedgerow,' Zoe said. 'Remember? You were hedging. Judy and I brought you your tea.'

Harry nodded. It came to him that he hadn't got his teeth in.

'I asked to come,' Zoe said. 'I asked Dilys if I could.'

She came round the bed, the other side from Dilys, and looked down at him. She was still smiling.

'D'you want your teeth?'

He nodded again, staring at her. He'd remembered that odd hair but he'd forgotten her big eyes, big eyes like a cow except they weren't soft eyes, but sharp, eyes that saw things.

Dilys handed him his teeth in a tissue. He put one hand up to his mouth to shield his gums while he slipped them in, awkwardly, because of the drip.

'You staying with Robin?'

'Yes.'

'Judy there?'

'No,' Zoe said, 'she's working. But she sent you her love.' She sat on the edge of the bed. 'She wants to know how you are.'

'The nurses won't like that,' Dilys said. 'They don't

207

like you sitting on the beds.'

Zoe glanced at her. She was still smiling.

'I'll wait till they throw me off.' She looked back at Harry. 'What'll I tell Judy? About how you are?'

'Tired,' Harry said.

'But you're not eating.'

'Don't want to.'

'Who's that going to help?' Zoe said. 'Who's going to have a better time if you don't eat?'

Dilys pulled up a grey plastic stacking chair, and sat down in it, leaning back, Harry noticed, as if his reply was no concern of hers.

'None of your business,' he said to Zoe.

'True.'

'Nobody's business,' Harry said. 'Nobody's business what I do. Not now.'

'Except other people have to look after you. And you're a pain when you won't eat, a pain for those people.'

He grinned suddenly.

'Always been a pain,' he said. 'Been a pain all my life.'

'Me, too,' Zoe said.

She looked down at him. Somewhere, in that collapsed old face, lay Robin's, the same bone structure, the same fleeting smile, the same private eyes. Harry was quite a small man, certainly a small man to be the father of such tall sons, but he had a large head, the head of a much bigger man than he was, a head, Zoe thought, full of things right now that he couldn't bear and was imprisoned with. She gave a quick glance across Harry's bed at Dilys. It was the same for her. She sat there in her organised way on her grey plastic chair and she too was shackled to her thoughts just as Harry was, or Robin, or the girl Zoe had had tea with, who was now Joe's widow. She folded her hands in her lap.

'You know something?' Zoe said.

Harry watched her.

'You don't eat,' Zoe said, 'and in the end you'll die. Is that what you want?'

Harry's gaze wavered.

'Can't decide?'

His mouth opened and shut, soundlessly.

'OK then,' Zoe said, 'I'll decide for you. While we're alive, we live. That's what you're going to do.' She looked across at Dilys. 'Isn't he?'

CHAPTER THIRTEEN

Lyndsay lay on a sun lounger in the garden of her parents' house on the edge of Stretton. The sun was out, but it was a nervous, late-spring sun, and Lyndsay's mother had brought her a rug, and a cardigan and a vacuum flask of coffee. She had also brought her a magazine. She was treating her, Lyndsay thought, as if she was ill.

Lyndsay's father had built the house thirty years before, on a plot of land that had once been the orchard to a big house that had been pulled down to make way for a tennis club. Lyndsay's brother and sister, both rather older than she, had been members of the tennis club when they were growing up, and her sister had married someone she had played mixed doubles with there, and had gone to live in Droitwich with him. They had had two children and Lyndsay's sister had become Personnel Manager in a company manufacturing garden machinery. Lyndsay's brother was an accountant. Lyndsay's mother, who had always done the books for her husband's building firm, said that her son had inherited his head for figures from her.

Nobody commented on what Lyndsay had inherited. She looked rather like her pale, pretty maternal grandmother, but that grandmother had been artistic, with a talent for water-colours and embroidery, and Lyndsay, although good with her hands, wasn't inclined to pick up either a paintbrush or a needle. She had been so very much the youngest child, both by temperament and by treatment. Babied, her brother and sister said, indulged. Photographs of Lyndsay at every stage of childhood still stood about the sitting room of her parents' house, and clustered on radiator shelves. They embarrassed her now, those images of the party-frocked child, all hair ribbons and white socks. It didn't surprise her that her sister got so irritated.

They'd all been amazed and relieved when she brought Joe home. She had only embarked gently on the beauty business, done a two-year course at Stretton College after leaving school and was waiting for her father to decide to buy her premises for her own salon, when she met Joe. It had been at a petrol station. She was filling her mother's car, which she had borrowed, and the automatic cut-off mechanism in the pump hose had failed, and petrol had suddenly leaped out at her all over her clothes, splashing her shoes, and she had screamed. Joe, filling the farm truck with diesel across the forecourt, had dashed to her rescue. She stank of petrol for days afterwards, reeked of it. Joe said—at least, for some time, he said—that petrol had become the best perfume in the world to him.

He asked her to marry him after three weeks. She said yes almost before the words were out of his mouth, indeed, she later realised, had been waiting for him to propose almost from the second he wrenched the gushing hose out of her paralysed hand and thrust it into a drain. To her parents, he was everything they could wish for, older, steady, handsome, apparently prosperous. He would take over where they could now thankfully leave off, in looking after Lyndsay. He'd said, smiling, looking at the clutter of silver-framed photographs, that she wouldn't have to get her hands dirty. They had all believed him.

They were all, now, in a state of shock. Something as savage, to them, as this thing Joe had done had never crossed their lives, entered their minds. They had asked Lyndsay to come and stay for a few days because she was, well, their daughter, and there were the children as well, but it was too bad, really it was. There was something outrageous in it, something extreme that left them bereft of attitude or opinion. When Lyndsay had arrived, they had welcomed her tenderly but also dutifully, as if she were in some way slightly contaminated. And then they had proceeded to treat her like an invalid, breakfast in bed, cups of tea and thimbles of sweet sherry, little lie-downs in the garden, under a tartan rug.

Her father, who was now retired, was very patient with the children. She could hear him now, from the house, singing old war songs to Rose. Rose loved singing. She loved anything that made a racket, music, motor bikes, barking dogs, rugby on television. Probably Hughie would be listening, too, but he wouldn't shout along with the singing, as Rose did. He had wet his bed the last two nights and

211

Lyndsay's mother had put a rubber sheet over the mattress, silently but pointedly.

'It was a mistake,' Hughie had told her. He wouldn't say sorry. 'A *mistake*.'

He had said several times to Lyndsay that he hoped they could go home soon.

'Are you missing playgroup?'

'No,' he said.

'Then why do you want to go home?'

He had turned Seal upside-down and eyed Lyndsay over his tail.

'I live there,' he said patiently.

I wonder if I do, Lyndsay thought now, looking up at the clean, pale sky. I wonder where I live. She let her gaze travel gradually downward in a curve, past the tall evergreen hedge that hid the courts of the tennis club from view, to rest on her parents' house, brick, neat, solid, decent. I certainly don't live *here*. Not any more.

The french windows to the sitting room opened, and Lyndsay's mother came out, limping slightly from the arthritis that she endured and about which she would never speak. She was carrying a light folding garden chair. Lyndsay sat up a little and tried to look more positive, less of a victim. Her mother shook out the chair, tested it for stability and sat down.

'There, now.'

She looked across at Lyndsay.

'You warm enough, dear?'

Lyndsay nodded.

'Dad's singing to the children. Can you hear him? Rose likes "Pack Up Your Troubles" best, bless her.'

Lyndsay said, 'She likes anything loud.'

Sylvia Walsh looked at her hands. They were nice

212

hands, as Lyndsay's were, well kept, and when she wasn't doing housework she always wore her engagement ring—two sapphires and three small diamonds—and the Celtic lovers'-knot ring which Roy had given her on their silver wedding day.

'I think we'd better have a little talk, dear. About your future. Obviously Dad and I want to do all we can to help.'

Lyndsay pulled the rug over her own hands, so that she could clench them in private.

'What do you mean?'

'Well,' Sylvia said, 'what is your position? Can you stay there? At the farm?'

Lyndsay said, without thinking, 'Of course I can stay! It's my home!'

Sylvia adjusted her cardigan so that the edges hung parallel over her bosom.

'But things are different now, aren't they? I mean, you can't work on the farm. Can you, dear? Perhaps the Merediths will need your house, you see, for a worker.'

'Nobody's said anything—'

'No, I don't expect they have. After all, things are at such sixes and sevens, with—with your father-in-law in hospital. But they'll have to think about it, won't they? Won't Robin be thinking of it?'

Lyndsay said deliberately, knowing her mother would flinch from hearing his name spoken, 'Joe had shares in the farm. His father had some, and he had more. Those will be mine, won't they?'

Sylvia stared at her.

'But you wouldn't want shares in the farm, would you?'

Lyndsay sighed.

'No. No, I suppose I wouldn't—'

213

'I mean,' Sylvia said, leaning forward, 'you can't stay there now, can you, not now, not now that—well, you'd have to deal with your parents-in-law, wouldn't you? You'd have to go into business with them.'

Lyndsay looked away.

'I couldn't do that. Anyway—' She paused, and then said, very quietly, as if uttering a disloyalty, 'Anyway, I hate the farm.'

Sylvia said carefully, 'Dad and I just wondered what you'd think of our little plan. It's only a suggestion, mind. It's only something for you to think about.'

Lyndsay took her hands out from under the rug and folded them on her stomach.

'We wondered,' Sylvia said, 'if you'd like to pick up again where you left off seven years ago. We wondered if you'd like to come back to Stretton and we'd see about a little salon again. Just something small. Even part-time that you could do while the children are little.' She paused. Then she said, in a voice intended to be kind, 'We just thought it might be good for you to have a complete change.'

Lyndsay put one hand flat on top of the other and pressed them both, hard, into her stomach. Her stomach felt concave, yielding, between her hip bones. She didn't think she had ever, in her life, been so thin.

'It wouldn't be a change,' she said to her mother. 'Would it? It would just be going back, back where I began—'

'Except that you have the children now, you have little Hugh and Rose. And you never finished what you'd begun before, did you, because—because you got married.'

214

Lyndsay turned her head aside. There were moments, sudden, unbidden moments, of so longing for Joe that she felt nothing short of frantic. Marriage, oh my God, marriage, *marriage* . . .

'Just think about it,' Sylvia said. 'I know how hard it must be to decide anything. But it has to be done. Life has to go on again.'

'And if I don't want it to?' Lyndsay said. 'If I just don't want there to be tomorrow?'

Sylvia stood up, adjusting the edges of her cardigan, and the waistband of her skirt, with the little deft plucking movements she had used all Lyndsay's life.

'You can't think like that,' Sylvia said. 'Not with children. If you've got children, you can't even begin to think like that.'

*　　　*　　　*

'I do staring,' Eddie said to Zoe.

He was squatting in front of her, holding a red plastic water pistol shaped like a handgun. Zoe was cross-legged on the ground, her back against the farmyard wall, her eyes closed. She had just had her first tractor-driving lesson from Gareth, on the old slurry-scraping tractor, and hadn't shown much aptitude for it.

'I can stare longer than you,' Eddie said. 'I'm gonna stare at you *now*.'

Zoe opened her eyes. Eddie's face was some 6 inches from hers, contorted with the effort of staring. His eyes were blue grey and small.

'Why?' Zoe said.

He didn't budge.

'What d'you want to stare for?'

'I'm gonna stare till you're scared.'

'I don't scare easy,' Zoe said.

She looked back at him. He had tiny features in a narrow face, and freckles. She put her tongue out at him. He took no notice.

'This is boring,' Zoe said.

He inched forward a little until she could smell him, faintly rank and babyish at the same time. He looked a bit like Gareth, she thought, but he had Debbie's slight build, the sort of build Zoe associated with city children, darting and zigzagging in howling packs through the housing estate where she'd grown up. She'd thought it perfectly normal then, perfectly natural to grow up in a world full of walls and walkways and stairwells and scuffed spaces and other people. Only now, out here, did it seem just one idea, one way to grow up rather than another. Judy had grown up here, after all. Judy had had air and fields and stony tracks and a river. And solitude. And she'd hated it. Zoe leaned forward and gave Eddie a little push.

'Give over.'

He rocked on his heels, but recovered himself and lurched in closer, his nose almost on Zoe's.

'You're a pain,' Zoe said. 'It's time you went to school and got thumped for being a pain.'

There was the sound of a car engine, and the Land Rover came into the yard at speed and stopped, as Robin always stopped it, on a swerve in towards the back door. Zoe lifted her gaze to look at it.

'I won,' Eddie yelled. 'I won! I won the staring!'

Zoe unfolded her legs and stood up, sliding her back up against the wall. Robin got out of the Land Rover, and went round to release the tailgate. Zoe moved across towards him. Behind her, Eddie fired

216

two squirts of his water pistol not quite in her direction.

The Land Rover was full of bales. Zoe peered.

'What's that?'

Robin picked the nearest bale up by its girdles of plastic twine and indicated with his head that she should do the same.

'Barely straw. I want it stacked by the maize on those pallets.'

Zoe lifted a second bale.

'What's it for?'

'For calves. I'm buying in calves this year to rear them for calving themselves.'

He began to stride away towards the barn. Zoe followed him, and behind her, Eddie, dribbling his water pistol.

'Haven't you got enough calves of your own?'

'Too many bulls.'

'But can't you tell? Beforehand, I mean. If you inseminate a cow, can't you tell what she'll have?'

'No.'

'Why not?'

'Because we haven't got that far scientifically yet. Because buying a straw of bull semen is a pig in a poke. Because I bought thirty bloody straws at twenty-two quid each and they were all bulls but two. Because to buy heifers of calf-bearing age would cost me seven hundred each.' He swung round on her, still holding the straw bale. 'Seven hundred. Each. OK? Enough? Enough? Enough bloody questions?'

Zoe put her bale down.

'Sorry.'

'Just get on with it, will you?' Robin shouted. 'Just stop jabbering and get on with it? Haven't I got enough to do without being questioned like you were

217

some damn journalist? I know what I'm doing and I can promise you that everything's for a reason and nothing's for fun!'

Zoe stooped over her bale again. Out of the corner of her eye she could see Eddie's small figure skittering for cover, away from trouble. She looked down at her hands and arms sticking out of the short black sleeves of her T-shirt, and they looked weird to her suddenly, white and thin and uncanny. She swallowed hard.

'Sorry,' she said again. 'I was only asking.'

Robin grunted and swung away from her into the dimness of the feed store. She followed him, carrying her bale, and dumped it precisely beside his.

'I'll finish these,' she said, not looking at him. 'I'll empty the Land Rover.'

There was a small silence. He took a step or two away.

'OK,' he said.

*   *   *

When she had emptied the Land Rover, she got into the driver's seat and sat looking at the dashboard. It was crammed with stuff, leaflets and chocolate-bar wrappers and squashed juice cartons and parking tickets and a small battered red notebook with 'Calf Management' scrawled on the cover. The passenger seat and the floor weren't much better, littered with straw and scraps of paper and oily rags. Over the back of the passenger seat, tossed all anyhow, was an old blue jersey, presumably Robin's jersey. Zoe pulled it down and bundled it loosely into her lap, like a cat, patting it down.

She put out a hand and touched the ignition. She nearly—but not quite—dared to turn the key. She

218

thought that, if only she could drive, she could take the Land Rover up to Dean Place Farm and collect the supper. Crisis or no crisis, Dilys was still making supper, and biscuits and cakes to take into Harry which Zoe thought he gave to the nurses. Dilys had even offered to teach Zoe to cook.

'What?'

'Well, you'll have to learn one day.'

'Will I?' Zoe said. 'What for?'

'For living,' Dilys said. 'For looking after yourself. For looking after other people. Can you turn out a room?'

Zoe grinned at her.

'Never heard of it.'

'Or iron a shirt?'

Zoe shook her head.

'I suppose,' Dilys said, 'you have these ideas that women shouldn't keep house any more.'

'No—'

'That it's all careers and so on.'

'I don't do it,' Zoe said, 'because I don't need to. When I need to, I should think I'll learn.'

Dilys had been over by the sink in her kitchen during this conversation, rinsing the dark heads of purple sprouting broccoli under the tap. She lifted her gaze and looked out of the window above the sink, and then said, in quite a different voice, 'When Harry comes home, maybe I could use some help. Maybe I could do with an extra pair of hands then.'

There was a pause.

'I see,' Zoe said.

She got off the edge of the table where she had been perching.

'That's different. I mean, if you need me to learn ironing, I'll learn.'

219

Two days later, Dilys had taught her to scramble eggs. It had been fine, Zoe thought, except for washing the pan. Washing the pan made you see the point, abruptly and forcefully, of sandwiches and plastic cartons of noodles and hamburgers in take-away boxes. She looked down at Robin's jersey in her lap. It had bits of straw caught in it, and frayed cuffs and a ragged hole. She picked it up and put her face in it. It just smelled of wool, dust and wool. She had been sorry when Robin shouted; not frightened but just sorry, plain sorry she'd made him shout. She didn't want to do anything to make him shout but rather the reverse instead. She picked the jersey up again and shook it out, as she had seen Dilys shaking out the laundry before hanging it on the clothesline, and then folded it and put it back over the passenger seat, patting it into place.

'What place,' Zoe thought suddenly. 'What place? What am I *doing*?'

* * *

'What's she doing here?' Debbie said. She had put Gareth's tea on the table. The children were eating theirs in front of the television. Debbie disapproved of this but today she had had enough of the children. She didn't care where they ate their tea, she didn't even much care if they ate tea at all, particularly Eddie. Eddie had discovered the bleach bottle which she had mistakenly left in the bathroom after cleaning, with the top insufficiently screwed on. He had filled his water pistol from it, and then aimed the pistol at his bedroom curtains, which Debbie had only made six months before, out of dark-blue cotton patterned with aeroplanes. Eddie had been

220

fascinated by the effect of the bleach trails on the dark-blue cotton, so fascinated that he had returned to the bathroom to refill his water pistol where Debbie caught him.

'I dunno,' Gareth said. He bent over his plate. 'I gave her a driving lesson on the tractor this afternoon.'

'*Gareth*,' Debbie said. 'Don't you damn well start—'

'Wasn't much good—'

'That's not what I mean.'

Gareth put in a forkful of chips and winked at her.

'Not my type. Looks like a boy.'

Debbie sat down opposite Gareth and poured herself some tea.

'What about Robin then?'

'What about Robin?'

'Robin and her?'

Gareth shrugged.

'Nothing as far as I can see. He gave her an earful this afternoon. He doesn't care who's here and who isn't right now. He doesn't notice.'

'I notice,' Debbie said.

'You and who else?'

'Velma,' Debbie said. 'Half the village.'

Gareth shook tomato sauce liberally over his plate.

'So what are you going to do about it?'

'You know what,' Debbie said, 'I want us to leave.'

Gareth sighed.

'I thought we'd been through all that. I thought you were going to help Lyndsay with the baby.'

'She's gone to stay with her mum.'

'She'll be back.'

'Gareth,' Debbie said, 'that's not the point. The point is, it's all changing. It isn't like it was once.'

Gareth took a swallow of tea.

'Look,' he said, 'I've got a good job. I don't mind the boss, this is a decent house, the kids are doing all right at school, you've got a job, we're settled.'

'I don't feel settled any more. I keep thinking something's going to happen. I think something will happen if we stay.'

'It's been nasty. A nasty patch, that's all—'

'*No*,' Debbie said. 'No. Things have *changed*. It'll never be the same again.'

He looked at her. Her blonde hair, which he'd always liked her to wear loose, was pulled back behind her head and tied with something, and it hardened her face, aged it. She was still good-looking, Gareth told himself, still a bit of a looker, but she'd changed, too, like her body had, and her mind and her attitudes. Ten years ago, she'd never have been like this. But then, ten years ago, she'd hardly had any kids, only Rebecca as a baby. She'd been chuffed to bits with that baby, she was like a doll to her with all her little clothes and stuff. But she got worried now. Those three kids had made her worried. They'd changed her, just as having them had changed the way she looked. He put his hand out across the table.

'Can we wait?' he said.

'What d'you mean?'

'Can we wait a bit before we think about it seriously? Can we wait a few weeks?'

She looked at his hand. It never did, she had discovered, to think in too much detail about where Gareth's hands had been that day.

'You mean until something else happens—'

'Maybe.'

222

She sighed. She picked up her mug and looked into it.

'All right,' she said.

*　　　*　　　*

When Robin came in, in the evening, Zoe had decided she wouldn't say anything much. She wouldn't sulk, but she wouldn't emphasise her presence either. She would just be there. In fact, when she heard the kitchen door slam, and then, almost immediately, the murmur of the television, she was upstairs in her bedroom, clipping her nails where they'd been broken heaving the straw bales. It didn't matter. They'd been too long anyway. She'd taken to growing them too long to emphasise to herself the admirable fact that she didn't bite them any more.

When she went down to the kitchen, Robin was standing on one leg, half out of his boiler suit, staring at the television. He turned slightly as she came in.

'Hi.'

'Hi,' Zoe said.

Robin pulled off the last leg of his overalls and bent to pick them off the floor. He said, over his shoulder, 'Sorry I bawled you out, earlier.'

'It doesn't matter,' Zoe said. 'I asked too many questions. At the wrong time.'

She moved over towards the cooker where she had left, on instructions from Dilys, two baked potatoes and a casserole.

'I think,' Zoe said, 'I'd better go. Back to London. I didn't mean to be in the way but I think I am.' She opened the oven door and reached gingerly inside. 'Would you like me to go?'

There was a pause. She heard Robin move a chair and sit down on it, to put on his shoes.

223

'We start making silage on Monday, dawn to dusk, all hands to the plough. We—we could use all help.'

Zoe straightened up, shutting the oven door.

'But I don't think I'm very useful.'

He looked directly at her, for the first time since her arrival.

'No,' he said. He was grinning. 'But you could be.'

'Did Gareth tell you about the tractor?'

'No, but I can imagine. Better next time.'

Zoe leaned against the cooker.

'You don't have to be kind. I came uninvited and I can go away the same way. I only want you to be honest.'

'I'm not being kind,' Robin said. He stood up, and leaned across the table to turn the television off.

'I'd like to be kind,' Zoe said. 'I'd like to help. I'd like to make you feel better.'

Robin sat down again, half turned away from her, riffling through some papers at his elbow.

'You'd have a job on. Quite apart from everything else, I've now had a fine imposed by the River Authority. Twelve hundred pounds and instructions to improve the slurry disposal within six months. Or else. Legal summons and all that.' He put his hand up and ruffled his hair. 'Sometimes I think—' he said, and then he stopped.

'It's a bugger,' Zoe said. 'Isn't it? A complete bugger.'

'I can't think where it all comes from,' Robin said, his voice almost inaudible. 'It seems now we've turned the tap on, we can't stop it, I can't—'

Zoe straightened up. Very quietly she moved across the kitchen and stood very close to Robin's chair, not touching him, but almost.

'I think,' she said, and her voice was quite matter of
224

fact, 'that you haven't turned it on for years.'

He looked up at her sharply. She herself looked as she always looked, and not remotely sentimental.

'When did you last have sex?' Zoe said.

He blinked. Startled into frankness, he said, 'Last year.'

'Where?'

'After the Smithfield Show. In London.'

'With a hooker?'

'No,' Robin said, amazing himself, 'with a girl from the Ministry. Fisheries Department if I remember correctly.'

Zoe moved very slightly and then lowered herself on to Robin's knees. She put her arms around his neck. He didn't move. He simply let her.

'I could be useful. *There*, at least.'

He was almost laughing. He was also, he noticed, putting his arms tentatively round her in return, shaking.

'Why—'

'I'd like to,' Zoe said. Her face was inches from his. 'Wouldn't you?'

'But I'm old,' Robin said. '*Old*. Too old for you. I'm old enough to be your bloody *father*—'

'So?'

'So it's indecent.'

'For you?'

'No, stupid, no—'

'I'll decide, thank you,' Zoe said, 'what's decent for me and what isn't. On the whole, what isn't is going to bed with crap boyfriends. Age doesn't come into it. You're shaking.'

'Of course I am,' he said. He tightened his hold on her, pulling her in so that their faces were pressed together, cheek against cheek. Damn, he thought, I

225

need shaving, I need a shave—'

'You had a bad time,' Zoe said, over his shoulder, 'didn't you? All those years. A bad time.'

'Not her fault—'

'Not yours either.'

She moved a hand up into his hair. He said, 'This is crazy.'

'Not as crazy,' she said serenely, 'as separate bedrooms.'

'I don't want to be a dirty old man—'

'I'll be the judge of that.'

'Hell,' Robin said. 'Oh *hell*—'

He dropped his face so that he could push it into her shoulder, into the dark grey wool of her jersey over her young and bony shoulder. The tears were coming, thick and fast and unstoppable.

'Sorry,' Robin said, gasping. 'Sorry. Oh Zoe, sorry—'

She said nothing at all. She sat there on his knees with his arms around her, and hers holding his head and neck, and waited while he wept. Then she got up and went over to the roll of kitchen paper pattened with smudgily printed mushrooms that Velma had bought in the village shop, and tore off a long strip.

'Here,' she said, holding it out.

He blew his nose ferociously.

She said, 'Don't say anything. There's nothing to say.'

He blew again. She waited until he had finished and then she sat down on his knees again.

'Where were we?'

'God knows,' Robin said, putting his arms around her. He was laughing weakly, 'God knows—'

She regarded him.

'Your nose is red.'

226

He nodded. He closed his eyes. She leaned forward and licked his nose and then kissed him slowly and softly on the mouth.

'Luckily,' Zoe said, 'it isn't your nose I'm much interested in.'

CHAPTER FOURTEEN

The ambulance came into the yard at Dean Place Farm and stopped by Dilys's flower tubs. There was in it, besides the driver in his precisely ironed pale-blue shirt, a nursing auxiliary, also in uniform, and Harry. Harry was in a wheelchair. He was dressed in clothes Dilys had taken in the day before, except for his feet which were in bedroom slippers. Dilys couldn't think why the sight of his slippers was so offensive. She'd taken his shoes in yesterday, his brown brogue shoes which she'd polished. Why couldn't they have put his shoes on, instead of slippers?

'Hello, dear,' she said.

She stood at the foot of the ramp they had let down at the back of the ambulance. Harry looked very small to her, smaller than ever.

'There we go,' the auxiliary said to Harry, releasing the wheelchair brake. 'Ready for the ride?'

They needed the bed at Stretton Hospital, they'd said to Dilys. Harry had stopped losing weight, had actually gained a pound or two, and he'd gain more once he was up and about. It wasn't good for him to be in bed any longer. It was time for him to come home.

'That's OK, isn't it?' Zoe had said to Dilys. 'I'll

come up when he comes back. I'll be here when the ambulance comes.'

But she wasn't, and Dilys's pride had forbidden her to ring Tideswell and ask why not.

'You'll need help,' Zoe had said. 'You'll need help getting him out of that wheelchair. I'll help you.'

She did need help. She actually, though her mind shrank from admitting it, needed help that was nothing to do with the physical. She needed Zoe there as a diverson to reconcile her to having Harry back; Harry, and not Joe. She thought Zoe understood this. It was odd, really, with Zoe being the last sort of person Dilys would ever have, in her right mind, dreamed of relying on. But there was something about her that suited the moment, fitted Dilys's need, soothed Dilys's anguish at finding herself so helpless.

The wheelchair came down the ramp and into the yard.

'There's someone in the kitchen who'll be pleased to see you,' Dilys said.

She put a hand on his shoulder. She couldn't kiss him, especially not in front of the ambulance men. There was a brief mad gleam of hope in Harry's eyes and then it died and he said, 'Kep? Old Kep?'

She nodded. The auxiliary began to wheel Harry towards the open back door.

'I thought Zoe was coming. She said she would.'

Harry said, 'In the hospital they asked if she was my granddaughter.'

'She's been good,' Dilys said. She pushed the back door flat against the wall to allow the chair to be wheeled through.

'We've got a diet sheet,' the auxiliary said, 'and a walking frame. Haven't we?'

'I'm not using no frame,' Harry said. 'I've got
228

sticks. I've got my old dad's sticks. Sticks is what I'll use.'

The auxiliary winked at Dilys.

'Frames are steadier—'

'I don't want to be steady,' Harry said. 'I don't want no more molly-coddling.'

In the kitchen, Kep rose creaking from his bed and came towards Harry, heavy with relief, wagging and grunting.

'There's a lad,' Harry said, touching his head. 'All right, boy? All right then?'

The auxiliary took a sheaf of neatly folded papers out of his uniform pocket and laid them on the kitchen table.

'All the forms—'

'What forms?'

'For the loan of the chair and the walking frame, dear. Hospital property.'

'You can take them now,' Dilys said. 'We don't want them. Help him into his chair by the table and take that thing away.'

The auxiliary looked at her.

'You'd be better, you know, for ten days or so—'

'No, thank you,' Dilys said. It was alarming to kick away the props but it had to be done. If Zoe had been there, she wouldn't have had a single qualm. 'You take them back. We'll manage.' She looked at Harry. 'He's only seventy-one, you know. He isn't a hundred.'

The auxiliary shrugged. He picked up all the forms but one, a sheet of pale-green paper printed in neat columns.

'I'll leave you the diet sheet, then.'

'I'm a farmer's wife,' Dilys said. 'Do you think I don't know about nutrition?'

229

The auxiliary sighed.

'As you say,' he said and then added with an edge of exasperation, 'Madam.'

He went back out into the yard, clumping Harry on the shoulder as he went. They heard him calling for the driver.

'Do you want that thing?' Dilys said to Harry, pointing at the wheelchair. He shook his head.

'I got your sticks out. Zoe polished them. The blackthorn and your father's with the stag-horn handle.'

The ambulance men came back into the kitchen.

'OK then,' the driver said to Harry. 'All for independence then, squire? Which is your chair? That one? Very well, squire, that one you shall have.'

Dilys watched as the two of them stooped and lifted Harry smoothly from the wheelchair and into his accustomed wooden carver at the head of the kitchen table. He looked so light in their hands, as if he were made of paper or balsa wood, light and perishable.

'You going to manage, dear?' the driver said to Dilys. 'Baths and the toilet and all that?'

'He's going to manage himself,' Dilys said. 'He's home and he's going to get better.'

'Better take it easy for a day or two. Better have a bit of help, just for a while—'

'I have help,' Dilys said. 'She couldn't be here this morning, but I have help.'

'Good,' the driver said. 'That's the way.' He gave Harry a wave. 'Cheerio, squire. Take care.'

The auxiliary looked at Dilys. She was plainly on his mind.

'You sure?'

She nodded emphatically. 'Thank you for bringing

him home.'

They grinned.

'All in a day's work,' the driver said. 'No problem.'

They went out into the yard and could be heard banging up the ramp and the rear doors of the ambulance, and then the driver and passenger doors slammed and the engine started.

'They're off then,' Harry said. 'They're going.'

He was leaning forward, his hands clasped in his lap. Dilys couldn't look at him. The ambulance turned slowly in the yard, reversing, as everyone always reversed, towards the old poultry-feed store, and then drove away, its engine getting fainter and fainter as its sound was swallowed up by the hedges either side of the lane, and then by distance.

In the kitchen, neither of them moved. It was quite silent, except for old Kep, panting under the table where he lay across Harry's feet.

Harry looked at Dilys.

'Lyndsay back yet?'

'No.'

'Men in today? Men from the agency?'

'No,' Dilys said. 'Robin sacked them. He's trying to sort something else out this morning.'

'Bad, that,' Harry said. 'Bad, with silage starting next week.'

Dilys said nothing. Harry went on looking at her.

'So there's no one?' he said. His hands moved a little in his lap. 'No one but you and me?'

*   *   *

Velma left her bike where she always did, leaning against the fence by the back door at Tideswell Farm. She propped it up with a brick under the pedal and

231

then put an old supermarket plastic bag over the saddle in case it should come on to rain. There were, as Caro and then Robin had endlessly pointed out to her, plenty of places nearby where Velma could put her bike under cover, but, as with electricity, Velma preferred to do things her own way, and to leave her bike in the open, in a particular spot, with its saddle shrouded in a supermarket bag.

She took another bag out of her bike basket. It contained, at Robin's request, a box of cornflakes, a carton of orange juice, a loaf of bread and a jar of marmalade. The loaf was sliced white and both the juice and the marmalade were the cheapest the village shop provided. Velma couldn't vouch for their quality but then, their quality wasn't of any consequence. Robin didn't notice and anything was good enough for that girl, that girlfriend of Judy's. When Velma had looked up at the house as she parked her bike, she'd seen that Zoe's bedroom curtains were still drawn across. Nine o'clock in the morning and still in bed and on a Thursday. Sundays would have been different, Sundays were excusable for a lie-in, but not Thursdays. Velma opened the back door. Better not, maybe, think about Sundays. Sundays were, as far as her husband and son and son-in-law were concerned, days for lounging about half dressed until noon and then going down to the pub and coming home legless three hours later to snore in the front room. It meant she had her daughters and her daughter-in-law round her neck all Sunday, smoking and moaning. She dumped the carrier bag on Robin's kitchen table. Sundays had come to be almost the worst day of the week.

The little red light on the telephone-answering machine was winking and the liquid crystal display

232

said that there were three messages. Velma considered whether to play them back and decided not. That madam upstairs could do it when she deigned to appear. It was, after all, one of the few things she could do, apart from take up space. Debbie said she was being quite a help up at Dean Place, but Velma doubted it. She couldn't see that Zoe could possibly be a help anywhere, she'd never met a girl that useless except perhaps for Patsy who'd married her Kevin and spent her whole life whining for fitted carpets and holidays in Ibiza. Kevin had to come home if he wanted a square meal since Patsy refused to do more than open packets. Patsy and Zoe, Velma thought, looking resignedly into the sink, were two of a kind, and not a kind she had any time for. If you weren't even going to wash a casserole dish, what prevented you from even running water into it to stop everything sticking on hard? At least the casserole had been eaten. Robin must have eaten a decent meal at last because Zoe wouldn't have eaten it. Zoe lived on rubbish, like Patsy did. Good food was wasted on someone like Zoe.

Velma ran hot water into the sink and attempted, as she did every morning, to marshal the chaos of papers on the table into some kind of order.

'Putting mess into squares,' Caro had called it. 'Makes you feel better, somehow, doesn't it? As if you're in control and not the muddles.'

Velma thought of Caro most days, whether she wanted to or not. It was something about the house, she supposed, being the place where Caro had lived all those years. Women did leave their mark on houses, even houses they didn't like, and Caro hadn't liked Tideswell. But she'd somehow had to live there, all the same. She'd been a puzzle to Velma. Nice to work for, considerate, but not quite with you, somehow, always a bit, well, foreign. She'd never belonged. Even if she'd never got that tumour and had lived to be an old lady, she'd never have belonged. Not like Joe. Joe had belonged, through and through. Velma still couldn't think of him without wanting to cry her eyes out.

She added washing-up liquid to the sink of hot water and whipped it up to a foam with a bottle brush. She'd thought she'd leave everything there for a while, to soak, and she'd go upstairs and give the bathroom a bit of a go, loudly, to wake that dratted girl up. Robin left the bathroom like a pigsty every morning anyway, you'd have thought he brought half the farm home with him every day. It had never been like that when Caro was alive. But then Caro had been an American, and Americans had strict notions of hygiene and dream bathrooms, she'd seen them in magazines and on the television.

Velma collected her cloths and spray bottles from under the sink, and went slowly upstairs. There was a shoe on the stairs, or a boot rather, one of the ugly great things Zoe wore. Velma picked it up, and then put it down again. Zoe could pick it up for herself. Velma climbed on and emerged on to the landing. All the bedroom doors were open, except Zoe's and the one that had been Caro's. Velma could see that Robin hadn't made his bed, she could see the end of it, all tossed and rumpled, and the duvet half on the floor. Most days he made an attempt, at least, to straighten it. Perhaps today he'd been in an extra rush what with having to turn those fellows off from Dean Place and now find replacements. She thought she'd just go in and make his bed for him before she started on the bathroom. He had, she reflected, a lot

234

on his plate just now.

She put her cloths and bottles down on the floor outside the bathroom and went into Robin's bedroom. Only one set of curtains was drawn back; the others, at the window closest to the bed, were still pulled across. Velma looked at the bed. It wasn't made at all, and it wasn't empty either. Zoe was in it, fast asleep, with her back to Velma, her dark-red head deep in the pillows. It was warm in the room, with the sun coming in through the east window, and Zoe had pushed the bedclothes down; not very far down, but quite far enough to reveal to Velma that she was completely naked.

*   *   *

'I came to see how you are,' Robin said.

He sat in Lyndsay's parents' sitting room in his usual position, on the edge of an armchair with his elbows on his knees. He looked, Lyndsay thought, different, though she couldn't quite define why. Less tired, somehow, less unhappily preoccupied.

'I'm OK,' she said.

Hughie sat on the floor at her feet. He wore his baseball cap and boots his grandfather had bought him, tough-boy boots of brown suede with brass eyelets where the laces went. He found these boots quite amazing. He couldn't recognise his feet in them at all. Some distance away, Rose was taking books out of a bookcase, rapidly and rapturously, supposing it to be forbidden. Her excited guilty pleasure made her, temporarily at least, very quiet.

'When are you coming back?'

Hughie looked up from his boots.

'Soon,' Lyndsay said.

'We've got a lot to talk over,' Robin said. 'There's a lot to be sorted. Dad came home this morning.'

'Oh,' Lyndsay said. She looked down at her lap. 'I'm not sure I'll be staying—'

'Where?'

'At Dean Place.'

Robin leaned forward.

'Not staying?'

'I don't know,' Lyndsay said. 'It's only an idea, an idea my parents had. Of—of a new life, in a way. A new life for me.'

'Lyndsay,' Robin said, 'you own fifty-two per cent of the shares in that farm. Joe's shares are your shares.'

'I—I'm not sure that I want them.'

Robin got up and crossed the thick, pale patterned carpet to the sofa where Lyndsay sat. He sat down beside her.

'You can't think like that.'

She looked sideways at him.

'Lyndsay,' Robin said, 'you can't decide something like this so soon. In a way it isn't even your decision.' He glanced down at Hughie. 'There's him, and there's Rose. Farms—' He paused. 'Farms aren't like other businesses, they aren't, in a way, ours to get rid of. I suppose it's because they're a way of life.'

'And death,' Lyndsay whispered. She turned a little on the sofa, so that she was half towards Robin. 'I don't think I can face it.'

'What?'

'Taking it on. Dealing with your parents.'

'I said,' Robin said, with a touch of his old weariness, 'I said I'd help you.'

'Will you? Will you really stand by me?'

'Why else do you think I've come? Why on earth,

236

with about a million things screaming to be done, should I come all the way into Stretton unless it's to see you and prove I meant what I said?'

'It would make a difference,' Lyndsay said. 'But I don't know—'

'I know,' Robin said, 'and you're not selling those shares.'

'You could buy them.'

'I can't. And I don't want them. I don't want all that arable.'

He stood up. She stood, too, more slowly. Behind them, Hughie crawled up on to the sofa and lay across the cushions where they had been sitting.

'But you must come home,' Robin said. 'You must come back.'

'Yes,' Hughie said.

'Soon. Tomorrow or the next day.'

'I could,' Lyndsay said, looking up at Robin. 'I could, now I know you'll help me.'

'I *said*—'

'I know. But I was so emotional then, you could have said anything, just to pacify me. But today is different. I believe you today. It was nice of you to come.'

He stooped to kiss her cheek. She put her arms up and held him for a moment.

She said, 'Is Zoe still there? At Tideswell?'

He stiffened slightly under her hands.

'Yes.'

'Is she a nuisance?'

'No,' Robin said. His voice sounded odd, slightly constrained. 'She's actually been pretty good with Mum.'

'So I heard.'

Robin stepped back, to release himself.

237

'You give me a call. About coming home.'
'I will.'
He looked down at Hughie, on the sofa.
'You keep her to it, old son. OK?'

*   *   *

Gareth, in the store beside the milking parlour where Robin kept all the drugs and foot-treating equipment for the cows, was testing a balling gun. He hadn't used it for a year almost, since the herd was last out at grass, but Robin had left instructions that the heifers were to be dosed with an anti-worm bolus before they were turned out. Half a dozen boxes of the bolus were stacked nearby, clean and white and medical-looking in the cobwebby muddle of the store. Robin never threw anything away. There must be stuff up there on those shelves past their use-by dates by a decade. Gareth slapped the gun against his palm. He could do with another pair of hands, shooting the pills down all those reluctant throats. Maybe Zoe could help. He'd ask her when he went over for his mid-morning break.

'*Well*,' Velma said from the doorway.

Gareth turned round. Velma was standing there, hands hanging down, in her usual uniform of leggings, daps, and tunic jersey.

'What's up then?' Gareth said.

'I went up,' Velma said. 'I went up to make Robin's bed and all, and there she was.' She sounded out of breath.

Gareth's face lit up.

'Zoe?'

'In his bed,' Velma said. 'In Robin's *bed*. Fast asleep and mother naked.'

238

Gareth grinned.

'Robin there, too?'

Velma said vehemently, 'She didn't stir. She didn't even flicker an eyelash. I knew it. I *knew* it would happen. I saw it coming a mile off. Who does she think she is?'

'Young,' Gareth said. He felt oddly stirred by the news. 'Willing.'

Velma snorted.

'Willing, all right. Set her cap at him from the start.'

Gareth stuck the balling gun into a pocket of his overalls.

'Takes two to tango.'

'You men—'

'Give him a break,' Gareth said. 'Will you? Just give him a break.' He stepped forward and thrust his face at Velma. 'Debbie and I came here when Kevin was a baby, eight years ago, and I can tell you Caro was in her own bedroom by then. Eight years ago. Maybe she'd moved out of his room years before that, *years*. What's he had to put up with then? And you ever heard a word about him locally? One word? All these years.'

Velma looked at him. She drew a huge breath.

'Well, they're going to hear now.'

'Not from you, Velma Simms—'

'It's my *business*,' Velma said. 'I work here. I've been looking after Robin and this house since long before you came.' She put a finger up to Gareth. 'Don't get me wrong. I've no objection to Robin settling down. Fact is, I'd like it. I'd like to see this house with a woman in it again, I'd like to see him looked after. But it's this little bitch. Who is she, I'd like to know? Just someone Judy's picked up in

239

London. I knew she'd be trouble, I knew it from the beginning. And I'm right. Robin'll make a fool of himself, you see if I'm not right, you just *see*.'

Gareth turned away and began to fiddle with the boxes and bottles on the dusty shelves of the store. It occurred to him to say that Zoe wasn't trouble, that she wasn't playing games, that in an odd way there was far less malice to Zoe than there was to Velma or any of the other women in Dean Cross, or even to his Debbie. But there wouldn't be any point saying such things. No point at all. Velma would just say he'd got an itch for Zoe himself and in a way, she'd be right. To look at, Zoe was nothing, nothing at all. But there was something about her you couldn't help fancying, something free, a bit oddball. It had occurred to Gareth once or twice that, if you were involved with Zoe, she'd stay free, somehow, she wouldn't start clinging and making demands. In fact, in any kind of relationship with Zoe it might well be the other way about.

'You leave them alone,' Gareth said. 'You leave them be. She'll do no harm and he deserves a bit of nookie.' He paused and then he said, surprising himself, 'She probably makes him laugh.'

'Laugh?' Velma said. 'Laugh? What's laughing got to do with it?'

'A lot,' Gareth said. He had a sudden vision of all those recent sessions at home, all those half-tearful pleadings from Debbie to find a new job, to get away from Tideswell, to escape what she increasingly insisted was a curse. His voice rose to a shout. 'A lot! A whole bloody lot, you interfering old cow!'

*   *   *

240

On the way back to Dean Place Farm, Rose went to sleep in her baby seat. Lyndsay could see her in the driving mirror, bright pink with warmth and drowsiness, her big pale-curled head bobbing and lolling, and her arms stuck straight out sideways, like a rag doll. One arm brushed Hughie every so often as the car swayed round corners, and as he was strapped into his own car seat, he couldn't avoid it. Lyndsay saw him pressing himself away from Rose into the far side of his seat, away from the possibility of being touched by her. Even asleep, she was confident, and her confidence quite simply offended him.

Lyndsay's parents had been very surprised at her sudden decision to go home. In fact they'd been slightly shocked, as if she was behaving discourteously and ungratefully after all they'd done for her and for the children. Lyndsay's father had said, looking at Hughie, 'But we were planning to go swimming, weren't we?'

'Another time,' Lyndsay said. She said that Robin's visit had made her feel she was making everything worse for Joe's family, that decisions had to be made and they were decisions that couldn't be made without her. Her father had asked what Joe's shares in the farm were worth. Robin had said a lot.

'But they don't own the farm,' Lyndsay's father said, 'do they?'

No, she had said, they didn't. She didn't understand it. Robin had said several things she didn't understand. He said he really needed over a million pounds of capital to farm comfortably the way he did, which was why he was so in debt and why he couldn't buy any of Joe's shares. She had gazed at him. It meant nothing to her. Money in millions was not compassable, especially when they lived so

241

decently, modestly even, compared with the kind of lives one usually associated with having millions. In farming, she supposed, the millions didn't go on anything a wife and children could see; they went on land and machinery and buildings and stock which then all ended up belonging to the bank anyhow. Yet whatever she did or didn't understand, Robin had made her feel she must go back and decide something, face to face. It was referring to Hughie that had done it, Hughie and Rose.

'Are you asleep?' Lyndsay said to Hughie.

'No.'

'Are you pleased to be going home?'

Hughie nodded. He wondered whether to ask if Daddy would be there and decided against it, simply because Lyndsay always said no, he wouldn't, and Hughie didn't much want to hear her say it again, for the hundredth time. He waved Seal in the air.

'Seal, too.'

'You can go to playgroup in the morning.'

'Perhaps,' Hughie said.

'Maybe Mary will be there. Maybe Mary'll have come to welcome us home.'

Hughie looked out of the window. There were fields out there again, fields and some sheep. At Granny Sylvia's house there were no sheep, and when you ran about in her garden, you had to run quite carefully. It was difficult to be an aeroplane in that garden.

'There,' Lyndsay said, 'the church and the shop.'

Rose's swinging arm caught Hughie lightly on the shoulder.

'Ow,' he said loudly, right at her, to wake her up.

She opened her eyes very slowly and looked at him, adjusting herself from sleep. Her expression was as it

242

always was, whatever she looked at, full of calm and determination. She rubbed a hand across her face, squashing her nose. Then she gave a little shout.

'Home!' Lyndsay said, mistaking her.

The car turned off the road down the lane towards Dean Place. Across the field to his right, Hughie could see his house, looking as it always did, always would.

'Out!' Rose yelled, tugging at the webbing straps of her baby seat. 'Out, out, out, *out*!'

'In a minute—'

Mary had hung some washing out, Lyndsay could see it, sheets and a towel or two, and a row of yellow dusters. How kind of her, how kind when she was only ever supposed to babysit once in a while, once in a blue moon when Lyndsay and Joe went out, really out ... Lyndsay bit her lip and changed down a gear to drive up the smooth ramp towards the house, parking where she'd always parked for years, sometimes several times a day, after going to the village, going to Hughie's playgroup, going to Dean Place and Tideswell, going to the supermarket, going to see Caro in hospital, going out, coming back, going out, coming back, and now coming back in a way she'd never even contemplated, a way that was so hard that she thought for a moment she mightn't be able to get out of the car.

'Out!' Rose bellowed.

'Let her,' Hughie said, turning his face away. 'Oh just let her—'

Lyndsay climbed slowly out of the car and then stooped in through one of the back doors to release Rose. Rose, breathing heavily, kicked and thrashed, desperate to be on the ground, to be independent.

'Careful,' Lyndsay said. 'Wait—' She propped

243

Rose on one hip and put her key into the lock of the back door. Inside the back door was the little lobby they had designed so carefully, a lobby for boots and coats and shovels, and fishing rods. Joe's boots still stood there, his old boots, the ones he'd said were leaking round the foot welt. He'd been wearing his newer ones that day, of course, and then they'd gone with him, to the police station, to the morgue, and then to wherever Joe had gone after that, to the empty place where Lyndsay couldn't follow.

She opened the door to the kitchen. It was tidy and shining. Lyndsay put Rose down on the floor and went back for Hughie.

'Seal likes you,' Hughie said.

'Oh good. I like Seal, too.'

She unbuckled his straps and lifted him on to the ground beside the car.

'In you go.'

He put his face up, sniffing like a little animal, recognising familiarity. She watched him trot into the house ahead of her, suddenly full of purpose, almost of certainty. The telephone was ringing. Lyndsay leaned into the car to retrieve her handbag and then ran into the house, stumbling over Rose to get to the telephone before it stopped.

'Hello?' she said. 'Hello? Dean Place Cottage.'

Rose stopped taking potatoes out of the vegetable rack and looked up, her attention caught by the eternal potential of a telephone call.

'Oh,' Lyndsay said. 'Velma. Yes, yes, I've just walked through the door, just this minute—'

She paused. Rose put a potato in her mouth and then took it out again, frowning. Her mouth was smudged with earth.

'Oh dear,' Lyndsay said. 'Oh heavens, oh *dear*—'

244

Rose put the potato down and began to crawl rapidly towards the sitting-room door.

'Dear, dear!' she shouted. Her fat hands slapped on the floor. 'Dear, dear, dear, dear, *dear!*'

CHAPTER FIFTEEN

Judy sat on a bench in St James's Park, holding a plastic bottle of mineral water. At the other end of the bench, an old man was asleep, a rather seedy and shabby old man whom Judy had already resolved she would abandon if he woke up and became conversational. She had not come into the park for conversation; she had come into the park to think.

Ahead of her two willow trees were brushing the grass with their long soft fronds, and beyond them was the flat shine of the water. It was a prospect Judy knew extremely well since the park was only fifteen minutes' walk from the edge of Soho, where her office was, and she often came there because it was green and you could breathe. When she had first come to London, she had avoided the parks, almost elaborately, as if defying all rural associations of any kind, but gradually, she had found herself in them, and noticing the trees, almost without meaning to be there. She had got to know St James's Park very well, and the best-placed benches and the regular people who came there. But today, sitting on her second favourite bench—a boy with an immense red backpack was stretched out asleep on the best one—nothing, however well known, looked familiar. She might, she thought, have been looking at it all for the first time.

She unscrewed the top of the mineral-water bottle and took a swallow. The water was too warm, which made it taste somehow less clean. Last night Lyndsay had telephoned. She had telephoned in something of a state, not tearful, but over-excited, wired up, to say that Zoe had started sleeping with Robin, that Velma had found her, stark-naked, in Robin's bed at nine o'clock in the morning.

Lyndsay had sounded outraged. Even in the midst of her own enormous reaction, Judy couldn't help noticing that Lyndsay sounded very much like a wronged wife.

'How dare she?' Lyndsay had cried. 'How dare she? Just come down here, uninvited, and take him over like that?'

When Judy had put the telephone down, she had felt quite extraordinary. She didn't know whether she was angry or offended or simply shocked. She couldn't decide if she felt she had been exploited or if she'd been betrayed. She couldn't analyse what she felt for a very long time beyond the unquestionable realisation that she'd known all along that this might happen, and that part of her, at some level, had simply been waiting until it did.

She had tried to ring Oliver, but he had had to go out to dinner with a client from the gallery and wasn't back yet. She wasn't at all sure what she was going to say to him, she just urgently needed to tell him what had happened and to hear his reaction, if only to see whether it tallied with any of the things she thought she was feeling. When she finally spoke to him, around midnight, he sounded almost offhand.

'So?' he'd said, 'what else did you think would happen?'

'But it's my *father*—'

'And,' Oliver said quietly, 'my ex-girlfriend.'

The conversation had stopped soon after that. There'd either been nothing much more to say, or far too much. And there was certainly a lot of thinking to do, thinking that had preoccupied Judy half the night, and which had driven her at one point to go into Zoe's room and stare intently, almost fiercely, at Zoe's few and impersonal possessions, to see if a clue lay there as to what Zoe was after.

It couldn't just be sex. Could it? In Zoe's life, in Zoe's world, sex wasn't a big deal; you just had some when you wanted some. Simple. But with *Robin*? Thinking about Zoe and Robin made Judy think of Robin disconcertingly as a man, a man who was capable of sex, a man who might actually at that very moment be having sex, with Zoe, at Tideswell Farm. Judy had always tried not to think about sex as being in any way connected with her parents—their separate bedrooms were simply a fact, always had been, and her sympathies had always lain with Caro, because Caro had subconsciously asked for them, had laid subtle emphasis upon her own differentness, her fastidiousness, her liability to become sullied by the grosser mortals among whom she now dwelt. It struck Judy with an angry shame that she had never thought of Robin from Robin's point of view, so seduced had she been by Caro's, and then with an even greater wave of feeling that Zoe had seen what she had not and had imagined what she had declined to visualise. Zoe had wanted something, and in her straightforward way had gone out to get it. But it wasn't as simple as that, it wasn't as selfish. Pushing her thumbs into the sides of the mineral-water bottle so that the plastic dimpled with small cracking sounds, Judy had to admit that Zoe had shown

247

compassion. Unmesmerised by either the presence or memory of Caro, Zoe had seen Robin's situation for what it was and had had sympathy. He was just a human being to her, a nice bloke in a delicate but deep kind of trouble. So she'd gone in there, to help, and to get something she was after, too, in the process. And in so doing, whether she had intended to or not, she had made Judy, quite purely and simply, jealous.

*　　*　　*

At Stretton Market, the young auctioneer who usually dealt with the calves told Robin he thought there'd be a falling trade on the week. He peered at the trailer in which seven bull calves and two barren cows waited to be unloaded.

'Friesians'll average a hundred and twenty, maybe. Sixty or so more for top grade. Got a Belgian Blue in there? They'll do better. Averaged nearly two-fifty last week. Prices are always on the move with the change from yard to grass cattle in the summer.'

'I'd like a hundred and forty for these,' Robin said. 'Minimum.'

The auctioneer grinned. He was a cheerful, quick-witted young man who, when he wasn't selling off cattle, did farm valuations, quotations on buildings and change of land use and pipelines. He had been to Joe's funeral, Robin had seen him standing beside Stretton's chief agricultural auctioneer, respectful in a dark suit and a Mid-Mercia Farmers' Co-operative tie.

He said now, to Robin, 'How's your old man?'

'Picking up,' Robin said. 'But it's slow. Very slow.'

'Will he be able to carry on?'

Robin sighed.

'I don't know. I honestly don't know. It's a hand-to-mouth arrangement right now, but I can't push him—'

'And you?'

Robin looked away, in case his extraordinary lightness of heart should show in his eyes.

'By all accounts,' the auctioneer said, his voice a mixture of teasing and envious admiration, 'not so bad.'

Robin groaned.

'You can't change your socks in peace round here—'

'You should be so lucky,' the auctioneer said. 'You should be so bloody lucky. The rest of us spend our lives chasing the skirt and a bit of it just walks straight into yours. Luck? It's indecent.'

Robin muttered something. The auctioneer gave him a quick slap on the shoulder with the clipboard he was holding.

'It's only envy. I'm just choked with it, green as grass.'

He went off, whistling, towards the auction ring. Robin released the catches at the back of the trailer, and lowered the ramp to the ground. The two barren cows peered mournfully at him through the slatted retaining screen. One of them had been sickly all her life, a feeble calf, then a dispirited heifer and now a sunken-eyed cow with poor lungs, her great wet nose always festooned with loops of phlegm. He shouldn't have kept her this long, he shouldn't have let her get this far, but it was hard, when you'd bred an animal, not to keep giving them one more chance, not to hope that one more costly round of antibiotics would do

249

the trick. It was the vet who had sealed her fate really, saying that she must go while she still had something left, before she succumbed to summer mastitis and became truly ill as well as worthless.

'It's called cutting your losses,' the vet said.

'I know,' Robin said. 'I've been cutting them all my life.'

Except in one respect, at this particular moment. It hardly seemed safe to reflect upon it, so used had Robin become to one trouble being relentlessly followed by another, but he appeared to have been awarded a bonus, a gift, a prize almost, for uncomplaining endurance and quiet persistence. When he had woken the morning after Zoe had first taken him to bed, he had lain in the clear dawn light and looked at her for some time with delight, relief and amazement. He had to tell himself, over and over again, that that really *was* a girl in his bed, a warm, breathing, naked girl, and that she had been there all night and had, when out of some obscure sense of belated propriety he had suggested she should go back to her own room, declined to leave.

'Why?' she said. 'Why? What have you got to hide?'

Then she had gone to sleep against him as easily as if she had been sleeping there for years, and when he had lunged out at the alarm clock, fearful of it waking her, she hadn't stirred. He had lifted himself on one elbow, to crane over her and see her face.

'Nice,' she'd said, after they'd made love. 'Really *nice.*' She was smiling then. Something of the smile still lingered, in her sleep, seven hours later. He'd bent to kiss her ear, with its fringe of silver hoops, and thought, swinging himself out of bed on the far side, that to leave his bed, his own bed, on an ordinary

250

weekday morning with a girl still asleep in it was something he had never, in his wildest dreams, thought could ever, ever happen to him.

But it had. It had happened that night, and the next, and all the subsequent nights. Zoe continued to keep her sparse black wardrobe in her own bedroom, but she slept in his. She seemed perfectly comfortable, trailing yawning out of the bathroom damply wrapped in a towel, nicking his pillows, pushing herself against him to get settled in bed, peacefully conversational.

'Velma's got the hump,' he'd said to her last night.

Zoe had been in the bath, holding one foot out of the water to inspect the length of her toenails.

'Well, you'd expect that. Wouldn't you? I spell urban decay to her. I'm poison. I'm corrupting you.'

'Without doubt,' Robin said, smiling at himself in the mirror above the basin. 'I think she's spread the word. Gareth's been slightly respectful and Debbie won't look at me. What about Mum?'

Zoe put her foot back in the water and lifted out the other one.

'What about her? What about everybody?'

'They'll have opinions,' Robin said. 'And they'll let us know what they are.'

'Do you care?'

'Not for myself—'

'For me?'

'You,' said Robin, turning towards her and dropping a kiss on the top of her head, 'can take care of yourself.'

'Right. Then who are we worrying about?'

'It's not worry—'

'We aren't hurting anyone,' Zoe said. 'We aren't taking each other away from anyone else. There

251

aren't any kids involved.'

'You're a kid.'

Zoe stood up in the bath and held out her arms for a towel.

'I'm as old as the hills. You don't want to think about what people think. What they think is their problem. We aren't responsible for other people's hang-ups.'

Robin wrapped the towel round her and lifted her out of the bath.

'I said I'd go,' Zoe said, 'whenever you tell me. I still will.'

'I won't tell you. I don't want to.'

'Fine.' She stood there, waiting for him to dry her. 'That's all we need. I'll tell Velma that, if you like. I don't mind. I don't mind what I say to Velma. I like her. She's entitled to her opinion and we are to ours but she can't expect us to adopt hers, even if she could explain to us, which I bet she can't, why she holds it.'

He kissed her shoulder.

'Shut up.'

She looked at him.

'I was only talking.'

He said, 'About Velma. I don't want to talk about Velma.'

'You started it.'

He dropped the towel and put his arms around her.

'And now I'm tired of it.'

'Look,' Zoe said. She put her hands up and held the sides of his face, 'I expect the whole neighbourhood's been talking about you for years. OK? And now, after all that's happened and the funerals, they're talking some more. And because of me, it's more more. But you don't have to listen. Do you? It's your life, Robin. Maybe for the first time in

252

your life, it's your life so why don't you just live it for a bit?'

Was that, really, what the auctioneer had meant when he talked so jovially about envy? Was it the sight of someone not only doing something for themselves, but that they were free to do, that made him tell Robin he had the luck of the devil? Robin wasn't used to being free. He was used to independence, to be sure, but independence made its own disciplines, created its own structures and demands, so that one was never, in a sense, free of one's own burdens, of the consequences of one's own decisions, of the path one had set oneself to follow. He moved up the ramp and looked at the beasts inside, waiting, as they had waited all their lives, for the next thing to be done to them, the next decision made by somebody else, the next pen or trailer or yard. Perhaps he'd been like that for years, got used to waiting, to reacting, to gritting his teeth and getting by, to obeying himself mindlessly. One of the calves stirred in the straw round its feet and looked at him, fourteen days old, produced out of a tube without touching or coupling, without sex. Robin looked at it with real sympathy.

'Poor little sod,' he said aloud.

*   *   *

'You can do the cleaning yourself,' Velma said. 'High time you learned, anyhow.'

She dumped a pile of dusters on the kitchen table to emphasise her point.

'Hoover's under the stairs. Dustbin men come Fridays.'

'OK,' Zoe said. She looked at the dusters. No

253

doubt Dilys would tell her what to do with them. Or Debbie.

'Robin can drop my money in when he's passing. Two weeks, he owes me.'

'I'll tell him,' Zoe said. She picked the dusters up and put them down again 6 inches away as if to acknowledge that responsibility for them had been transferred. 'Will you get another job?'

'Of course,' Velma said.

'Round here? Or will you have to go to Stretton?'

'What business is it of yours?'

'None,' Zoe said. 'I just don't want you to lose out. You don't have to leave.'

'Don't I?' Velma said, her eyes widening in indignity. 'Don't I just?'

'No,' Zoe said, 'you don't. Robin doesn't want you to. Nobody does. What's changed?'

'You've got a nerve,' Velma said. 'You've got a bloody nerve, standing there asking me that!'

Zoe said reasonably, 'But I'm not marrying Robin. Am I? I'm just here. And he's better. You can see that. Even if you can't stand me, you can see that Robin's better.'

Velma went over to the kitchen door, where she hung her anorak. She wore it every day, winter or summer, because, she said, it was cold on her bike, she felt it cold even on the hottest days.

'I'm going,' she said. 'I'm not taking any more of this.'

Zoe stayed by the table.

'I'll tell Robin. I'll tell him about your money.'

Velma was struggling into her anorak. Her face was almost hidden from Zoe but something about her angry, jerky, muddled movements made Zoe think she might be close to tears.

'I wish you wouldn't,' Zoe said. 'I wish you wouldn't go—'

Velma thrust her second arm triumphantly into its sleeve.

'I'm glad to be shot of it,' she cried. 'I'm glad to be going. I'm glad to be getting out of it all.'

And then there was a whirl of plastic carrier bags and the door opened and immediately slammed after her, deafening and final. Zoe looked at the table. Beside the dusters lay Robin's post, arranged in Velma's graded manner, and beside that her final lunch for him, pointedly for one only, a Scotch egg, cut in half, and a handful of pickled onions. Zoe picked it up. It seemed to her food so alien that she couldn't think who it was intended for. She peeled away the covering of plastic film, and used the film, like a protective glove, to pick up the onions and drop them in the rubbish bin. Then she found a knife, and cut up the egg into very small pieces and carried the plate outside to the garden Caro had once made and which now languished neglected under a riot of new weeds, to give it to the birds.

* * *

'Where's Dad?' Robin said.

'Out. With one of the new fellows. He doesn't know much but he's willing to learn. Barley doesn't look too good.'

'I know,' Robin said.

Dilys had lost weight. As she sat at the kitchen table surrounded by the farm accounts as was her wont the last week of every month, Robin looked at her hands moving slowly among the papers and saw

255

that her rings were slipping up and down her fingers with little clinking sounds, like light coins clashing together.

'We'll have to think about some permanent help, Mum.'

She said nothing. Robin lowered himself into the chair opposite her and put his elbows on the table.

'We have to have a meeting, Mum, now that Lyndsay's back. We have to talk.'

'You're not a shareholder,' Dilys said, not looking up.

'No. But I'm your son. And I'm also virtually running this farm as well as my own just now.'

'We're doing that,' Dilys said. 'Like we always have.'

Robin said gently, 'No, Mum. Not like that any more. You know that.'

'Dad's a lot better. He was out for four hours yesterday.'

'But he didn't do much. Did he? He can't.' Robin paused. It was in his mind to say, 'His heart's not in it. Nor is yours,' but he held back.

'We'll have your meeting,' Dilys said. 'Even if it won't change anything. How can it? What can Lyndsay do?'

'We have to ask her. She's a shareholder. She's got Joe's shares.'

Dilys gave him a quick glance.

'You've upset Lyndsay.'

Robin waited.

'God knows what she expected,' Dilys said, 'but you've upset her all right.'

'She wanted my support,' Robin said, 'and she'll

256

get it. She knows that.'

'And Zoe?'

'What about Zoe—'

'What's upset Lyndsay about Zoe?'

'You know what, Mum. Don't pretend you don't.'

'I'm not pretending,' Dilys said. 'I've thought this would happen all along.' She gave Robin a glimmer of a smile. 'She's a good girl, Zoe. I never thought I'd say it, but she's a good girl. She's patient with your father, patient as a saint. Lyndsay can't see that, of course. Nor will Judy.'

'I haven't spoken to Judy yet.'

Dilys picked up several invoices and clipped them together.

'Women don't like letting go. They get used to the men in their lives, they get used to having them there.'

'I'm not any less there because—because—'

'Because you're having a fling with Zoe.'

'Yes.'

'That's not how it seems to Lyndsay. Or Judy. Or Velma. Velma's just been in, all of a tizz. She walked out of Tideswell this morning.'

'Damn woman—'

'Didn't like being upstaged,' Dilys said.

'Zoe wouldn't upstage anyone—'

'Didn't need to. Didn't try. She just had to move into your bedroom.'

'Mum,' Robin said, 'what's made you so philosophical? I thought I'd get an earful about Zoe.'

Dilys lifted her head and looked at him.

'I'm tired, dear.'

'Of course.'

'Things aren't what they were, the life's not there, the colour's gone.' Her hand, holding the sheaf of invoices, was trembling very slightly. 'We've just got

257

to make the best of what's left. Haven't we? We've just got to do what we can, Lyndsay included. And you.'

Robin came round the table and stood close to Dilys's chair.

'You send Zoe up to me this afternoon,' Dilys said. 'I could do with her this afternoon, now that the cricket's finished on the television. Dad'll be tired by this afternoon.' She glanced up at him. She was almost smiling. 'That is, if your new housekeeper can spare the time.'

*   *   *

Zoe wasn't in the house. The kitchen looked oddly distracted, somehow, even above and beyond the chairs standing about at angles unrelated to the table, and a tower of washing-up drying in the rack, perilously balanced.

'Out with Gareth,' a note on the table said. 'Back later. Vet coming at three-thirty. Velma's gone. Sorry about that.' And then three kisses and a huge flourishing Z. Robin looked at the answering machine. Three messages, one from a feed salesman, one from an adviser on alternative uses for arable land whom he had contacted on behalf of Dean Place Farm, and one from Judy.

'I need to talk to you,' Judy said. She sounded very emotional. 'I need to talk to you when you're on your own. I suppose I'm sorry for you, but I don't know. I just don't know. Ring me, will you? Ring me tonight.'

Robin sighed. She was sorry for him, was she? Sorry for what exactly, sorry for what he'd been through or for what she had, so much of the time, put him through? He sat down at the table and picked up

Zoe's note. The kisses and the Z must be at least three-quarters of an inch high. And all Judy could feel was pity. Pity! Pity, for God's sake! 'Pity if you must,' Robin said aloud to the ghost of Judy in the empty kitchen. 'Pity if you want to. I can't stop you. But I have to say that the best response, the kindest, most useful response is just, for once in your life, to accept. To accept, without damn well judging.'

CHAPTER SIXTEEN

Lyndsay's father had made a list of four properties in Stretton that might be suitable for use as a small beauty salon on the ground floor with a flat on the first floor above. One of them had a balcony and another a small garden, fenced with woven wooden panels, with a square of shabby grass and some tired flower borders and a lilac bush. Both Lyndsay's parents had said that they would help her with the capital needed until she could extricate herself financially from Dean Place Farm, and also that they would be very happy to help with the children while Lyndsay got her business going. Her father also said that the building with the garden, though small, was structurally sound and that he had plenty of contacts left in the building trade who would do her a reliable and reasonable conversion job.

'And when the children need a big garden,' said Sylvia, 'they can come to ours. Can't they?'

Lyndsay had given a small smile and nodded. Her mother's garden measured perhaps a quarter of an acre, the scrap behind the building in Stretton maybe 15 feet. She stood in the first-floor flat of the building in Stretton and looked out of its windows, down into the street or the garden, or sideways, on its detached side, at the brick side of the next building, looming very close and pierced by two small windows only, shielded by slatted plastic blinds. Everything seemed very near and very airless. She thought of putting the children to bed in one of the tiny bedrooms, and then of coming into the small front sitting room, alone, on weekday evenings, and turning the television on, as she so often had in the last alarming lonely months of Joe's life, just for its company.

'Nice joinery,' her father said, slapping the heel of his hand into a window frame. 'Solid. A proper job.'

'It's a bit small—' Lyndsay said faintly.

'Bound to be,' Roy Walsh said. 'Bound to be, dear. After living on a farm. You can't expect 16 acres of oats to look at in the middle of Stretton. This is a nice little property. Sound. And a good location, too, just off the high street.'

Lyndsay began to say, pointlessly, that Joe had never grown oats, and stopped herself. She touched a nearby wall, where the wood-chip paper had lifted a little, at a join, exposing green emulsion paint underneath.

'Is it fair to the children?' Lyndsay said. 'Is it fair to bring them in from the country and ask them to live here?'

'Of course it's fair. As long as they've got their mother with them, it's fair. And you've got us ten minutes away, and the park. It's far more than most children have got, far more.' He looked at Lyndsay. His heavy, kind face creased with mild anxiety as it always had when he looked at her and told himself how defenceless she was, unprepared, and how unfitted for this age when women seemed to have

260

taken their own lives over to such effect, their own and anyone else's they could lay their hands on. Lyndsay wasn't fitted for this, she wasn't made for modern womanhood. But she had to live it, all the same. She'd had a man to take care of her, but now he'd gone and she'd got to face the world for herself.

He said gently, 'You can't put the clock back, dear. You can't pretend you're still a wife because you're not now. You're a widow. A widow with young children and maybe thirty working years ahead of you.'

She picked at the stiffened flap of wallpaper with a fingernail.

'You said,' Roy persisted, 'that the meeting at Dean Place Farm didn't go very well.'

She said, 'No, it didn't. They wanted me to become a partner, to stay there in the cottage, to keep the farm in the family.'

'And you don't want that?'

She said nothing.

'Lyndsay,' Roy said, 'if you don't want to stay on the farm, then you have to do something else. Don't you see?'

She turned away from him and crossed the grubby flower-patterned carpet the last occupier had left, to the window. Below her, on the pavement, two girls with babies in strollers were leaning against a litter bin and smoking. An old man was going past, very slowly, towing a tartan shopper on wheels, and so, rather faster, was a middle-aged woman in a striped shop overall. And there was traffic. Cars and vans and a delivery messenger on a motor bike. For the last six years, when Lyndsay looked out of her windows, she'd hardly ever seen anybody except the postman or Rose in her pram, and the traffic had been Joe's Land Rover and her car and the weekly travelling fishmonger. Sometimes she'd hated that, hated the emptiness and the shimmering uniformity of the fields. But she hadn't thought of trading it for this; it had never crossed her mind that, if she had to give up the blank agricultural view, this was the alternative.

'I asked you a question,' Roy said patiently.

'I'm afraid of the change,' Lyndsay said.

'But the change has already happened, dear, nobody can help that—'

'Robin could,' Lyndsay said angrily, without having intended even to mention his name.

'Robin?'

'He persuaded me to go back,' Lyndsay said, rushing on, 'and now he's made it impossible for me to stay.'

Roy waited. Robin had always seemed a nice fellow, quieter than Joe, a bit less friendly, perhaps, but a nice fellow all the same.

'Why's that?'

'I can't explain,' Lyndsay said. She put her hands up to the combs in her hair. 'He's just let me down.'

'Do you mean he took his parents' side in your discussion?'

Lyndsay shook her head. He hadn't really, beyond saying that their future had to be thought of, that they, with their chief administrator and workhorse gone, needed to think about how they were going to manage their lives, lives they had never had even to consider might change.

'It's worse for them, in a way, than anyone,' Robin had said to Lyndsay. His voice hadn't been unkind, but it had been firm. 'Because they're too old for change. They're too old to have a future but they've still got to keep going.'

262

'They've still got each other!' Lyndsay had screamed.

Robin had barely glanced at her.

'And do you think,' he'd said, 'that that's what either of them really wants?'

'He's got to look to them,' Roy said now. 'He's all they've got. Like your mother and I are looking to you. You've got your family and Joe's parents have got Robin.'

Lyndsay said foolishly, 'Robin's got a girlfriend. She's young enough to be his daughter.'

'Has he? Well, well. Nice for him to have a bit of company.'

But not nice for me, Lyndsay thought savagely, abandoning for me, displacing. She thrust her combs back in.

'I felt he wasn't thinking about me,' Lyndsay said. 'He wasn't putting himself in my shoes, he wasn't concentrating. That's all.'

'But you've got to concentrate. You really have, dear. You might not like responsibility but you've got to take it. You've got to take the next step.' He moved heavily forward and swung the door of the room back and forth, eyeing the level of the floor below it. 'They're asking eighty-eight thousand for this and I reckon I could get it for eighty-two or three. And then a bit more for the conversion downstairs and a spot of decorating up here, after we've applied for permission to use the place as business premises.' He looked at her. It wasn't a particularly fatherly look, but more one of shrewd speculation, as if he were discussing a business tender. 'Well, dear,' he said, 'what do you say?'

*   *   *

Oliver was carrying yet another slender paper cone of freesias and a bottle of New Zealand Chardonnay. He sat on the bus going out towards Judy's flat right down the Fulham Road with the wine held upright between his thighs and the flowers balanced against it, lightly, so that they didn't crush. He was sweating slightly. It wasn't a particularly hot day, but he noticed that, when he touched the plastic bag that the wine was in, his fingers slipped a little. He supposed that that was because he was nervous.

He was nervous because of the things he had spent the last few weeks screwing his courage up to say to Judy. He wanted to be kind in the way he said them, but he also wanted to leave her quite clear about what he was saying. He wanted to tell her that he loved her, and that she aroused interest in him as well as protective feelings, but he also wanted to tell her— and here he had to peel his hand away from the wine bottle—that he couldn't, for the moment, go on having a relationship with her, not a relationship of constant companionship and willing sexual fidelity. There wasn't anyone else, he would say, he could promise that. It was simply that he couldn't go on loving someone who kept sucking him down into the bog of her own personality problems—or at least, he could love them, but he couldn't live with them.

He thought Judy had had quite a hard deal in life, but not as hard a one as she seemed to believe. Of course it was hard to be abandoned by your natural mother, but if that mother had plainly not wanted you, and had then patently never regretted giving you up, could you possibly, unless you were mulishly obstinate about being made happy, insist that your life would have been better with her? Oliver had seen

264

a photograph of Judy's real mother, and several birthday cards of flamboyantly flowering South African plants, and had thought that both looked loud and insensitive. Whereas Caro had clearly been neither and had, into the bargain, wanted Judy as badly as her own mother hadn't. And Oliver liked Judy's father. Judy had complained about him a lot, especially with reference to his treatment of Judy's dead mother, but to Oliver, none of her complaints seemed quite to square with the man he had met during the uncle's funeral. On the way back to London, after the funeral, it had occurred to Oliver that her persistent attitude to her father was just one more of Judy's excuses, excuses for not putting up with things or just getting on with things the way other people did. And Oliver, holding the cone of freesias with his fingertips, was getting pretty tired of Judy's excuses.

The bus stopped just short of Fulham Broadway Station and Oliver got off, holding his wine and his flowers. It was ten or twelve minutes' walk to Judy's flat from the bus stop, time enough, maybe, to rehearse what he was going to say and how he was going to say it. He didn't want to emphasise the effect of her defeatism on him, nor indeed, any other of her deficiencies, but he wanted to make her think. He wanted to jolt her out of her rut of assumptions about herself, to make her see that, if she was resolute in being so sorry for herself, nobody else—and certainly not people she wanted and needed—would ever be sorry for her, for the right reasons.

'I don't want never to see you again,' he planned to say. 'I just can't see you for a bit. Not until you've got something to give me back.'

He swallowed. The paper cone of freesias was

265

becoming damp in his damp hand. His mother, he realised, would have admired him for what he was going to do, would have told him that he was acting with courage and principle. The trouble is, Oliver thought, pausing on the pavement and looking up at the house opposite, to the two attic windows of Judy's sitting room, that she'd be wrong. And on both counts.

*　　*　　*

Zoe stood in the bedroom that had once been Caro's and looked about her. She had obediently brought with her both a duster, recommended by Dilys, and a damp cloth, advised by Debbie. She had put both on the windowsill. Then she had walked to the centre of the room, somewhere near the end of Caro's bed, and looked about her, examining things, tasting the atmosphere. It was not, she decided, as interesting nor as revealing a place as Caro's grave. She had come in as a deliberate experiment, to see what she could detect in the room. Two days before, she had found Dilys in Joe's room, at Dean Place Farm, and Dilys had said, without self-consciousness, that she came in every day, for herself really, just to see. Zoe had wondered if people who had lost someone they loved often went into their bedrooms, because bedrooms were the most intimate places, the places where little essences or traces might cling. And that was perhaps the reason why bedrooms sometimes stayed untouched after a death, so that whatever fragile memory still clung there wouldn't be torn away, like a cobweb.

'Why don't you use Caro's room?' she'd said to Robin.

266

He had his reading glasses on and was engrossed in a dairy magazine.

'Too soon.'

'For you, you mean? That you still feel she's in it?'

He put the magazine down. Zoe could see a photograph of a yellow calf with a white blaze on its poll scratching its chin on a fence.

'Too soon for her,' Robin said. 'It was her room for so long.'

'But she's dead.'

He looked at her briefly, over the top of his glasses, and picked the magazine up again.

'That doesn't necessarily finish things.'

'It does,' Zoe said, 'for the person who died.'

'Look,' Robin said, 'I don't want to do anything about that room. I don't want to think about it. I've got enough to think about.'

Zoe began to stack plates.

'Farm things—'

'Yup.'

'But not people things.'

'Not if I can help it.'

'Why not?'

'Because,' he said, and his voice sounded sad to her, 'there's so much I can't change. Especially about the past.'

The past had lived in this bedroom for years, years and years, in fact ever since Caro had moved out of Robin's bedroom when Judy was three. He'd told her that, quite openly. Twenty years of separate bedrooms, almost all of Zoe's lifetime. Zoe gripped the footrail of Caro's bed. What had Caro thought, lying here alone? What had she thought, if indeed she thought at all, of Robin lying there across the landing, alone, too, accepting her decision because he

267

had no option and because, and certainly in the early years, he had loved her. But what had she loved, really loved? Judy, maybe, and this bedroom with its American quilt and the idea of being buried in a plot of earth no one could ever take away from you? But not Robin, not really. Robin had not turned out to be the kind of person she could love, although maybe she'd tried. There were plenty of people in Zoe's life she'd tried to like or love, and failed. Wanting to wasn't enough. There had to be something else, some other bond or spark, something that kept you really interested. Like she was, herself, in Robin, and he, she thought, was in her. She went over to the windowsill and picked up the duster and the cloth. Velma had said she gave Caro's room a quick once-over, each week, implying that Zoe should do the same. But was there really a point in dusting a room where nobody was and nobody came and Robin didn't want to think about? None, Zoe decided, absolutely none. She did a dance step or two across the floor on her way to the door, flapping the cloth and the duster. You can't change the past, Robin had said, and therefore, in inference, you have to leave it to get on with itself. Zoe pirouetted in the doorway, flourishing the duster towards the bed.

'So long,' she said. 'Byeee,' and then she slammed the door behind her.

*   *   *

'We've got to face it,' Dilys said, 'haven't we?'

Harry didn't look at her. He leaned his back against the old sycamore at the top of the 15-acre Joe had planted with linseed, and drank the tea Dilys had brought him. She hadn't brought him tea in years, not herself, not toiling up that half-mile along the headland from the point where the farm track stopped. He could see the roof of her car shining in the faint sun and then the acres of peas and barley stretching away to the point where Dean Place Farm gave way to Tideswell, and the fields in the distance, dotted with fat black plastic bags where Robin was making silage. He had done it alone with Gareth this year, day in, day out. All previous years, of course, Joe had helped him at silage time, just as he, Robin, had helped in return with the harvest.

'It's no good us pretending,' Dilys said. 'Is it?' She was sitting some distance from him on a big stone that emerged from the hedge where the sycamore grew, a big ancient stone that looked as if it had once had significance for somebody. 'We can't go on like this.'

'We're managing,' Harry said. He put his face into his tea mug again. 'We're getting by.'

Dilys stooped forward and brushed grass seed off her skirt. She said, very quietly, 'We aren't, you know.'

He waited.

She said, 'In a month or two, we'll be losing money, we won't have the money to pay for the men, to pay the bills. We never had to pay for men before. We never had to pay for other people's labour.'

'They're no use,' Harry said, 'those boys. They're no use at all. You can't teach them.'

'And we,' Dilys said, 'can't learn new ways.'

He gave her a quick glance. She was unscrewing the lid of the tea flask again, deft but slow. She said, 'We've got to face it. We've got to admit that if we wanted to keep the old life we'd have to learn new ways. But there's no point admitting that because

269

there isn't even an old life any more. It's gone. We'd be fooling ourselves if we thought otherwise.' She held the flask out to him and he offered his mug to her in silence.

'Joe kept this place going,' Dilys said. 'More than even we knew it, he did. He never stopped working, he gave up his life to it. Without him we can't manage. We can't even begin to manage.'

Harry took a swallow. He said stubbornly, 'There's Robin.'

'It isn't the same,' Dilys said, 'and you know it. He's got his own place and his own troubles. He's been as good as gold to us since Joe's accident, but he can't perform miracles, he can't be more than one man, he can't work more than twenty-four hours a day.'

Harry put his mug down. Something dark and heavy was settling inside him, and he was afraid of it.

'When I came back from the war,' he said, 'I thought I'd never have anything bad to face again, I thought I'd done all that, for one lifetime.'

Dilys laid her hands on the big stone either side of her.

'We've got to give up the farm.'

Harry said nothing.

'I don't want to be the one who says it, but one of us has to. We can't manage any more. We haven't the body or spirit and Lyndsay can't help us. We probably should never have asked her to, expected it of her. But if she can't then there isn't anyone else and we have to face it.'

There was a long silence. Harry looked at the view which he could have described minutely, every tree and hedgerow and fold of land, with his eyes closed. He knew it wasn't lovely land, he knew it wasn't like

270

those beautiful Herefordshire farms he and Dilys had once seen on a brief touring holiday, rolling away towards the dark mountains of Wales, but it was land that he had touched every working day of his life, and it was as familiar to him as his own self, his own body. The word 'dispossessed' came into his mind and hung there. He shut his eyes.

'Where'd we go?' he said.

He heard her sigh.

'Stretton, maybe,' she said. 'A bungalow, in Stretton.'

* * *

Debbie had *Farmers Weekly* open at the 'Situations Vacant' page. 'Herdsperson,' one advertisement ran, '70-cow unit, loose housed and herringbone parlour. Cottage available. Mid-Surrey.' Below was another. 'Attractive salary, 3-bedroom centrally heated cottage offered to capable herdsperson for 160 Friesian/Holstein unit. Experience of DIY AI preferred. Essex.' She drew rings round both, and then another that asked for experience in foot-trimming, in Oxfordshire. Gareth could do that. Gareth could do all the things these ads asked for, and more. One of the good aspects of working at Tideswell Farm had been that there was nothing involved in looking after cows that Gareth hadn't had to learn to do, one way and another.

But he didn't need to learn any more. He didn't need to work for Robin Meredith any longer, he'd paid all the dues of loyalty while Caro was ill, and then after her death, and after Joe's. Gareth wasn't family, after all, he was only an employee and there was a limit to the loyalty expected of an employee. If

271

he stayed at Tideswell any longer, Debbie reasoned, he'd get stuck there, he'd never advance to a bigger herd, a better unit with progressive technology and automatic scrapers. He'd just moulder away, increasingly stuck in his ways, and she, Debbie, and the children would have to moulder with him, tied to his stubbornness and lack of enterprise.

Debbie got up from the kitchen table and filled the electric kettle at the sink. She'd stopped begging Gareth to leave on account of her own instinctive dread of the place because she could see she wasn't doing any good that way. He'd told her she was being superstitious and he despised superstition, twitching the newspaper out of her hands if he caught her reading her horoscope. So she had changed tack. She had dropped her own fears and begun emphasising Gareth's future, and with it, the future of Rebecca and Kevin and Eddie. She said the job at Tideswell was for a young single man, a beginner, not for an experienced father of three. She was careful not to mention the precariousness of matters at both the Meredith farms, nor Lyndsay's defection to Stretton. She was especially careful not to mention Zoe.

The back door opened with the stealth peculiar to Eddie and he slid in.

'Well,' Debbie said.

Eddie put a packet on the kitchen table, a big envelope stiffened on one side with cardboard.

'What've you got there?'

'Pictures,' Eddie said. He had a rag tied round his head like a hippie bandanna.

'What pictures?'

'Pictures of me,' Eddie said. 'Zoe did them.'

He upended the envelope and several black-and-white photographs slid smoothly out on to the table.

272

Debbie peered.

'Did she give them to you?'

'Yes.'

'Have I got to pay her?'

'I dunno,' Eddie said, 'she just gived them me.'

He heaved himself on to a chair and leaned, breathing heavily, over the open copy of *Farmers Weekly*.

'Cor,' he said triumphantly, 'you've gone and drawed in this book. You're not supposed to draw in books.'

'It's not a book,' Debbie said, 'it's a magazine.' She picked up one of the photographs. Eddie, halfway up a gate, had turned to look at the camera over his shoulder. It was excellent. It was Eddie precisely. If Zoe hadn't taken it, Debbie would have been thrilled with it.

'I don't think you should have accepted these.'

Eddie wasn't listening. He picked up Debbie's felt-tip pen and was doodling across the advertisements for pig managers and flock assistants.

'I'll get Dad to give them back. I'll get him to take them to the house in the morning.'

Eddie drew a dense blob, and then another one close to it. He sniggered.

'Cow's jobs—'

Debbie whipped the pen out of his hand.

'Dirty little brute. Where've you been all afternoon, anyway?'

'Nowhere.'

'Time you went to school,' Debbie said. 'Time you had some discipline. Time—' She stopped. Eddie watched her. Something about her suggested to him that what she had been about to say affected him and was therefore worth focusing on. He regarded her

273

steadily, not observing her so much as staring at her, to make her finish what she had been saying.

Debbie tossed her head. What did it matter? Eddie was hardly five after all, and it would be a relief to give vent to her feelings. Telling Eddie could do no harm.

'Time we were all moving on,' Debbie said.

*   *   *

Robin was very tired. When he flexed his shoulders and back against the driver's seat of the Land Rover, he could feel the bones and muscles cracking and creaking in protest, stiffened by those hours and hours of mowing, day in, day out, and with a mower he should have replaced four or five years ago. When he'd stopped, at dusk, and sent Gareth home, he'd gone into the house for a shower and a mug of tea, and then told Zoe he had to go up to Dean Place, to see how things were.

'Fine,' she'd said. She always said fine. Sometimes, when he went back into the house, she wasn't there, but quite often she was, drawing at the kitchen table, or casually involved with her own newly devised and eccentric version of domesticity. But she never seemed to be waiting for him; she was just there, pursuing her own life until there should be occasion for it to collide with his again. She'd got quite useful around the farmyard lately, could manage the slurry tractor and the milking machine. Robin wouldn't let her anywhere near the feed, though. Nobody touched the feed but him, not even Gareth. Too much depended on it.

He put the key into the ignition of the Land Rover and turned it. Outlined against the lit kitchen window

274

of Dean Place Farm, Dilys stood waving. She never used to wave to him and if—as it seemed to him—her waving was a sign of how she'd changed, then he wished she wouldn't. She was altogether softer to him, and it unnerved him, as if something of spine had gone out of her and she was turning to him as Lyndsay had tried to. Robin was uncertain, driving the Land Rover steadily out of the yard and up the lane, that he could stand any more dependency just now.

Yet he'd known, sitting there with his parents that evening under the harsh overhead light, that their dependency was inevitable. Slowly, as if reciting something learned by rote, Dilys had told him that they'd decided to give up the farm. They couldn't manage it alone any more, and they couldn't manage hired help either. They would move as soon as the landlord could find a new tenant, sooner than the six months' required notice of quitting had expired, if possible. They'd start looking for somewhere in Stretton, somewhere manageable but with a bit of garden so that Harry could grow some vegetables. Perhaps Lyndsay's father would help them.

'I never thought,' Harry said, 'I never thought it would come to this.'

'No.'

'I thought I'd die in my bed here.'

'Now, Harry,' Dilys said, but there was no reproach in her voice.

On we go, Robin thought wearily now, on we go because we don't really have a choice, it's all we can do. You can assume nothing, take nothing for granted because nothing is certain as it once used to seem. In a few months, the face of our lives, of our farms, will be utterly changed, Mum and Dad gone,

275

Lyndsay gone, only me left doing whatever it is I think I'm doing. I knew once, I know I did, but once was long ago.

He swung the Land Rover in through the yard gates at Tideswell, tiny moths dancing in the headlight beams. The light was on in the kitchen, and in the bathroom on the first floor, and he remembered, with a sudden unbidden pang, how it had been to come back, in those first weeks and months after Caro's death, to a dark house, an empty house, with only the house cat offering her composed and silent company. He got out of the Land Rover stiffly, slammed the door and leaned against it for a moment, collecting himself. Then he moved slowly forward and opened the back door and let himself into the house.

Zoe was standing by the cooker, holding a mug in both hands.

'Hi,' she said. She was smiling. She took one hand away from the mug and motioned towards the table where Gareth sat, unfamiliar in an off-duty leisure shirt with his hair parted and smooth. He stood up when Robin came in.

'He's been waiting nearly an hour,' Zoe said. 'I thought you'd be back long before now.'

Robin looked at Gareth.

'Sorry,' Gareth said. 'Sorry to come so late and without warning. But I wondered—' He paused and then he said with difficulty, 'I wonder if I could have a quick word with you?'

CHAPTER SEVENTEEN

'No,' Hughie said.

Lyndsay put a hand on his shoulder.

'Lie down, Hughie. Lie down. It's bedtime, it's time to go to sleep.'

Hughie didn't move. he sat bolt upright in bed in his grandmother's smallest bedroom wearing his baseball cap. That day, he had been taken somewhere he had not liked, not at all, and told that this would be his new bedroom. He had said no. He didn't need a bedroom, he already had a bedroom in his own house where his bean bag was. It was his own room with his own bed in it. In the place where they had been today with Granny Sylvia, the bedroom they said would be his wouldn't be his at all because Rose would be in it, too. She would have to be because the only other room would have Lyndsay's bed in it. Hughie quite saw why Lyndsay didn't want Rose in her bedroom, but by the same token, he couldn't see why he was expected not to mind having to have her. He did mind. He wasn't sleeping in that room and he wasn't sleeping with Rose. In fact, he wasn't going to sleep anywhere at all until he was taken back to his proper place for sleeping, in his own room.

'No,' he said again.

'Please,' Lyndsay whispered. She dared not speak too loudly in case her parents heard her, and drew conclusions. Her mother had always said she thought Rose was out of control; now she had begun to hint that Hughie was, too, implying that Lyndsay was failing already in her task—hard, said Sylvia, but not impossible—of bringing the children up alone.

277

'If I lie down with you,' Lyndsay said, 'will you lie down then?'

'No,' Hughie said. He held Seal against him.

'You'll be so tired, if you don't sleep—'

'Sleep at my house,' Hughie said babyishly.

'We can't.'

Hughie said nothing. When Lyndsay began to talk rubbish like this and not to make sense, as she hadn't when Daddy went away, he had learned to say nothing, but just to wait. Hughie had got good at waiting recently. Uncle Robin had said he had to do it, to feel better, and it had seemed to be something Hughie could do, as long as things stayed the same, as long as he was in his house and Seal was there, and Lyndsay didn't keep putting him in the car and telling him, in a bright voice he mistrusted, that he was going to see Granny Sylvia. He didn't want to see Granny Sylvia, he didn't want to see any grannies. He had grown tired, just recently, of being carried about like a parcel and given instructions. When Rose was told to do things she didn't want to, she roared. Hughie wasn't going to roar, he wasn't going to do anything Rose did. In fact, he wasn't going to do anything at all, and he wasn't, if he could help it, going to be where he didn't want to be either. He gave a quick glance at his left shoulder. Lyndsay's hand still lay there. He could see her ring with the blue jewels in it, and her plain one, golden colour, that she said you got given when you were married. Hughie wondered, briefly, who gave you the golden ring when you were married, and then he darted his head sideways, quick as a flash, and bit Lyndsay, as hard as he could, on her hand.

*   *   *

Bronwen was engaged. The whole features department at the magazine had erupted in excitement and were clustering round her, admiring her ring—Victorian, set with pearls and garnets—and drinking sparkling white wine out of paper cups.

'He said he was going to wait until our holiday to propose,' Bronwen said, 'and then he couldn't. He said he just couldn't wait. So we'll have a honeymoon before our wedding, and another one afterwards.'

'You make the most of this,' the features editor said. 'This is a wonderful time, before reality sets in. You relish it.'

Tessa was keeping an eye on Judy. She noticed that Judy had admired Bronwen's ring just like everyone else, and that she had her paper cup of wine, and she looked all right. But Tessa also knew Oliver had stopped phoning. Comforting Judy over the death of her mother had been one thing, an awkward, inarticulate, impossible thing, but comforting her for the loss of Oliver was quite another. This was territory Tessa understood. Being chucked had a currency of comforting Tessa was perfectly easy with. She watched Judy carefully and prepared heartening, who-cares, sisterhood things to say if Judy looked as if she needed them, if the sight of Bronwen's triumph became too much to bear. Tessa had a new boyfriend herself in fact; she'd known him for three weeks and he was shaping up quite nicely considering that he was younger than she was, and going prematurely bald. But before him there'd been no one for almost ten months, and the memory of those ten months made Tessa very anxious indeed to be kind to Judy. She leaned across from her desk and touched Judy's arm.

'You OK?'

Judy glanced at her and nodded. She was looking good, Tessa thought, especially now she was growing her hair a bit. It was dramatic hair, thick and shiny, not the kind you could cut into a bob like half the office, but the kind you had to have more of and let go a bit wild.

'I just wondered—'

'It's OK.'

'Do you want to talk about it?'

Judy drank from her paper cup.

'There isn't much to say. I don't even know if I was in love with him, not properly. I liked him. You couldn't not like him, but he wasn't—well, he wasn't—'

'A passion,' Tessa said. 'The big pash.'

'No.'

'But nobody wants to be chucked, all the same.'

Judy said, surprising herself, 'He did it very nicely. In a funny way, I wasn't even altogether surprised.'

'But you must be hurt, you must be—'

Judy gave her a quick smile.

'Sorry to be disappointing,' she said, 'but I don't seem to be. Not badly, anyhow.'

Tessa said, determined to get some mileage out of her need to sympathise, 'And so soon after your mother—'

Judy took a pen out of her pen mug and balanced it carefully on its end.

'Oliver was good about that. He made me talk about her. He made me think about her as a person, not just as my mother.' She let the pen fall. 'He made me think about a lot of things.'

'Don't you want to kill him?' Tessa said. 'Don't you want to wreck his car and ruin his career and cut

280

the crotch out of all his trousers?'

'Isn't it funny?' Judy said, 'but I don't. I'd have thought I wanted to, but I don't. There are people I want to kill, but not Oliver.'

Tessa looked round, with elaborate furtiveness.

'Starting in here—'

Judy said, 'I'm wondering whether to stay.'

'What!'

'I don't know but I'm thinking about it. I'm not sure why I'm here, if you know what I mean, I'm not sure what I'm doing.'

Tessa finished her cup and crushed it up between her hands.

'It's a job, isn't it? Pay's OK, work conditions OK, people pretty lousy, but what d'you expect on a magazine like this? And you're good at it. I wouldn't be prepared to say this every day, but you're better than Bron and me. You've got more ideas.'

'Pointless ones, most of the time,' Judy said. 'I can't help feeling the whole thing is pointless.'

Tessa threw her crushed paper cup in a competent arc into Judy's waste-paper bin.

'Don't tell me you've got a social conscience, next stop Greenpeace activist—'

'Not that,' Judy said. 'But not this, either. Not this sort of life which just passes the time.'

Tessa was growing bored. A broken heart had powerful potential conversational charm, but a meaning-of-life discussion had, by its very definition, absolutely none. She gave a tiny yawn.

'You let me know then,' she said, 'when you're sorted,' and then she got up and sauntered over to Bronwen's desk, to perch on the edge of it in the little crowd that still lingered, and ask Bronwen if she

281

intended, when she married, to take her husband's name.

*   *   *

A small building firm, known to Roy Walsh, had provided Lyndsay with an estimate for converting the ground floor of the building in Stretton into a beauty salon. There was room for a reception area, two cubicles, a lavatory and a secluded space at the back for a sunbed. The conversion costs were not, Roy Walsh thought, unreasonable. It was the equipment that was going to be costly, the sunbed and the adjustable treatment couches and the electrical slimming gadget with its pads and control panels and loops of pastel-coloured wire. Roy wanted Lyndsay to sit down and work out costs with him, to see how long it would take to recover the initial investment and whether it was worth taking a girl on, to answer the telephone and make coffee and do the manicures. But Lyndsay seemed reluctant. She agreed to a lot of the things he suggested, but with an acquiescence that was hardly encouraging.

'It's early days,' Sylvia said to him, 'very early. It's very soon for her to be able to put her heart into anything. And the children are worrying her.'

The children were worrying Roy and Sylvia, too. Rose they thought very unfeminine, a very overpowering baby, almost brutal. And as for Hughie—well, Lyndsay hadn't wanted them to know Hughie had bitten her, but how could they help it? They'd heard her cry of pain and surprise and, when they'd hurried upstairs to see what was the matter, he had tried to do it again. Biting, on top of bed-wetting. Of course he'd lost his father, poor mite, but he was only three and couldn't really have understood the

282

reality of that. It was more, they were sure, that Hughie was reacting to Lyndsay, reacting to her uncertainty and inability to make decisions. She made him feel insecure, you could see it, she made him anxious. The sooner they could all be settled above the salon the better because only then would the sense of order return that the children needed so badly.

'I'm going to push her to sign,' Roy said. 'She'll think I'm hard-hearted, but I'm going to. It's for her own good, after all. She has to face the future. It isn't as if she's destitute after all—she's a very lucky young woman in that respect.'

His voice had an edge of impatience. Sylvia knew it well, remembered the relief they had both felt—but not liked to express—when Lyndsay had announced she was going to marry Joe. It wasn't that they didn't both love Lyndsay dearly, nor feel very sorry for her, but they had hoped so much that that stage of parenthood was over for them, that with all their three children settled in their own homes and with their own children, they could have some freedom at last, some time to do the things that there was never time to do before, what with a family and a business to see to. Sylvia had thought of a spring trip to Holland to see the bulb fields in bloom, and Roy had bought new fishing rods and had talked of the local golf club. But if Lyndsay was in Stretton, they'd have to look after the children for her, especially at the beginning. Of course they would do it, they'd do it gladly, but they couldn't help knowing that it wasn't what they'd planned.

'I've got to push her,' Roy said, 'haven't I? I don't want to, but it's for her own sake. I've got to push her to sign, so we can all get on with it, with what has to be done.'

* * *

Zoe parked the slurry tractor under the lean-to roof of battered corrugated iron where it lived. She'd got quite good at manoeuvring it and she'd noticed that the men who had come with the earth mover to dig the new slurry pit had stopped work to watch her. She'd put a bit of a performance on for them, a few flourishes, like a girl on the back of a circus pony. It gave her a little buzz to find herself good at something she hadn't even known about six months before, especially as she couldn't even drive a car. But cameras and tractors—now those she could handle.

She went back into the house and washed vigorously at the kitchen sink. Velma had hated to see Robin or Gareth washing at the sink after being out with the cows, but Velma wasn't here to impose her likes and dislikes any more, and Zoe was perfectly happy to use the sink as the men did, for hands and faces as well as dishes and pans. She sniffed her hands, to see if the last faint echo of cow had gone. They smelled of washing-up liquid. Then she took off her jeans and T-shirt—no point going all the way upstairs to do this if you then had to bring the dirty clothes straight back down again—and dropped them in the corner where the dirty washing had peaceably begun to collect in a random pile.

Upstairs, in her bedroom where she still kept her clothes, Zoe put on a less weary pair of black jeans and a clean grey T-shirt. She looked, she thought, regarding herself in the mirror let into the front of the wardrobe door, different, less skinny and washed-out, less like something that had been kept in the damp and dark too long. She hadn't exactly got fatter, her clothes fitted just the same, but the lines of her face and body looked smoother, less spiky, and she had a few freckles scattered across her nose and cheeks. She used to hate her freckles, but now, on skin less green-white than usual, they didn't look too bad, somehow. She gave herself a smear of lipgloss and a squirt or two of the men's cologne she liked, made, said the label on the bottle, from Caribbean limes. Then she went downstairs and out into the yard.

Gareth's cottage lay 400 yards from the farmhouse across a flat field planted with a rustling crop of maize. A track had been left through the middle, and along this Gareth walked or cycled half a dozen times a day. Zoe could see his boot prints in the earth, and the swooping tracks of his cycle tyres, and when she raised her eyes, the flat red-brick façade of his cottage, with its shining windows and the television satellite dish suspended on one side like a great white saucer. It was a very ugly cottage. Zoe had asked Robin why, if he was going to build a cottage, it had to be so ugly. Robin had been mildly amazed.

'Ugly?'

'Yes. Very. Colour, proportion, setting, everything.'

'But it works,' Robin said. 'It does what I need it to do.'

Like his car, Zoe thought, and his clothes, and his poor neglected garden where the roses Caro had planted were now suffocating in the relentless coils of bindweed. Things had to work, had to perform their function and earn their keep; beauty, if present in any form, was an accident.

Zoe came up out of the maize on to the little

sloping garden Debbie had made around the house. There was a paved path in faintly coloured stone slabs, and a scattering of tubs and pots planted with petunias and French marigolds. There were also several items from Eddie's arsenal lying about, plastic guns and shields and something that looked like a rocket. Kevin, Gareth had said, wasn't interested in all this war-games stuff, it was only Eddie and you couldn't keep him away from it, try as you might.

Zoe went round the house, past the never-used front door with its lace curtain behind a glass panel, to the back. The door to the kitchen stood wide open, and there was a mop and bucket on the step, and a mat hung out to air. Zoe put her head inside.

'Debbie?'

There was a pause. Zoe waited. After a moment or two, Debbie appeared from the living room, neat in a sleeveless pink T-shirt and a short denim skirt. She stared at Zoe.

'What are you doing here?'

'I've come to see you,' Zoe said.

'What about?'

'I've come to ask you something.'

Debbie moved a little closer across the kitchen and put her hands on the back of a chair.

'You'd better come in—'

'I don't need to,' Zoe said. She leaned against the doorframe. 'I'm OK here.'

Debbie shrugged. She put her hands up to her hair, and pulled it more tightly through its elastic band. Then she smoothed down her skirt.

'Well?'

'It's about Gareth.'

'What about Gareth?' Debbie said sharply.

286

Zoe leaned her back against the doorframe and put her hands in the pockets of her jeans.

'He came to give in his notice—'

'What's that to do with you?'

'Nothing. But it's bad for Robin. Everything's bad for Robin just now, I don't understand the half of it, but I know it's money and his parents and Lyndsay going and the farms. And now Gareth.'

'Gareth's got to think of himself,' Debbie said quickly. 'Gareth's got responsibilities, he's got a family—'

Zoe watched her for a moment, and then she said, 'Did *you* want him to leave?'

'No.'

'I just wondered,' Zoe said. She leaned forward a little, as if inspecting the toes of her boots.

'It was time he got a better job,' Debbie said. 'It was time he moved on.'

Zoe didn't look at her.

'But why now?' she said to her boots.

Debbie said nothing. She looked down at the kitchen table where Gareth's first two job applications waited to be posted.

'If I went away,' Zoe said, transferring her gaze from her boots to Debbie's face, 'would Gareth stay on? Just for a bit, until Robin's sorted? Would he?'

Debbie gave a little gasp.

'I don't know—'

'I thought it might be that, you see,' Zoe said. 'I thought it might be me. The last straw.'

'No,' Debbie said. 'Yes.'

'But would Gareth change his mind?'

Debbie looked at the letters. She held on to the chairback hard.

'No,' she said, 'he wouldn't.'

'And you wouldn't?'

'No,' Debbie said, 'it's too late.' She shot Zoe a quick glance. 'There's a limit to what you can do for other people.'

'Oh I know,' Zoe said, 'I know that. It's just that this is such a bad time for Robin—'

'It's bad for all of us!' Debbie cried. 'It's been bad for ages, months and months, long before you came!'

Zoe eased herself upright from the doorframe.

'Yes.'

Debbie moved suddenly. She went over to the kitchen worktop where the electric toaster stood, and retrieved a big envelope that was balanced behind it.

'Here.'

'What's that?'

'It's the pictures. The pictures you took of Eddie. He shouldn't have taken them—'

'But they're his,' Zoe said. 'They're of him. Who else do they belong to? They aren't any use to anyone else.'

'We don't want them,' Debbie said.

Zoe took the envelope. She said slowly, 'What's bugging you?'

Debbie said nothing.

'Is it the sex?'

Debbie made a little gesture.

'You want to let that go,' Zoe said. 'It doesn't affect you, it doesn't interfere with your life.'

Debbie shut her eyes.

'Good luck,' Zoe said.

She turned, and Debbie heard her walking away, down the little path, past the flower tubs and the plastic guns, towards the maize field. She opened her eyes. The letters still lay there, two white squares with Gareth's careful, unpractised handwriting across

288

them, and first-class postage stamps. She picked them up. She'd said to Gareth that she'd post them.

'If you like,' he'd said.

She turned, and went into the sitting room, still holding the letters. From the big window, which she kept so scrupulously polished, she could see Zoe still, walking without hurry down the green aisle of maize. She wondered how she would tell Gareth of the visit, how she would colour it, how she would try and explain her own reaction, justify it. Then she wondered if she would, in fact, tell Gareth about it at all.

*   *   *

'In the morning,' Lyndsay said. 'I have to sleep on it.'

Her father sighed.

'It will be the same in the morning—'

'I can't,' Lyndsay said. 'I can't do it just now. I'm tired.'

Roy glanced at his wife. She was sitting in her accustomed armchair, embroidering a fire screen. She'd been at it for over a year and Roy couldn't think why her absorption in it was so profoundly irritating. But it was.

'Help me, dear.'

Sylvia said, pushing her needle in and out, 'Lyndsay, we're only trying to help you. Your father hasn't done all this for himself, he's done it for you.'

'I know.'

'You'll do no good by putting off signing. It has to be in your name because of the business. If I could sign for you, I would, but I can't.'

Lyndsay stood up. She said in a voice that was almost angry, 'I *said*. I said I'd do it in the morning.'

289

She glared at them. 'I'm not a *child*.'

Silence.

Roy took off his reading glasses and laid them on the unsigned contract. He said, 'Then you have to stop behaving like one.'

'By doing what you say?'

He glanced again at Sylvia, but she was negotiating an auricula and wouldn't look up.

'Not necessarily,' he said tiredly, 'but by doing something. We only came up with the plan because you hadn't got one of your own.'

'Not yet,' Lyndsay said furiously. 'Not *yet*. Joe's been dead six weeks. Six *weeks*. Why should anyone have to decide anything when their husband has only been dead six weeks?'

Sylvia threaded her needle neatly in and out of the canvas, and folded it up.

'No need to upset yourself—'

'I am upset,' Lyndsay said, 'of course I'm upset! I'll probably be upset, as you call it, for years and years. I don't *know*. None of us do. But I do know sometimes what I can't do, and I can't sign that contract. Not tonight.'

Sylvia stood up. She didn't look at Lyndsay.

'Then we'll wait till the morning.'

'But,' Roy said, 'it has to *be* the morning.'

Lyndsay looked at them both. She opened her mouth to say something, and then she shut it again. Instead of replying, she walked to the sitting-room door and opened it.

'Night,' she said.

They waited for her to say something else, to say sorry. But she didn't.

'Good-night, dear,' Sylvia said.

Upstairs, Hughie lay asleep propped up on four

290

pillows. It was his compromise over lying down. Sylvia, Lyndsay knew, disapproved of this, but Lyndsay didn't mind. She didn't mind, either, the fact that Hughie had bitten her. It was startling, but she wasn't hurt, certainly not in her feelings. In fact, when Sylvia and Roy had burst into the room, Lyndsay had been looking at Hughie with something little short of admiration.

She sat down by him now. He looked miserably uncomfortable, half sliding off the precarious pillow mountain he had made himself, his baseball cap tilted upwards by the angle at which he lay, so that the peak stood straight up, scraping his fair hair up behind it. Lyndsay was glad he was asleep, however awkwardly. Only when he was asleep, could she be sure he wasn't oppressed by all the things he chose to be alarmed by.

But did he choose? When she looked at him now, and saw Joe's colouring, if not his features, she was very doubtful that Hughie invented anything. If he was afraid of things, he had good reason—those things were alarming to him. Just as the black spectres in Joe's life had been alarming to him. Lyndsay might have chosen not to see Joe's shadows, nor to believe in them if she did, but she couldn't so choose with Hughie. Hughie was her child, and for the moment wholly dependent upon her for his faith in life. And now he was pitting himself against her because, quite simply, he had to, to survive. He wasn't being troublesome, he was being truthful. It was almost as if, in his childish instinctive way, he was trying to force her to see that what she was about to do was as wrong for her as it would be for him. He loved her. Young as he was, Lyndsay knew that no one in her life had ever loved her as Hughie did, and

291

that, even if he grew temporarily ashamed of such love as he grew older, she would never forget the intensity of it and the utter trust it placed in her. She put a hand out and held his foot. In some way, she knew she had failed Joe. She had never meant to and would have done everything in her power not to have done so, but, for whatever reason, she had failed him because she couldn't reach him. Well, she could reach Hughie. She could reach him because he allowed her to, he let her in, in a way that Joe had never been able to. And if he could let her in, she must make sure that she proved trustworthy, so that he would, as a grown man, be able to let in someone else and not be driven to the edge of a fatal isolation as Joe had been. Whatever she chose to do in the morning, she must remember that. She had the chance now not to let Hughie down, when he needed her, and she must take it.

*   *   *

They hadn't really spoken all evening. Robin had come in late, and tired, and sweaty, and had gone up for a shower, and come down to ruffle her head as he passed her, as if she were a dog that he was very fond of which could be relied upon not to speak. She put soup and a sandwich in front of him, and while he ate, he went through the pile of papers that had been collecting recently on the table, weighted down by a small monkey wrench that happened to be lying around. The papers were mostly invoices, bills. They were for sums that seemed improbable to Zoe, just too big, and for things that had gone, been used up, feeds and vet's visits, drugs and machinery repairs. Robin went through them steadily, over and over.

She watched him for a bit and then she looked away, at the television, which was on, but with the sound turned right down, so that people were mouthing silently out of the screen, like fish in a tank. Zoe felt badly for Robin, but there was nothing she could do, not in this department. She had tried that afternoon, and failed—failed, really, because of the effect that the help she really could be to Robin in another department had had on everybody else.

'Coffee?' she said.

He shook his head. She stood up and collected his bowl and plate and took them over to the sink. It was still quite light in the yard outside, and there was a little thin hard new moon hanging above the barn like a sharp, curved blade. She watched it for a while. After a moment or two, she realised that there was another light coming from somewhere, a moving light coming down the drive from the lane above. It was a car, and it was coming slowly, as if it didn't know the way. She watched it until it emerged into the yard and stopped. There was one person in the back, and the driver.

'A taxi!' Zoe said.

Behind her, scribbling figures on scrap paper, Robin grunted. Zoe leaned forward, holding on to the edge of the sink. A girl got out of the taxi, a tall girl in black, pulling a bag out behind her, one of those big, soft rollbags with canvas straps.

'Robin,' Zoe said, and her voice shook a little, 'Judy's here.'

CHAPTER EIGHTEEN

Everything was late this year, Harry thought. He stood looking across the acres of linseed and observed that they were hardly yet in flower. Too much rain earlier, now not enough. And a warm, choppy wind on and off for weeks, drying everything up. He leaned his arms on the top of the five-barred gate giving on to the field, and felt the folded papers in his pocket crackle. He had said he'd read them. He'd promised Dilys he would.

'On my own,' he said. 'Out there. I can't read them with you watching.'

The papers were the particulars of two bungalows in Stretton that Dilys had chosen from a great sheaf sent to her by the estate agency. At first glance, they looked not only indistinguishable from one another, but also from almost any other bungalow Harry had ever seen. It was so difficult to care where he lived, if he couldn't live here, and difficult to the point of impossibility to imagine life after Dean Place. It seemed to him that there might, quite simply, not be a life. That was why he hadn't written yet to their landlords giving notice of quitting Dean Place. Dilys had drafted a letter, but he couldn't bring himself to sign it. It appeared to be like signing some kind of death warrant. Dilys told him he was stubborn. He probably was, but there was more to it than that. There was the belief that he had lost so much already that nothing and nobody could or would expect him to lose any more. Certainly not the last shreds of his freedom.

He pulled the folded papers out of his pocket and

slowly opened them up. 67 Otterdale Close and The Lindens, 20 Beech Way. 'Better garden', Dilys had written on one and 'Sun room and bigger kitchen' on the other. What did it matter? What was he going to do with a garden, he'd like to know? And kitchens were Dilys's affair, as were sun rooms, whatever they were supposed to be. Sun rooms! The very words put him in mind of geriatric outings in coaches to Llandudno. He folded the particulars back up again, clumsily, and stuffed them in his pocket. Dilys could decide. He didn't care and nor, he suspected, did she at bottom. But she could decide, all the same, and then he could grumble.

He heaved himself back up into the tractor cab, and rattled his way rowdily down the track towards the house. It was like a cantankerous old horse, his tractor, every joint stiff and cracking, full of aches and pains and obstinacies, but familiar. He'd always refused to think of replacing it, citing the ludicrous price of new ones as an example and concealing its frequent breakdowns with furtive evening tinkerings when Joe had gone home. Well, now he wouldn't have to replace it. It and he would be put out to grass together, except it wouldn't be grass, it would be some damned suburban garden, round a bungalow. He'd a good mind to take the tractor with him. He'd say to Dilys, 'All right, 67 Otterdale Close it is, as long as there's room enough in the drive to park the tractor.' He'd said he'd give Dilys his answer by dinnertime but, fired by the notion of taking the tractor, he thought he'd go and tell her right now.

There was a car in the yard. It was, to his surprise, Lyndsay's car. He thought she was in Stretton, signing up on some beauty parlour her parents wanted her to have. Harry hadn't much time for

Lyndsay's parents. Nice enough people, but not his sort. He'd been to their house once, at Dilys's insistence, during Joe and Lyndsay's engagement, and had never seen a sitting room so full of knick-knacks. Little thises and thats on every surface. Dilys had put him in a chair and told him not to move, or else. She'd been afraid he'd break something.

'Well,' Harry said, clumping into the kitchen, 'surprise, surprise.'

Lyndsay was sitting at the kitchen table with Rose on her knee. Rose, breathing heavily, was strenuously kneading a lump of Dilys's bread dough on the tabletop. Lyndsay had tied her hair back with something and looked different on account of it, a bit older, more alert. Across the table, Hughie was drawing big red Hs all over an old agricultural seed catalogue.

'Hello,' Lyndsay said. She smiled at Harry, but shyly, as she used to when Joe first brought her home.

'Nice to see you, dear,' Harry said. He bent over Hughie. 'Kiss for Grandpa?'

Obediently, Hughie held up his face.

'Mmm,' Rose said urgently, leaning across the table for equal attention. 'Mmm, mmm, *mmm*.'

Harry went round to her.

'Nah,' she said, craning away from him. '*Nah*.'

'Rose. Oh, *Rose*.'

'Leave her.'

'She's so awful. My parents—'

Dilys put two glasses of fruit juice down in front of the children.

'Never mind, dear.'

Hughie pulled his glass towards him, and tipped it towards his mouth without lifting it from the table. He watched Lyndsay over the top of it.

'I'm—I'm rather in disgrace,' Lyndsay said to Harry. 'I was just telling Dilys—'

Harry sat down in his accustomed chair.

'Who with?'

'My parents.'

Harry waited. Rose began to slap the bread dough first with one fat palm, and then the other.

'I wouldn't sign the contract,' Lyndsay said, 'on the building in Stretton.'

'Perhaps,' Harry said, uncertain where this was leading, 'it wasn't the right one.'

'No it wasn't. But there won't be a right one, you see. The whole idea wasn't right, the whole idea of Stretton.'

'No,' Harry said heavily, thinking of the bungalows.

Hughie set his glass upright again, very quietly. Dilys had come to sit next to him and he felt that she was being very quiet, too; extra quiet. Only Rose was making a noise, slapping the dough.

'I've changed my mind,' Lyndsay said. She looked down, at the back of Rose's curly head, and her stout and solid little body in its green-spotted dungarees. 'I've changed my mind and I'm not going back to Stretton.' She gave Dilys a quick glance. 'I'm staying here.'

'Well,' Harry said.

'I want to try and farm. I want to try and run the farm. Like Joe did.'

Dilys and Harry exchanged glances.

Dilys said, gently for her, 'But you don't know anything about it, dear. You've never taken any interest. You wouldn't know where to begin.'

Lyndsay said nothing, just stared down at Rose's back.

297

'It's a mug's game, now, farming,' Harry said. He'd felt a leap of hope when she first spoke, but he knew it was an insane leap. Lyndsay farm! A girl take on a farm like Dean Place, a town girl with soft town ways who'd never been able to do anything for herself! He couldn't help feeling fond of her for thinking of it, but he couldn't let her think it, all the same. 'It's not what it was. It's all paperwork and subsidies. You can't grow food to eat like we used to, like farming used to be.'

Lyndsay looked across the table at Hughie.

'I could get a manager. For a few years anyway, while I learn what to do.'

'You'd have to pay him.'

'I know.'

'What'd you do that with?'

Lyndsay took a breath.

'If I lived here,' she said, 'I could have lodgers. Or people for holidays, family holidays. Couldn't I?'

Harry heard Dilys gasp.

'Live here—'

'Yes,' Lyndsay said, 'here. Because you're going to Stretton, aren't you? Buying a bungalow?'

Harry closed his eyes.

'You'd live here.'

'I'm a major shareholder now,' Lyndsay said. 'And you are moving out.'

'We're giving up the lease,' Dilys said. Her voice sounded faint, as if she couldn't quite remember how to use it.

'But you can't,' Lyndsay said, 'without my consent. Can you? And I don't want to give up the lease. I've decided. That's what I've come to tell you, you see.' She looked at Dilys. 'I thought you'd be pleased.'

298

Dilys nodded, speechless.

'Flabbergasted,' Harry said.

'People learn,' Lyndsay said. She sounded almost certain. 'Don't they? All their lives changes happen and then they learn something else, either because they want to or they have to. Well, I'm a bit of both. I may not succeed, but I'm going to try.'

'Why?' Dilys said suddenly. 'Who for?'

'You don't need to know,' Lyndsay said. She glanced at Hughie. 'Only we need to know that.'

'What about our shares?'

'Can't you keep them? Or, if you don't want to, sell them to someone else?'

Dilys leaned across the table.

'*Tell* her,' she said urgently to Harry. 'Tell her she can't do this. Tell her it won't work.'

He regarded her for a moment and then he looked at Hughie, very still, and Rose, now sticking her fingers into the dough and then peering into the holes she'd made.

'Sorry,' Harry said.

'What do you mean, sorry?'

'I can't do that,' Harry said. 'I can't tell her that.'

'Why not?'

'Because,' he said, closing his eyes again and feeling for the words, 'I can't tell her from my heart that I think she's wrong.'

* * *

From the garden at Tideswell, Judy could see Zoe's red head, high above the hedge, going back and forth in the cows' yard, on the slurry tractor. Judy had never driven a tractor in her life, never wished to; at least, all the years of her growing up she had never

299

wished to. She wondered if Zoe was doing it on purpose, showing off. If so, whatever Judy's feelings, it was the only bit of showing off she had done so far. In fact, she had been absolutely unobtrusive since Judy's return, quiet and quietly occupied. On the very first night when Judy had prowled the landing full of offended resentments, Zoe had come out of Robin's bedroom, fully dressed, and had slipped past Judy without a word and gone into her own room, closing the door and leaving Judy in a silence that frustrated her of all further action. She had stood there for ages, under the bleak central light outside Robin's bedroom door, raging with the desire for a scene and the knowledge that there was, at this precise moment, nothing to have a scene about. Zoe had pre-empted her. Judy had come back, so Zoe had withdrawn from Judy's father's bed and left Judy furious, and empty-handed.

Judy bent among the roses and grasped another tough and flexible clump of bindweed. It came up with suspicious ease, in a tangle of spidery white roots, confident in the knowledge that it had left far more of the same roots comfortably behind than Judy could ever hope to pull up. There was something about it, in Judy's present mood, that reminded her of Zoe, with its invasiveness and lawlessness and untouchableness. You couldn't affect Zoe, you couldn't make her *mind*. She would simply slip away from you, if confronted, into her own world and challenge you to prove any harm she was accused of doing. Of course she wasn't doing any harm, except to Judy, and the harm she was doing to Judy was entirely of Judy's own permitting, even creating. 'I hate this place,' Judy had said to Zoe. 'I don't want to be here.' But Zoe hadn't hated it, and she hadn't taken anything Judy had wanted, as her own. Up to now, that is. Judy yanked out another spiralling green tangle of weed. Now was so very, very different. It was so different that for the moment Judy couldn't think what to do about it.

She couldn't, to start with, think what to do about Robin. He had been surprised to see her but kind, in a wary way. In her anger, she'd thought he was wary because he had bloody good reason to be, sleeping with Zoe as he was. But she soon saw that he wasn't remotely self-conscious about that, just as Zoe wasn't; he was wary because he'd never got her right, never known how to handle her, even in her baby days. She had made it plain, all her life, that as far as she was concerned he got it wrong, all the time, and all he was doing now was waiting to get it wrong again and then for her inevitable offended reaction. But, for the first time, she was slightly awed by him. She didn't feel able to confront him. She told herself that this was Zoe's fault but she knew that wasn't true. She knew the change wasn't in Robin or in Zoe. It was in her.

She bent to scoop the huge, light pile of bindweed off the grass and dumped it in the wheelbarrow. It was a cloudy day, but heavy and hot. She wheeled the barrow part of the way towards the corner where Caro had made a compost heap, and then left it there and went into the house in search of a drink of water. Robin was in the kitchen, opening his mail with his thumb.

'Oh—'

He looked up.

'What?'

'I thought you were out—'

'I was. I will be again in a minute. Does it matter?'

'No,' Judy said. She felt she was blushing. 'No. Of course not.'

He said nothing. She went across to the sink and turned the cold-water tap on.

'Dad—'

'Yes?'

'Can I ask you something?'

'Of course.'

She turned round, holding a dripping tumbler and fumbling in a trouser pocket with her other hand.

'I went into Mum's room. I don't know why, but I went in and I looked in the drawers and things—'

Robin waited, his thumb in a half-torn envelope.

'And I found this.'

She held out to him a small, thin, battered cardboard folder.

'Yes.'

'Do you know what it is?'

'It's an air ticket,' Robin said.

'Yes. But what is it?'

'It's the return half of the air ticket your mother was given in 1971 to come to England.'

'Which she never used—'

'No.'

'But you knew about it?'

He hesitated. Then he put down the envelope he was holding.

'Yes.'

'Did you look in her drawers?'

'No,' he said, 'but she showed it to me.' He paused, and then he said quietly, 'Often.'

'Often?'

'Judy,' Robin said, 'I don't want a row but the truth is that the ticket—that ticket—was produced several times a year, and shown to me.'

302

'But it was only valid for six months—'

'I know.'

'Dad,' Judy said, 'did she sort of threaten to leave all the time?'

He looked at her briefly, unhappily, but said nothing.

'And she never did—'

'No.'

'She just liked the idea.'

'Maybe,' Robin said. 'It doesn't matter now.'

Judy said, almost as a cry, 'It does! It does to me!'

'Why?' he said guardedly.

'Because I didn't know her! I only knew the bits she let me know!'

He bowed his head.

'She couldn't settle,' Robin said, 'and she couldn't leave. Perhaps the ticket gave her the illusion that she could.'

'Oh Dad—'

'It's OK,' Robin said.

'But she taunted you—'

'Not taunted.'

'Didn't it drive you mad?'

He turned away and began to shuffle through the mess on the table.

'I got used to it.'

Judy threw the ticket in the vague direction of the kitchen wastebin, and then she moved closer to Robin. Tentatively she put out a hand and touched his sleeve.

'Dad,' she said, and was aware that her voice was little more than a whisper. 'Dad, I'm so sorry. So *sorry*.'

*　　*　　*

303

'Satisfied now?' Gareth said. He stared at Debbie long and hard. 'Got what you want?'

Debbie held the washing basket on her hip. It was full of laundry she'd been on her way to peg out on the line when Gareth had found her. He'd been holding a letter, and when he saw her, he chucked the letter into the basket on top of all the damp T-shirts and socks and said, 'Read that, then. *Read* it.'

The letter came from near Melton Mowbray in Leicestershire. It offered Gareth, subject to interview, a place on a four-man team managing 400 cows. '32-point polygon,' the letter ran, 'cubicle housing, automatic scrapers and mixer wagon feeding. There is an excellent modern house close to your work. We shall require, of course, the names of two referees.'

'You've got an excellent modern house *now*,' Gareth said. 'And I'm my own man, not part of a team. But if that's what you want—'

Debbie nodded, silently. Gareth was seldom angry and it disconcerted her when he was, but for all that, she wasn't going to lose the ground she'd gained.

'It'll be less lonely, working with other people—'

'I'm not lonely,' Gareth said.

She thumped the laundry basket down on the ground.

'You're not the only one.'

Gareth snatched the letter up.

'Look,' he said, 'it's only the same bloody money.'

She said obstinately, 'But it's a bigger place, more technical, more modern—'

'You're not going to give in, are you? You've made up your mind and that's that.'

She bit her lip. She had made up her mind. Her

instinctive fears had hardened into a resolution nothing would shift now. Nothing.

'So,' Gareth said, 'we take the kids away from an area they've settled in, from schools—'

'They'll settle again,' Debbie said. 'So will we.'

Gareth came a step or two nearer and pushed his face into hers.

'You haven't had to do the dirty work in any of this. Have you? It was me that had to see Robin, had to tell him all this stuff about a joint decision, when it wasn't, when it was you. And it's me that's got to uproot from work I know, work that suits me, and start again in bloody Leicestershire. You insist I do this, but you don't have to do anything yourself. You just tag along.'

Debbie muttered, her head bent, 'I'm not doing it for nothing.'

'Telling me you're not,' Gareth said. 'Telling *me*.' He drew a breath. 'We're going to look such fools,' he said. 'Such fools. It's all going to settle down round here, and I need never have bothered myself.'

She gave him a sharp glance.

'What do you mean?'

'Lyndsay's back. Velma saw her. And now Judy's home.'

'What difference will that make?'

'Maybe they've come back for real. To stay.'

Debbie gave a little snort.

'Don't make me laugh. What use will those two ever be? Of all the family, those two are the most useless of all and in any case, Robin and Judy have never got on, never.' She bent and picked up the washing basket again. 'It'll be worse chaos than ever round here, if they're back. You'll see.' She paused, and then she said to Gareth with emphasis, 'And here's still that Zoe. Isn't there?'

*　　　*　　　*

Zoe was sitting up in bed. She wore an old collarless flannel shirt of Robin's which she had found at the back of the airing cupboard, while looking for an old towel in the course of a hair-dyeing session. The shirt was huge and worn, and she had rolled up the sleeves so that the cuffs formed big soft pads round her elbows. She had put the bedside lamp on the floor and the light from it threw the room into weird relief, with huge, jagged shadows and a spooky glow across the ceiling. She had her knees drawn up, and a sketch pad balanced against them. She was drawing, in soft black pencil, the head of a cow, from memory.

It was well after midnight. The evening had been constrained, as all evenings had been since Judy returned. It seemed to Zoe, watching Judy, that Judy was bursting with something, overflowing with a need to ask or to tell, but holding back at the same time. Zoe wasn't going to help her. Or at least, she wasn't going to say anything that might help Judy until she had made things plain with Robin. When that might be, she couldn't tell. You couldn't hurry Robin, you couldn't corner him and insist upon his talking something through. You had to wait, in a way that reminded Zoe of waiting for weather, for the moment to be right, like the time of the moon.

She shifted in bed a little, and heard, simultaneously, the creak of floorboards out on the landing, a quiet creak, almost secretive. She held her breath. There was another step, and then a knock, a tap almost, on her door.

'Come in,' Zoe said.

The door opened silently, revealing Robin in the pyjamas she had teased him about, blue-striped and schoolish.

'Hi,' Zoe said, 'I thought you might be Judy.'

Robin closed the door softly.

'Has she spoken to you?'

'Hardly,' Zoe said, 'though she's busting to. I'm kind of waiting.' Robin sat down on the edge of the bed and regarded her.

'You look about ten.'

'People always say that. I'm older than all of you.'

He grinned.

'I know.'

She picked up her pencil and her pad and bent sideways to put them on the floor beside the lamp. Then she twisted herself until she was on her knees and could put her arms around his neck.

'Robin—'

'Yes,' he said, holding her.

'Robin, I've got to go.'

There was a tiny pause, and then he said, 'I know.'

'I always did have to,' Zoe said, 'even when I came, I knew I had to go. So did you.'

He held her hard.

'I've been right for now,' Zoe said, 'but I wouldn't be right for ever.'

'I know that. But I don't want now to be over.'

'It is over. It's changed. It's changed already. It changed when Judy came.'

'She's given up her job,' Robin said, his face against Zoe's shoulder.

'I thought she might. That's good.'

'And she kissed me.'

'Yes?'

'And she said she was sorry. I don't know quite

307

what for.'

'For everything,' Zoe said.

'She's never said such a thing before in her life.'

'Maybe she never felt it.'

'Zoe,' Robin said, turning his face and kissing the side of her neck, 'you've been like a holiday.'

'When did you last have one?'

'I never did.'

'And will you have another?'

'Maybe. But not immediately. I don't need one for a while.'

'Good.'

He put his hands under her arms and held her away from him.

'Where will you go?'

'London,' Zoe said, 'back to London.'

'What will you do?'

'What I was doing. But more. I'll travel next. I'll go and find things I've just thought about before and I'll look at them and take their pictures.'

'Drifting—'

'No,' Zoe said, 'not that. I've learned about that. I know I can't get rooted yet, but I know I can't drift either. I'll find people who need me.'

'Lucky them.'

She held his ears, lightly.

'Are you going to go forward now?'

He nodded.

'Yes. Don't quite know how, but yes.'

She leaned towards him, still holding his ears, and kissed him.

'I've liked it,' Zoe said, 'I've really liked it. Being here, with you.'

*   *   *

Judy heard Robin's bedroom door close. And then silence. The whole house was suddenly drenched in silence. While he had been in Zoe's room, she thought she could hear murmuring, steady, quiet, private murmuring, but she couldn't be sure. Maybe they hadn't been talking anyway. Maybe they'd ... Stop this, Judy told herself, stop this. None of your business. That's what Dilys had said to her that day, quite plainly. It had amazed her.

'It's your father's life,' Dilys had said, 'and you're not a child any more. You've made it plain you wanted nothing to do with him, ever since you were little, and if you've changed your mind now, and you find you don't like what's going on, that's your problem. Not his.'

Judy had been very startled. She had gone to Dean Place to tell them she had decided to give up her job in London, and was coming home, and she expected a welcome due to the return of a prodigal daughter. But they had been preoccupied and fretful, and had told her there was nothing to come home for.

'We're moving on,' Dilys said. 'We're moving in to Stretton. Lyndsay's informed us she's coming here. Says she's going to farm. I don't know what your father will say.'

'He won't say anything much,' Judy said spitefully. 'He's too busy—'

Dilys had looked at her sharply.

'If you mean Zoe—'

'I do.'

'There's nothing wrong with Zoe,' Dilys said.

'She's changed him—'

'She's put a bit of heart back in him,' Dilys said, 'if that's what you mean.' She had given a little laugh then, a short, barking sound as if she wanted to take the edge off what she was about to say. 'Heart,' she said. 'We could all do with a bit of that round here.'

Judy turned now, on her side. She hadn't pulled the curtains across properly and she could see a slice of early summer night sky, dim but not quite dark. Out there, the farmyard lay, and the cows, some in the barn, the young ones in the field below the house, and beyond them still was Gareth's house where Gareth might even now be awake as she was, thinking about his future, anxious that he was doing the right thing, afraid of change.

'He had no choice,' Robin had said. 'He didn't want to, but Debbie did. He never said so, but you could tell. He didn't want to move.'

But he was moving, and so were Gran and Grandpa, and so was Lyndsay, amazingly, away from the dependency she had always known, away from waiting for someone else to make the choices, away, indeed, from some of the strongest bonds of the past, gripping bonds that had done as much harm as good. Like me, Judy thought, like me. Or, at least, as I must make like me.

CHAPTER NINETEEN

'Come in here,' Lyndsay said.

She pushed the door open, and Hughie could see a big room with windows and a bed. He stood in the doorway and looked at it. There were photographs on the walls, lots of them, and a cupboard thing and a bee droning about on the windowsill. Hughie didn't like bees.

Lyndsay stepped into the room past Hughie and began to walk about in it, slowly. Every now and then, she stopped near one of the walls and looked at a photograph. They appeared to be full of lines of people, Hughie thought, lines all standing behind one another with the smallest in the front, like the Christmas play photograph at his playgroup. He held Seal, and waited.

Lyndsay went on looking at the photographs. She walked very slowly about the room, very softly, and her skirt swung behind her. It was blue. Hughie knew what it would feel like if he grabbed at the folds of it as Rose had done just now, just before she'd been put down for her morning rest, leaving a smear on one side. Rose always left smears. Her hands had always been somewhere else, first.

'Come and look at this,' Lyndsay said.

Hughie came forward very slowly.

'Put Seal down.'

Hughie gripped him.

'No,' Lyndsay said. 'Put him down. I want to show you something for a boy. A real boy.'

Hughie hesitated.

'Seal is for bedtime,' Lyndsay said, 'not for all day, too. There are going to be other things for all day now.'

Hughie turned and began to walk back towards the door. Lyndsay waited until he had almost reached it, and then she said, 'There's a picture of Daddy here. I should think he was a bit bigger than you but not much. He's got a cricket bat.'

Hughie stopped, but didn't turn.

'This room was Daddy's room. All the time he was a boy. When he was a little boy and then when he was a bigger one. All these pictures have got Daddy in them.'

Hughie half turned and stood with one profile to her.

'This can be your room,' Lyndsay said. 'This can be your bedroom now. Just yours. You can have all the pictures of Daddy and you can put your own pictures in here, too. You can have that bed.'

Hughie looked at it. It seemed very high, and it had black legs and the bedspread was made of caterpillary stuff.

'Or,' Lyndsay said, 'we can bring your own bed over from the cottage and you can have it in here instead and we'll put this bed somewhere else.'

'Take the bee away,' Hughie said.

'Please.'

'Please.'

Lyndsay opened the window nearest to the bee, and scooped it out into the air quickly with her hand.

'It's gone. It was very sleepy.' She looked at Hughie. He was swaying slightly, as if he was thinking, pondering.

'Do you like this room?' Lyndsay said.

He was silent.

'I'll be next door, you see. I'll be in Granny's old room. I'm going to put my bed in there. And Rose can have the room beside the bathroom.'

Hughie went over to the nearest wall and looked up. There were four photographs up there, four blocks of men in rugger clothes. They all looked the same. Hughie couldn't see which one was Joe, but he was in there, being a rugger man like all the others. Next to the rugger pictures was the window, a big window that didn't have bars across like his little window did now. The glass in this window looked very empty and clean. He turned round. Lyndsay was

312

standing quite still, watching him. He walked quickly up to the bed and climbed on to the chair that stood beside it, a bare wooden chair with no cushion on it. When he was kneeling on the chair, he paused, just for a moment, and then he reached across and put Seal down, on the pillow. Then he scrambled off the chair again and ran out of the room on to the landing.

*   *   *

Zoe was packing. Her clothes, her few clothes, lay in dark piles on the floor and she was kneeling beside them taking forgotten things out of the bottom of her rucksack, socks and rolls of spare film and an out-of-date coach timetable, before she put everything else back in.

'Oh,' Judy said.

She stood in the doorway, holding two mugs of coffee.

Zoe sat back on her heels. She said, without resentment, 'Were you coming to tell me to go?'

Judy swallowed.

'Yes.'

'Well, here I am, going.'

'I wasn't going to tell you. I was going to ask you. I thought—'

'What?'

'I thought that we couldn't live together like this. Now that I've come back.'

'No,' Zoe said, 'I know. I knew that before you did.'

'Don't,' Judy said with some edge, 'always be right. Please.'

'I'm not always right. I'm just not fixed.' She looked at Judy. 'Are you still going to want your father when I'm gone?'

'Shut up—'

'Well, are you?'

Judy put both coffee mugs down on the little chest by the bed, spilling some as she did so. She took a grip on her temper, and said carefully, 'There was a lot I didn't see.'

'You're bloody lucky,' Zoe said, 'to have a father at all.' She reached out and picked up a handful of T-shirts and lowered them into the rucksack. 'In fact,' she said in a voice which lacked its usual composure, 'you're bloody lucky anyway. You're a bloody lucky spoiled bitch.'

Judy lowered herself, very quietly, on to the edge of the bed.

'I haven't taken anything,' Zoe said, and her voice was still ragged. 'I said I wouldn't, and I haven't. But that doesn't mean I didn't want some things. Things you've got. Things I'll never have. You can tell yourself you don't need this stuff, this family stuff. You can tell—' She stopped and turned away abruptly, putting one arm up across her eyes.

'Zoe—'

'You shut up,' Zoe said. 'Don't make it worse by trying to tell me it'll be OK.'

'I won't,' Judy said. 'But I'm sorry—'

'Of course you are, of course. You never meant this to happen. Nor did I. Nor did your dad.' She shifted her balance to extract a paper tissue out of her jeans pocket, and blew her nose hard. 'Well, it's happened and now we've got to do the next thing.'

Judy leaned forward.

'Have you got any money?'

'No,' Zoe said, 'but it doesn't matter. I don't mind about money. I'll get some—'

'You can have the flat, if you like,' Judy said diffidently. 'I've given a month's notice. I've paid the rent. So it's all there, if you want it, for a month. And—and, well, your herons are there. And your quilt.'

Zoe picked up a grey sweatshirt and held it against her eyes.

'Thanks.'

'And I can let you have some money—'

Zoe shook her head.

'Robin's done that.'

Judy closed her eyes.

'Are you in love with him?'

'Probably,' Zoe said, 'I don't know. I've got nothing to measure it by.'

'No.'

'He's been good to me. I've been good to him.'

'Yes.'

'And it's hard to leave that.' She looked up at Judy again and her face was pinched and small. 'But I'm going to.'

                    *   *   *

Later, Judy offered to take her into Stretton to catch the London coach but she said it was OK, thanks. Gareth was taking her. Robin was lending Gareth the Land Rover because there were various things that needed picking up in Stretton anyway, and he would take Zoe to the coach station. If he wasn't back to start the afternoon milking, Robin said, then he, Robin, would start it himself. Robin had then looked at Judy, as if considering whether to ask her to help, but had plainly decided against it. Judy then went back into the house to let them say goodbye to each

315

other without her there, watching.

When she heard the Land Rover go out of the yard, she went upstairs and into Caro's bedroom so that she could watch it drive up the track to the lane, and then turn left towards the village, and after that take the road to Stretton. She felt no relief at seeing it go, only a strange small pain, and a sense that she owed Zoe more than she had acknowledged, that it was too late, now, to unstitch what had happened and try to smooth her responses.

She turned from the window and looked at Caro's bed with its red-and-white American quilt. It was just a bed. Extraordinary, after all these obsessive years, that the bed in which Caro had slept and been so sick should simply have become a bed, and no more. Maybe, Judy thought, I'll sleep in it. Maybe I'll come in here and turn all the furniture around and sleep here. If Dad—if Dad doesn't mind.

From downstairs, the telephone was ringing. Robin clearly hadn't plugged in the extension by his bed. Judy waited, counting the rings. He hadn't, it appeared, switched on the answering machine either. Judy leaped forward and raced down the stairs to the kitchen, seizing the receiver.

'Hello? Hello? Tideswell Farm—'

'That Judy?' Velma said.

'Velma—'

'You home then?'

'Yes.'

'You home for good?'

'I've only been back three days,' Judy said. 'I haven't even talked to Dad. Not yet.'

'Not while she was there,' Velma said. 'Madam.'

'What?'

'I knew she'd go,' Velma said, 'I knew it. I've just

316

seen Gareth driving her out, not three minutes ago. Going to London, is she?'

'Yes. Yes, I think so—'

'And not coming back?'

'Velma,' Judy said, 'it isn't really anything to do with you.'

'I didn't ring to speak to you,' Velma said, 'anyway. I rang to speak to your father.'

'He's out in the yard—'

'Give him a message, will you?' Velma said. 'Will you? Tell him I'll be down as usual. Like before.'

'Oh—'

'You tell him,' Velma said. Her voice was comfortable with complacency.

'Sorry,' Judy said.

'What d'you mean, sorry?'

'I mean the job's not open any more,' Judy said. 'I mean that there's no "like before" to come back to.' She took a breath and shut her eyes, picturing Zoe on the coach to London, staring out of the window. 'You walked out,' Judy said to Velma with decision, 'and now you can stay out.'

*   *   *

'Dad?'

Robin turned. In the dim light of the barn, he couldn't see her very clearly, especially silhouetted against the light as she was.

'Hello.'

'Dad, I've just done something. I've sacked Velma.'

'Velma!'

'She saw Gareth driving Zoe off. So she rang to say she'd be back and I said she wouldn't.'

317

He smiled.

'Good for you.'

'You don't mind?'

He shook his head.

'I'll do what she was doing.'

He smiled again.

'What nobody was doing—'

'Dad,' Judy said again, 'you OK?'

He bent and picked up the mallet lying in the straw at his feet.

'I will be.'

'I don't know if this is the moment to ask you, but—' She stopped.

'Well?'

'Can I ask it, can I ask you something?'

'Of course,' he said. He put out the hand that wasn't holding the mallet and took her arm. 'Come outside. Come out into the light.'

'I haven't any business to ask, in a way, I haven't any right—'

'What is it?'

He guided her out into the yard, to the sheltered space by the feed store where Gareth left his bike.

'Can I stay?' Judy said.

He stared at her.

'Stay?'

'Yes. Live here. Live with you.'

He dropped his hand from her arm, turning his face up towards the sky for a moment before he said, 'Judy, dear, I've got to sell the farm.'

'Sell it—'

'Yes,' he said. 'Sell it. I'm hoping to sell it and then lease it back. And the milk quota. I don't know if I can do it, but I've got to try.' He gave Judy a quick glance and then he said, 'I can't afford to replace

318

Gareth, you see. And the debts are—well, better not to think about them. The new slurry pit's just a detail. I've seen it all coming and, at the same time, I haven't. Haven't wanted to. I've got to go back to where I started, milking myself, full-time. It's the only way.' He squinted up at the sky again. 'At least it'll give Grandpa a chance to say I told you so.'

Judy leaned against the warm grey wall of the feed store and spread her hands flat on it, at either side.

'I'd no idea—'

'No. Why should you?'

'I just assumed you were managing, that you always would, that there was a kind of permanence here.'

'There isn't permanence anywhere,' Robin said.

'When you sell up,' Judy said, 'could you go somewhere else?'

'I don't want to go somewhere else.'

'Because of the continuity? Because of the change?'

'It isn't much here,' Robin said, 'but I made it, what there is. And—' He paused, and then he said, 'And I know it.'

'Even though it's so hard. Even though it's always been so hard—'

'Yes.' He bent down and wrenched a clump of weeds out of a crack in the concrete floor of the yard. 'I don't think it's going to be any harder, in a way. Physically it will be, because I'm older, but maybe in other ways, I'll—well, I'll get fewer things wrong.' He hurled the weeds away into a corner. 'I wouldn't want to live any other way now. I suppose I may have to, one day, but I'll only give in at the last ditch.' He turned his head slowly and looked at Judy. 'There'll always be room for you here, Judy. Or wherever. You know that. But there's no money. Farmers never pay

319

themselves anything anyway and I couldn't pay you.'

'Suppose I don't want that—'

He smiled at her, a tired, faraway smile.

'You think about it. Don't rush into anything. Changes of heart—' He stopped.

'Well?'

'Changes of heart are heady things.'

'I mean it.'

'Yes.' He leaned forward and kissed her, very lightly, on the cheek. His own cheek was rough. 'Got to get on now, Judy,' he said. 'Things to do. You know how it is.'

*　　*　　*

Lyndsay had spread a map of Dean Place Farm on the kitchen table in the cottage. The fields, irregular in shape and linked haphazardly to one another, were marked out in acres and hectares, with their gateways and stiles. The stiles were part of the local footpath system, but Joe hadn't liked walkers, hadn't liked footpath associations, and had managed, without actually closing them, to make both paths and stiles subtly unwelcoming. There'd been a battle or two over this; letters in the local press and a stand-up shouting match with two formidable women armed with statutory rights and wire-cutters. But Joe, with the doggedness of one who was both on the spot and had closed his mind to any change of heart, had won. Looking at the double-dotted lines of the footpaths on the farm map, Lyndsay thought she might re-open them and even, perhaps, make a farm trail for visitors. Maybe Robin would join in, and let his cows be part of it. You couldn't imagine visitors getting much satisfaction out of nothing but acres of barley and rape seed.

The kitchen was quiet. Rose was asleep upstairs and Hughie had gone, for the first time in weeks, to his playgroup. He had, moreover, gone without his baseball cap, and without Seal. Seal lay on Hughie's bed carefully swaddled in Hughie's pyjamas and wearing, Lyndsay could have sworn, an expression of palpable relief on his plush face. She had considered putting him in the washing machine—he badly needed it—but had refrained. Hughie was creeping forward, inch by inch, and she must not, because of a senseless whim for hygiene, knock him back.

A car drew up outside. She raised her head from the map and looked out of the window. It was Robin. She hadn't seen him for weeks and certainly not since she'd come back to Dean Place. She straightened up and waited for him, by the table, watching his shadowy form come into the house through the patterned glazed doors of the outside porch, and then the kitchen. He opened the door, without knocking.

'Hello,' he said.

She nodded.

'I'm glad to see you,' Robin said. 'I'm glad you're back.'

He was wearing an old checked shirt with a frayed collar, and corduroy trousers.

'Judy's back, too,' Robin said.

'I know.'

'Has she been to see you?'

'No—'

'She will,' Robin said. He looked round. 'No children?'

'Asleep,' Lyndsay said. 'Or at playgroup.'

'And you are counting your acres?'

'Trying to.'

He came round the table to stand beside her and look at the map. He said, 'What'll you do with the land you can't get subsidy on?'

There was a tiny beat.

'I don't know.'

'Trees?'

She said nothing.

'Not advisable,' Robin said. 'Stock?'

She said nothing.

'Too expensive. You need manpower. Grazing?'

She said nothing.

'The best idea, really. I could tell you who to approach.'

'I'm going to get a manager,' Lyndsay said tightly, 'to begin with.'

'He'll want a share—'

'I know. I know that. I mayn't know much but I'm not a complete fool.'

'Nor am I,' Robin said.

She moved away from him a little.

'What do you mean?'

'I'm not such a fool,' Robin said, 'as not to know why you'll hardly speak to me.'

She put her hands flat on the map, and leaned on them, looking sternly downwards.

'Zoe,' Robin said. 'Right?'

There was a pause and then Lyndsay said, 'It made me feel so lonely—'

'You were lonely anyway,' Robin said. 'So was I. We both are. We have to be, for a while.'

She gave a tiny nod.

'I thought—well, I suppose I thought you could be there for me, you could—'

'No,' Robin said gently. 'Who'd I be helping?'

She straightened up and pushed her hair back over

322

her shoulders.

'Hughie's a bit better. He went to playgroup today without Seal.'

'Good.'

'My parents are hardly speaking to me—'

'They will,' Robin said. 'It's hard to offer help and have it turned down—'

Lyndsay looked at him, for the first time since he had come in.

'But was it real help? Was it what was best for them or best for me?'

He shrugged. There was something about the shrug, something humorous and appealing that made Lyndsay say suddenly, 'Oh Robin, I'm sorry, I'm so—'

He put a hand out. He was laughing.

'Don't you start.'

'What?'

'Saying sorry. First Judy, now you. She wants to say sorry all the time and I can't take the both of you—'

'Suppose we mean it?' Lyndsay said indignantly. 'Suppose we really do?'

'Then I'll know,' Robin said, 'won't I? I'll know. If, that is, that I think either of you have any cause. If I don't think that we all of us, one way and another, had our reasons.' He put his hands in his pockets. 'Judy wants to stay.'

'At home? At Tideswell? You and her?'

'Yes.'

'Lord,' Lyndsay said.

'And she wants this at the very moment I've got to try and sell it.'

'Have you?'

'Yes.'

323

'Oh Robin—'

'Maybe to your landlords here. I don't know. And then lease it back, get put on the tenancy with you.'

She said, uncertainly, 'I'd like that.'

'Would you?'

'It's frightening, taking all this on—' She paused and then she said, 'Joe's debts, those loans. He never said a word—'

'No,' Robin said, 'he wouldn't have.'

'The bank didn't know either. They've taken the loans on for now, but not, of course, for ever.'

Robin grunted.

'I'm going to do an evening accountancy course,' Lyndsay said. 'Accounts and book keeping.'

'Good girl.'

'Please,' Lyndsay said, 'don't talk to me like that.'

'Sorry. Habit.'

'We haven't got any habits now,' Lyndsay said. She moved away from the table and went across to the window, looking over Robin's Land Rover bonnet to where Joe had planted the barley all those months ago on that great sloping field opposite which she had gazed and gazed at, the field he had insisted on top-dressing their very first Christmas Day together while she waited and watched, frustrated and impotent and, now it seemed to her, almost ridiculous, in a new red velvet dress with the candles lit and the table laid with ivy trails. 'There aren't any habits left. We've got to make new ones.' She turned from the window and looked straight at him. 'We've got to make our own.'

CHAPTER TWENTY

You couldn't, Dilys thought, fault the condition in which Debbie had left their house. When Robin and Lyndsay had first suggested that she and Harry move into Gareth's house, she had been horrified, and more than horrified; offended. For her and Harry to move out of Dean Place Farm into a herdsman's house seemed an affront she couldn't even contemplate because it was, in essence, so improper. And then it was made worse by Harry leaping at the chance. She'd sat opposite him, at the kitchen table round which all farm and family business had been conducted for over forty years, and seen his face light up at the suggestion. There was no mistaking it. He looked, no more no less, like Rose did, when you offered her a biscuit. Rapturous.

She had said, at first, that there was no question, that the idea was not to be contemplated, not mentioned again. And then something even more disconcerting had happened, which was that Lyndsay—Lyndsay of all people—said that there was no money in any case to buy a bungalow in Stretton, and then Harry had looked as if he wanted to jump from his chair and hug her.

'The business side of this farm,' Lyndsay said, not looking at either of them, 'is in an absolute mess. There isn't any money to buy a bungalow.'

Dilys stared at her.

'Nonsense.'

'No,' Lyndsay said. Her voice was flat, as if she was reciting something dull. 'True. Fact. Joe was in debt, deeply in debt. Money you didn't know about, money that didn't go through the books, private loans.'

Dilys clenched her hands together.

'How much?'

Lyndsay looked at her, directly, for the first time.

'You don't need to know how much. You just need to know there isn't the money to buy a rabbit hutch, let alone a bungalow.'

Dilys went upstairs then. She left them and went upstairs, and sat in the dusk at her bedroom window and waited for one of them—Lyndsay or Robin or Harry or Judy—to come up and find her, and apologise. But no one came. She sat there, upright, her hands folded deliberately in her lap, and thought of those hours she had spent over the farm books, hours and hours with her meticulous columns, her attention to detail, her obedience to Joe's progressive wishes. It seemed to her impossible, outrageous, that she might have got things wrong all those years, that Joe might not, after all, have known what he was doing. Out of the question, like moving to a herdsman's house. She must have sat there for over an hour. The intimately familiar landscape outside the window sank into darkness and, she could no longer see the swoopings of the house martins which nested each year, so faithfully, beneath the eaves of the house. Finally, she had gone downstairs again and found them all there, still talking, still resolved. Judy had smiled at her, a smile, Dilys supposed, intended to convey sympathy in the face of the inevitable. But Dilys wasn't ready for such sympathy. She had put the kettle on, noisily and pointedly, and banged cups down on the table, and clattered spoons.

But for all that, here she was, in the bedroom that

had once belonged to Gareth's Eddie, peeling stickers of martial arts practitioners off the window. Debbie had left the room spotless, but the stickers were there, and some very odd curtains that looked as if someone had sprayed bleach on them, and two different sorts of wallpaper. Debbie had liked wallpaper, plainly. It was everywhere, even in the bathroom, a design of shells and sea-horses, impractical and fanciful. Yet for all the wallpaper and the window stickers, Dilys couldn't dislike the house. She had tried to, and she couldn't. She had tried, very hard, to feel that they had been rescued but in quite the wrong way—but had failed to feel that, too. She had wanted, at some level, to feel that nothing whatsoever could or should be salvaged from the loss of Joe, and in that wish, the one closest to her heart, she had succeeded least of all.

She laid the stickers in a row on the windowsill. Perhaps Hughie would like them. Perhaps, on the other hand, he should not be encouraged to like anything both so ugly and so violent. There was nothing, after all, remotely violent about Hughie. In fact, quite the reverse. Often, when Dilys went up to Dean Place for the children's bedtime, and was reading to Hughie in Joe's old room, she had a feeling of peace she could neither account for nor remember ever having had before. Triumph she'd had, satisfaction, a sense of achievement, of victory, but not peace. Sitting on Hughie's bed and reading the funny little stories he liked, of moles and tigers in shoes and scarves going about their accident-prone but ultimately secure anthropomorphised domestic lives, unquestionably gave her peace. She felt a state of quiet there, a freedom from disturbance, a tranquillity and ease of mind. There was no
327

explaining it, but there it was, lying round her and Hughie, sitting up in Joe's bed, like still water or a snow field, silent and unbroken.

She unscrewed the top of a bottle of white spirit she had brought upstairs with her, and dipped a cloth in it, to rub away the smears of adhesive the stickers had left on the window. In two weeks' time Lyndsay's new farm manager would move in, to Joe and Lyndsay's former house, a young chap, two years out of agricultural college, on a three-year contract. He hadn't got a wife, but he had a live-in girlfriend who was also in the farm business, a specialist, apparently, in quality salad crops. Once, Dilys told herself, she'd have put her foot down about the couple not being married—but not now, not since Zoe, not since this strange advent of calm that made her feel less urgent, somehow, about putting her foot down about anything.

There, across the maize field, and in her direct line of vision, lay Robin's house. She hadn't lived within sight of Robin for twenty-five years and had never, she thought, looked at the house except to feel, with disapproval, how different its appearance and management would be in her care. She didn't feel that any longer. He was negotiating to sell it, and the land and the house she was in herself, right at this moment, and she felt full of the most fervent desire that he should succeed. The omens looked good, but you couldn't tell, you couldn't be sure. If the last six months had taught Dilys anything, it was the folly of being sure of the future.

Dilys picked up all the cleaning things and looked at her watch. Ten to twelve. In ten minutes, Harry would be in for his lunch, her transformed Harry who had set his face against keeping stock all the years she

328

had known him and who had now taken to Robin's cows with a vengeance. He'd become Robin's right-hand man, going off down the track through the maize field half a dozen times a day and returning with that look of almost sleepy satisfaction she couldn't remember seeing on his face in years. He had all the work he wanted, and none of the care. Robin had the care. Robin, Dilys now thought, had always had the care, all his life. Yet in the singular way that things had turned out, maybe he had had a reward or two as well, not least in Judy, going off to agricultural college in September, financed half by the bank and half by her Aunt Lyndsay. What would my father have thought, Dilys wondered, treading carefully down the stairs, what would he have thought to see these girls, these *girls*, on a farm? Judy in a boiler suit, Lyndsay talking of buying a computer...

Dilys went into her little kitchen. The sun was coming in through the south window and lighting up the parsley pot she had put on the sill and the washed jam jars and the folded dishcloth. She had never had a south-facing kitchen window before, never lived in a room where the sun was a presence, a factor. She turned on the taps and washed her hands slowly, dreamily, looking out across the tall rustling heads of maize to the roof of Tideswell, to the barns and the buildings. Change and loss, she said to herself, change and loss, like a chant, over and over, life carrying you away, carrying things away from you, then bringing something back, some little thing you didn't look for, didn't know you needed until you saw it washed up there, waiting at your feet. Change and loss. And growth. Growth where you had never looked for it before, never thought to look. Because you weren't ready. Because you hadn't known the loss. Dilys turned off the taps and dried her hands carefully, polishing her thin, old, pinkish-gold wedding ring. Then she began to open cupboards and drawers in search of the bread board, and a loaf, and a knife.

The LARGE PRINT HOME LIBRARY

If you have enjoyed this Large Print book and would like to build up your own collection of Large Print books and have them delivered direct to your door, please contact The Large Print Home Library.

The Large Print Home Library offers you a full service:

☆ **Created to support your local library**

☆ **Delivery direct to your door**

☆ **Easy-to-read type & attractively bound**

☆ **The very best authors**

☆ **Special low prices**

For further details either call Customer Services on 01225 443400 or write to us at:

The Large Print Home Library
FREEPOST (BA 1686/1)
Bath BA2 3SZ